SHERLOCK HOLMES AND THE GREAT DETECTIVES

SHERLOCK HOLMES AND THE GREAT DETECTIVES

Edited by
Derrick Belanger

Belanger Books

2020

Sherlock Holmes and the Great Detectives
© 2020 by Belanger Books, LLC

ISBN: 9798662862456

Print and Digital Edition © 2020 by Belanger Books, LLC

All Rights Reserved. No part of this book may be used or reproduced in any manner whatsoever without written permission except in case of brief quotations embodied in critical articles or reviews.

This book is a work of fiction. Names, characters, businesses, organizations, places, events, and incidents either are the products of the author's imagination or are used fictitiously. Any resemblance to actual persons, living or dead, events, or locales is entirely coincidental.

For information contact:

Belanger Books, LLC

61 Theresa Ct.

Manchester, NH 03103

derrick@belangerbooks.com

www.belangerbooks.com

Cover and Back design by Brian Belanger

www.belangerbooks.com and www.redbubble.com/people/zhahadun

Table of Contents

An Introduction to the Great Detectives *by Derrick Belanger*   10

The Adventure of the Grey Seal *by Will Murray*   13

The Wilhelm House Curse *by Derrick Belanger*   47

Done With Mirrors *by Dan Andriacco*   70

Pipes, Bonnets and Pieces of String *by Robert Stapleton*   95

The Case of the Watery Wife *by Lorraine Sharma Nelson*   131

The Esau Ladies *by Robert Perret*   163

The Adventure of the Edinburgh Professor *by Stephen Herczeg*   185

The Chapel of the Holy Blood *by Chris Chan*   211

The Adventure of the Philanthropic Crook *by D.K. Latta*   232

The Wet-Nosed Irregular *by Harry DeMaio*   260

The Stanforth Mystery or The Adventure of the Felonious Fiancé *by Paul Hiscock*   283

The Inner Temple Intruder *by David Marcum*   305

The Curate's Curious Egg *by John Linwood Grant*   348

The Case of William Wilson *by Richard Zwicker*   380

The Case of the Spanish Bride *by Brenda Seabrooke*   402

Special Thanks to Our Kickstarter Backers   427

COPYRIGHT INFORMATION

All of the contributions in this collection are copyrighted by the authors listed below, except as noted. Grateful acknowledgement is given to the authors and/or their agents for the kind permission to use their work.

"The Adventure of the Grey Seal" ©2020 by Will Murray. All Rights Reserved. First publication, original to this collection. Printed by permission of the author.

"The Wilhelm House Curse" ©2020 by Derrick Belanger. All Rights Reserved. First publication, original to this collection. Printed by permission of the author.

"Done With Mirrors" ©2020 by Dan Andriacco. All Rights Reserved. First publication, original to this collection. Printed by permission of the author.

"Pipes, Bonnets and Pieces of String" ©2020 by Robert Stapleton. All Rights Reserved. First publication, original to this collection. Printed by permission of the author.

"The Case of the Watery Wife" ©2020 by Lorraine Sharma Nelson. All Rights Reserved. First publication, original to this collection. Printed by permission of the author.

"The Esau Ladies" ©2020 by Robert Perret. All Rights Reserved. First publication, original to this collection. Printed by permission of the author.

"The Adventure of the Edinburgh Professor" ©2020 by Stephen Herczeg. All Rights Reserved. First publication, original to this collection. Printed by permission of the author.

"The Chapel of the Holy Blood" ©2020 by Chris Chan. All Rights Reserved. First publication, original to this collection. Printed by permission of the author.

"The Adventure of the Philanthropic Crook" ©2020 by D.K. Latta. All Rights Reserved. First publication, original to this collection. Printed by permission of the author.

"The Wet-Nosed Irregular" ©2020 by Harry DeMaio. All Rights Reserved. First publication, original to this collection. Printed by permission of the author.

"The Stanforth Mystery or The Adventure of the Felonious Fiancé" ©2020 by Paul Hiscock. All Rights Reserved. First publication, original to this collection. Printed by permission of the author.

"The Inner Temple Intruder" ©2020 by David Marcum. All Rights Reserved. First publication, original to this collection. Printed by permission of the author.

"The Curate's Curious Egg" ©2020 by John Linwood Grant. All Rights Reserved. First publication, original to this collection. Printed by permission of the author.

"The Case of William Wilson" ©2020 by Richard Zwicker. All Rights Reserved. First publication, original to this collection. Printed by permission of the author.

"The Case of the Spanish Bride" ©2020 by Brenda Seabrooke. All Rights Reserved. First publication, original to this collection. Printed by permission of the author.

An Introduction to the Great Detectives

by Derrick Belanger

Sherlock Holmes —the name immediately brings to mind an image of the great detective sitting in his rooms in 221B Baker street, his fingers steepled before his hawkish nose, his sharp grey eyes focused on the client who has brought a little puzzle for him to solve. Unfortunately, the same cannot be said when one reads the names of the other literary detectives of the time period, sometimes referred to as the rivals of Sherlock Holmes. Sadly, names like Lois Cayley, Professor Augustus S. F. X. Van Dusen, The Old Man in the Corner, or Dr. Thorndyke are meaningless to all but the most ardent admirers of Victorian and Edwardian mysteries.

The Great Detective Universe series hopes to rectify this problem and expand the world of Sherlock Holmes by bringing the consulting detective and his purported rivals into a *shared* universe, in other words, a universe where not just Holmes and Watson lived but also Carnacki, Father Brown, The Grey Seal, and many other great detectives. This expansive universe also includes "new" traditional sleuths such as Professor Carlo Stuarti, Augustine Dalrymple, and

Marcel Berengar. They all join Holmes and Watson on the foggy, cobblestone streets of London, solving troubling problems, righting wrongs, and bending chaos into order

With this being a shared universe, not every story has Holmes working closely with his fellow great detectives. In Dan Andriacco's "Done with Mirrors", Holmes is only mentioned. It is his associate, Inspector Tobias Gregson who is more involved with the case. Also, we felt that we could play a bit loose with strict rules and have two stories in which Sherlock Holmes meets Jimmie Dale, the Grey Seal. Both stories are excellent, and in a multiverse of opportunities, there's no reason why we can't have two different first encounters. Just think of how many first meetings Batman and Superman have had.

Sherlock Holmes and the Great Detectives is the third book in *The Great Detective Universe* series; however, it is the first that is fully traditional. The previous two books, *Sherlock Holmes and the Occult Detectives Volume One* and *Sherlock Holmes and the Occult Detectives Volume Two*, had Holmes sharing his world with sleuths such as Professor Van Helsing and John Silence, great minds studying worlds beyond our own. The stories in *Sherlock Holmes and the Great Detectives* follow Holmes's mantra that ghosts need not apply. These mysteries follow the standard formulas and are grounded in our Earthly realm. The next book in the series will have Holmes teaming up with his Praed Street successor, Solar Pons.

We hope to have several of *The Great Detective Universe* books published each year. Plans are already in place for a third collection of *Sherlock Holmes and the Occult Detectives*. A collection of Carnacki, the Ghost Finder stories in 2021 will be our first in the series which does not have a specific connection to Sherlock Holmes. There are also ideas for new collections featuring Professor Carlo Stuarti, the Thinking Machine, Lois Cayley, and The Old Man in the Corner. Of course, there will continue to be many more featuring Sherlock Holmes and his dear friend, Dr. John H. Watson.

Until next time, dear reader. Many games are afoot!

Derrick Belanger

June, 2020

The Adventure of the Grey Seal

by Will Murray

Millionaire Clubman Jimmie Dale entered the exclusive St. James Club on Fifth Avenue and went directly to the reading room, where he sat down with a fresh copy of the *Morning News-Argus* he plucked from the wooden rack.

Engrossed in the front page, he failed to notice the lean gentleman seated in a wing-chair not very far distant. This individual, too, was also perusing the *News-Argus*.

Not recognizing the man, Jimmie put down his paper and said, "Pardon me, I did not notice you. My name is James Dale."

"I find that not being noticed has its advantages," said the other fellow in a distant voice. He did not put down his paper.

Jimmie laughed shortly, reflecting to himself that this had often been true in the course of his peculiar existence.

"I will not disagree with you on that point," he returned lightly. "I do not recall ever seeing you at the St. James Club prior to today."

"That is because I am a guest," the other said in a cool tone. The newspaper dropped, and the man turned his head to reveal a mature face dominated by penetrating grey eyes.

"You may call me Mr. Altamont," he stated.

"No first name?"

"I do not find first names necessary when I am not on intimate terms."

Jimmie frowned. The man had a trace of an accent. But he could not place it. His dark eyes grew thoughtful.

Jimmie offered, "I have the impression that you come from the Continent. Am I mistaken?"

"Yes, you are. But no matter. I am very glad to meet you."

Jimmie nodded politely. "And I, you."

The young clubman gave Altamont a thorough visual examination. He was a hawk-nosed individual with lean features surmounted by a high forehead, suggesting a great intellect. His age was difficult to judge. Jimmie thought that he could land comfortably on either side of sixty. The St. James Club was so difficult to get into, he could not imagine who this man could be. Guest cards issued by the club were rare. Rarer than memberships, in fact. He was on the point of asking Altamont who sponsored him, but decided the question impolite.

"What is your line, Mr. Altamont?" Jimmie asked instead.

"Presently, I am a traveler. My destination is Chicago. I have only lately arrived in New York City. I do not expect to remain here more than a fortnight."

"Chicago is an interesting city. What attracts you to it?"

"Only that I have never before visited the windy city."

"I see," said Jimmie. But he failed to truly understand. There was something odd or perhaps amiss about this man. He could not put his finger on what, but concern caused his interested expression to turn pensive.

While Jimmie was contemplating the fellow, Altamont's penetrating gaze went to his hands.

"You have remarkably sensitive hands," Altamont pointed out.

Jimmie smiled politely. "I am a man of leisure. I do not work with my hands."

"And yet they appear to my eyes to possess dexterous fingers that turn to specialized work from time to time."

"What makes you think so?"

"They have a certain sensitivity. I might call them artist's hands, but scrutinizing your features, I do not sense or detect an artistic soul. I notice that your fingernails show signs of having come into recent contact with paint, I would venture to say oils of the type used by portrait artists."

"That is a remarkable observation," said Jimmie, growing tense, "if erroneous. I am not a portrait artist."

"And yet you paint," the other murmured. "I also note traces of wax under two of your fingernails and one thumb. It is the left thumb, and yet you appear to be right-handed. Also, your manner is rather brisk, which runs contrary to your assertion that you are a man of leisure."

"Are you a detective, Mr. Altamont?"

"Why do you ask?" countered the other.

"You appear to be very observant."

The other nodded without replying directly.

Instead, he said, "I would have to examine your fingertips to be certain, but I fail to notice abrasions upon the tips of your fingers of the kind found in certain specialists who habitually sandpaper their digits."

Jimmie forced out a ragged laugh. Inside, he was hardly laughing.

"Whoever would apply sandpaper to their fingertips?"

"That is a common practice among professional safecrackers," the other said pointedly. "I understand that it makes the fingertips raw but sensitive, the better to feel the tumblers drop into place."

Altamont's intelligent eyes bored into Jimmie's own. For a moment neither man spoke.

Jimmie's heart skipped a beat. He forced himself to be calm. "I believe I asked you a direct question a moment ago."

"I am not a Headquarters man, if that is what you are thinking. Far from it."

"Yet you are very observant for a tourist passing through New York City on his way to Chicago."

"I have followed your career for some time, Mr. ...Seal."

Now Jimmie could feel his mouth drying up.

"I beg your pardon. I believe I told you that my name was Dale."

"Ah, yes. The moneyed scion of the Dale safe manufacturing company, one of the largest in America. No doubt you learned a great deal of the trade, being the son of your illustrious father."

"I fail to see your point," Jimmie returned thinly, "for a man always learns from his father. It is only natural."

"Yet you did not go into your father's business."

"It was not to my taste. May I ask why so many personal questions from a perfect stranger?"

"As I informed you, I have been following your career from afar. Useful data need not be collected in person, for a great deal of insight can be gleaned at a distance — if one possesses the correct reports and the perspicacity to sift through them and glean facts from those reports."

"I do not believe I am following your trend of thought," said Jimmie, carefully choosing his words.

"Allow me to enlighten you," said Altamont, folding his newspaper and standing up. He strode over. Jimmie came to his feet, bracing his athletic body against the necessity of defending himself.

Instead, the man merely offered an open palm to Jimmie's scrutiny. In the center lay a small diamond-shaped piece of paper. It was grey in color.

"This is not an original, of course," stated Altamont calmly. "Merely one cut from grey construction paper in order to make my meaning plain. For there is no need to speak of deep secrets here, even though we are perfectly alone."

Now Jimmie felt as if he could not — dared not — speak. His heart was pounding. The man's gesture was unmistakable.

Returning to his chair, Altamont continued casually.

"I became interested in the daredevil doings of the Grey Seal when news of his existence first reached London. This audacious rascal intrigued me, and so I set my mind to deducing the reasons why a seemingly sane man would undertake such Robin Hood exploits."

Jimmie said nothing. He simply listened.

"When the Grey Seal first made himself known, cracking difficult safes and leaving behind his gummed paper seals, he did so without taking anything from the boxes he had penetrated. I realized immediately this man was no common crook. But who would perpetrate such outrages? Someone with a knowledge of safe construction and their mechanisms, surely. A charming rogue with the most up-to-date knowledge of the new combination locks coming into use."

Altamont's keen eyed glittered.

"Actually, this narrowed down the suspects to a tender few. That is when my attention went in your direction, Dale, given your unique background. You were in the perfect position to understand the inner workings of the latest in safe design. Your failure to steal also pointed an accusing finger, although a polite one. For you enjoy the unsullied reputation of a gentleman."

Jimmie examined his fingernails and saw minute bits of wax left there when he removed the disguise of his alter ego, the down-and-out painter, Smarlinghue. He was amazed that these bits could be detected at such a distance.

Altamont continued casually.

"Then the exploits of the Grey Seal changed character. After a pause of a year, he resumed his gentlemanly depredations. His *modus operandi* altered. At first, I suspected that a copycat was stealing his thunder, as it were. But these crimes were too perfect. This could only be the same individual. Now he was a modern Robin Hood, preying on criminals and exposing them.

"I asked myself what could have wrought such a change, and while I considered many theories, I rejected most of them and came up with only one possibility: Blackmail. The plucky fellow was being coerced into doing their dirty work for someone else. Even if the dirty work was in the cause of right. That these new crimes were directed against evil men did not change my original conclusion."

Jimmie forced a thin smile. "Being a stranger to these shores, Altamont, you could be forgiven for not being up on the latest news. Several months ago, the person who called himself the Grey Seal died in a horrific tenement fire. After which it was revealed that the personality behind the silk mask was a rather low fellow going by the name of Larry the Bat."

"I did read those accounts. As well as the follow-ups. Nothing was ever discovered of who Larry the Bat really was. No last name was ever attached to the fellow. Absent those particulars, I could only conclude that Larry the Bat was a fictitious individual — the creation of the actual Grey Seal. No doubt wax was involved in his development."

Altamont's keen eyes went to Jimmie's fingers.

"I do not know what you call yourself when you are not being Jimmie Dale, but I am forced to conclude that the Grey Seal is not deceased, and may be poised to rise from his grave at any moment."

Jimmie confirmed none of these damning theories. Instead he asked, "What do you want of me?"

"To blackmail you."

"Damn you!" he bit out. "I will pay you nothing! For you can prove nothing!"

"I am madly indifferent to proving anything, my dear fellow. I only wish to avail myself of your special skills. In return, I will be on my way to Chicago and no one will be the wiser."

"I am forced to state boldly that I am reluctant to accept the guarantees of a self-admitted blackmailer," Jimmie returned stiffly.

"I should like you to crack a safe for me and remove from it certain papers," Altamont continued, unfazed. "These documents have to do with an espionage ring I am battling. Before I can continue on my way, I must have these papers."

Against his better judgment, Jimmie asked a simple question: "Where are these papers?"

"In the German consulate here in Manhattan. I assure you that if you provide this assistance, it will be to the benefit of the civilized world, and no one will be the wiser."

"I doubt very much that I or anyone else can get into the German consulate unchallenged, much less escape with their freedom intact. For these are tense times, and relations between the United States and Germany are strained."

"I admit that mine is a difficult request, but I am prepared to help you gain entry. For I am known there and, furthermore, am on intimate terms with certain trusted consulate staff."

"And if I refuse?"

"If you refuse," returned Altamont, "I must undertake this task myself. And I fear that although I have some modest skills in common with the Grey Seal, I am not as up-to-date as

I would like to be. Are you familiar with the new double combination locks?"

Jimmie nodded. "I own such a safe. The outer dial is an arrangement of letters, while the inner ring is governed by a series of numbers. Without getting both sequences correctly lined up, a safe equipped with such a lock cannot be opened — except perhaps by cold chisels and nitroglycerin."

"Would you say that your present skills are equal to such complicated mechanisms?"

"I am familiar with these latest developments and their construction," Jimmie retorted.

"Excellent! From your facial cast and by the weary look in your eyes, Dale, you appear to be bereft of rest. Let me suggest that you catch up on your sleep and rendezvous with me here this evening, promptly at 7 o'clock. From this charming spot, we will embark upon our little adventure."

"If I refuse?"

The other's eyes hardened. "War is raging the length and breadth of the Continent. Our efforts tonight may help bring the awful conflict to a swift and satisfactory conclusion and restore the peace. That would be a benefit to your nation's security, as well as to other democratic countries which are friendly to America. I need not remind you that Germans are engaged in acts upon these shores calculated to discourage American intervention on behalf of her allies."

Jimmie considered this carefully.

"If I did not know better," he remarked, "I would think that you were the famous Sherlock Holmes of London. But I have read that Mr. Holmes is no longer consulting with Scotland Yard, or anyone else."

"This has been reliably reported in newspapers around the world," offered Mr. Altamont, smiling thinly.

Abruptly, he stood up. Jimmie did likewise. Despite his deep suspicions, he clasped the offered hand, which he shook resolutely.

Altamont smiled tightly. "Tonight then."

"Seven o'clock sharp," agreed Jimmie.

With that, Altamont exited the St. James Club, and Jimmie Dale returned to his chair, a worried look on his youthful features.

*****

Jimmie Dale returned to his Riverside Drive home in a foul humor. Benson, the chauffeur, drove the limousine in respectful silence.

By some rotting miracle, someone had penetrated his deepest secret: Jimmie Dale, graduate of Harvard and member of the exclusive St. James Club, was in reality the most wanted cracksman in Manhattan's checkered history.

That the world presently believed the Grey Seal was an unmourned dead man named Larry the Bat was immaterial. Larry the Bat was a fictitious impersonation created out of slovenly clothes, artful makeup, and bits of wax — a police informer no one would ever miss. Nor did they.

The police force did not miss the Grey Seal, either — although they would have preferred to consign him to the Tombs, if not Sing Sing.

For several months, after the tenement blaze that had consumed the last vestiges of Larry the Bat, alias the Grey Seal, Jimmie Dale had begun to breathe easy.

In the beginning, he had applied his skill at opening safes "for the sheer deviltry of it" — as he liked to say. Then *she* entered his life. The splendid and enigmatic Marie LaSalle. In the beginning, he did not know her true name. He called her the Tocsin, and she had dubbed Jimmie her

"Philanthropic Crook." For she knew his secret and had been blackmailing him into committing actual crimes against his better judgment.

That these crimes were against other criminals, most notably the corrupt cabal known as the Crime Club, would not spare him from prison. The motivations behind his Robin Hood-style forays mattered nothing in the eyes of the Law. If the Grey Seal had ever been apprehended by the police and stripped of his black silk mask, it would have been all over for Jimmie Dale, his high public standing and great wealth notwithstanding.

Had the underworld found him first, it would have been even worse.

"Death to the Grey Seal!" That was the cry below the Dead Line, where gentle society gave way to the rough and rowdy. The Bad Lands, some called it. There, the gangs ruled and crime ran rampant.

Now, the great fear that his improbable imposture would come to light had returned in the form of a strange foreign man named Altamont.

Who was he? Jimmie wondered. How had he penetrated this deepest secret? As Jimmie rolled along Riverside Drive, these questions became of lesser concern to him.

He was being blackmailed again. That his blackmailer might possess high and lofty goals was small comfort. Jimmie must once more don the black silk mask and girdle of burglary tools that he fashioned himself. He must risk all in the service of an unknown manipulator.

It was fantastic, this scheme, to penetrate the German consulate and make away with secret documents. Jimmie had no qualms about cracking the safe. No combination lock known to man could defeat him for long. But to get in and out of a guarded consulate successfully seemed impossible.

Yet this Altamont claimed to have the ability to accomplish this feat of daring.

Jimmie arrived at his sumptuous home and went directly upstairs to his den, which ran the length of the building, boasting a fireplace and a rosewood desk.

None of his many servants shared his secret with him. He looked up at the portrait of his father on the wall — a man who died years before the Grey Seal had been born in Jimmie's clever and mischievous imagination.

What would he say if he could see his son now? The elder Dale had wanted Jimmie to follow in his footsteps. Instead, he had sold off the family business, choosing to live upon the proceeds, which were considerable.

In the beginning, the Grey Seal was but a lark — a thrill pursued by a young man who had learned the innermost secrets of safes and their mechanisms at his father's feet. In that, the canny Altamont had been correct in his surmise.

Once again, everything was put at risk. It was maddening. Jimmie began to regret ever creating the Grey Seal.

There was one comfort — a cold one. If the mysterious Altamont was able to pull off this scheme, the risk afterward would be minimal. For Jimmie had burned all of his specially-prepared grey seals.

The Grey Seal might live again — this one last time. But he would not leave any trace behind; he would remain dead. Jimmie was determined that the Grey Seal be left forever behind him, a wraith undeserving of resurrection.

He hoped that Altamont was telling the truth about his Chicago itinerary. Once the man had moved on, there should be no more trouble.

But even as he thought this, Jimmie's blood began racing and a fresh sparkle came into his dark eyes. It had been months since he last became the notorious Grey Seal.

In the interim, he had created a new identity, that of a disreputable dope fiend named Smarlinghue. A painter by trade. It was necessary, for Marie LaSalle had vanished after the supposed death of Larry the Bat, disappeared in order to preserve him from police suspicion. Jimmie was determined to find his beloved Tocsin, with whom he had fallen deeply in love. Smarlinghue was the means by which he combed the underworld in search of her trail.

By the most minute of clues, this Altamont had correctly reasoned that Jimmie had been experimenting with an alternate identity. He obviously possessed a formidable mind — one as sharp as a saber's edge.

Jimmie had no intention of underestimating him.

He went to an alcove holding a squat, barrel-shaped steel safe of his own design. Opening the fabulously-complicated outer and inner doors with practiced fingers, Jimmie removed a folded leather girdle of burglar tools, black slouch hat, and matching silk mask which were the only survivals of the late, unlamented Grey Seal.

Placing them into a black valise, he concealed it in the inner vestibule, ready for the evening's activities.

He began looking forward to this adventure, despite his deep misgivings.

*****

The winter darkness descended upon Riverside Drive early.

This was the evening of the Winter Solstice — the shortest day of the year — and Jimmie dreaded the coming of night. Dreaded or not, it soon arrived. Street lamps were lit, indoor electric lights came on, but nothing dispelled the darkness nor the cold of encroaching winter.

Jimmie had finished a dinner of steak and baked potato when his butler, the faithful Jason, entered the dining room.

"A man to see you, Master Jim. He said that you were expecting him."

Jimmie frowned. He was expecting no one. No one and no thing, except to venture out into the cold and the dark and rendezvous with Mr. Altamont in another hour.

"Did he present his card?"

"He did not, sir. His name is Altamont. He did not state his business."

"Altamont! How could I have forgotten? Yes, show him in, Jason."

Jimmie followed the butler into the drawing room and then dismissed him once Altamont was presented.

The man was bundled up against the cold and looked rather unprepossessing, being thin as a rail in face and form. He appeared nearly elderly, Jimmie saw with a shock. Much older than he had earlier reckoned. His features were red from the cold.

"I thought we were to meet at the St. James Club in an hour?" Jimmie blurted out.

Altamont said briskly, "There has been a change in plans. I am unable to enter the premises through my own recognizance. So, I have improvised an alternative plan. But fear not. I believe it to be foolproof."

"Before I risk my freedom," Jimmie returned levelly, "kindly lay this plan of yours out for my examination. And please keep your tone low. I have servants."

"The person who would normally permit me to enter the consulate has been called away on urgent business. As unfortunate as that may sound, it means one less person we would have to manage if matters should go awry."

"Come, come — the plan," urged Jimmie impatiently. "Out with it."

"I am coming to that. Parked a short distance away, as if making its rounds, is a common coal truck. I propose to bury you in anthracite, and slip you into the basement of the consulate through the coal chute. Since it is now dark, no one will be the wiser."

"Preposterous!"

"I thought it rather clever," mused Altamont, betraying a hint of a British accent. His mode of speech was an attempt at American English. It was passable, but only that.

"The safe of which I speak is not the consulate's office safe," he continued, "but a clandestine one that is secreted in a corner of the basement under a work bench and covered by a housepainter's drop cloth. Therefore, it is not normally guarded. Once you have been deposited to the coal chute, it should be no great effort to traverse the cellar undetected to the northwest corner and apply your remarkable skills to the combination dial."

"And if I refuse to do this?"

"Have we not already had this discussion? The risk is, in fact, a modest one. For I will leave the coal-chute window unlatched, permitting you to exit at your own liberty. Darkness will aid you. I will be waiting two blocks away to pluck you up, as it were."

Jimmie considered the matter at length.

"I do not like this," he said at last.

"But you will accomplish it. For I have faith in you. And if not you personally, in your innate patriotism as an American. Shall we go?"

Altamont's simple words penetrated Jimmie's brain. In an instant, he made his decision.

"Let me change clothes and fetch my valise."

"Very well."

Retreating to his bedroom, Jimmie carried his black valise and swiftly changed into clothing that was dark and disreputable, first donning a pair of grey leather gloves in order to keep his garments free of fingerprints. He wrapped around his waist the girdle of upright leather pouches that held so many of the slim blue steel lockpicks that made the Grey Seal such a formidable safecracker, securing it with straps to his shoulders, in the manner of a life preserver. A small-calibre automatic pistol went into a pocket. He might not need any of these tonight, but he dared not chance it.

A topcoat of warm black wool went over his girdle, and he took up the valise, joining Altamont. They swiftly left the dwelling, saying nothing to Jason.

Outside, the air was bitter. But Jimmie's heart was more bitter still. He did not like this adventure. He did not trust this Altamont. Yet there was something in his compelling manner, the calm confidence with which he comported himself, that made Jimmie think that this undertaking had a reasonable chance of success.

Briskly, they walked to a coal truck almost as red as a fire engine and displaying a fashionable amount of automotive brass. Jimmie climbed into the open tonneau, where he donned the black slouch hat calculated to half-conceal his hair and features.

Altamont gave the engine a good cranking, then joined him, slipping behind the steering wheel. With a coughing grumble of the motor, they were off into traffic.

The German consulate was uptown, and they rode in silence for a time. Jimmie found himself staring at the man's stiff profile. He did not appear to be wearing a disguise, yet there was something not quite human about his hawk-like features. But for the cold-reddened cast of his skin, Altamont might have been a Red Indian — a war chief of a bygone era.

"On the seat beside you," Altamont stated as they pushed northward, "you will discover a manila envelope, secured with string. Do not open it. Hide it in your topcoat.

When you remove a similar envelope, you will find on the safe's top shelf, replace it with this one."

Jimmie inserted the envelope carefully into his leather girdle where it would not be dislodged.

"You are swapping false documents for genuine ones?" he asked.

"It is more complicated than that, Dale. These documents were removed from the safe by myself. I am having you replace them before their absence is noticed. For, if noticed, suspicion might glare in my direction. In order that my mission in America succeed, I cannot permit this. The papers you are taking will surely be missed in due course, but their loss cannot be traced back to me. This is also critical to the success of the endeavor."

"Did you crack the safe in question?"

Altamont shook his solemn head. "I did not. Conceivably, I could have. But to do so would take considerable time and effort, during which I might be discovered. No, this job requires the skill and finesse of a man who has done it many times over without mistake. As for the papers in your hand, I merely purloined them when the safe was open in my presence and no one was looking my way. For the man in charge of the safe — whom I carefully will not name — happened to be preoccupied with other more enticing documents I provided him at the time. The documents you are to remove are the documents I provided him."

"I do not understand the purpose of such a subterfuge," Jimmie confessed.

"The purpose, my dear fellow, is to sow confusion and confound an adversary of my country and your own. Also, it will further the larger plan in which I am engaged."

"You are a spy, then."

"I prefer to think of myself as an honorable emissary of my native country."

An impressive mansion loomed ahead, its many windows aglow.

"Now here we come to our destination," snapped Altamont. "I will pull over in this convenient alley where you will draw on your silken mask — I trust you brought it — and crawl into our heaped cargo of coal, concealing yourself with my assistance. I assume that your own imagination will supply the remaining details of our little operation."

Stepping out, Jimmie said dryly, "I am glad that I wore my best evening clothes."

The other man chuckled at the wry jest and exited the truck.

"When you have finished your work," he directed, "return to this alley. I will be waiting."

"You had better."

Altamont had parked with the truck's rear facing the back bricks of the alley, so no one saw Jimmie Dale don the black silk mask that completed his alternative identity as the Grey Seal and then crawl into the truck's wide bed while Altamont used a shovel to further bury him in cold nuggets of grimy anthracite.

Jimmie had the foresight to use a grey handkerchief to cover his mouth and nose, otherwise he would be breathing coal dust, and his lungs would be wracked with convulsive coughs that could only betray him.

"You appear to be well situated," remarked Altamont. "I daresay you will need no further instruction. And so off we go."

The truck motor had been left idling. Altamont shortly had it lumbering back into traffic. It traveled only a short distance, paused, and then began backing up into a driveway, turning sharply to align the back of the truck with the foundation wall.

Jimmie heard the tramp of footsteps and a rattle indicating the coal-chute aperture had been opened.

Then, the bed of coal began to tip forward as Altamont cranked the mechanism which would permit the coal to flow through the wide aperture at the rear. This was opened by yanking a lever.

After that came a clinking and crunching as the man employed his shovel. He had climbed into the back and straddled Jimmie's concealed form. As he shoved coal down the inclined bed, he used his shovel to propel Jimmie through the rear aperture and into the waiting coal chute built behind a narrow open window in the consulate's granite foundation.

Fortunately, the consulate was a large building and required a great deal of anthracite to heat its titanic furnace. Using his hands and feet, Jimmie propelled himself down the tin chute and into the cellar, landing in a coal bin constructed of plain barnboard. Coal continued tumbling down upon him. Jimmie found a corner in which he could hunker until the clattering torrent ceased.

The coal-chute window was left slightly ajar, then Jimmie heard the truck soon drive off.

Handkerchief clamped over his mouth and nose, Jimmie waited. He knew that someone might descend to check the delivery. But no one did. After twenty minutes of waiting, he stirred and groped his way to the coal-bin door.

It was padlocked on the other side. Jimmie's tools were useless, since he stood on the opposite side of the lock. Fortunately, the walls did not go all the way to the rafters. Therefore, it only took a bit of climbing and wriggling to ease over the top edge and drop carefully on the other side.

The close air had a familiar musty smell that belonged to cellars alone. He could make out shapes and shadows, but that was all.

Plucking out a small electric flashlight, Jimmie put his grimy handkerchief over the lens to throttle the telltale illumination. With this weak light as a guide, he crept to the northwest corner, brushing aside dusty cobwebs, and by touch located the steel safe underneath the workbench littered with ordinary carpenter tools. Using one grey-gloved hand, he pulled away the concealing drop cloth, exposing the combination dial to the mellow glow of his torch.

Crouching before the safe, he removed the handkerchief from his flashlight, shielding its back glow with the wings of his coat. Hunkering down, he studied the combination dial, and with his tapered and sensitive fingers began working the outer ring. Back-and-forth, listening carefully, he plied his secretive trade.

Once he was satisfied that the tumblers had clicked, he went to the inner ring and commenced twirling the digits.

This was careful, painstaking work, and it was almost done when there came the creak of a door opening, followed by a splash of electric light, then slow, measured footsteps pressing down upon wooden risers.

Someone was entering the cellar!

Clicking off his torch, Jimmie pivoted, but remained in a crouching position. Slowly, he drew the drop cloth over the safe front, masking the gleaming dial.

Only a vague light came through the cellar windows. Thus, Jimmie could barely see the hulking figure moving about. Peculiar that he did not turn on the light switch.

But then he did. It was one of those rheostat-style switches, situated mid-way down the steps. When the light came on, it was of low wattage. Crouching underneath the workbench, on the opposite side of the still-shut safe, Jimmie kept immobile.

The coal dust smeared all over his lower face kept it from being revealed by the light. At the same time, the stuff had caked around his nostrils and Jimmie began to feel a compelling urge to sneeze.

Pinching his nostrils shut, he quelled the impulse. But this forced him to open his firm lips in order to take in air. And he began inhaling coal dust through his mouth.

When the impulse to cough started creeping up on him, Jimmie shut his mouth, pinched his nostrils and prayed that the man's business was routine.

As it turned out, it appeared to be so.

The hulking shadow went directly to the coal bin, unlocked it and, taking up a coal scuttle, began carrying mounds of the black stuff to the coal furnace.

Once he had filled the great cavity, he ignited the furnace with a match.

The device began to roar pleasantly, and yellow-red flames were leaping around the vented feed-door of cast iron.

Jimmie could no longer hold back his cough. In one inner pocket, he carried a flat flask. Taking this out, he unscrewed the cap and drank from the reservoir. It was simple tap water, but it did its job, washing his throat and clearing it.

In the act of replacing the cap, it fumbled free from his gloved fingers, making a tiny sound on the concrete floor.

Jimmie froze. He shut his eyes, afraid that they would catch and reflect the cherry-red light coming from the furnace. He waited.

No sound alerted him to approaching danger. So, Jimmie opened one eye. It fell on the man looming only a few yards away.

Oblivious to all sound, the silent fellow stood watching the operation of the furnace for several minutes. It was roaring throatily. The steady noise had masked his mistake. Then, evidently satisfied, he locked up the coal bin and returned to the first floor, after extinguishing the electric light.

He had no sooner departed than Jimmie started coughing in a restrained manner. He downed more water, found the fallen cap and replaced it, pocketing the life-saving flask.

Returning to the safe door, Jimmie brushed aside the drop cloth. Bringing his electric torch back into play, he finished working on the combination dial. Finally, the last tumbler clicked. Then he reached for the steel handle with one gloved hand, giving it a quick twist.

The handle rotated all the way and Jimmie eased the heavy door open.

Using his flashlight, he found the top shelf and removed the envelope containing the documents. Before he could replace it with the one he had brought tucked into his girdle of tools, he froze.

For his gloved fingers left dusty coal smears on the first envelope!

Momentarily stymied, he considered the problem. To remove a glove meant leaving fingerprints. The prints of Jimmie Dale could be found in no police file. That did not mean they might not incriminate him at a later date.

The solution proved deceptively simple. Dipping into his tool kit, he extracted a simple set of tweezers, and then removed the envelope with it, carefully placing it on the top shelf.

This accomplished, he closed the door and spun both dials, satisfied that he had completed his unwanted assignment.

The drop cloth was replaced last. Then Jimmie stood up.

Now to escape.

Carefully, Jimmie crept toward the coal bin. He would have to scale the wooden wall again and slip over. This proved more difficult, since he did not have a mound of coal to raise him up to start with.

He took his time, for to lose his grip and fall would mean disaster. Again, his coal-smeared gloves made him pause. He decided that leaving coal marks on a coal bin did not matter.

Taking the top edge firmly in both hands, he lifted his lithe body, hooking the top with his right leg, then pulled himself up.

Eventually, Jimmie got himself balanced upon the edge. He rolled over and landed rather clumsily on the coal pile. From there, it was a matter of stepping cautiously to the back and pushing open the long narrow window that let in cool air that he needed desperately now.

Wriggling out was not so simple as sliding in. Jimmie took the precaution of poking his head out first. He saw no one in the side yard. So he began pulling himself up, pushing his head and shoulders out and then using his elbows to lever up and out.

The awkwardness of this means of escape forced him to sprawl on the ground at the end. There, he lay for a moment, looking about with anxious eyes and not daring to stand up until he was certain no observers lurked about.

Jimmie squandered ten minutes with this precaution. Finally, he got to his feet and started creeping toward the street.

Jimmie had gotten only a dozen paces when from around the front of the entrance, a towering figure stepped up, a revolver gleaming in his right fist.

A guttural voice spoke heavily, urgently. "You will stop where you are. Upraise your hands. Do not make foolish moves."

As if to emphasize the threat, the warning click of the revolver being cocked came distinctly.

Caught!

This was Jimmie Dale's greatest nightmare. Not only was he apprehended with documents belonging to the German government on his person, but he was wearing the black silk mask and unique tool kit that marked him as the Grey Seal.

Or did it?

He had not left behind any of his trademark seals. But did that matter? When they unmasked him, they would see the features of the respectable society man, Jimmie Dale.

The German growled, "You will be so good as to walk to the back and we will enter through the rear door. Turn about!"

Having absolutely no alternative, Jimmie obeyed. The hard muzzle of the gun pressed into his back, impelling him forward. His footsteps were leaden as he trudged his way back.

Turning, he was prodded through the rear door and into a back room that seemed to have no particular function. There was no furniture. And only one window. The ceiling light was not turned on. Only street illumination pervaded. He wondered if he was to be murdered here.

"Now we will see who you are," his captor sneered.

Keeping his gun trained on Jimmie's chest, the man reached over and removed the slouch hat. He tossed this aside. Jimmie's hair was exposed, but his haircut was no different than any other man's. The silken mask concealed his upper features.

The gunman's free hand reached out abruptly and yanked the black silk mask from his head — revealing all!

Jimmie had considered resisting, but the man would have shot him at point-blank range. Disgrace was one thing, death quite another. He would deal with disgrace. He would survive to live it down, if he could. Visions of steel prison bars materialized in his tense brain.

The man gave a curt curse as his eyes fell on Jimmie's exposed features.

"I fail to recognize you! Who is the devil are you? Answer now!"

Jimmie did not hesitate. "My name is Bannister. That is all that I will confess."

"I do not know you."

"I do not want you to," retorted Jimmie.

The man lifted his voice and called for assistance.

"*Achtung*! Come and see here!"

Footsteps came loudly, and two firm-faced men entered the dim room. They looked like officials — diplomats or attachés. They possessed hard features under shaven bullet skulls. Jimmie took them to be the type of spies who inhabit foreign embassies.

"Who is this man?" one demanded harshly.

"He purports to be named Bannister. I have never heard of him."

"Who do you work for?" asked the other.

"I am a freelance," replied Jimmie, going along with their suspicions.

The two newcomers studied Jimmie carefully. One said, "Bring a washcloth. This man's face is so black with coal dust, it is not possible to properly make out his face."

And then Jimmie realized the truth! They could not discern his true features!

As if energized by this knowledge, Jimmie waited for one of the men to rush away for a washcloth and soap. Then his grey-gloved fist struck out and knocked the revolver from the first man's fingers.

This daring move took the pair by surprise. The revolver sailed across the room, rebounded off one wall, and because the hammer was cocked, the weapon discharged.

The bullet jumped into the ceiling. Plaster spilled downward. That was enough to send the two men scrambling, fearful of a ricochet.

While they were so preoccupied, Jimmie ducked out the back door, raced toward the rear fence and vaulted it with a strength born of sheer desperation, landing in a backyard belonging to another home.

He ran for his life. Certainly, for his freedom. He rushed to the street, around a corner, and attempted to get his bearings.

Behind him lifted exclamations — cries in German that Jimmie recognized as commands that he be hunted down.

Using his gloved fingers, Jimmie smeared more coal dust on his exposed face, for that was the only thing that preserved his true identity and the reputation of the Dale family.

There was no sign of Altamont, but Jimmie had left by the rear, which put him on a back street. He knew he could not hail a cab, dressed as he was. He would have to walk until he located the coal truck or figured something out. And so he walked on, wondering if Altamont had heard the ruckus.

If so, would he rush to his aid, or flee the vicinity?

Blocks along, his heart leapt. The headlamps of a coal truck came around the corner, illuminating him like a scarecrow caught in a searchlight.

"Altamont," he breathed.

Sprinting for the truck, he jumped into the open tonneau, landing on the passenger seat.

"I was discovered!" he panted.

"So I gathered," the other man said without undue concern. Gears grinding, the truck began rolling, and Jimmie ducked down, endeavoring to keep out of sight.

"Do you have the envelope?" Altamont demanded.

"In my tool kit."

"Capital! Then we have succeeded."

"But the Germans are in hot pursuit."

Altamont yanked the wheel hard to the left and sent the cumbersome delivery truck trundling up a narrow alley.

They progressed three-quarters of the way up the alley when a knot of figures appeared at the street behind them. One raised his revolver. There came a sharp report, and some of the coal in the truck bed jumped and fractured.

Altamont gunned the engine, then took a right at the other end, swerving ahead of a follow-up bullet. It struck the dull brass work, then went singing off into space harmlessly.

Taking out his automatic, Jimmie twisted his body about, preparing to return fire.

Altamont's grip stayed him. "No bloodshed! I must work with these men in the future."

"I would not dream of it," retorted Jimmie, firing two quick shots into the night sky, the weapon sounding like a spiteful dog barking.

Behind them, the Germans ducked and scattered in as many directions as were available. Wild bullets flying about in the dark had a way of cowing even armed men.

Pulling onto a thoroughfare, Altamont said, "Quick thinking. Our friends dare not pursue us now. They may or may not call the police. Most probably, they will check the contents of their safe. When they find the documents you replaced, they will breathe a sigh of relief. They may or may not notice the absence of the envelope that you procured. If they do, they will likely conclude that this is not a police matter."

"They saw my face," said Jimmie, still crouching down where no one could see him in the dark. For he knew the coating of coal dust made him a marked man.

Taking his eye off the road, Altamont looked down and appraised him carefully.

"We are of short acquaintance," he allowed. "Even so, I doubt I would recognize you for who you truly are. Strangers would be unable to match your coal-smeared face with that of your washed visage. All that matters now is to whisk you safely homeward."

"I cannot return home looking like this," Jimmie insisted. "I am covered in coal dust and no doubt leave footprints as black as India ink. They would be damning."

"Remove your shoes and wipe the bottoms of your shoes' soles. This will solve one problem."

Struggling to stay out of sight, Jimmie complied.

As he was wiping, he urged, "Take me to the Bowery."

"As you say."

It was several minutes before they were rocking through the Bowery below the Dead Line, where Gangland held sway.

By this time, Jimmie had used his flask of water and the lining of his dark coat to wipe his face. It was hardly a thorough job, but in the darkness any remaining traces could be mistaken for mere city grime.

The tool kit was back in the black valise and Jimmie began breathing more easily.

"I see that you have lost both your hat and mask, Dale. I trust that you left no fingerprints?"

"I never put on my hat or mask unless I am wearing gloves," assured Jimmie. "Up ahead. That is the building — the brick one."

Altamont slowed the truck. "This is where you have your hideaway."

Jimmie said nothing. His new Sanctuary was a secret. Or so he believed.

"I should be able to slip inside without any trouble," he breathed. "My makeup kit is there. I will exit again in disguise, find my way home, and no one will be the wiser."

"Very good," said Altamont. "I trust you to conclude the night's activities with the skill and aplomb you have displayed thus far. I want to assure you that our business is now concluded."

Jimmie eyed the man's solemn profile. "How can I trust you?"

"You need not. Time will show you the truth of my words. Nothing else will suffice. I am bound for Chicago on the morning train. And you are bound for what is no doubt a comfortable bed. It is unlikely we will ever meet again."

The truck pulled over and Jimmie picked up his valise, while the mysterious Mr. Altamont took the envelope of documents and placed it inside of his topcoat.

"It is important that no one knows that the Grey Seal walked one more time," Jimmie said in parting.

"I have taken certain steps to confuse the issue."

His hand on the dashboard, Jimmie paused before exiting.

"Certain steps?"

"If the Germans summoned the police, you will read about it in the morning newspapers. If you do not, then consider it all a dead issue. Either way, you have my profound thanks, as well as the gratitude of my humble nation."

Wearing a puzzled frown, Jimmie hopped out and made for the vestibule of the ancient rat-trap building containing his hideout. He did not look back as the truck rumbled off, disappearing into the night.

Jimmie mounted the dim staircase to the squalid room rented to the imaginary drug-wrecked artist named Smarlinghue.

This was his new Sanctuary, for the old one had burned up.

Locking the door, he doffed his coal-smeared duds and changed into fresh clothes. Only then did he light the gas-jet that sputtered out fitful yellowish illumination. Carefully, he stowed his black valise in a hiding place behind a removable section of baseboard.

Relief washed over him as he removed more coal deposits from his hands and face, using a rickety washstand and cloth.

Sitting at the table, he applied makeup to his features, changing them into a semblance that was neither Jimmie Dale nor the imaginary Smarlinghue, whose easel and paints stood nearby.

Once satisfied that his face was not his own, Jimmie doused the gas-jet and took up the bag into which he had stuffed his incriminating coal-dusted clothes. This bundle he carried into the basement.

Opening the cast-iron feed door of the massive coal furnace, he tossed the bundle in and watched through the vents as the greedy flames licked and consumed the last traces of the Grey Seal's latest, most wicked adventure.

Returning to the first floor, he stepped out into the night and hailed a taxicab which took him to Riverside Drive. The driver let him off two blocks north of his address, where Jimmie removed his makeup under cover of darkness.

Then he struck for home, once more himself.

Faithful Jonas met him at the door, saying, "I did not realize you were out, Master Jim."

"I was showing Mr. Altamont the sights of New York," Jimmie said with forced jauntiness. "He was quite pleased with the evening's diversions. I believe that I will retire early, Jonas. Good night."

"Very good, sir."

*****

Jimmie slept well that night. When he woke up, a folded copy of the *Morning News-Argus* rested beside his breakfast setting.

Unfolding it, he scanned the headline. His heart gave a trout-like leap.

GREY SEAL RETURNS FROM DEAD
Master Cracksman Strikes Again

Fearfully, he read the front-page story. The German ambassador had complained that a masked man had entered their cellar and burgled an auxiliary safe, taking away confidential documents. The man had been briefly detained and unmasked, but his features had been unreadable, owing to a coating of coal dust.

Then Jimmie's heart quailed.

According to the story, the burglar had left behind a taunting sign of his handiwork. An untouched envelope had been opened. Within lay a diamond-shaped seal made of grey paper that could not be accounted for.

"Altamont!" Jimmie cried. "Only he could have —"

The enigmatic Mr. Altamont had gone out of his way to point the stern finger of guilt at the Grey Seal. But for what purpose? It was unfathomable.

For the next two days, Manhattan buzzed with the word that the notorious Grey Seal had risen from the dead.

Some claimed that this was a copycat crime. Others, that the infamous super-crook had not died in the tenement fire that had supposedly claimed the life of Larry the Bat.

The police were frantic. A city-wide dragnet had been cast. The usual police characters were rounded up and questioned closely under the hot glare of Headquarters lights.

Owing to the international complications, Washington was apoplectic. The President of the United States was determined to keep America out of the growing war in Europe. All efforts were made to reassure the German ambassador in Washington that this was not the work of U.S. secret agents. Suspicions were intensifying between the warring Kaiser and neutral America.

Jimmie laid low, avoiding his usual haunts — the Bowery and the St. James Club equally. It was too chancy to do otherwise.

*****

One week after the burglary of the German consulate, Jimmie braved the dining room of the St. James Club to have lunch with Herman Carruthers, the managing editor of the *Morning News-Argus* — despite his not yet having reached the age of thirty. The uproar had simmered down. Carruthers had a pipeline into official police matters. It was high time, Jimmie thought, to probe where the investigation stood. His fellow clubman was the surest source of information.

"This has been quite a profitable story for you, Carruthers," Jimmie remarked calmly. "You must be selling twice the number of papers as usual."

Carruthers should have been smiling. Instead, he was profoundly glum of mien.

"Would that this charade had continued another week — another day," he sighed. "But Headquarters informs me this morning that their detectives have concluded a thorough examination of the grey paper seal found in the German safe. It is a clumsy fake, not even gummed on the back. The paper is of poor quality. As you know, they have on file authentic examples of the original Grey Seal's trademark. Those are of uniformly good quality. Now they have concluded that this daring burglary is not the Grey Seal's handiwork, after all. I am forced to report this in an extra. Our headline will proclaim: 'Grey Seal still deceased.' " Carruthers glanced at his wrist watch. "It should land in the streets at any moment."

"This revelation will certainly sell a lot of papers," Jimmie observed. "No doubt about it."

Carruthers nodded. "But after that extra is issued, circulation will fall back to normal numbers. Such is the life cycle of a newspaperman."

"I'm sure New York will be all the happier for that news."

"Personally," said Carruthers, "I doubted it myself. As you know, I have followed the exploits of the Grey Seal since his beginning. No one could have survived that terrible tenement fire. And if the Grey Seal had, he would have resumed his nefarious operations long before this. As it stands, the police are searching for a yegg who may or may not be named Bannister."

Settling back into his chair, Jimmie Dale relaxed. The Grey Seal might or might not return, but for the moment, Headquarters considered him still buried in the past. This was a relief, and more than he could have hoped for.

*****

A few days later, Jimmie received a letter postmarked Chicago. It was typed. There was no return address. Only two typewritten words: Altamont Hotel. Jimmie doubted any such establishment existed.

The envelope was marked: *Confidential.*

"My dear Dale," it began.

"I have been reading reports out of New York. It appears that I was mistaken. I did not think the German diplomat would be so bold as to report the intrusion. But I read that he has. No doubt you have been wondering why I left a certain crude seal in the envelope you so kindly restored to the German safe. Perhaps the truth has occurred to you by now.

"If not, permit me to explain. In investigating criminal activities, police detectives pay a great deal of attention to what they call a *modus operandi*. The *modus operandi* of the mysterious craftsman who opened the German safe, I reasoned, would point the finger of suspicion at the Grey Seal — for they are one and the same. The best way to neutralize any theories in that direction, I believed, would be to leave a seal that would make them think this from the start. Yet upon more careful examination, dispel the premature theory for all time. Thus, I manufactured an example of a grey paper seal too cheap to pass muster. I am pleased to learn that my good opinion of New York City detectives is not misplaced.

"I remain grateful for your assistance. I think it unlikely that we shall meet again. No doubt you will burn this letter."

It was signed, "Yours sincerely, Sleuth Hound."

Jimmie fed the letter into the den fireplace, considering the strange signature with its capitalized letters, S. H. It seemed to suggest another personality entirely.

"If I did not know better," he murmured, "I would think that Mr. Altamont was in reality Sherlock Holmes. But Holmes has disappeared into retirement. Or at least so the London newspapers have reported."

As Jimmie watched the paper curl and darken, the typewritten letters melting forever from sight, he began to doubt the normally reliable reports out of London....

The Wilhelm House Curse

by Derrick Belanger

I received a card with a brief message from Carnacki requesting my presence that evening at Cheyne Walk, Chelsea. He did not explain the topic of conversation nor why he had provided me with such short notice. It didn't matter, for I never missed a dinner party by Mr. Carnacki. The man was a detective who investigated strange occurrences possibly supernatural in nature. When called upon, I would go to his home joined by our three mutual friends – Jessop, Arkright, and Taylor. We would dine together and then Mr. Carnacki would regale us with a fanciful tale of one of his extraordinary investigations.

This night was no different. The detective welcomed us and we dined on a delicious meal of cod pie. Carnacki talked on many different topics from the impact of recent storms on the construction of lighthouses to the unstudied traits of a cunning wicketkeeper. While we all politely engaged in conversation with our host, we really wanted to know the reason he had called us there.

It was not until we had retired to Carnacki's library and sat in our respective chairs with glasses of brandy that he sated our curiosity.

"That tome," Carnacki said, pointing to an ancient, gnarled leather book he had on display in his locked cabinet of biblio curiosities, "comes from the Wilhelm House. You, of course, are unfamiliar with the small Tudor estate in Marylebone. That is the setting of the little matter which is the topic for this evening."

Carnacki had been filling his pipe. He paused and struck a match. "A simple matter, really, but one of perspective. From a distance, it was easy enough to sort out, but like an eye held to a flame," here he paused and held the match to his face, "I was too closely involved in the matter and therefore, blinded by the light." He shook the match out and deposited it in the ash tray.

"I was visited by a member of the stock exchange. Mr. Xavier Walsh was a broker with exquisite tastes as I could tell from his fine pressed suit, perfectly molded hair, and expensive cologne. His girth also matched his appetite, and he came to me over a property he had inherited. The man rambled as he introduced himself and it took him awhile to find the point he wanted to make."

"'Do you know of Mr. Jessop Hartley, sir?' he enquired in his barking voice, asking as though the answer would determine if he made a sale. 'No? Well, my friend, he knew you. He spoke highly of Mr. Carnacki. Hartley was our associate jobber. We didn't have a jobber, Benson and I, we were both brokers, and so a few years ago we went into it together, "Walsh, Hartley, and Benson," perhaps you've heard of us? No, well, you should get into investments, my friend. Buy low. Sell high. Easy enough to do, but few do it.

"'You want me to get to the point, I can tell by your furrowed brow. I can't say I blame you. In my profession, time is money, and one delayed trade can mean a difference from gaining a hundred pounds to losing a thousand.'

"'You said this Hartley knew of me,' I said, trying to get the blowhard to focus. 'Very few know of me in the way you describe, that is, of my knowledge of the ghostly realm.'

"'Well, Hartley was into all that mumbo jumbo gobbledy gook. Poor man was a widow. A few years after his wife's death but still before he joined my partner and I, he also lost his son. Poor fellow. That's when he turned to the spiritualists. He used mediums to speak to the dead, practiced seances, and travelled often to Africa. The man came back with all sorts of bizarre trinkets. It's all a bunch of hooey if you ask me.

"'Our other partner, Benson, was a devout Anglican and it always bothered him to be in partnership with a heathen, as he'd whisper to me behind Hartley's back. To be honest, Mr. Carnacki, I'm a practical man. I like to see things with my own eyes to believe it, as they say, so I was just as suspicious of Benson's beliefs as I was of Hartley's.

"'Anyhoo, about a year ago, Hartley was very pleased with himself. He had purchased a house in Marylebone, supposedly a haunted house, if you believe that. Oh, you probably do, don't you, Mr. Carnacki? Don't answer. Let me finish. This house, The Wilhelm House, was a simple Tudor that had been around for hundreds of years. It originally was part of the Wilhelm family as it had to be. That's where the curse comes in. According to legend, Malaki Wilhelm was a warlock who was a practitioner of black magic. I know this all sounds ridiculous. But the story goes a tax collector claimed Mr. Wilhelm was behind on his payments and therefore the property would be seized. Wilhelm was furious and put a curse on the house saying that only a member of the Wilhelm family could ever live there. If another man lay claim to the house, then the dark beasts he commanded would slay the man in his sleep and take his soul to Hell. All very dramatic, isn't it? The tax collector was found dead a few days after trying to take Wilhelm's property. Thus, the Wilhelm house stayed in the Wilhelm family for centuries. Whenever an owner of the house fell on hard times and someone tried to take the house by money or by force, they ended up dead a few days later. This went on until about twenty years ago when the last descendant of Maliki Wilhelm passed out of this world. The house has exchanged hands with several owners since then until, at last, it landed in Mr. Hartley's care.'

"I stopped Mr. Walsh and asked the man how a cursed house that had to stay in the Wilhelm family could have multiple owners over the course of twenty years.

"'I wondered that myself. Hartley explained that it ends up Old Wilhelm hadn't just said that his descendants could lay claim to the house. He had said his descendants or one the spirits deem worthy could claim ownership of the house. There was a ritual that had to be performed, and if the new owner of the house passed the test, he could claim the house. If he failed, well then...' Here Mr. Walsh stopped and ran his pointer finger across his neck to emphasize what happened to those deemed unworthy."

Carnacki paused in his storytelling to take a sip of brandy. His eyes took a quick glance over at the book in his cabinet, and I noted a sense of unease about the man. It made me feel queasy, for what could that book contain which caused such a sense of foreboding in the Ghost Finder.

"Walsh's story," Carnacki continued, "struck me as having many elements of folktales: the haunted house, the curse by a wronged or dying man, the smiting of those who broke the rules. These are elements told to children by adults to keep them out of mischief. 'Don't go into the old Magully house or you'll be cursed,' and such like that. Clearly, Mr. Walsh was using his salesman skills and setting up the pitch, as they say. I was waiting to see what he wanted me to do about this supposedly haunted establishment.

"'Now, you're probably wondering why I am spending so much of your precious time on this silly story of a curse,' Walsh correctly surmised. 'Well, here's where things get interesting. About two months ago, Mr. Hartley, God rest his soul, died while traveling in the Congo.'

"'Cause of death?' I inquired, interrupting my vivacious storyteller.

"'He complained of an upset stomach the night before and pains in his chest. The next morning, he had passed on.'

"'Any witnesses?'

"'You mean besides the savages? Yes, a few of the sailors he had travelled with, British citizens, confirmed the death and his request to be buried in the Congo.'

"'So, his body did not return to England?'

"'Correct. Is that important?'

"'Oh,' I said coolly. 'I'm just trying to get all of the facts. So, what happened after Mr. Hartley's untimely death?'

"'That's where things get really interesting. Benson and I were visited by the executor of Hartley's estate. A young man by the name of Ferguson. Benson and the executor got along fine as both had served in the royal navy. I was also impressed with Ferguson because, like me, he was practical, and seemed almost embarrassed by the terms of Hartley's will. He explained, and tried not to scoff, that Benson would inherit the entire Hartley estate if he followed the rules set forth in claiming the Wilhelm House."

Carnacki explained the rules to us. The inheritor of the estate must spend the night in the house. In the Tudor, there is a small chapel room. In the chapel is an ancient leather-bound tome which the inheritor will find open on the pedestal. When Carnacki explained this part, he motioned to the book he had locked away in his cabinet, and we all knew that the ancient tome of the story and the book in the cabinet were one and the same.

"Walsh explained that at the stroke of midnight, the inheritor must prick their finger, and sign their name in their own blood inside the book. After spending the remainder of the night in the house, the inheritor may leave any time after first light. The spirits will then convene and make their decision if the claimant is worthy to inherit the Wilhelm House.

"'We all had a laugh, the lawyer included, after he finished his explanation,' Walsh told me. 'Benson then signed the paperwork, half of which was in some ancient tongue, typical of good ole Hartley, and then he was given the key to the house. Benson is a fine man, and he told me that after he spent the night in the Wilhelm House and inherited Hartley's portion of the business, he'd let me buy half of Hartley's share so that we both would remain equal owners.

"'Benson spent that night in the Wilhelm House. He followed the directions with fidelity, and signed his name in blood precisely at the stroke of midnight. The next day, he told me the house was quite small and the bed old and uncomfortable. Nothing odd occurred that night, and his only complaints were about the cramped quarters, lack of electricity to the home, and how he had to draw blood to sign the infernal book. Benson said he'd sell the house soon and be happy to be rid of it. Poor soul never had a chance. He was found dead in his home the next day. His heart had stopped in the night.'

Carnacki shivered slightly thinking back to the look on Mr. Walsh's face. "The man was terrified, and with a quivering hand, he reached into his pocket and took out an old, rusty key. He explained that a much more nervous Mr. Ferguson had come to see him to provide him with the key to the Wilhelm House for he was next in line to inherit the property."

"'My business is stocks, Mr. Carnacki," he continued, "which makes me a gambling man. Some gambles are safe and others risky. With the death of Benson, this gamble moved quickly from the realm of a safe bet to that of a risk. Mind you, I still don't believe in this curse and believe that there is most likely a rational explanation to all of this, possibly even coincidence. Still —"

"'You'd rather that I make certain that there is, to the best of my knowledge, nothing to the curse.'

"Relief swept over the man when I said this.

"'Yes, you understand perfectly Mr. Carnacki. I'd like to hire you to inspect the house this evening before I arrive to make sure all is well. I checked, and there is nothing in the rules about having more than one person in the house when I sign the book. So, I'll give you some time to inspect the house, and then I'll arrive around eleven o'clock tonight. If you detect nothing wrong, I will join you and I'll sign the book, and if all goes as expected, in the morning I'll inherit Hartley's estate and reward you handsomely for your trouble.'"

*****

Carnacki paused his narrative so that we could refill our glasses of brandy. Jessop, Arkright, Taylor, and I exchanged glances which said as much as if we were having an open discussion. *What unholy spirit awaited Carnacki in the Wilhelm House?* we asked, through raised brows and shifting jaws. *What horror did Carnacki have locked away in his book case?*

The answers to our questions would come soon enough for our host leaned back in his recliner and continued his tale.

"I agreed to Hartley's terms and at dusk I travelled to the Wilhelm House. It was an old dilapidated building, much out of place in its neighborhood. The houses around it had been knocked down and rebuilt, I'm certain, a number of times through the years, and the current models must have only been a decade or two in age. The Wilhelm House, in contrast, only showed cosmetic changes over the hundreds of years, and even those changes would have been out of date twenty-years ago. The grey paint on the house's exterior was chipped revealing bug infested boards. The shingles on the roof were pulled up in parts, and a soft green mold creeped from roof to base, coating the establishment in a sickly hue.

"The yard was wild and overgrown, yet I could tell it had been cared for within months, not years. That meant Mr. Hartley had done some upkeep before his untimely death. Perhaps, he planned to do more, but did not have the opportunity.

"The two front steps squeaked as I stepped on them, and the door looked so worn that I wondered if I might be able to push it open without the use of the key. I gave it a shove to see if it would give, but the lock held, and so I removed the rusty key from my pocket and used it in the door. It took a few twists to get the lock to work, but it did. The door slowly fell open and a loud creak cried from the hinges. With my bags in hand, I entered the establishment.

"The interior of the house was in much better upkeep than what had greeted me outside. The house was small, perhaps a total of 800 square feet, and it was sparsely decorated. I stepped into the main room, which acted as both parlor and dining room, which contained a couch and a small table with two splintered wooden chairs. I set my bags down and pushed the couch against the east wall, giving myself enough room to lay out my electric pentacle.

"Before setting up, I decided to explore the house. Off to the west side was a small tiled kitchen, with a stove and sink. I noted a change in the plaster from the main room to the kitchen, showing that the kitchen, though old, was a much more recent addition. The house originally was probably just the single room.

"I slipped back into the main room and eyed the walls which were barren. There were no holes from hanging portraits or pictures and so I surmised that the room had been recently painted. There was the outline in the ceiling of the attic entry at the back of the room. Beyond that, there was little to note of the room.

"There was a door in the rear of the dining room leading me to an addition. Here I found a tidy, small bedroom with a trundle and small side table, next to that was the water closet and then on the very end was the chapel. It was a tiny chapel, not much larger than a telephone booth. There was a pedestal on which rested that accursed tome opened to the most recent signature page. I noted the last signature was that of Mr. Benson and before him, Mr. Hartley. Resting next to the book was a gnarled wooden pen, the tip of which contained a pointed, sharp thorn. I could see that the man who would sign the book was intended to prick his finger with the thorn and then sign his name in his own blood.

"Having satisfied myself in knowing the lay of the land, I went back to my bags to get to work. I first removed the Sigsand manuscript and used it to perform a basic protection spell on myself. I did not feel any spiritual presence of ill or good, and thinking back to the chapel and how it was not part of the original house, I thought that the Wilhelm curse was probably nothing more than a fairy tale. Still, with the death of Benson, I couldn't rule anything out. So, I knew I had to try and summon whatever might be lurking on the edges.

"From my bags, I next removed a brass urn and the pieces of my electric pentacle including a battery. The Wilhelm house, though it contained some modern amenities, surprisingly had never updated to electric power. I assembled the pentacle and placed the urn in the corner of the room facing the direction of the planet Mercury.

"When all was ready, I went about the domicile lighting candles in each room as twilight was beginning to fade to darkness. I then returned to the pentacle, powered it up, and turned to the Sigsand manuscript. There was a particular spell to summon spirits haunting a house. It is challenging in that the spell combines chanting with very specific movements similar to that of the Indian yogi. If all was successful, I would bind whatever spirit was in the house to the brass urn that lay outside the pentacle. From my safe circle, I would be able to question the spirit, and if I found it to have evil intents, banish it from the house. The spell took no less than an hour to complete.

"As I performed the ritual, I noted scratching sounds seeming to come from the walls and ceiling. From those sounds, I knew there was something in the house with me. At the conclusion of the spell, I bowed before the vassal, exhausted, and kissed my hand in a salute to whatever I had trapped. But the vassal remained empty. I meditated, expanded my mind, tried to connect with the creature that had evaded capture. All was silent. I could not grasp whatever was in the house with me. I heard the scratching noises again in the ceiling. Then, there was a thunderous crash!

"I snapped out of my meditation, and if I hadn't been sitting with my legs crossed, would have surely jumped outside of my protective pentacle. The sound came from the back of the room. I turned to find that the entry to the attic was open, the crashing sound was the stair case falling open and hitting the wood floors. Nervously, I looked to those stairs which ended in the dark abyss at the attic entryway. The scratching sounds continued echoing from above.

"What manner of creature is this? I wondered. It had evaded my binding spell and was now inviting me to follow it up into the darkness of the attic. Beads of sweat coated my brow, and I fidgeted with my fingers trying to decide my next course of action. If the spirit was benevolent, then it could be trying to show me something of importance. If the spirit was malicious, then it was leading me to a trap. Whatever the creature was, it had to be powerful to evade the ethereal binds from the manuscript's spell. If I left the electric pentacle, the protection it provided would be lost. The other protection spell would not be enough to hold off the force. If this being was evil, then it would be my body that would be discovered in the morning with my soul trapped in whatever Hell this beast had created. But if it was good....

"Gentlemen, it was not a decision I took lightly. In the end, curiosity won out, and I stood and stepped outside of my protective pentacle. I took a candle and holder from the wall and with the flame quivering in my shaking hands, slowly approached the stairs. The floorboards creaked underneath my weight. Each step seemed to take a minute or two at a time, as I paused with each footfall, listening for that infernal scratching noise. I finally found myself at the base of the stairs, looking up into the absolute darkness, not knowing what awaited me.

"It took all of my will to ascend those steps, my heart pounding in my ears, my head twitching from side to side making sure nothing was about to pounce upon me. Then at last, I made it up the stairs and used the light to scan the room. I saw nothing but a barren space. Then, the thing loomed up from the shadows, a massive black form with demon wings, I winced, ready for it to strike when I was greeted by...honking.

"The sound was so unexpected that I lost my balance momentarily and almost stumbled back down the stairs. I know not how, but I was able to compose myself, maintain my balance, and even keep the candle in my hand. I held the light toward the sound and saw the familiar brown, black, and white markings of a goose. The fellow honked at me again, but not in an unfriendly manner. I looked about the room and found that boards in one part of the wall had rotted away. A tarp loosely was draped over the opening. That is how my feathered friend had entered the attic. I laughed aloud and gave a slight bow to the bird who had caused me so much angst.

"Not long after, I descended the stairs. It didn't take long to disassemble my pentacle, pack up my bags, and move the furniture back to its proper place. When Walsh arrived around 11, I explained the situation to him. He had a good laugh at my expense, snickering as I explained how I had been fooled by a common fowl.

"'That's a good one,' the man chortled, his nose flaring like the snout of a pig. He was quite pleased when I told him with certainty that the curse was no more than a fairy tale.

"I gave him a brief tour of the house, and just before midnight we stood at the chapel entryway. 'So that's it then. Just a bit of theatrics. Well, I don't mind playing my part and inheriting the wealth.'

"'I'm sure you don't,' I said jovially. I had grown fond of Walsh, despite his being a blowhard. He was amiable, and I appreciated his healthy sense of skepticism.

"Walsh picked up the pricking pen. It was about a minute before midnight and Walsh held the tip just above his finger, ready to impale it and draw blood. He lifted and was about to strike when a realization dawned on me, and I smacked the blade from his hand before he injured himself.

"'What in blazes, man?' he snapped.

"'Because there is no supernatural explanation for the death Mr. Benson does not mean there isn't a natural one. The curse may not be true, but that thorn could still have been used for a hundred years. With all of those people's blood on it, there could be a deadly disease that passes into one's body when the skin is broken.' I reached into my pocket and removed a small knife I carry. 'Use this instead.'

"Walsh thought of my explanation for a second, then he took the knife from me. 'Thank you, Mr. Carnacki,' he said in a voice of great respect.

"The hour turned to midnight, and Walsh made a small cut on his left hand. He then dipped his right pointer finger in the blood and signed his name in the book.

"'That's done,' he said with happy finality. 'This is my house now, Mr. Carnacki, or it will be soon. I guess it will still belong to the goose for a couple of days until I get the final estate paperwork.'

"With the hour being late, we talked just for a few minutes more about some logistics of the estate, including the cost of adding electricity. Then, we turned in for the night. Walsh preferred a soft cushion, and he found that the bed had a very firm mattress, so I ended up sleeping in the bedroom while Walsh took the couch.

"We rose the next morning, said our goodbyes, and then headed out for our homes. Walsh gave me payment for my services, and he invited me to come for dinner once he had added power to the house and repaired the attic.

"I left the Wilhelm House in high spirits. I breakfasted at a highly rated French bakery in Marylebone, and afterwards, deposited my payment in the bank before returning home. A pleasant day out was had and when I returned to Cheyne Walk, I thought the events of the previous evening left for a rather dull case. However, 48 hours after I said my goodbye to Mr. Walsh, I read in *the Times* of his death.

*****

"Carnacki paused in his retelling, and I could see great pain on his face for failing Mr. Walsh. How, I wondered, could the man have died when my host had ruled out both occult and supernatural explanations for the curse?

The Ghost Finder looked to each of his guests. "You are all asking yourselves the same question. It is the same question which went through my head. What did I miss that could explain this outcome?

"The article in the Times explained that Walsh had been meeting with a client when he clutched his chest and collapsed. Foul play was not suspected, and the article went on to say how odd it was that in a short amount of time all three members of the Walsh, Hartley, and Benson brokerage had died so closely together.

"I spent the morning trying to come to some conclusion, something that I had missed which would explain all, but I could not. I was stumped."

Carnacki leaned back in his chair, his intense gaze softened, and he shook his head, thinking back to his predicament. "You may think of me as a proud, man, my friends, but I am not so proud to admit when I am beaten. I could not solve this mystery without some help from a friend. So, I wrote to the man formerly known as the greatest detective in all of London. I wrote to Mr. Sherlock Holmes."

The Ghost Finder stood from his chair and talked as he went to his desk. "I had worked with Holmes on a couple of occasions, once helping him on one of his cases. Another time, an incident involving his Praed Street friend required all three of us to work together to solve a caper which I am not yet ready to speak about. Carnacki opened his top desk drawer and removed an envelope. He then walked back to his chair. "I should say that the world is not ready for that particular tale." Our host took his seat and removed the letter. "I had written to Holmes with all the details of the case, and the man, I should say my friend, responded quickly. I had this letter in my hand just two days after I had written to him."

Carnacki unfolded the letter and read:

Dear Mr. Carnacki,

It was a pleasant surprise to hear from you, my friend. Your case certainly is an intriguing one, and I believe that just as you supplied me with the answers I needed to finally bring the case of the cutter Alicia to a close, I have enough answers to help you do the same in this little puzzle around the Wilhelm House.

Let us review the facts which you so eloquently provided me. We have all three members of the brokerage Walsh, Hartley, and Benson appearing to die from natural causes. Two of the deaths are directly connected to the Wilhelm House, and the third death appears only connected to the house in a secondary way as Mr. Hartley was the owner of the establishment before his demise. All three men seemed to have died under similar circumstances, expiring from a heart condition.

If we start by examining the two most closely linked deaths then we shall look to

Mr. Benson and Mr. Walsh. Both died shortly after staying the night in the Wilhelm House. How similar were their times in the house? We know that they both spent the night, but they slept in different locations; Benson slept in the bed and Walsh slept on the couch. Since you slept on the bed, Mr. Carnacki with no ill effects, we can rule out the bedroom being involved in their deaths.

We know that they both signed the Wilhelm book; however, they both signed the book in different manners. Benson signed his name in the book using his pricked finger. Walsh, on the other hand, cut his left hand, and dipped his uncut finger on his right hand in the blood and used it for signing. Your idea that a disease could be spread through the jabbing device was well devised. I would have suspected the same thing; however, we have now ruled that out as a possibility.

Since have ruled out the needle as an instrument of death, we have to look at *what still remains as a possibility. There is only one thing left that we know for certain both Benson and Walsh touched, and that was the book in the chapel. Both men signed the book on a specific page. It should also be noted, my friend, that you did not touch the signature page in the book. If you had, I believe you would not have had the opportunity to write to me about this case. For, the evidence points to the book, at least the signature page in the book, being the cause of death. I fear that the signature page is laced with a deadly poison.*

If indeed I am correct and a toxic element was added to the page in the book then we need to ask ourselves a number of additional questions: What poison was used? How long had the poison been in the book? Is there a connection between Hartley's death and the deaths of Benson and Walsh? Let us start with the latter question and work our way to the former.

Hartley, we know, passed away on a voyage to Africa, specifically the African Congo. The jobber, we are told, complained of chest pains before dying, just as Mr. Walsh clutched at his chest before his death. We also know that Benson, while he died at home, died from heart failure. From these similar circumstances, it is more than likely that all three members of the brokerage died from the same means. What means was that? There happens to be a frog in the Congo sometimes nicknamed Death Chess because it has a black and white pattern similar to a chess board. The animal is rare, and little is known of the creature in the Empire. The amphibian secretes a liquid which is seemingly harmless, but stops the heart of those who come in contact with it in a matter of days. I surmise that someone killed Hartley with that poison, and then they added it to the signature page of the Wilhelm book. Anyone who touched the page with a bloody or clean finger would ingest the poison through the skin and would die soon after.

Knowing the means and method of the murder of the men, we have to ask ourselves the final questions: Who is responsible? Why did he do it? While I have enough data to answer these questions, it will be up to you, my friend, to answer them in their entirety.

I surmise that the man responsible is the executor, Mr. Ferguson. We know from Walsh that Hartley travelled with a few sailors when he visited the Congo. They were the witnesses of his death. We also know that Ferguson was a former Navy man, and therefore, was a sailor. Ferguson went with Hartley and arranged for his death. He then returned to London and acted as the solicitor for Hartley's estate. The contract that Benson and Walsh signed contained some sections in an archaic language. Walsh thought it was part of Hartley's air of mystery. If you obtain a copy of the will and translate it, I am sure that it will say Benson and Walsh signed over their share of the brokerage to Ferguson upon their deaths. This means that Ferguson has murdered three men for the purpose of gaining the brokerage.

We do not have enough information to know why, exactly, he wanted the ownership of Walsh, Hartley, and Benson. It would be pure speculation to come to a conclusion, and so I leave it to you, Mr. Carnacki, to find the answer and bring Mr. Ferguson to justice.

Sincerely,

Mr. Sherlock Holmes

Carnacki folded the letter from Sherlock Holmes and placed it back in its envelope. "Holmes may be verbose, but he most certainly has earned his reputation for greatness. He had untangled the web before me so perfectly that I couldn't believe I hadn't seen it myself. I was blinded by the flame, gentlemen, but now I had clarity and I had to act.

"I returned to the Wilhelm House. I still had the key that Walsh had given me. I entered the house and found it exactly as I had left it. I hoped that I would still find the book in the chapel, though I knew there was a good chance the executor had taken it. All depended on if Ferguson wanted to enter the Wilhelm House and remove the evidence before he could claim ownership, or if he did not want to raise suspicions by entering the house again before he could claim it, and would wait until the property had transferred into his possession.

"I entered the chapel and found the book still resting on its pedestal, open to the signature page. I put on two layers of gloves for my own protection and slipped the book into a sack as carefully as the hero Perseus put Medusa's head into his leather bag, for like the Gorgon, the book could instantly end my life by turning my heart to stone.

"With the book in hand, I left the house the way I had come, through the front door, not thinking in the least that someone may be watching me. I returned to my house, to this very room, and lay the book open upon the desk. Looking at the signature page, I thought the best thing to do would be to have a sample of the page analyzed for the poison. With that evidence, I could prove that Benson and Walsh had been murdered. I could then have their bodies exhumed and checked for the poison as well. I was contemplating whether I should carefully cut a section of the page for analysis or perhaps use a razor to slice out the entire page. My mind debated these options for a few minutes. Then it was interrupted by a sound of footsteps from outside the room.

"Who is there?" I called out.

"I heard the footsteps stop. Then they quickly moved to the library, and the door was thrown open. In walked an impeccably dressed young man sporting a top hat and cape. He was tall, and physically well built. His green eyes were piercing, yet he kept a blank visage as if he were in the midst of a hand of poker.

"'You have something of mine,' the man said in a level voice. He removed the white glove from his right hand and then held it out to me. 'I wish to have it back.'

"'Who are you?' I asked. 'What business do you have entering my house without permission.'

"His lips curled into a twisted grin at my statement. 'That's good, coming from you. I saw you enter my property and use a key to get in. I don't know where you got it from, but I want it back. If you meant to rob the house, surely you discovered that it contained nothing of value less you consider used candlesticks to be worth something.'

"'Your name, sir,' I commanded.

"'Ferguson,' he replied.

"'The solicitor to Hartley's estate?' I questioned.

"Ferguson's eyes widened in surprise. Then his gaze steadied. 'What do you know of Mr. Hartley?'

"'I know that a solicitor should not claim ownership of his client's property.'

"Again, Ferguson's eyes widened, less so this time. His demeanor remained cool. 'What is it you want, Mr...?'

"'Carnacki,' I responded, 'and what I want is justice for the men you murdered.'

"This time, Ferguson remained cold at my insinuation. He gave a slight nod of the head as though he expected me to make such a statement.

"'That is a slanderous accusation,' he responded. He approached me as he spoke. 'If you must know, I am the son of Mr. Hartley, and the heir of his estate.'

"I was now taken aback by this revelation, but I remembered Walsh's words to me, that Hartley had said he lost his son. That had been interpreted to mean the son had died. In reality, they had become estranged.

"'Yes, Mr. Carnacki. My father and I quarreled and drifted, so much so that I took my mother's maiden name as my own. I assure you I have the documents to prove my heritage.' He stepped closer to me, just a few footsteps from the desk.

"'But your father left you nothing. He left it all to his associates at the brokerage.'

"Ferguson as now at the desk, looming over me. 'That is correct, Mr. Carnacki.' He put his hands down and leaned into me, keeping his intense eyes focused upon me. 'Due to the untimely death of his associates, I now have inherited the entire brokerage as laid out in the wills that they signed.'

"'You tricked them into signing away their business. You killed them all just to get revenge on your father for disinheriting you. What kind of a —' I froze midsentence. Ferguson saw the look of horror on my face, the direction of my focus. He glanced down as well, and he jumped back in fright, for Ferguson, when he leaned in to intimidate me had put his ungloved hand upon the open signature page of the Wilhelm book.

"The man held his hand out before his face, and with a blood curdling scream, completely lost his composure. He fled from my house. I thought perhaps he was running to treat himself with an antidote, but it was not to be. I read his obituary in the paper two days later.'

"After these events, the brokerage was shuttered, and the Wilhelm House was finally knocked down, replaced by a more modern, larger brick house. I kept the Wilhelm book for myself as a memento of the strange case."

Carnacki stood, put out his pipe, and collected our brandy glasses. We also rose and collected our hats and coats.

"Out you go!" our host genially commanded using the recognized formula. And we went out, away from Cheyne Walk, the four of us, returning to our homes.

Done With Mirrors

by Dan Andriacco

"You mean he lives in a tree house?" I said.

"No, he merely maintains his study and his collection in one."

"Oh, well, that's completely different then."

Professor Carlo Stuarti, a mentalist and magician of extraordinary skill and no small fame, acknowledged my sarcastic rejoinder with a smile. "He designed it himself, of course. I suspect that Mr. George Washington Hill III is one of those wealthy men who is determined to be eccentric."

"I would have thought his hobby of collecting magic tricks was enough to establish that, without the arboreal construction."

An American by birth like me, and a highly successful architect by profession, Hill had lived in England for more than four decades. I had heard something of the man and his unusual pastime before Stuarti mentioned him to me that day. A fellow didn't hang around the music halls as much as I did back then without picking up interesting tidbits.

"Tricks?" Stuarti echoed. "You do him an injustice, Jack. According to those who have seen it, Hill has amassed a stunning collection of stage illusions, memorabilia, and rare books about the art of prestidigitation. Some of it reportedly goes back to the great Robert-Houdin himself, the father of modern stage magic. Hill's pocketbook is apparently sufficient to accommodate his fancies. And now word is about that he has acquired the Turk, the famous chess-playing automaton long thought destroyed in a fire."

"So that's why you're paying him a visit."

"*Esatto.*"

"But you said you've never even met him. What makes you think he'll show you this machine, if he really has it?"

"Oh, I am quite certain that he will not, at least not on my inaugural visit. In fact, Hill made it clear that he only agreed to see me at all because he is familiar with my reputation as a conjuror. However, what my host chooses to show me and what I will see are most likely two different things."

Stuarti was a dab hand at big stage illusions – levitations and such – but his best stunt was mentalism. He had mastered "cold reading," the skill of drawing inferences from close observation of an individual. When done right, the subject (a member of the audience in a stage performance, or a "mark" in the hands of a confidence man) will swear that the practitioner of cold-reading is a mind-reader. And nobody did it better than the boss. The ability had even helped him to solve a particularly horrifying homicide at the famous Madame Tussaud's wax museum. His confidence that it would also enable him to unravel the secrets of George Washington Hill did not seem far-fetched.

He stood up and looked in a mirror to adjust his white tie. I had dropped in on Stuarti in his dressing room at the Alhambra Theatre about an hour before his performance, as was my habit in the late 1880s. He was Alhambra's top draw then, touted on a big poster outside the hall as "the Count of Conjuring." Still, there is no such thing as too much publicity, and it was my happy job to boom the magician just as I had once boomed Buffalo Bill on his English tour. His elegant appearance and subtle Italian accent didn't hurt. Stuarti cut a fine figure in his white tie and tails, tall and handsome, with pure white hair except for a dramatic streak of black that matched his mustache. In his early sixties, his penetrating brown eyes gave evidence that he had seen and done a lot. Not all of it was on stage.

"What is so special about this Turk?" I asked. "Maskelyne unveiled his whist-playing automaton more than a dozen years ago, if I remember right."

John Nevil Maskelyne was one of the great magicians of his or any other age. But Stuarti, who was even better at mental magic and knew it, bristled at the very name. He abandoned his sartorial task before the mirror to set me straight.

"Maskelyne's Psycho was exposed almost immediately by a writer on games as being operated by air pressure. An ingenious invention, although not Maskelyne's. The mechanical man and the chest beneath were each too small for anyone to be inside, and both sat on a clear glass cylinder. Who would have thought that it was compressed air which moved the mechanical hands? But Maskelyne and his partner, Clarke, made the great mistake of applying for a patent. You cannot keep a patent secret."

Stuarti dismissed the whole topic with a wave of his nimble hand, a typically Italian gesture. "The Turk, on the other hand, remains one of the world's great mysteries. It was presented as a mechanical man capable of playing chess at the highest level. The truth of its operation has been the subject of much speculation, including an article by the American writer Edgar Allan Poe. Most theories assume that somehow a man was hidden inside or beneath the machine, but that was never proved.

"This much is known: A Hungarian nobleman, Baron Wolfgang von Kempelen, created the Turk to impress the

Empress Maria Teresa of Austria more than a hundred years ago, around 1770. He exhibited it here in England, as well as in France, Germany, Russia, and America. The Turk defeated most of its opponents, including the Emperor Napoleon and your Benjamin Franklin. After the Baron's death in 1804, Johann Mälzel bought the device and showed it widely in the United States. Mälzel died at sea in 1838. The Turk changed hands several times after that until it burned up in a museum fire in Philadelphia in 1854 – or so it has been thought."

"But wrongly?"

"Perhaps. I am a magician. I believe that anything is possible. Would you like to accompany me on my visit with Mr. Hill, Jack?"

I shrugged. "Why not? I've never been in a tree house."

And that's how I happened to be on the scene shortly after a particularly puzzling murder.

*****

George Washington Hill III resided in a handsome brick house in the London suburb of Upper Norwood, within a short ride from the train station. It was an unusually warm but rainy Saturday morning in October when we showed up there ten minutes early for our nine o'clock appointment. Paying scant attention to the domicile, we walked around the back to the tree house as Hill had instructed. Armed with an umbrella big enough to shield both of us, I didn't mind the brief amble in the gentle rain. The grass was slightly mushy beneath our feet.

"It does not disappoint," Stuarti said, pointing ahead of us with his silver-handled walking stick. The tree house, nestled in a sturdy old English oak, was a wood structure probably about fifteen feet square. Instead of steps or a ladder, a metal shaft connected it to the ground.

"Is that an elevator?" I asked, incredulous.

"A lift, yes, and electric-powered from the looks of it."

"An electric elevator, not steam-powered or hydraulic? I didn't know there was such a thing."

"Well, it is certainly rare. Werner von Siemens built the first one in 1880, but an American –"

He stopped dead at the sound behind us. Two men were approaching from the Hill house, a tall, fair-haired figure in a raincoat and a younger man, about my height with a military mustache and a bearing to match.

"You must be Professor Stuarti," the latter told the boss. "I'm Henry Carr, Mr. Hill's private secretary. And this is Inspector Tobias Gregson, of Scotland Yard."

"Inspector Catchpool speaks very highly of you, Stuarti," the older man said.

Stuarti acknowledged the compliment with a modest bow. "He is too kind. I present my associate, Mr. Barker. What has happened?"

"Hill is dead," the Inspector announced. "Shot himself."

"The blood was still fresh when we found him," Carr informed us. "But we didn't hear the shot." He shook his head in bewilderment. "His business affairs were in sound shape, although he'd spent a lot of money lately, and he was going to be married in two months. I don't know why he would kill himself, least of all on a morning when he had an appointment he was looking forward to – the one with you."

"Then why do you assume that he did such a thing?"

"Because he was alone up there, Professor. Nobody could have been with him and got away. When Miss Turner – that's his fiancé, Abigail Turner – and I arrived here at almost the same time, about a half-hour ago now, the lift-cage was at the top. We had to call it back down so that we could use it. If someone had been there with Mr. Hill this morning and left, the cage would have been at ground level when we got here."

"Couldn't someone – a hypothetical killer – have ridden the cage down and then pushed the button to send it back up?" Stuarti asked. He hadn't spent a lot of time in elevators, nor had I.

Carr shook his head. "The only way the cage will move up or down without somebody in it is if it's summoned from the other end of the lift."

"Why is that?"

"Neither the 'up' nor the 'down' button inside the cage will work until a passenger closes the door from the inside. It works just like a lift in an office building, except that there's no paid lift-operator."

"Couldn't a killer have jumped out of the tree house?" I said. "Sure, it's maybe forty feet up, but –"

"Why would anybody in his right mind do that?" Gregson objected.

"It couldn't happen anyway," Carr said, almost apologetically. "There are no windows in the tree house, and no door except for the door of the lift-cage. Mr. Hill has some special books – scarce or unique, I guess – that he said sunlight would hurt. He had electric lighting installed instead. He is a very wealthy man, you understand."

He *was*, I thought.

"Yes, I understand," Stuarti said dryly. "Where is this Miss Turner?"

"I left her in the tree house. She was being sick in the W.C."

The Inspector's eyes bulged. "The tree house has a W.C.?"

His home probably didn't. Carr ignored the interruption. "I didn't want to leave her there alone, but I thought the police needed to be notified right away since it was suicide. I told her not to disturb anything."

"Well, all this talk is very nice," Gregson said, in a tone that suggested just the opposite, "but I need to have a dekko at the body. Care to come along, Professor? Catchpool says you were of some help in that wax museum business."

Stuarti executed a small bow at this gross understatement. "Of course, if you will permit. The true magic of life and death is always of interest to me."

"As you can see, the lift is only large enough to take two people at a time," Carr said. "The Inspector and I will take it up, and then you two can call it back down. It's easy to operate. I'll show you how."

We watched as Carr, inside the lift-cage with Inspector Gregson, closed the door and pushed the "up" button. When the cage reached the top and those gentlemen exited it, Stuarti pushed the button outside the lift to bring the cage back down. It returned to ground level with the door still open. Stuarti stepped in, pushed the "up" button, and then stepped outside. The elevator cage stayed put, just as Carr had said it would without the door closed. Only after we got in the cage and Stuarti closed the door did pushing the button have any effect.

"Didn't you believe –"

"I like to see for myself, Jack. Seeing is believing. No, that's not quite true. I don't believe what I see, either!"

At the top, the cage door opened into a large room with a wall full of bookcases to our left and all kinds of magic paraphernalia scattered about – a top hat suitable for producing a rabbit, a three-legged table with mirrors on the sides and a head-sized hole in the top, a guillotine, and much more. In the corner where the bookcases met the wall opposite the elevator, behind an angled desk, sprawled a crumpled body with a bloody head. Gregson knelt beside it. That tableau was the first thing I noticed. The second was an attractive young red-headed woman in a pale blue frock clinging to Carr the way I would like Miss Aurora O'Reilly to cling to me. Her body trembled.

"I see why you called Scotland Yard rather than a doctor," Stuarti observed, his dark eyes on the body.

Gregson stood up and confronted Carr and the presumptive Miss Turner. "What did you do with the gun?"

"I never saw any gun," Carr said. "But, then, I wasn't looking for it. I never thought of that."

"I didn't touch anything," the young woman asserted.

Gregson looked around helplessly. "There has to be a gun somewhere." The room was sizable, but not so big it couldn't be taken in with the sweep of an eye. The wall opposite the elevator contained what we later learned was a discreet door to the W.C. along with shelves holding some of Hill's smaller acquisitions in the way of stage-magic apparatus. The wall to our right off the elevator contained several large mirrors, reflecting the bookcases and creating the illusion that the room was larger than it was.

"Perhaps there has to be, but there isn't." Stuarti chuckled. "No gun, no suicide, my dear Inspector."

Gregson swore.

"It couldn't be murder!" Carr got so excited he took his hands off the dead man's fiancé. "I told you that. The lift-cage is the only way in or out of this room, and a killer couldn't have used it to escape. If someone else shot Hill, that would be like murder in a locked room. That's impossible!"

Stuarti walked over to the wall of bookcases and studied them intently, occasionally touching one here and there.

"Right you are," Gregson said. "It couldn't be murder – unless one or both of you did it. A blind man could see that you two are mighty cozy with each other."

"I resent that!" Miss Turner cried.

"I'm not saying you meant to do it, Miss. Maybe one of you got into an argument with the victim and shot him in the heat of the moment, or even in self-defense. And the other one is being protective; it's only natural."

"That didn't happen," Carr insisted. "I told you what happened."

"What were both of you doing here?"

"I work here. I helped Mr. Hill with his correspondence and cataloging his magic collection."

"And I came to speak to him about plans for our wedding," Miss Turner said. "We were to be married nine weeks from today. It was just happenstance that Henry and I arrived at the same time."

Stuarti looked up from an old book he had picked off the shelves behind the body, an action reflected in a mirror on the opposite wall. "It hardly seems likely that these young people would attempt to make Hill's death seem like suicide – saying they found the lift-cage at the top when they arrived this morning – and then get rid of the gun, does it, Inspector? This is an excellent first edition of Robert-Houdin's *Confidences d'un Prestidigitateur,* by the way." He re-shelved the book.

"People do strange things when they commit their first murder. Look, by Carr's own account nobody else could have done it – not unless he was a . . . a magician."

Stuart emitted a slight cough. Gregson glared at him. "Are you volunteering?"

"I didn't know Hill, but a lot of magicians must have. Mr. Carr, Miss Turner, can you suggest anyone who might have wanted to kill Mr. Hill?"

"I don't know about killing him," the woman said, "but he did have a rival – a man named Rowan Kirk."

"Ah, yes," Stuart said. "An amateur magician and another collector. I know the name."

"I think it's fair to say that Kirk hated Mr. Hill," Carr said "but not Mr. Hill's former wife, Olympia. Far from it. And I guess I should also tell you that Mr. Hill didn't get along very well with his son, Wash – George Washington Hill IV."

"And why is that?"

Carr glanced quickly at Abigail Turner. "Really, I don't want to engage in unseemly gossip about a dead man."

"In your position you would do well to cooperate," Gregson warned.

"Oh, all right, then. Wash is the son of the first Mrs. Hill. He's never forgiven his father for carrying on a dalliance with Olympia while his mother was dying of consumption. Wash is Hill's solicitor and handles his investments, but they argue all the time. They did, I mean."

"Who inherits from Hill?" Stuarti asked. "As his secretary, you must know that."

"As a matter of fact, I do. Mr. Hill had an appointment with Wash for next week. I believe that he planned at that time to change his will in the light of his upcoming marriage. Since that didn't happen, Wash inherits everything under the existing will, despite their differences."

Stuarti eyed Miss Turner, which was surely no chore. "Hill's death is certainly untimely from your point of view, then."

"Well, of course it is. We were going to be married!"

"Be all that as it may," Gregson said heavily, "you two are going with me to Scotland Yard to talk about this some more."

With the Metropolitan Police under heavy criticism that year for the inability to stop Saucy Jack's reign of terror in Whitechapel, two suspects and a dead body must have seemed like manna from heaven to the unimaginative police official.

"Do you mind if we chat with the other suspects, Inspector?" Stuarti asked.

"They aren't suspects as far as I'm concerned. You remind me of Mr. Holmes and his little theories, Professor. Chat away!"

*****

The rain had stopped by time we were back on terra firm. Stuarti looked mournfully at the ground. "Damp earth is perfect for holding footprints, but – *Dio mio!* – look at this mess, Jack!" He pointed with his walking stick. "My footprints! Your footprints! The Inspector's! Henry Carr's! The young lady's! What hope is there of finding the killer's, or even proving that there was another person in that tree house this morning? If only we had known this was a matter of murder before we trampled the evidence!"

"Spilt milk," I observed.

"And no use in crying over it? English aphorisms are so expressive! Well, then, on to Mr. Kirk, who seems to have shared the deceased's taste in women as well as his hobby."

Rowan Kirk was "something in the City," but did not work a full day on Saturdays. His large villa in Kent, near Lee, was a seven-mile ride in a dog cart. I was grateful that it had stopped raining, for it would have been a soggy ride otherwise. We stopped along the way at a telegraph station, where I dispatched a wire to Miss A. O'Reilly at *The Daily Telegraph*: **MURDER IN UPPER NORWOOD. STUARTI INVOLVED.** That would be enough to get her started. I never missed a chance to boom the boss.

And he never missed a chance to lecture. The subject on the way to Kent was Hill's collection.

"The round table with the three legs was the Sphynx illusion, first presented by Colonel Stodare at the Egyptian

Hall," he informed me. "The angled mirrors behind the table legs reflect the curtains on either side of the stage. But to members of the audience, it appears they are looking through the table to the curtain behind it. The head, appropriately made up to look like the ancient Egyptian monument, seems to be bodiless as it answers questions from the audience. The body is, of course, concealed by the mirrors. Some illusions really are done with mirrors! The guillotine effect, however . . ."

My mind wandered. I was more interested in how someone could shoot George Washington Hill to death in a tree house and then evaporate – presuming that Stuarti was right to believe that Carr and Miss Turner had told the truth. And they must have! As Stuarti had argued, why would they lie about the position of the elevator cage and then dispose of the gun? Or, to look at it another way, why get rid of the weapon and then lie about the position of the cage? And Miss Turner had every reason to want Hill to live long enough to change his will.

Rowen Kirk's villa, The Larches, stood on its own property. Kirk appeared in the large entrance foyer with a lady at his side shortly after being summoned by a servant. He welcomed us with a warmth I hadn't expected.

"I've had the pleasure of seeing you perform four times at the Alhambra and once at the Palladium in Edinburgh," he told Stuarti, smiling broadly. "Marvelous! Marvelous!"

"You are too kind, *signore*."

Kirk, a man of about sixty, wore a golden pince-nez on a black ribbon, the lenses a bit too small for his wide face. The buttons on his paisley waistcoat were strained by his growing girth. He spoke with the slightest of Scottish burrs.

"And this is my good friend, Mrs. Olympia Hill."

Stuarti kissed her hand. I shook it, not that her hand wasn't eminently kissable. Mrs. Hill may have been forty or so, topping my age by several years, by she was still a handsome woman with wide green eyes, soft chestnut hair done up in the latest fashion of that year, and a memorable figure.

"I am afraid that I come with some shocking news," Stuarti said. I watched his eyes watching theirs for their reaction. A hawk had nothing on Stuarti. "We have just come from the home of Mr. George Washington Hill III. I regret to tell you that he is dead."

"Dead!" Mrs. Hill gasped and put a hand on her admirable bosom. "Was it his heart?"

"No," said Stuarti, "it was his head. Someone put a bullet in it."

"Oh, dear, dear, dear," Kirk said. "Can that really be? Murder? Who can have done such a thing?"

"Inspector Gregson of Scotland Yard suspects that either Miss Abigail Turner or Mr. Henry Carr did the murder, and the other is lying about it."

"Well, they *were* engaged," Mrs. Hill said.

"Hill and Miss Turner, you mean," I said.

"I mean *Henry* and Miss Turner," Mrs. Hill corrected. "They were engaged for some weeks, perhaps a month or two, until it was broken off. I don't know why, although I could guess. Not long after, George announced that he was going to marry the beautiful Abby. We had been divorced about six months at the time. I was well rid of him, not to speak ill of the dead."

"I find your candor refreshing," Stuarti said with a twinkling in his eye.

"Then I will continue it. I knew that George was a thorough cad when I married him, but I had no choice. He threatened to ruin my reputation if I didn't. His first wife lay dying when we . . . when I made a mistake. It was the biggest mistake of my life."

Kirk squeezed her hand in a silent gesture of support. Stuarti, perhaps because he was a gentleman, didn't press the point. Divorced women had gained more legal rights in Great Britain in the previous decade, but social mores remained such that Mrs. Hill was fortunate to have found a respectable new suitor.

"Hill met Miss Turner through his secretary?" I surmised. Poaching on one's employee just didn't seem like cricket to me, as the English might say.

"I never asked," Mrs. Hill said. "But her father is a builder who worked with George. He built that silly tree house for him. Perhaps that's how both men knew her. Henry is a fine young man. I can't believe Abby gave him up for George on her own accord. Maybe it was her father's idea."

Stuarti had listened carefully, but now turned to Kirk. "You were a rival of Mr. Hill's in the collection of stage magic, as I understand."

"A rival? Nonsense." Suddenly, Kirk wasn't Mr. Pickwick anymore. "Oh, it's true that we've been competing on the same playing field, as you might say, for more than twenty years, but I beat him at every turn. He even let his greatest treasure escape him."

He looked meaningfully at Mrs. Hill, who blushed prettily. I wouldn't have thought she had that in her.

"George was a man who went after whatever he wanted, using fair means or foul," she said quietly. "When he didn't get it, it wasn't a good idea to be around him."

"There is a rumor that Hill secretly acquired Baron von Kempelen's famous chess-playing machine, the Turk," Stuarti said. "That would also be a treasure to one such as yourself, would it not?"

Kirk, just about to light a cigar, paused to nod. Stuarti hates tobacco smoke. "It would be, certainly. But I'm sure the

Turk went up in smoke long ago and that Hill made up that rumor himself."

"I am of the opposite opinion. I see that you spent the morning in the City."

"Yes, but how the devil –"

"He's the Count of Conjuring, that's how," I said. I've always been proud of inventing that alliterative soubriquet. It looked great on the posters.

"The ticket stub from the train is sticking out of your waistcoat pocket," Stuarti said. I liked my explanation better.

Kirk chuckled. "And I thought you were reading my mind!"

Stuarti turned to Olympia Hill. "You, on the other hand, were not out and about this morning before you came here."

She raised a delicate eyebrow, which took on the appearance of a question mark.

"Neither your dress nor your boots show the slightest traces of the rain which only ceased about an hour ago, Mrs. Hill. Note how Mr. Kirk's trousers and boots are still wet. Ergo, you spent your morning indoors at home and only ventured out after the rain had ceased."

"How very clever of you, Professor!"

"I do even better on a bigger stage. Who benefits by your former husband's death?"

"Everyone, I should think. But I suppose Wash inherits, even though he loathed George and the feeling was mutual."

"Presumably the estate would include the magic collection."

"Presumably. George never told me much."

"I might pick up an item or two if Wash puts it on the block, if that's what you're thinking," Kirk said.

"Yes, that is what I was thinking."

*****

George Washington Hill IV lived in Lower Norwood, not far from his father. I expected Stuarti to want to talk to him next, but instead we headed to Scotland Yard to talk to the victim's secretary and his fiancé.

"But you said they're innocent!" I protested on the way.

"Nevertheless, they are central to the case. Mrs. Hill gave us a key piece of information about them that must be followed up."

Instead of asking what he meant, I said:

"About Mrs. Hill, couldn't she have gone to Upper Norwood, shot her ex-husband, and then simply changed her clothes before calling on Kirk?"

"She could have, but she didn't. I can read faces like you read dime novels, Jack. Hers betrayed no sense of relief that my deductions about how she spent the morning gave her an alibi for Hill's murder. She was amused by my little performance, nothing more."

We rode in silence for a while, and then I said: "If neither Carr nor Miss Turner is the killer, then maybe figuring out *how* it was done would lead to *who* did it."

"How? Surely that is obvious, Jack!"

"Not to me!"

"Well, think about the mirrors. And perhaps if I whispered *The Turk* that would give you a clue."

I was still thinking, to no avail, when we arrived at the Yard. Using powers of persuasion that verged on the hypnotic, Stuarti at length convinced Gregson to let us talk to his two suspects alone. He didn't like the idea, but his own interrogation had gotten him nowhere. We started with Carr, who looked about ten years older than he had that morning.

"You were formerly engaged to Miss Turner," Stuarti stated.

"What of it?" He spoke wearily.

"I am trying to help you, Mr. Carr, but that doesn't look good. It supports the Inspector's theory that you are covering up for Miss Turner, or she is for you. This has the makings of a very ugly love triangle."

"That's not true. I . . . I still love Abby, yes, but I'm not covering up for her, and I didn't kill Hill to get her back. Everything I said about what happened this morning was true."

"What happened to your engagement to Miss Turner?"

"I wish I knew. Abby just came to me one day and told me it was off. She said I should forget about her. Small chance of that, with me working for Hill!"

"She looked very fond of you this morning," I pointed out.

"I wish I could believe that, that she still feels the same way about me that I do about her. But I just happened to be there when she needed somebody to lean on."

Miss Turner, for her part, refused to enlighten us on the matter of her disengagement from Henry Carr.

"That is quite a personal matter," she said stiffly, pulling errant strands of pale red hair off her lovely face. "What difference can it make now?"

"All the difference in the world if a jury believes that you and Carr secretly remained lovers and Hill found out," I said, deliberately harsh. I was trying to wake her up. "You do realize that you and Carr could both go to the gallows, don't you?"

"Please just don't let my father know that I'm here," she said. "It would mortify him."

* * * *

After the interviews, we found Inspector Gregson deeply engaged in conversation with a beauteous blonde, her large violet eyes riveted to a notepad in which she scribbled his words of Scotland Yard wisdom. I enjoyed watching her for a while before she noticed we were there. My favorite lady journalist had exquisite ankles. Her other curves were in the right places as well.

"Hello, Miss O'Reilly," I said finally.

"Oh, Mr. Barker! I thought I might see you and the Professor. The Inspector was just telling me about his suspects. Such a romantic story!"

"I am a romantic myself," Stuarti said truthfully. After all, the man claimed to be the natural great-grandson of Charles Edward Stuart – Bonnie Prince Charlie. He may have even believed that himself. "But what do you mean?"

"Why, isn't it obvious? The Inspector's astute questioning has discovered that the man and woman who supposedly found the body were once engaged." If Gregson hadn't learned that on his own, I doubt that Stuarti would have told him. "Either Henry Carr is lying to protect the woman he loves, or Abigail Turner is lying to protect the man she loves. Either way, it's a wonderful story – murder for love. My readers of the gentler sex will adore it!"

The irony of what she had just said seemed to escape her, but I didn't think it would help my cause with Miss O'Reilly to point it out.

Gregson sat back with a self-satisfied smile.

Aurora O'Reilly had happily covered fashion, society, and gardening until she stumbled onto the Madame Tussaud's murder. Now her editor threw her any story involving blood and mayhem. She delivered the goods in print, I must admit. It was a leg up for a publicity agent like me to have a friend in the press, but I was more interested in her than I was in her journalism.

"I will have an even better story for you," Stuarti said, "the true one. Hill's fiancé and his secretary are completely innocent of anything except being foolish, which I am happy to say is not a crime. A third person shot and killed George Washington Hill III."

"But that's impossible," Gregson sputtered, echoing Carr's word earlier that day.

"So are all illusions until they are explained. Give me just a little time, Miss O'Reilly, and I assure you I will explain this one."

* * * *

"Who inherits? What bloody right do you have to ask me a question like that, eh? What bloody right?"

George Washington Hill IV appeared to be only about half a decade older than his stepmother, with a ruddy face, greying side whiskers, and the arrogance of a prosperous solicitor. He stood glowering at us, blocking the doorway of his capacious Lower Norwood home.

"I assert no right," Stuarti retorted, "but only a responsibility – the responsibility of every man to see that justice is done. Our friend Inspector Gregson believes that Henry Carr or Abigail Turner killed your father. I am convinced that he is wrong."

Hill emitted a sound somewhere between a grunt and snort. "Beautiful woman, Miss Turner. No wonder the old goat fancied her. I could fancy her myself. Don't see what she saw in him. Don't see it at all."

"Your stepmother suggested that perhaps the young lady's father suggested the marriage."

"Turner? Not bloody likely! He knows what the Dad was if anybody does. Worked for him for years. But what's all this got to do with the inheritance?"

"If your father didn't settle money on Miss Turner in his will," Stuarti said, "that's one less motive for her. Carr said he didn't, but Carr's testimony is somewhat suspect. Mrs. Hill thinks you inherit everything, but she might not be fully informed."

"Well, they're both right. It all goes to me, what's left of it. The Dad was a wealthy man, but he spent a lot of money to build a bloody tree house and buy a chess-playing mechanical man. Lot of nonsense, you ask me. He must have been in his second childhood."

Stuarti's eyes lit up like a lantern. "The Turk! He did have the Turk!"

"Right. That's what he called the machine, the Turk. I gather he bought it from a dodgy Russian prince or some such who didn't exactly have clear title to it."

"Where is the Turk now?"

Hill frowned. "In the tree house, isn't it? That's why he bloody built the bloody thing!"

"Mr. Hill, you have been a great help. Perhaps you will be interested in learning just how. As the heir to your father's tree house, I will need your permission to . . . . "

*****

It took five trips in the elevator to get us all up to the late G.W. Hill's tree house study that evening: the young lovers (Carr and Miss Turner), the older lovers (Kirk and Mrs. Hill), Wash Hill, Inspector Gregson, Miss O'Reilly, Stuarti, me, and a red-headed man of medium height introduced as Dick Turner. The latter held a set of blueprints in his rough hands.

"Thank you all for being here," Stuarti said in the smooth tones of a practiced performer. He was dressed as one, too, prepared to take to the stage at the Alhambra in little more than an hour. "Our purpose here, as you all know, is to solve the murder of George Washington Hill III. But I believe there is another mystery as well – the location of the most famous and most valuable artefact in his collection, the Turk."

"I say he never had it," Kirk asserted, sounding more Scottish than ever in his pugnacity.

"And I know that he did," Wash Hill said. "I liquidated some investments for him to get the bloody money for the bloody purchase."

The term "bloody money" reminded me that Wash himself had a gold-plated motive – he was presumably about to be replaced in his father's will by a new stepmother young enough to be his daughter.

"I didn't know for certain when I entered this room for the first time ten hours ago that Baron von Kempelen's Turk was in the dead man's possession," Stuarti said, "but I thought there was a good chance of it. The story seemed too unbelievable to be false. And yet –" the great man waved his hands around the room – "the machine was nowhere to be seen amid all this paraphernalia of stage magic."

"Pardon me, but what does this have to do with the murder?" Mrs. Hill asked, impatience writ large on her handsome face.

"The Turk was missing. Hill's murderer, who should have been in this room when the body was found because the lift-cage was at this level, was also missing. Perhaps both were in the same place. The younger Mr. Hill confirmed for me that this tree house was built essentially to house the Turk. I suspected there was a secret hiding place for it. In fact, I conjectured that as soon as I walked into the room and saw this magnificent wall of books. Priest holes were quite commonly concealed by bookcases. That is why I asked Mr. Turner to join us this evening. He built this grand tree house to George Washington Hill's specifications and knows its secrets."

"I built it all right," that individual asserted, "and I can assure you there's no hidden compartment. I brought the blueprints to show you." He spread them out between his two hands and held them up to show us in an almost dramatic gesture.

The small audience displayed varying degrees of surprise. They were under the mistaken belief that all was not going according to Stuarti's plan.

"Then I am undone!" Stuarti cried. "For once, Stuarti was too clever." That was laying it on a bit thick, I thought. But then, I knew what he was up to. "Inspector, your simple solution was the right one. Miss Turner and her lover must have committed the murder."

Miss O'Reilly, enraptured, scribbled furiously in her journalist's notebook.

Gregson ostentatiously pulled out a set of handcuffs and approached the dead man's fiancé, who instinctively clung to Carr. "No!"

"No!" her father shouted at the same time. "No, no, no! I did it, damn it. I killed the evil bastard. I couldn't let him get his filthy hands on Abby."

Never have I seen a look of shock to match the one on Abigail Turner's face. She started to say something, then stopped, lost for words.

Stuarti worked hard to suppress a triumphant smile. "And there is a secret room, which Hill didn't include in the blueprints."

"Yes, with a door like none other." Turner was wilting before our eyes, like a dying plant. "Nobody would have ever found it. It's held fast by an electromagnet and can only be released by a button hidden in the desk. Hill said he got the idea from an illusion by Robert-Houdin."

"That would be the famous 'light and heavy chest'– a small box that could be lifted by the weakest boy but not by the strongest man when the concealed electromagnet was turned on. That illusion convinced the marabouts in Algeria that Robert-Houdin had supernatural powers. To you it meant something quite different, a way out when you needed it. You hid in the secret room after killing Hill."

Turner nodded. "I shot him dead, to his great surprise. He told me I didn't have the nerve. When he turned out to be wrong, I guess he wasn't the only one who was surprised. I sat there with the gun in my hand for about ten minutes, just staring. Then I heard the lift cage going down and I knew that somebody would be coming up. There was no way out, so I had to hide. I ducked into the secret room. Somebody came into the library, but I couldn't make out their voices and didn't know who it was. After the cage went down again, I heard the sound of someone being sick in the W.C. I waited a minute or two and then peered out. The coast was clear, so I summoned the lift-cage. I rode it back down with my gun still in my hand. When Carr came back with you a few minutes later, he found the cage on the ground just as he'd left it. I had no idea that I would be setting up Abby and Henry to take the blame." He looked at his daughter. "I still don't understand why you would agree to marry that blackguard."

"Oh, Papa! He told me he had evidence that you stole money from him, and that he would expose you if I didn't break it off with Henry and marry him."

"That's a damned lie! I never broke a law in my life." He swallowed. "Until I murdered a man."

*****

Miss O'Reilly accompanied the boss and me in the cab to the Alhambra, a mad dash to get there by the opening curtain.

"Yes, I could have been mistaken in my conviction that Abigail Turner and her obvious admirer hadn't killed Hill," Stuarti conceded in response to the lady journalist's question. "But logic and my reading of their faces told me that I was not. Therefore, a third person killed Hill and left the scene, yet somehow left the lift-cage at the top." He lifted a slender finger. "Or perhaps not! Perhaps the killer was still in the tree house when the young lovers arrived, and only left afterwards when Carr had departed and the young lady was occupied in the W.C."

"So, you thought of a concealed compartment," Miss O'Reilly said.

He nodded. "They are not uncommon. Such a hideaway would also explain the whereabouts of the Turk. Hill obtained it under somewhat questionable circumstances and therefore may not have wished to display it openly. I suspected the bookcases from the first, but I couldn't find a latch to open the way. Nevertheless, I did not lose faith. And if there was a hidden room in the tree house, who – other than Hill – had to know the secret?"

"The builder of the tree house!"

"Precisely, Miss O'Reilly! And since that builder was also Miss Turner's father, who Wash Hill assured us knew the dead man's foibles, I was reasonably sure that I knew the killer's identity. Perhaps it was unsporting of me to set a trap by making him think the Inspector was going to arrest his daughter, but I had no real evidence. A confession was the only way."

"Not quite the story you expected," I told Miss O'Reilly, all sympathy.

"No, but it is far better! Now the young lovers will be headed to the altar instead of to the gallows. And it was a murder for love after all, you know."

"How so?"

"Dick Turner loved his daughter too much to see her married to a man that he knew was a scoundrel. My readers will be enthralled."

I had hoped to help Miss O'Reilly celebrate this good fortune over dinner at Goldini's, but she reminded me that she still had to write the story for the next day's edition of her newspaper. Just as the cab pulled up to the offices of *The Daily Telegraph*, I remembered something.

"What about the mirrors?" I asked Stuarti. "You told me to think about the mirrors. The mirrors in the tree house had nothing to do with the secret room!"

"Oh, but they did," Stuarti assured me with a chuckle. "You must know from your own experience that mirrors always make a space look larger. Without them, surely it would have been obvious that the study in the tree house was bigger on the outside than on the inside."

Pipes, Bonnets and Pieces of String

by Robert Stapleton

I am obsessed. At least that's what my uncle Charles keeps telling me. The truth of the matter is that I have taken to spending my lunchtimes at a fashionable London teashop, in the company of a most peculiar old man. My fiancé, Richard Frobisher, tells me it's an unhealthy interest. Perhaps he's jealous. But then again, I really cannot imagine why he should be. I'll readily admit that the old man seated at that corner table is not the sort of person any ordinary young woman is likely to want to spend much time with. But then again, I am no ordinary young woman. No. I am a journalist.

"So, you're still wasting your time chatting with that amateur detective, are you, Polly?" asked Uncle Charles when he came round to my lodgings early one morning. "Some boring old man in a tearoom."

"I am not wasting my time, Uncle. And he's not boring. Far from it. He puts most of the professionals to shame."

"Then it's high time you met a proper detective for a change. Now, as it happens, a man I know at my club has managed to arrange for you to meet a detective of a very different order."

I hate it when people try to organize my life for me, especially when they claim to have my best interests at heart. I bridled. "It is extraordinarily good of this friend of yours to go to all that trouble for me, Uncle, but I am really not interested."

"There might even be a story in it for you," he added. My curiosity can sometimes overcome even the most temperamental aspects of my personality. "Really?" I replied without much enthusiasm. "And when am I due to meet this detective?"

"The arrangement is that you should meet him at his residence this very morning," said Uncle Charles, consulting his pocket watch. "In fact, you have just enough time to make the appointment, if you hurry."

Disgruntled at being bullied in this way, I swallowed my irritation and decided that, if I was going to meet this detective at all, then at least I should try to look respectable for the occasion. With that in mind, I powdered my nose, tidied my hair and put on one of my more stylish bonnets; the one with the feathers sprouting out of the middle. A few minutes later, with a coat wrapped around me against the cold March breeze, and a hatpin securing the bonnet to my mop of brown hair, I set off to attend this unexpected meeting.

*****

A corporation omnibus dropped me off at Baker Street, where I made my way along to 221B, and rang the doorbell. A woman opened the door, who told me she was the landlady of the property. I handed her my card, and told her I was there to meet the famous detective, and that he was expecting me.

"He is retired now, you know," said the landlady, as she led me up a flight of seventeen stairs, "and he normally lives in Sussex, but he spends a few days several times each year back here in Baker Street."

On reaching the landing, the landlady knocked upon the door, and opened it to reveal a most extraordinary room. A table in one corner of the room was laden with laboratory paraphernalia, whilst another held a large aspidistra, together with a copy of the *Evening Observer* newspaper. Beside the fireplace stood a tall, slim man, with an aquiline nose, and sharp facial features. I estimated him to be somewhere in the middle years of his life.

All this I observed through a cloud of tobacco smoke, rising from the briar pipe the man was smoking. As a newspaper reporter, I am of course quite used to men smoking. I have even occasionally indulged in the practice myself, so I resisted the temptation to cough loudly.

The landlady, on the other hand, proved rather less indulgent, as she gave an almost theatrical splutter, crossed the room and threw open the window.

"Miss Margaret Burton is here to see you, Mr Holmes," she added as if by way of an aside.

"Thank you, Mrs P," replied the man with the pipe, as we all stood watching the fresh air chase the smoke around the room, and finally pursue it outside to mingle with the fumes of the Baker Street traffic.

The moment we were alone, I accepted Mr Holmes's invitation to take a seat beside the glowing fire, whilst he took his seat facing me.

Then I waited for something to happen. This visit had not been my idea, so I saw no reason why I should initiate the conversation.

Mr Holmes removed his pipe, and broke the silence. "You are certainly a young lady with the most unusual abilities, Miss Burton."

"I hope that is a compliment, Mr Holmes," I replied.

"Indeed. A lady whose business lies in the handling of words."

"True." I raised an eyebrow, inviting him to explain this comment.

"That is quite evident from the ink-stains on your right hand, the notebook protruding from your bag, and from your articles published regularly in the daily Press. He indicated the copy of the *Evening Observer*.

"My work is always keeping me busy, Mr Holmes."

"And now you have developed a singular interest in the work of detection. I understand you are interested in meeting a proper detective for a change."

I returned his gaze. "That is entirely my uncle's idea. He hopes you might deflect the attention of this innocent young girl away from another detective whom her family considers totally unsuitable for her."

"Another detective?" Sherlock Holmes raised an eyebrow in what I took to be mock surprise. "And where exactly do you meet this other detective?"

"At an ABC teashop."

"ABC standing for the Aerated Bread Company?"

"That's right. They have a teashop in Norfolk Street. Just off the Strand. Conveniently within walking distance of my newspaper's offices in Fleet Street. Merely an ordinary, though quite fashionable, London tearoom. But the man I meet there is far from ordinary."

Holmes sat back in his chair, drawing deeply upon his pipe. "Pray, tell me more about this detective. For example, can you give me his name?"

"I have no idea of his name," I replied. "He has never revealed it. To me he is simply the old man in the corner. He wears a rather loud tweed suit, and an extraordinary shapeless hat. He is elderly, pale in complexion, thin in both face and limb, balding, but with mild blue eyes that betray a keen intellect. And he possesses decidedly large ears. In fact, he bears a striking resemblance to a scarecrow."

Mr Holmes chuckled. "You are an observant young lady."

"I am a journalist, Mr Holmes. It is my job to observe things."

He nodded. "And what is there about this man that so intrigues you?"

"He analyses crimes reported in the daily newspapers, considers the facts and, with myself as his audience, he solves those cases which have left Scotland Yard completely baffled. He loves to show the professional detectives in an extremely poor light."

Mr Holmes laughed. "That would not be a particularly difficult task."

"But he seems to be able to read the minds of those people recorded in the newspaper articles. He sometimes even attends the court hearings, in order to gain a better insight into the accused and their crimes."

"This man sounds a most fascinating character," said Sherlock Holmes. "When will you next be meeting him in that Norfolk Street teashop?"

"I generally see him at around lunchtime. I have been doing so fairly regularly for several weeks now."

Sherlock Holmes consulted his pocket watch. "Then I suggest we repair to that tearoom for our own luncheon. If this man is there today, then I should certainly like to listen to what he has to say. And then come to my own conclusion about him."

*****

We alighted from our cab in Norfolk Street at around lunchtime. As usual at such a popular hour, the teashop was crowded with patrons, but my own customary corner table was left unoccupied, save for a single solitary figure. The weird old man was sitting quietly in his corner, reading a newspaper folded on the table in front of him, with his usual glass of milk and slice of cheesecake beside it. He looked up as I led Mr Holmes toward him, but remained seated, holding in his scrawny hands a length of string which he was absentmindedly tying into a series of complicated knots.

Before I had time to introduce my guest, the old man said, "You must be Mr Sherlock Holmes."

"Indeed I am," replied Mr Holmes, taking the seat directly opposite the old man.

"Even now you are a recognizable figure in London."

"And, although I have no idea of your name, I can immediately tell that you are a man with an interesting life. Your coat and trousers are in need of a brush and an iron, and your shirt requires the tender care of a launderer. I must therefore conclude that you live on your own. Your mind is usually upon other matters, since the eyeglasses you wear have seen better days, and the right side-arm has been repaired in a decidedly utilitarian manner."

The man in the corner remained almost completely impassive, apart for a twitch at the edge of his mouth, which I took to be his appreciation of the keen mind he had now encountered.

I ordered my usual midday meal: coffee, a roll with butter, and a plate of meat. Mr Holmes declined to order, but continued to sit, watching the withered old man. I sat watching the two, with keen interest, to see how they might interact.

Abruptly, the man in the corner put down his string, opened the newspaper he had been reading, and spread it out upon the table.

Pipes, Bonnets and Pieces of String by Robert Stapleton

"Mr Holmes," said he, "allow me to ask you what you make of this recent burglary; the ongoing story reported in the *London Mail*. It is supposed to have happened at number 24 Melgrove Gardens."

"It seems a very commonplace crime to me," replied Mr Holmes. "On the surface."

"Aha! On the surface." The man in the corner reached for his glass of milk, and immediately drank down half its contents. Then he picked up his piece of string, and continued to tie knots along its length. "Having read the report about the incident, you will recall the fact that the burglary occurred only three nights ago, at the home of Admiral Pulverholm and his wife. It appears that somebody entered the building by breaking a window in the scullery downstairs. According to the newspaper reports, the intruder, whoever it was, then proceeded to make his way upstairs to the bedroom, where the admiral and his wife, lay asleep in bed. According to the report, it seems the thief then removed an ornament from the mantelpiece, a figurine in the shape of an elephant, a souvenir of the admiral's time serving in the Indian Ocean, and escaped with it into the night. In the morning, although a thorough search was conducted of the premises, it was discovered that nothing else in the house had been touched. Except that the admiral reported that the door of the safe in the corner of his bedroom had been unlocked and left ajar. He declared that nothing whatsoever was missing from the safe."

I watched as Mr Holmes fixed his attention upon the man in the corner, intrigued, as the eccentric old man continued to fidget with his piece of string and tied it into ever more complicated knots.

"Odd, would you not agree?" asked the old man.

"Singular," replied Mr Holmes.

"Puzzling," I added, attempting to remain a part of the conversation. "But a man was arrested for the theft."

"And the newspapers record the proceedings that took place at the magistrate's court on the following day," continued the old man. "Lady Pulverholm revealed that she had been out shopping later on the morning following the overnight robbery, when she happened to pass a certain pawnbroker's shop, and her eye was caught by an item on display in the window. It turned out to be the missing statuette. The one taken from the bedroom. The owner of the pawnbroker's shop, a Mr Walter Hallibred, provided a detailed description of the person who had brought in the object. Within the hour, the local police, who had been investigating the break-in and theft, had arrested a young small-time crook by the name of Danny Crumb. This was the man who now stood before the magistrate in order to answer the charge of burglary. Although admittedly no saint, young Danny Crumb claimed to be completely innocent of this particular offence. Yes, he had indeed pawned that object, but no, he had no idea that it had come from the home of Admiral and Lady Pulverholm. He claimed to have discovered the missing figurine in the garden of a neighbouring house. What he had been doing in that garden remains a matter for speculation, which Crumb has so far refused to clarify. Then came the question of the open safe in the bedroom. The defendant appeared puzzled by the suggestion that he might have opened it, and once more claimed that he had nothing whatsoever to do with the matter. And, with nothing having gone missing from the safe, the investigation passed over that particular charge. With no further evidence to consider, but with his suspicions by no means assuaged, the magistrate felt he had no choice but to remand the accused into custody, whilst further investigations were made by the police."

"Which will of course take them nowhere," said Mr Holmes.

Pipes, Bonnets and Pieces of String by Robert Stapleton

The old man in the corner nodded. "But now we come to the point of it all. Tell me, Mr Holmes, why would anyone do something so strange?"

"What exactly do you mean?"

"Of all the things that were vulnerable to being stolen from that house, including from the open safe, why would anyone choose to take a ceramic elephant, and why not, at the same time, take the opportunity of stealing some or all of the other valuable items and ornaments in the rest of the house?"

"Did the elephant have any particular value?"

"None at all, above a few shillings."

"I agree. It is very strange. The only conclusion has to be that, whether or not this was indeed a burglary, then it was no mere common or garden crime. We might safely reject the improbable scenario, suggested by the Press and investigated by the police, that this rather naïve young man, Danny Crumb, actually carried out the robbery."

"Agreed. Then consider this proposition, if you will," continued the man in the corner. "This apparently minor crime could well have been a cover for the theft of some other item in the house. Danny Crumb was merely the hapless petty criminal who was used as a scapegoat to divert attention away from some much more serious crime."

I was now completely fascinated by this developing conversation. "If so, then what else was taken?" I asked.

"Precisely the question we need to ponder."

The two men sat quietly watching each other, until Mr Holmes concluded, "It is too early to propose any conclusion without further information. More facts. We must therefore conduct more detailed inquiries."

The man in the corner finished off his milk, stood up, and left like a shadow, stopping only to settle his bill at the counter.

"I must also leave," said Mr Holmes.

"Are you going to follow up the case?"

"Oh, certainly."

"Then may I come with you?"

"Of course. Your presence will be of the greatest value."

*****

The moment we stepped out through the front door of the teashop, Mr Holmes and I noticed a motorcar draw up beside us. It was a large, black city car, driven by a smartly dressed chauffeur. The rear passenger door of the Packard opened, and a head looked out. "Ah, there you are, Sherlock. Your landlady thought I might find you here. Would you care for a lift?"

"Where are you going?"

"Melgrove Gardens."

"Then we should be delighted to join you."

We climbed into the back of the vehicle and I found myself in the company of a man I vaguely recognized from an article I had once researched at the Foreign Office.

"This is my brother," explained Sherlock Holmes as the motorcar set off again. "His name is Mycroft, and he works with several government departments, most frequently at the Foreign Office."

"How do you do, Mr Holmes," I said by way of greeting. "I believe we have met before."

Mycroft leaned closer. "And I recognize you, young lady. You are Miss Polly Burton, of the *Evening Observer*. A journalist. And a professional busybody."

"You are quite correct, Mr Holmes," I averred.

"Then, if you are going to accompany us this afternoon, I hope you will be circumspect in your reporting of today's events."

"I can make no promises," I told him. "But I am a fulltime reporter."

"Then remember this, if you allow your creative imagination to run away with you, I shall be forced to deny everything."

"Naturally."

Sherlock Holmes sat back in his seat. "Now, Mycroft, what is this all about? Why are you interested in such a minor infringement of the law as occurred, or did not occur, in Melgrove Gardens?"

Mycroft Holmes took a deep breath. "We have recently received information that a certain European power, who in view of Miss Burton's presence here I shall refrain from naming, is seeking possession of a set of government documents giving details of a recently designed steam propulsion system being developed for use in our new generation of torpedo-boat destroyers. These documents are extremely sensitive, and are of course in the highest category of secrecy."

I found this revelation intriguing. Which foreign power was he talking about? As though I and my prospective readers could not make an educated guess. And what was so important about this new propulsion system? It raised more questions than answers in my mind.

"Only three copies of these plans exist," continued Mycroft Holmes. "One set is kept at the admiralty, whilst a second remains under lock and key in my own office."

"And the third is undoubtedly kept at the home of Admiral Pulverholm," concluded Sherlock Holmes.

Mycroft Holmes chuckled, and turned to me. "Do you see now why my brother is considered to be the greatest detective in the world?"

"You exaggerate, Mycroft," objected Sherlock Holmes. "The matter was simple enough to deduce."

My eyes lit up as I came to the obvious conclusion. "And one of these sets of plans has gone missing."

"That is precisely the matter we are investigating," said Mycroft Holmes. "One of our agents working in Europe has discovered and retrieved a carefully reproduced copy of the contents page, along with a promise of payment on delivery of a replica of the full set of documents."

The Packard rolled into Melgrove Gardens, and stopped beside another vehicle parked outside the front of Number 24, a large town house with well-maintained lawns and shrubbery both front and back.

The housemaid admitted us to the ground floor of the building, where we were immediately greeted by Lady Pulverholm. A tall, respectable woman in her later years.

"An Inspector from Scotland Yard has arrived," she informed us, "and is at this moment talking with my husband upstairs."

"Who is this Scotland Yard man?" asked Sherlock Holmes.

"An Inspector Hopkins."

"Ah, yes. I know the fellow well."

"Then we must join them upstairs immediately," said Mycroft.

"No," asserted Sherlock Holmes. "I should first of all like to examine the site of the break-in."

The housekeeper, a lady called Mrs Wellenough, who apparently carried a great deal of weight in the household, appeared and called for the kitchen maid to conduct us to the scullery.

This storage room lay close to ground level, and the single window, still jagged with broken glass, had recently been covered over with a sheet of canvas, and was currently awaiting the attention of a glazier.

The kitchen maid, a young girl named Prue, led the way into the scullery, where Sherlock Holmes set about a most unusual method of investigation.

He knelt down, and examined the floor. "There appears to be no sign of broken glass inside this room," he noted.

"That's right, sir," said Prue. "Mrs Wellenough told me I needn't bother brushing up in here just yet. She says I'll have plenty to sweep up after the glass has been replaced."

"Interesting," said Sherlock Holmes. "Now, may we proceed outside?"

Prue led the way out into the backyard, and there we came across the main debris left from the broken window.

Sherlock Holmes pointed to the shards of glass lying on the ground immediately beneath the shattered window. "As you can see, the window was broken by the use of a sheet of newspaper, covered in molasses, which had been pressed up against the glass in order to keep it largely in position whilst the intruder broke it."

"That seems obvious enough," said Mycroft. "In that way, the intruder would not have woken the rest of the household."

"Or so it would appear," continued Sherlock Holmes. "But look at this. When we examine the glass which is still attached to the newspaper, we find that it is the wrong way round. Observation, and a moment's consideration, will tell you that glass on the outside of a window attracts dirt of a quite different in nature from that on the inside of the window. I am sure that Prue does an excellent job of cleaning the window. But only on the inside."

"Yes, sir," said the kitchen maid. "It's the job of the window cleaner to clean the outside. But he often overlooks this part of the building."

"Even so, if the glass had been broken from the outside," continued Sherlock Holmes, "we should expect to find a scattering of broken glass inside the scullery. Both fallen from the glass itself, and scraped from the window frame by the intruder as he climbed inside."

"But it isn't there," I exclaimed.

"Which is why," continued Sherlock Holmes, "we can be certain that the window was broken from the inside rather than the outside."

I gasped. "But that means that somebody inside the house must have deliberately broken the window to make it look as if an intruder had done it."

"Bravo, Miss Burton."

"And Danny Crumb has to be innocent."

"At least of this particular case of breaking and entering."

I now had at least one newspaper story from today's activities. But the day was far from over yet.

"Now we must find out what Inspector Hopkins has to tell us." With a look of satisfaction upon his face, Mr Sherlock Holmes led the way back to the entrance hallway of the house, from where the butler escorted us up the main staircase.

In the master bedroom, we found Inspector Stanley Hopkins talking with another man who was seated in a comfortable armchair. This man's air of authority indicated that he was the owner and master of the house.

"Inspector Hopkins," said Sherlock Holmes, with a knowing smile.

The Inspector seemed astonished to see two men by the name of Holmes. "Mr Holmes," he gasped. "I thought you were well and truly retired these days."

"Indeed I am, Inspector," replied Sherlock Holmes. "But I am always prepared to make an exception when national security is at stake."

The policeman did not look happy. "Well, I hope you won't be disappointed by this little conundrum."

"We shall see," he turned to the other man. "And Admiral Pulverholm. Allow me to introduce myself. I am Sherlock Holmes. And this is my young friend, Miss Polly Burton."

The admiral did not appear to be impressed.

"My brother has provided me with some background information on this case," Sherlock Holmes told him. "But I sense that there is more going on here than meets the eye."

"Maybe less," replied Inspector Hopkins dolefully. "That is what we are here to determine."

"In that case, be kind enough to explain yourself, my dear Inspector."

"As Mycroft will have told you, certain highly sensitive information has been leaked to a foreign military power possibly bearing aggressive intentions toward this country."

The admiral stirred uncomfortably in his chair. "And your brother, in the company of half the detectives at Scotland Yard, is accusing me of being responsible for leaking this information."

"Certainly not you personally, Admiral," said Mycroft Holmes defensively. "As I have already explained, it is just that yours is one of only three possible sources of the leak."

"And why could it not have been leaked from your home rather than mine?" demanded the admiral.

"Because my papers are still inside the safe at my house."

"As are mine," roared the admiral. "Let us see, then, shall we?" With that, the admiral stood up, removed a key from the watch-chain attached to his waistcoat, and approached the safe in the corner of his bedroom. "See, gentlemen," he announced. "Apart from one held for security purposes by my bank, this is the only key that will open this safe." He slid the key into the lock, rotated the mechanism, turned the brass handle, and pulled the safe door wide open.

Pipes, Bonnets and Pieces of String by Robert Stapleton

The admiral examined the contents. "Here, on the top shelf, I keep loose cash, which is necessary for meeting everyday expenses. I use it to pay the servants, outside utilities, shopkeepers and traders who supply us with our daily dietary and other necessities."

He turned to the second shelf. "And here I keep items of greatest value, including those papers entrusted to me by the admiralty. See. Here they are, safe and sound." I watched him push aside another bundle of documents, and lift out a cardboard folder. This he held up for us all to see. The folder carried the words "Top Secret" printed in red letters on the outside. He opened the folder, and removed a pile of official-looking papers.

"Gentlemen, and the lady present," he announced with exaggerated grandeur, "these are the papers we are talking about. And they are all here. Every one of them."

Inspector Hopkins looked embarrassed, whilst Mycroft Holmes gave the impression of being confused beyond reason. Only Sherlock Holmes remained impassive, pensively watching the papers, whilst I shrank back into the shadows.

"It certainly looks as though we owe you an apology, Admiral," Inspector Hopkins replied sheepishly.

"It does indeed seem to be that way, Inspector," replied the admiral, with an expression of triumph now upon his face.

"In which case, we must extend our investigations elsewhere in our search for this leak of information," admitted Mycroft Holmes.

Mumbling their profuse apologies, both Mycroft Holmes and Inspector Hopkins turned, made their way back down the stairs, and hurried out into the fresh air.

The admiral turned to face Sherlock Holmes. "Well, Mr Sherlock Holmes, are you going to join them? If not, then why are you and the young lady still here?"

"We shall of course take our leave of you shortly," said Sherlock Holmes. "But first I have a few questions I should like to put to you, Admiral."

The admiral glowered back. "Very well. Ask your questions, and then be off with you."

Unperturbed, Sherlock Holmes asked, "How many sheets of paper are in that Top Secret folder, sir?"

"In the folder? Half a dozen. Why?"

"Do you check those papers every day, Admiral?"

"Of course, I do. Religiously. Every single day, without fail."

"And do you count them every time you check them?"

"No, sir, I do not. I usually have better things to do with my time."

"Then you would never know if just one single sheet had been removed."

"True enough, I suppose."

"In that case, perhaps you might agree that somebody could have removed a single sheet one day, and then replaced it again on the following day. If this were to be done every day for a week, then you would never have been any the wiser."

"Do you always make such wild speculations, Mr Holmes?"

"I never make speculations of any kind, Admiral. I employ the science of deduction."

"But you have no evidence whatsoever to support this ridiculous idea."

"True."

"And, much more to the point, who would do such a thing, and why?"

"I have not yet come to a definitive conclusion about those matters," said Mr Holmes.

As the admiral turned his attention to reattaching the key to his watch-chain, Sherlock Holmes asked if he might examine it for a moment.

The admiral handed over the key without objection.

Sherlock Holmes then held the key to his nose, and sniffed it gently. His eyebrows rose slightly, and the hint of a smile appeared upon his face. He knelt down beside the safe, and sniffed at the lock.

"This lock has been recently oiled," he observed.

"I do try to keep it in working order," declared the admiral.

"Indeed. The aroma of lubricating oil is strong here. As it is upon the key."

"With the two having recently been in close contact, the presence of oil would hardly be surprising."

"Except that the key carries another scent."

He passed the key to me. "What is your opinion, Miss Burton?"

I took the key, and held it close to my nose. I sniffed. "Yes, oil," I decided.

"And?"

"It also carries another smell. Wax. Distinctive."

"Suggestive."

"Of what?"

Holmes said nothing.

"Wax?" demanded the admiral.

"Oh yes," replied Sherlock Holmes. "Now, let us try to imagine what might have occurred here. Somebody managed to gain access to that key."

"Impossible," declared the admiral. "That key is upon my person at all times."

"Except when you are in bed."

"Even then, it is always close at hand."

Sherlock Holmes brought out his magnifying glass, and studied the key in greater detail. "There are even traces of wax still adhering to parts of the key. That too is suggestive."

"What are you proposing, Mr Holmes?"

"It is clear that anyone wanting access to your safe would need only a moment's contact with this key in order to make a wax impression, so that a duplicate could then be quickly made."

"That is a preposterous idea, Mr Holmes," cried the admiral.

"Not really. If the person involved in this crime were to be a member of your own household, they might have plenty of opportunities to gain access to your bedroom, and to the safe itself."

"But no crime has been committed," insisted the admiral. "Nothing has gone missing, as you and your colleagues have already agreed."

"Perhaps," said Mr Holmes. "But something unexplained has occurred here."

"We have a busy day ahead of us, Mr Holmes," said the admiral. "So, I must ask you to leave."

"Certainly. But one final question, if I may," said Mr Holmes.

"Very well."

"Why did you report the open safe to the police when you knew that nothing had been taken?"

"It was entirely my wife's idea. She considered a full disclosure to the police to be essential."

"And whose idea was it to incriminate the young thief by planting that elephant in your neighbour's garden?"

The admiral scowled. "Now, unless you have any other unfounded allegations to make, I think you should leave now, Mr Holmes."

Pipes, Bonnets and Pieces of String by Robert Stapleton

*****

It was late the following morning when I next encountered Sherlock Holmes. We met at my habitual corner table in the ABC teashop. On that occasion, after a morning sitting at the typewriter, I was wearing a more workaday bonnet. We were alone, and I had already begun my luncheon, when the diminutive figure of the amateur detective arrived, and assumed pride of place in the corner seat we had reserved for him.

The little man took a fresh piece of string from his pocket, and began to tie knots along its length. "The presence of Mr Holmes here suggests that you are making some progress in the case involving 24 Melgrove Gardens," he told us.

As Sherlock Holmes remained in pensive silence, I tried to explain. "It seems that somebody has made a copy of the key to a safe there containing government documents. We even discovered traces of the wax left on the key when we examined it."

"Really? I find your mention of the smell of wax intriguing."

"But nothing is missing from the admiral's safe."

"Or so he tells you."

"Mr Holmes thinks that copies of those papers must have been made, presumably without the knowledge of the admiral."

"So, they could be passed on to some foreign power perhaps?"

"It is not a matter to be discussed in public," said Sherlock Holmes as he leaned forward and riveted the little man with a steely glare. "But if the information on those papers were indeed to fall into the hands of some foreign power intent on gaining a military advantage over this nation, then this might already have become a matter of the international significance."

"As I suggested the last time we met, this is undoubtedly a more important case than the police are capable of dealing with."

"Serious."

"For the thief also. Who do you have in mind, Mr Holmes?"

"It is still too early to say."

"But you have some ideas."

"Indeed. Although I should need further information before I can be certain."

"Then permit me to supply that information," said the man in the corner, with an evident sense of pride. "Allow me to provide the single piece of information which will prove to be the key factor in unravelling this entire mystery."

I sat watching these two men as they once more faced each other across our corner table. Two detectives, with so much in common, and yet so very different in many ways. I was intrigued. My journalist's ears were alert. I wondered what great pearl of wisdom would now be revealed. I bit deeply into my bread-bun, and listened.

"Let us consider the household in general," said the little man. "They have a modest array of servants, including cook, kitchen maid, housemaid, footman, chauffeur, gardener, valet, butler and housekeeper. But let us concentrate upon the housekeeper."

"Mrs Hester Wellenough."

"That is indeed her name now. But it was not always so."

"Really?"

"Certainly not. I have spent a great deal of time, both yesterday and this morning, looking through newspaper archives and public records. It seems quite clear that Mrs

Wellenough was previously married to a man by the name of Mulberg."

"Tell me," said Sherlock Holmes, "did he have any connection with the firm of Milton and Mulberg, the brewers?"

The man in the corner continued to tie ever more complicated knots into his piece of string. "German immigrants," he said. "The Mulberg brothers. Heinrich and Joseph. Both proved to be intelligent and resourceful young men. They arrived in this country two-and-twenty years ago, met up with the Milton family, and went into business together. As you suggest; brewing beer."

"A profitable business, one would suppose," opined Mr Holmes.

"Perhaps. But it seems that Joseph Mulberg had a huge row with both his brother and the Milton family. Over some trivial matter. The two brothers never spoke again. Joseph found employment with a publishing company, met a young woman from Stepney, married her and settled down to a life of domestic bliss. They had only one child. A boy called Samuel."

"But Joseph died."

"That's quite right. After ten years of happy marriage, Joseph succumbed to pneumonia, leaving his widow with a young boy to raise and feed. However, within a year, she had met this man, Wellenough. A clerk at an insurance office in the city. They married and settled down. Then, after another four years of what we might assume to be a happy marriage, the new husband also died. Of a stroke."

"A tragic situation."

"Indeed. Hester Wellenough was once more left to fend for herself. Taking in washing and ironing amongst other things. And the growing son, who had until now been an assistant to an odd-job man, looked to his father's family for assistance. Whilst not prepared to assist the mother, the other

Mulberg brother wished to help the young man, and found his nephew a job at the coopers' workshop that supplied the brewery. Samuel's job was to make the barrels which were used by the brewery to hold and transport their beer."

"But that was an independent firm."

"Located in adjacent premises. But free to stand or fall on its own merits. However, the young man did very well there, and rapidly rose to a position of responsibility and seniority within the firm. At the same time, young Samuel kept in touch with his mother, and helped her find employment at the home of Admiral and Lady Pulverholm. As housekeeper. A highly respected and responsible position."

I now felt bold enough to make my own comment on the story. "Good for her. It seems that everyone was now happy."

Mr Holmes nodded slowly. "But recently things have begun to go wrong." He stared at the old man in the corner. "What can you tell us about that?"

The little man had come to the end of his piece of string, so he put it down, took out his notebook, and removed from it a couple of photographs. These he laid out upon the table, in full view of Mr Holmes and myself. They showed a young man, dressed in a smart suit and a bowler hat. "These photographs were published in the newspapers late last year," said the man in the corner.

"Then this must be Samuel Mulberg," I decided.

"Quite right. These two pictures were taken of him outside court as he arrived to answer a legal case. A sawmill firm was seeking settlement for a delayed payment from the coopers' workshop at which the young Mulberg was employed."

"They were having financial problems," concluded Mr Holmes.

"But the matter must have been settled quickly," I added, "or else we would have heard more about it in the Press."

The scarecrow sat back, with a self-satisfied grin upon his face. "That is the intriguing part of this whole business. Within a couple of weeks, the debt was settled, and nothing more was heard of the matter."

I watched as the man in the corner smiled, slipped quietly out of his place, and scuttled across the floor of the tea-room. A moment later, he had disappeared through the front door, and was gone about his own business.

Whilst my own mind was awhirl with so much new information, I turned to see Mr Sherlock Holmes, also sitting deep in thought. After a couple of minutes, he stood up abruptly, and also headed for the door. I adjusted my bonnet, picked up my notebook, and followed in his wake.

*****

I returned with him to his temporary lodgings in Baker Street, where Mr Holmes declared that he needed time to think.

"This will probably be a three pipe problem," he declared, as he took a clay pipe down from its place in a pipe-rack above the fireplace, filled it with a plug of tobacco, then lit it and drew heavily upon the lighted pipe.

"I am sure you would like a cup of tea, my dear," came Mrs P's voice from the doorway.

I turned, and smiled. "Yes, that would be an excellent idea. My cup at the ABC went cold before I had time to enjoy it."

Down in her own living room, the landlady sat talking with me for the rest of the afternoon, until I realized I was going to be late for my meeting with Dickie Frobisher, and would have to leave at once.

It was at this moment that Sherlock Holmes burst into the room.

"Ah, there you are, Miss Burton," said he. "Are you up for an adventure this evening?"

My plans for the evening were about to receive a shattering blow. "I'm always up for anything exciting, Mr Holmes," I declared.

"Even if it might involve breaking the law?"

I hesitated until, with a twinkle in her eye, Mrs P interposed, "Your young man will be able to visit you in prison."

That decided the matter. I took a deep breath and replied, "Of course."

"Splendid." Sherlock Holmes smiled, and led the way outside.

The cab we hailed took us to the southern outskirts of the city, and dropped us off at the gates of a building which pronounced itself to belong to "The Milton and Mulberg Brewery Company".

The smell of hops hung heavy in the cold atmosphere, but Mr Holmes reminded me that we had no argument with either Mr Milton or Mr Mulberg, but only with the latter's nephew.

After speaking with the man on duty at the gate, Mr Holmes followed the directions he had been given, and we shortly found ourselves standing outside another building close by. This time the gates were locked, and solid iron railings protected the place against entry by anyone who ought not to be there. Such as ourselves. The place betrayed itself as a coopers and barrel-makers' workshop, not least by the presence of lengths of wood, metal hoops, and half completed barrels standing outside in the yard.

With dusk now falling rapidly, Mr Holmes discovered a small door in the side of the building, and used his pick-lock to gain us entry that way. Then we were inside the main building itself, where a strong smell of sawdust greeted us.

Having broken into the place, I felt less inclined to object when Mr Holmes used the same method to gain entry to the main office of the premises. A brass plate fastened to the door declared it to belong to Mr Samuel Mulberg. I looked around, and discovered that the building was supplied with electric lighting, so I flicked the light-switch, and bathed the office in the glow of an overhead lightbulb.

After a search of the filing cabinets, Sherlock Holmes found a document detailing exports, both accomplished and planned. "The brewery is expecting to complete a shipment of beer to Europe within the next few days," he told me. "In which case we need to take a closer look at the barrels they intend to use for that purpose."

By the dim illumination from overhead skylights, together with an electric torch Mr Holmes had discovered in the office, we made our way through the rest of the building. We narrowly avoided tripping over further half-finished wooden barrels left in the construction workshop, and finally reached the storage room at the far end of the building, linking the workshop to the brewery itself.

There we discovered two rows of wooden barrels, each three or four feet in height, already containing approximately thirty-six gallons apiece, and all branded, "For Export".

"What exactly are we looking for?" I asked my companion.

"If Mulberg is supplying copies of those documents to some foreign power, then the best way would be to employ some channel of communication already in use. That way, no suspicion would be aroused."

"You mean that Mulberg was making use of his trade in beer. But how exactly?"

"Use your imagination, Miss Burton," replied Sherlock Holmes. "If you wished to hide a bundle of papers in here, where would you conceal it?"

"Inside a barrel?"

"Perhaps. But the liquid contents would inevitably render the paper unreadable."

"Then where?"

"Possibly a secret compartment hidden inside the top of the barrel. The entire purpose of this place is to construct wooden casks, so it would take very little extra labour to construct a false cavity in the top of one or more of these barrels."

"Then how can we discover which one it is? There must be a dozen of them in here."

Sherlock Holmes removed an iron crowbar from beneath his coat. "When struck, the noise resonating from a gap containing air will sound very different from one which carried only liquid."

He walked along the lines of barrels, striking the top of each as he came to it. The dull sounds emitted by the barrels showed that each contained only liquid. Until he reached the far end of the second row.

"Aha! Now, listen to this, Miss Burton."

I listened with great care as he again struck the top of the wooden barrel. The sound was indeed different. Distinctive. I could imagine a gap of air immediately beneath the wooden lid.

Using the sharp end of his crowbar, Sherlock Holmes broke open the top of the barrel. As the wood gave way with a crack and a sigh, we saw, in the light of the torch, a cavity which was separated from the liquid below by a secure wooden base.

Mr Holmes put his hand into the cavity, and drew out a sealed bundle wrapped in waxed leather. As I held the electric torch, and directed its beam, I watched him open the wallet, to reveal a package of papers, each carrying diagrams and technical formulae which meant nothing whatsoever to me.

"This is better than I had hoped," said Mr Holmes. "These undoubtedly are copies of the papers that were taken from Admiral Pulverholm's safe, and then replaced. Somebody has gone to extraordinary lengths to reproduce the information in exact detail."

"Six sheets."

"The full set listed in the paper Mycroft's spy found. For which Mulberg was to be paid on delivery."

"Quite right, Mr Holmes." A voice from the doorway interrupted our discussion.

We turned as a light switch clicked on, and the incandescent lightbulb above us glowed into life, flooding the room with stark illumination. In the entrance, we saw three men. I gasped when I saw them. Two were armed with metal tools which I later discovered were commonly employed in the coopers' trade. One man carried a flanging iron; a length of metal with a pair of claws at one end. The other man held a heavy hammer. Both carried their implements in a threatening manner which made my blood run cold. The third man I recognized from the photograph shown to me by the man at the teashop. It was Samuel Mulberg.

"So, you have worked out our little subterfuge, have you?" growled Mulberg.

"You are a dangerous man, Mulberg," cried Sherlock Holmes. "You are selling the interests and security of your country to an enemy power."

"In view of our firm's financial problems, it was a sad necessity, Mr Holmes. As indeed is your unfortunate death. And that of the young lady."

"But, if you fail to deliver these papers," said Mr Holmes, "your own life will be in grave danger."

"Then we must make sure they are delivered," said Mulberg as the other two men approached us. The one with the hammer closed upon Sherlock Holmes, who countered with his crowbar, forcing his opponent to drop his implement. Mr Holmes then leaned the crowbar against the side of the closest barrel, turned to face his attacker, and began to give a good account of himself using his wits and bare fists.

Fearing for my life, I backed away as the other ruffian now approached me. Until I tripped over the crowbar Mr Holmes had hidden in the darkness, and fell over backward between the barrels.

The man with the flanging iron drew closer, with a nasty expression distorting his face. I scrambled to my knees, and picked up the crowbar with both hands. As the man raised his iron, preparing to strike me dead, I held the crowbar up to defend myself. The flanging iron struck it with great force, jarring my wrists painfully. But, despite the pain, I gripped the crowbar at one end, and swung it. The man was too slow to move out of the way in time, so the crowbar made painful contact with his right arm.

I heard a bone crack.

The man fell back, uttering words that no young girl should ever be expected to hear.

So, I hit him again.

Another shadow now fell across me, and I looked up to see Samuel Mulberg himself standing between me and the light. Before I had time to react, Mulberg kicked the iron bar out of my hands, and reached down to grasp me by the collar. What he might have done to me next, I hardly like to imagine, but, at that moment, the air was filled with the piercing sound of a police-whistle.

Uniformed policemen emerged through the doorway, and soon had the two thugs in custody. Samuel Mulberg, on the other hand, had slipped away through an outside door, leaving it open, and himself nowhere to be seen.

Inspector Hopkins now took charge of the situation. "Ah, here you are, Mr Holmes, and Miss Burton. A little old man left us a message. He said we should come down here and arrest you two both for breaking and entering. I don't suppose you know who that might have been."

"I can hazard a reasonable guess," said Mr Holmes, as he dusted himself down. "But I must say, it is extremely good to see you, Inspector."

"And Miss Polly Burton here, as a reporter with the *Evening Observer*, will have to explain herself to the editor of her newspaper."

"But first we must hurry off in pursuit of Mulberg," said Sherlock Holmes. "We now have clear evidence of his involvement in the theft of secret government information. And now he is on the run."

Adjusting my bonnet, I accompanied Sherlock Holmes and the policemen out through the back door.

"He must have taken the footpath across the common," shouted Mr Holmes. "Quick! It is imperative that we catch him before he reaches the roadway, and finds some means of escape."

I was equally determined not to let the man escape. Now, emboldened by the presence of so many policemen around me, I gathered up my skirts and hurried on blindly into the darkness. After no more than a minute, I ran full-tilt into somebody hidden in the darkness, and screamed as rough hands grasp hold of me. I looked up, and saw, to my horror, that it was Samuel Mulberg himself. The man turned me round and held me firmly from behind, with his arm across my throat, almost strangling the life out of me.

As the policemen caught up with us, Mulberg shouted his defiance. "Call off you men, Inspector," he yelled, "and give me time to get away. Otherwise, I'll kill the girl."

"I don't think you will do that, Mulberg," shouted back Hopkins.

"I wouldn't be so sure if I were you, Inspector. If I have to stand trial for treason, and then face the hangman's noose, I have nothing further to lose by taking her life."

I knew I had to take the initiative in this standoff, so I lifted my right foot, and raked the edge of my boot down Mulberg's shinbone. The man holding me yelled in shock and pain, and momentarily loosened his grip on my throat.

I pulled away.

At that moment, from out of the darkness, and huge fist collided with Mulberg's face, sending the man who had been holding me in a death-grip sprawling across the ground.

I looked up, and saw Richard Frobisher step out of the night, and into the torchlight.

"Dickie!" I yelled. Then, with my insides turning to mush, I ran into his outstretched arms, and burst into tears. There are times in life when a girl is allowed to do that sort of thing, and this seemed to me the most appropriate moment ever.

"You were late for our date," he scolded me.

"I know," I sniffled. "I'm sorry. But we had these villains to catch."

"So, I see. A lady in Baker Street sent me a note, telling me to contact Scotland Yard about you. So, here I am."

"Good for her." I hugged him more tightly, whilst the policemen set about placing Mulberg, together with the other villains, under close arrest.

The man in the corner continued his nervous habit of tying knots in the string he was holding in his thin bony fingers. "You understand," he told me, "that it was very much against my nature to approach the police at all, and Scotland Yard in particular. But I knew exactly where you were going to be that evening, and I wanted to make sure they captured the chief miscreant. Samuel Mulberg."

"And you saved our lives in the process," I added, adjusting the new bonnet I had purchased in celebration of our success.

He merely smiled indulgently.

Sherlock Holmes had told me that, compared with the antics of that evening, he considered the keeping of bees to be much less hazardous to the health of a middle-aged man like himself. So, I was not particularly surprised when he failed to join us at the ABC teashop that lunchtime.

"The full story, or as much of it as we have discovered, can now be revealed," I told the old man. "Having been given extra time in which to raise the money he owed, Samuel Mulberg agreed to sell military secrets to a foreign power in exchange for enough money to solve all his financial problems. It seems that somehow his mother made a copy of the key to the admiral's safe, and so gained access to the folder containing the secret documents. Over a period of several days, Mrs Wellenough removed the pages from the document folder, one at a time, and gave each in turn to her son. After he had made a careful copy of that page, he brought back the original, so that his mother could return it to its place in the file, removing the next page for similar treatment. The contents page had already been sent abroad, but we managed to rescue the other six." I felt proud that I had finally gained a proper understanding of the affair.

"All very neat and tidy," observed the strange old man sitting in the corner across the table from me. "So, the police are happy."

"Indeed."

"And what about the other business? How do you explain the supposed break-in by the burglar, Danny Crumb?"

I blinked, and tried to remember the details of that case. "Mrs Wellenough and her son made it look as though a break-in had occurred, to distract attention after all of the sheets had been copied, and the originals returned to the safe. It can only have been a way for them to cock a snook at the police."

"If true, then it would certainly be an attitude which I myself would applaud. But there appears to have been more going on here than you have so far grasped, Miss Burton."

"More?"

The wizened old man leaned forward, his long neck and beak-like nose reminding me of a stalking bird. He opened up his newspaper, and laid in out across the table in front of me. "Now, Miss Newspaper girl," he said in a scathing tone. "What do you make of this latest entry in the Stop Press column of this morning's newspaper?"

I looked down at the column before me.

"It reports that, earlier today, Admiral Pulverholm was himself arrested for his part in passing government secrets to agents of a foreign power."

In complete amazement, I read, and re-read the article, just to assure myself that he had revealed its contents correctly. He had.

"It was, of course, quite obvious," the man in the corner told me.

"Was it?"

"Of course it was. And it all had to do with the wax."

I blinked in amazement. "The wax?"

"You identified the presence of wax by its distinctive smell."

"Yes, certainly."

"Then consider this. If the key had been impressed into a bed of wax, then returned to its place among its fellows on the keyring, then spent much of its time in the pocket of the owner's waistcoat, being brought out each day for practical use on numerous occasions, and all this for perhaps a couple of weeks, then it would carry very little trace of the original wax. If what you say really did happen, then you would never have been able to detect the smell of the wax at all."

My brain was working rapidly now. "In that case, the presence of the wax must have been staged. Somebody put it onto the key at almost the last moment, specifically so that we should find it there."

The old man chuckled. "Perhaps by the admiral himself."

My eyes opened wider, in even greater amazement. "Then perhaps there never was any second key at all."

"Even your friend Sherlock Holmes realized the truth of it. He should be at Scotland Yard as we speak, helping Inspector Hopkins detail the charges against the admiral. The Inspector is going to need every bit of help Mr Holmes can give him."

"You can be a very cynical fellow at times," I told the old man.

"Cynicism is the very first requirement necessary for any detective. But consider this, what if the point of the supposed break-in, which was blamed on that foolish young burglar, was to place something in the safe rather than take anything out?"

I buried my face in my hands. "I find this whole business utterly confusing."

"But it all becomes as clear as day the moment you introduce the idea of blackmail."

"Blackmail?"

"Supposing Mrs Wellenough and her son had secured possession of some letters which proved the admiral guilty of marital infidelity. He would be willing to do almost anything to secure the return of those letters."

"Certainly."

"Think back, Miss Burton, to the occasion when you saw the inside of the admiral's safe. Did you see a bundle of letters in there?"

I thought carefully. "Yes. I think I did. He had to move it to one side in order to reach the government documents."

"Now, suppose the mother and son promised to return those letters in exchange for access to his top-secret papers. With all the documents now having been copied, they returned the incriminating letters, leaving the door open as a sign that they had done as they had promised."

"How intriguing."

The man in the corner gave a lopsided grin. "Not really. It's all quite simple when you admit the possibility. Now I can hardly wait to see how the newspapers report the unfolding public humiliation of the admiral."

I continued to study the newspaper article, trying to come to terms with this latest turn of events. Had we all been wrong about those thefts from the admiral's home, or was it just I who had been too slow to realize the truth? As a journalist, I am accustomed to humbug, but here I had found deception at every turn. Had the admiral's unsuspecting wife let the cat out of the bag by insisting upon reporting the open safe to the police? And, more interestingly, would I be the one called upon by my editor to cover the case when it came to court, and to write the report that the old man in the corner would read?

I looked up again, only to discover that my companion had slipped away, and was already stepping out into the fresh afternoon air. I was alone, with nothing more than this newspaper article, and a piece of string, twisted into complicated knots, from one end of its length to the other.

The Case of the Watery Wife

by Lorraine Sharma Nelson

West Ashley, Dorset, U.K.

Something in the air shifted. She turned. And there it was. Suspended above the water. Like a macabre angel.

Augustine Dalrymple hesitated for the briefest of moments before stepping into the chill waters of Hammersley Pond. The cold pierced the leather of her boots, shocking her system. She bit her lip, taking two more steps into the murky pond. The sludge sucked at her boots, making it difficult to maintain her footing.

But she was not to be deterred.

She would find out who or what it was that hung there above the pond. It looked like a woman, but the air around it wavered, making it difficult to tell for sure.

Two more steps...

Augustine saw clearer now — a woman, with her hair twisted into a chignon at the base of her neck. Her lips moved but no sound issued forth. But it was her eyes that held Augustine transfixed. They were large, almond-shaped, and seemed to dwarf her tiny heart-shaped face.

And, they stared right at her.

"Who are you?" Augustine whispered.

The lips moved again.

"I'm afraid I can't hear you. What manner of creature are you?"

Still nothing.

Augustine shivered. The water lapped at her knees, the hem of her skirt clinging to her stockinged legs. Something moved beside her and she glanced down in time to see a frog hop a lilypad.

In the next instant, her eyes snapped open. She took a deep, shaky breath, running the back of her hand across her damp forehead. *Again?* How many times had she had this same dream? Four? Five times? More? Was it possible she was losing her mind? She turned over, pulling the covers close about her. If these dreams didn't stop, that was a distinct possibility.

*****

Augustine rode her bicycle up to the boarding house in time to see the front door open and her Aunt Wilhelmina step outside. "Gussie, dear, you have a guest." Her aunt's eyes gleamed, cheeks flushed.

"Who is it, Auntie Willie?" She hopped off the bike, straightening her skirt and untying the kerchief around her brunette locks. Released from their confinement, the curls sprung out in every direction, but Augustine barely noticed.

"You'll see for yourself. Come. Come. It's rude to keep such an illustrious person waiting."

Her brows drew together as the older woman ushered her into the old stone manse. "He's waiting in the Drawing Room," she whispered, gesturing.

Augustine's eyes widened. "The Drawing Room? Whatever for? Why didn't you ask him to wait in the Conservatory?"

Auntie Willie made an impatient sound, giving her a gentle push toward the room in question. "Did you not hear a word I said? He's illustrious."

Curiosity poked at Augustine as she ran a hand over her hair in a futile attempt to tame the tangled mane, then she opened the door and stepped inside.

The gentleman had his back to her, his gaze on Hammersley Pond.

"Sir, I believe you have been waiting for me? My name is Augustine Dalrymple."

The man turned slowly and for a split-second Augustine's world tilted. In the next second he was beside her, gently propelling her toward a chair. Augustine squinted up at him. For an older gentleman he moved with the speed and agility of a much younger man.

"You ... you are –"

"Sherlock Holmes, at your service, Miss Dalrymple," he said, his voice a deep baritone.

Augustine shook her head. "But ... I thought you were retired, sir."

He inclined his head, his famous Widow's Peak gleaming in the soft lighting. "Indeed, I am."

Augustine shook her head. "Well then – forgive me – but why are you here?"

He smiled, the gesture filled with a lifetime of secrets. "Why, to help you with your case, my dear Miss Dalrymple."

She stared at him blankly. "My case?'

His gaze flicked to the window. "The apparition you've been visited by in your dreams. The woman's head suspended above the pond."

Augustine's jaw dropped, until she saw amusement flicker in his grey eyes, and promptly closed her mouth. "Mr. Holmes," she finally said, "I am at a loss as to how you came by this knowledge."

He shrugged. "I have my ways…"

Augustine shook her head. "But I have told no one –"

"No, indeed. You have been the soul of discretion, dear lady."

"But then –"

"Forgive me, but the hour grows late…" His gaze flicked to the window again, before returning to her. "Perhaps you will be good enough to show me where you encountered this disembodied spirit?"

Augustine was once again rendered almost speechless. "They are merely dreams, sir. Don't tell me the famous Sherlock Holmes believes in the possibility of spirits?"

He smiled. For a man of advancing years, there was still a palpable virility about him. "There are more things in Heaven and earth, Horatio, than are dreamt of in your philosophy."

Augustine smiled. "I love *Hamlet*. Ghosts, murder, sacrifice…" She sighed. "Writers in the year of our Lord, 1912, cannot compete with the bard." She met the man's gaze. "And you are correct, of course, sir. One cannot dismiss anything as one has not encountered everything."

"Well said." Holmes held out a hand to help her to her feet. "Are you quite well, my dear lady? Shall I ring for some tea?"

"No, no. I am quite myself, thank you." Augustine's cheeks burned. "I'm not in the habit of swooning, you understand? It was just the shock of seeing you."

Holmes bowed. "I am flattered, Miss Dalrymple –"

"Gussie, please." He raised an eyebrow. "Or Augustine. Whichever suits your fancy."

He smiled, ever the gentleman and held out his arm. ""Augustine, it is, then. Shall we?" She slipped her hand into the crook of his elbow and allowed him to lead her into the back garden.

The Case of the Watery Wife by Lorraine Sharma Nelson

As they strolled toward Hammersley Pond, Augustine shot a questioning glance at the tall man in the deerstalker hat beside her. "Mr. Holmes if I may —?"

"Sherlock, please." He smiled. "If I am to address you as Augustine, then you must likewise address me by my first name, must you not?"

"Very well. Sherlock then. You are aware, I'm sure, sir, that I am not a real detective."

Holmes's eyebrows rose. "You have successfully solved some rather puzzling cases, have you not?"

This time Augustine was not surprised by the man's knowledge of said cases. "Yes, they have been ... daunting, but I was not approached to examine those cases because of my background as a detective –"

"Rather, because of your sharp intellect and your ability to solve problems. You are a keen observer of human nature, my dear. It is a detective's first and best trait."

This time, Augustine stopped walking and addressed him face-to-face. "Sir, I must insist on knowing how you came to know about my dreams."

Holmes raised himself to his full height, gazing down his nose at her in a most disconcerting, imperious manner. "My dear woman, I am Sherlock Holmes."

She waited for him to continue, but he merely offered his elbow and resumed his stroll to the pond. She bit back a smile as she accepted. It was true, then. All those stories about his ego and narcissism. They had only just met and she was already experiencing both.

"Dr. Symes is an old schoolmate of mine," he murmured, by way of a delayed explanation. "Ah, we have arrived. Charming spot."

Dr. Symes. Aunt Willie's paramour. Of course. How could she have forgotten? Just last week, when he had been at the manse for afternoon tea, he had mentioned that Augustine looked peaked, and she had briefly told him about her recurring dreams. His eyes had gleamed with interest, but he had refrained from comment, suggesting instead a tisane to help calm her nerves at bedtime. She had thought no more about it, but apparently, he had. Enough to mention it to an old school chum.

Who just happened to be none other than the World's Greatest Detective.

Bemused, Augustine smiled, and realized that the man in question was looking at her, one arched eyebrow raised. "Oh," she said. "Forgive me. Yes, this is Hammersley Pond."

"Most becoming. And, where did you encounter the ... ah ... spirit?"

She pointed to the middle of the pond, now calm and peaceful with lilypads floating serenely on top. "In my last dream, I attempted to reach it, hoping to find some clue as to why this was happening to me, but the mud was difficult to maneuver, especially in my skirts." She smiled ruefully. "It seems even in my dreams I am hampered by my garments."

Sherlock nodded. "I must confess that a man's wardrobe is far more suitably designed for most occupations than a woman's." He inclined his head toward her. "It is my belief that the time will come when women will not be constrained in their garments as they are in this day and age."

"I fear I will not live to see that day," she murmured, knowing she sounded wistful, but unable to keep the yearning out of her voice.

"You will permit me to help you with your case?" Holmes asked, and for the first time Augustine detected a note of uncertainty in his deep baritone.

She blinked. "Case? Sir, these apparitions exist only in my dreams. And, truth be told, since I have been taking Dr. Symes' tisane at night before retiring, my dreams of late have been quite normal."

"Nevertheless, dear lady. I believe there is more to your dreams than you realize. With your permission, I will help you uncover the reasons for it."

For a moment, Augustine was at a loss for words. Those dreams she had were the product of an overactive imagination playing out in her subconscious. Surely there was nothing more to them than that?

But...

She met the detective's eyes. Felt the intensity of his gaze all the way down to her toes. If this great man thought there was more to her dreams than meets the eye, then who was she to question him? She cleared her throat. "I would be honored to have the expertise of the World's Greatest Detective," she said simply. "But as I said earlier, I am somewhat surprised, sir, as I have read in the *London Times* that you retired some eight years ago, in 1904 to be precise."

Holmes inclined his head. "Yes, indeed, but as *I* mentioned earlier, your particular case called to me."

Augustine sighed. "Please do not misunderstand me, sir. I am flattered by your interest in this matter, but," she shrugged, "it is hardly on the level of the 'Study in Scarlet,' for instance."

"Permit me to be the judge of that."

She watched as he surveyed the area, his eyes narrowed to slits, his every sense on alert. He looked like a hawk swooping over the land, looking for prey, and Augustine shivered slightly. It would not do to have Sherlock Holmes as an enemy. It would not do at all.

"There are a great many gases being expelled from the pond," he murmured after a while.

"Yes. It is more of a bog than a pond, really." She eyed him critically. "I have considered that the apparition in my dreams was nothing more than the expulsion of gases and it is merely my overactive imagination that saw a face where there was none."

Holmes swung to her, his razor-sharp gaze pinning her where she stood. "And do you truly believe that? Are you prone to seeing faces in the gases released from the bog?"

She bristled. "No, indeed. I have lived here a good part of my life and am a frequent visitor to the pond. I have never spied a face in the bog gases."

"Then do not doubt yourself. Trust in your senses, dear lady, and they will serve you well."

At a loss for words, Augustine merely nodded.

"Did this spirit appear to you at a particular time in your dreams?"

"Yes. I could hear the clock in the village square chime four times at each encounter."

Holmes nodded, his eyes warming with approval, and Augustine felt as if she were back in school, receiving a pat on the arm from the headmistress. She watched as the dapper gentleman fished a watch out of his vest pocket. "It is now 4:20 p.m." He glanced up, surveying the pond again. Augustine tried to see it from his point of view: big enough to swim in if one were a child, so long as one did not mind the stew of leaves, twigs, and grasses that combined over time to create the gases that escaped at various intervals.

During daylight hours, the pond seemed very amenable indeed, with a willow tree on the bank providing a filigreed shade over part of it. With the summer sun streaming through the leaves, it created a most pleasing effect.

In the evening however, the pond took on a more sinister visage. The tree looked like a cloaked figure looming over the helpless pond. Its gnarled fingers spread over the surface as if deciding where to reach down and snatch up some unsuspecting creature.

"Does the time of your ghostly visit have any significance, I wonder?" Holmes murmured.

"It is usually the time the gases coalesce, but that is all."

"They seem to be late today," he mused. "Perhaps we will have more luck tomorrow." He roused himself, straightening his shoulders and smiling at Augustine. "In the meantime, there is research to be conducted and studied. May I assume you have been busy investigating the matter?"

Augustine shook her head. "I thought them merely dreams, Sir."

"Indeed." Holmes glanced back at the pond, eyebrows slightly raised as he watched the green, glowing gases swirl and combine as they rose from the soup. "I imagine this pond will not easily reveal its secrets to us."

"We will have to coax them out," she whispered, seeing again in her head the vision of the woman that haunted her dreams.

As they turned to return to the manse, Augustine glanced back at the pond, as she always did, for one last look. She took a sharp breath, garnering her companion's attention.

She felt rather than saw him follow her gaze, and heard from him a similar intake of breath.

Together, they watched as the gases rose from its murky depths, shifting, coalescing into various shapes.

They watched for a moment, before Holmes nodded. "Yes, it is easy to see how these shapes could resemble a head in one's dreams. I fancy I can see several as the gases shift and change."

"Yes." She could barely form the word.

Holmes strode rapidly back to the pond, eyes fixed on the gases. Augustine hurried after him, not at all surprised by the fact that he did not hesitate at the edge of the pond, but in fact plunged in. Biting her lip, she did likewise.

She tried not to think of the sight they presented – an unlikely duo wading toward the glowing green gases that wavered and wafted in the soft autumn breeze.

"Fascinating," Holmes murmured, cocking his head as he examined the gases. Here, at the very center of the pond, all was quiet, save for the rustling of dry leaves overhead and the croaking of bullfrogs. They stood as one, the otherworldly glow capturing their attention, until they heard a voice calling to them from behind.

They turned, and Augustine saw Auntie Willie on the banks of the pond, waving to them, a look of profound distress on her kindly face.

Holmes glanced at Augustine, one dark eyebrow arched. "It appears we have distressed your aunt. Come." He crooked his arm, offering his elbow to Augustine for support, and together they waded back to shore.

*****

"Whatever were the two of you thinking, wading about in that filthy pond?" Auntie Willie asked, handing Augustine a steaming cup of tea. Across from her, Holmes held a similar cup, his expression somber as he stared into the crackling fire by the hearth.

"As I told you, Auntie, we were looking for something," Augustine mumbled, wrapping her hands tightly around the hot cup, relishing its warmth.

Auntie Willie shook her head as she adjusted the crocheted wrap around Augustine's shoulders. "Whatever would people have thought had they seen you? You're very lucky, Gussie, that the manse is somewhat secluded."

"Yes, Auntie."

"May we have a moment to discuss the case we're working on?"

Holmes's words had the desired effect on Auntie Willie. She blinked at both of them, and Augustine saw the exact moment that the older woman realized her beloved niece was working with the great man himself.

Muttering something about baking some loaves, the woman beat a hasty retreat, but not before darting an appraising glance at Augustine.

"Wonderful woman," Holmes said as the door clicked shut behind her. "Reminds me of my own landlady, of whom I am especially fond."

"Mrs. Hudson?" Augustine asked, before she could stop herself.

Holmes's sharp features registered a flicker of surprise before it was replaced by his usual inscrutable façade. "Ah. I see you are indeed familiar with my life," he murmured over his teacup.

"As is most of His Majesty's kingdom," Augustine replied, surprised at the rush of sympathy that swept through her at the man's lack of privacy. So, why should she feel sorry for him? He was famous and admired the length and breadth of England. She should be so lucky.

"It is not all that you assume," he murmured, watching her closely. "Notoriety is an ugly beast that once discovered cannot be hidden away in some dark cave."

"I'm sorry," she said, hating the idea of the general public knowing every detail of her private life. "I cannot imagine what it must be like."

He smiled then, and once again Augustine was surprised at how it transformed his face, making him appear almost handsome. "And let us hope that you remain in the dark on that account." He set his teacup back down on the table and sat back. "My dear, if I may be so bold as to suggest something?"

Augustine inclined her head. "Please, by all means."

"Do not take the tisane Dr. Symes recommended for you. It is of the utmost importance that you see your ghostly friend again."

She frowned. "But why, Sir? You say we have a case, but there is no proof that it is anything more than a dream —"

"If Dr. Symes thought your dreams questionable enough to mention them to me, it is enough to peek my interest. I ask again that you do not take the tisane, starting tonight."

"Very well," Augustine said. "If you think it may help."

"It is my great hope that it will, my dear."

*****

The ghostly face beckoned to her, shimmering, shifting, as it hung above the pond. Augustine took a step forward. Then another. The sucking mud threatened to claim her boot and she struggled to maintain her balance and footing both.

"Please," she said to the disembodied head, which, up close, was considerably more disconcerting, "can you not tell me who you are? If I am to help you, your name would be most useful."

In response, the leaves rustled anew, but this time they carried a name on the breeze they created.

Forty…

Augustine's breathing quickened. "Forty what?"

Silence.

"Please. It has no meaning to me."

The Case of the Watery Wife by Lorraine Sharma Nelson

In the next instant her attention was riveted by the resulting response carried by the breeze filtering through the leaves.

Spell...

"Spell?" She whispered, trying to ignore the cold seeping into her limbs. "What does that mean?"

No answer.

In desperation, Augustine blurted out, "Are you the result of foul play?"

Yessss...

Noooo. Augustine sat up, chilled to the very marrow of her bones.

*****

Holmes once again sat in the chair across from the fireplace, having already claimed it as his own. "And now, to the matter at hand. What does the number *forty* and the word *spell* have to do with the … ah … disembodied spirit from your dreams?"

Augustine was at a loss. Much as she wanted to impress the man with her deduction skills, the mystery surrounding this particular case had her stumped. How was one supposed to solve a case with only two clues? And even then, those clues being whispers on the wind? Or, for that matter, something that did not exist in the real world?

"I believe a trip to the local library is called for," Holmes murmured. "Posthaste."

*****

Augustine massaged her temples as she contemplated the pile of newspapers strewn about the massive oak table in the village library. As libraries go, it was quite impressive. After all, West Ashley was not a large town. Heavens, it was barely a town. In fact, *village* described it quite adequately. The population varied between two thousand people in the winter months, and nearly five thousand in the height of summer. At that time wealthy Londoners escaped the heat of the city for the somewhat cooler climes of the west country.

She straightened in her seat, stretching her neck and shoulders. Gracious, but she was exhausted. She had been searching for any hint of a woman either missing or presumed dead through foul play in and around West Ashley, for the past week, but had not had any luck in the matter.

From Holmes's gruff manner of late, it appeared that he had fared no better than she. *What now?* she thought, rubbing her eyes. *Do we give up? Dismiss my dreams as nothing more than an overactive imagination, or do we persist in this affair?* She sighed as she sat back and picked up another stack of newspapers. They would forge on, of course. She would not admit defeat any more than would the great Sherlock Holmes.

"Ah, you are hard at it. Excellent."

She looked up, irritation sweeping through her. Holmes looked as dapper and crisp as a man taking tea with King George, whereas she felt as disheveled as a woman who…well…who had spent the night wading in a pond, talking to ghosts. Even if it had been in her dreams.

Dash it all. How does he do it? Does the man wake up impeccably dressed, ready for action?

"I take it from your disillusioned expression that you have had no luck either." It was a statement of fact.

"Correct as usual, sir."

Holmes smiled. "Even though there has been no progress, one must be patient in the pursuit of truth." His grey eyes gleamed. "I did, however, find a most fascinating article on the two Americans – the Wright brothers, I believe — and how they came about creating their flying vessel." He rubbed his hands together as he took the seat across from her. "What a miraculous age we live in, my dear Augustine." Before she could respond, he reached across the table, plucking a pile of newspapers from the stack strewn across the table. "Now then, let's see what we have here."

For three hours, the duo pored over accounts of every type of mystery happening across the length and breadth of Dorset. But, to no avail.

Finally, when Augustine thought she must have a cup of tea or expire where she sat, Holmes looked up at her, his piercing grey eyes considerably subdued. "I suggest, dear lady, that we retire back to the manse. No doubt, your charming aunt will have some delicious confections at the ready for teatime?"

She did not need to be asked twice. Augustine was out of her seat and into her coat before Holmes finished speaking. Thoughts of Auntie Willie's light-as-air scones and buttery jam tarts had her quickening her steps out of the library, and she noticed with satisfaction that Holmes had to hasten his steps to keep up.

*****

Augustine had just leaned her bicycle against the front wall of the corner shop that tripled as a newsagent's, a café, and a market, when she saw the face from the pond heading right toward her.

Same almond eyes.
Same heart-shaped face.
Same chignon.
Except this face had a body attached.

She tried not to stare – so rude – but failed miserably. She gaped, slack-jawed, as the woman, smartly dressed in a grey tweed suit, with matching pumps in the very height of fashion, breezed past her.

As Augustine stared after her, a woman with a small child paused to address the smartly-dressed woman. They exchanged a few words, but, much as Augustine strained to hear their conversation, they were too far away. She waited for the woman, who clutched the child's hand as they hurried by the shop, and stepped quickly toward her.

"Pardon me, Madam, but I believe I'm acquainted with the woman you addressed a few moments ago." She inclined her head toward the rapidly-retreating woman. "I can't quite recall her name, though."

The woman squinted at Augustine. "You mean Mrs. Folsey?"

Of course! Now she remembered, the connection snapping together in her head like a jigsaw puzzle. *The library sale.* "Oh, Mrs. Folsey. How could I have forgotten. She lives on…um…"

"Spedwell Lane," the woman supplied, looking at Augustine as if she were slow in the head.

"Yes, Spedwell Lane. One of those big houses over there." She sighed. "My, I would give anything to see inside one of them, wouldn't you?"

The woman's back straightened and something akin to pride flashed in her blue eyes. "I already been in 'er 'ouse. Work for 'er, don' I?"

"You do? Well, my goodness. She looks like a lovely woman to work for. Have you been with her long?"

"'Ere, what's with all the questions?" The woman's eyes narrowed to slits as she appraised Augustine.

"Oh, it's just that I'm sure I've met her at a social gathering. I don't want to embarrass myself if I run into her at some point."

The woman looked dubious, eyeing Augustine's attire. She bristled. What was wrong with the way she was dressed? Why, she was in a frock that she had only worn a handful of times thus far. It was practically brand new. She resisted the urge to pat down her unruly locks. "So, have you been with her long?"

"Long enough. Come along, Polly." She tugged on the child's hand, ushering her down the sidewalk.

Augustine glanced back at Mrs. Folsey, who was by now quite far along. Making a split-second decision, she dashed after the woman. People on both sides of the narrow street stopped to stare at her as she raced down the sidewalk, and she got more than a few 'tsks' and plenty of disapproving stares. No doubt Auntie Willie will have heard about her unladylike behavior by the time she got home.

"Excuse me, please." The woman didn't pause or turn around. In fact, she quickened her pace. "Mrs. Folsey?"

At the use of her name, the woman stumbled, raising a hand to steady herself. She turned slowly, sky-blue eyes wary. "Yes?"

"Please forgive my intrusion, but I thought I recognized you. I...um...wanted to thank you again for your generous donation to the library book sale this past July."

Puzzlement. Confusion. Fear. Augustine watched as these emotions played across the woman's face. With a supreme effort she gathered herself, jutting out her chin. "The library book sale? Oh, of course. I...I'm glad I was able to help."

"They raised more funds than ever, thanks to you."

"*They?* You don't work there?"

Augustine shook her head. "No, unfortunately. But, I help out whenever time permits, especially during the sale. They are sadly short-staffed."

A tight smile pulled at the woman's face. "Well, I'm ever so glad to help out. But, I am in a hurry, so if you'll excuse me..." She turned away, effectively ending the conversation.

"You did say that you had more to donate," Augustine blurted out, praying she wouldn't be struck down by lightning for the big fib.

Mrs. Folsey glanced back over her shoulder. "I did?"

Augustine nodded, her heart jack-hammering. This *was* the woman from her dreams. What did it all mean?

A brief hesitation, during which both women sized each other up. "I'll speak to my husband about it. If he agrees, I'll have one of the servants deliver a box to the library."

Augustine clapped her hands together, hoping she showed the right amount of enthusiasm. "That would be wonderful. Thank you so much, Mrs. Folsey. But, there is no need to send one of your staff. I would be most happy to pick up the box."

Mrs. Folsey's eyes widened. There it was again. Fear, darkening her eyes. The air around them suddenly rife with the stench of it.

"No." The word hung between them. The woman took a deep, shaky breath, her hands curling into fists as she strove to compose herself. "I mean, that won't be necessary. I don't know when I'll have the books ready. It will be easier if I have my manservant deliver —"

"Oh, it's no trouble, believe me. I can call on the telephone to check if it is ready for pick up."

The woman gave her an inquisitive look. "You have a telephone?"

Augustine nodded, pride swelling her chest. "Why, yes. My Auntie Willie — Wilhelmina Dalrymple — had one installed just this year. She runs the boarding house on the hill —" Augustine gestured toward the lone stone manse, visible from their vantage point — "with Hammersley Pond right behind it. Do you know it?"

Augustine's breath hitched at the change in the woman. Her face drained of color, her eyes wild, her jaw slack. She swayed, stumbled, and would have sunk to the ground had Augustine not reached out a hand to steady her.

"Mrs. Folsey, are you okay? Should I send for Dr. Symes?"

"Dr. Symes? No. No, please. I…I am quite well. Just a slight dizziness brought on by hunger. I neglected to eat lunch today. I…I must go." She put a gloved hand to her temple, pressing slightly.

"It would be my pleasure to buy you a cup of tea and perhaps a scone or two?" Augustine ventured, her hand still on the woman's elbow.

Mrs. Folsey shook her head. "You're very kind, but I must be going. I've tarried in town long enough. My husband will be expecting me. Please excuse me." She wrenched her arm away, hurrying down the sidewalk before Augustine could stop her. As she approached a fancy-looking automobile, a man in a uniform stepped out of the driver's side, and hurried to open the back door for her.

As the woman made to step inside, she hesitated, turned. "My man will deliver a box to the library by week's end. You need not concern yourself about it."

Augustine stared after the automobile as it made its way over the cobbled street and disappeared from view. Her skin prickled, every sense on high alert. The provisions she was sent to procure for Auntie Willie momentarily forgotten, she sped back to the manse as if twenty red devils were after her.

The Case of the Watery Wife by Lorraine Sharma Nelson

*****

"Identical to the woman in your dreams, you say?" Holmes raised an eyebrow. He puffed on his briar wood pipe, a contemplative look on his angular face. "So, logic dictates that if she is undoubtedly alive and well, there is no case."

"You did not see her, Sherlock. When I mentioned Hammersley Pond she almost swooned."

He gave Augustine a speculative look. "And what do you surmise from that?"

Frustration swept through her and she had the childish urge to stamp her foot. "I do not know. Why do I dream of her if there is nothing amiss?" She shook her head, slumping into a chair across from Holmes. "Maybe I am losing my mind."

"Maybe."

Her head whipped up.

"And, maybe not."

"Sherlock, please. I am in no mood for puzzles."

"And yet we have a daunting one right in front of us, do we not?"

Augustine frowned. "Did you not just say that there is no case?"

"I said logic dictates that if she is alive and well there is no case."

Augustine wanted to throw her cushion at him. "She *is* alive and well," she ground out through clenched teeth, "ergo, there is no case."

"I am afraid we must agree to disagree," Holmes said, pointing his pipe at her.

Augustine felt a throbbing in her temples. "You are speaking in tongues, Sir. I —" She stopped, her head snapping up. "Mrs. Folsey," she whispered. "Spedwell Lane." She was out of her chair and pacing, her breathing quickening. "Could that be what the apparition meant? Not *forty,* but *Folsey?*"

Holmes nodded, sitting back. "Yes, I do believe so. And you heard *spell* when what she perhaps meant was *Spedwell.*" He set his pipe carefully down on the side table. Standing, he straightened his vest, smoothed his hair back, and strode over to the coat rack, where hung his famous Inverness tweed cape, with the grey houndstooth pattern, and his equally famous deerstalker hat.

He caught her staring at the garments and, somewhat self-consciously, donned them. He then met her gaze. "I suggest you rouse yourself, dear lady. The game is afoot."

Augustine's breath hitched. The apparition, spirit, disembodied head – call it what you will – had effectively pointed them in the right direction.

Holmes was right.

The game was indeed afoot.

*****

Holmes lifted the heavy brass knocker, worn with age, and tapped it three times against the heavy oak door. The sound reverberated inside the house, sounding almost like a muffled heartbeat. Despite herself, Augustine felt a twinge of misgiving. She shivered, gathering her coat closer around her.

The door opened, revealing a slight woman with snow-white hair, dressed in a floor-length brocade robe. "Yes?"

"The Folsey residence, I presume?" Holmes said, projecting an air of intimidation.

The woman, however, was not easily intimidated. "Who wants to know?" She lifted her chin and stared down her nose at Holmes, then flicked a glance at Augustine. Deciding,

The Case of the Watery Wife by Lorraine Sharma Nelson

apparently, that the woman beside him was not worth her time, her gaze returned to Holmes, speculating.

"I am an acquaintance of Mrs. Folsey," he said, "and as I am in the area, I thought I would pay my respects."

The older woman's eyes widened and Augustine recognized the selfsame expression of fear that she'd seen in the younger woman. Whatever was going on here was worth investigating, and she aimed to get to the bottom of it.

"She ... she ain't ... she's not in."

"What a shame. When do you expect her back, pray tell?"

The woman shook her head and Augustine watched as the color slowly drained from her withered face, leaving it pale and sickly. "I ... I don't know. She didn't say. It may be a while. In fact, I'm sure it will be."

"Oh. Well, in that case, we'll wait." Holmes brushed past the astonished woman, deerstalker in hand. He smiled over his shoulder at Augustine, who joined the woman in staring at him in astonishment. "Come, come, Augustine, my dear. Don't dawdle on the doorstep. We mustn't be rude."

Augustine eased past the older woman, mumbling her apologies. What on earth was Sherlock up to? What was the point of being here if the person in question that they were here to interview was not home?

She noticed then the scope of the foyer and lost her train of thought. It was immense. Covered in what was surely imported marble, with an enormous crystal chandelier winking above them in the afternoon light, it reeked of wealth and privilege.

"Sherlock — ?"

But she was cut off by a deep baritone voice coming from her left. "Good afternoon."

Augustine turned to see a man emerge from one of the many rooms adjoining the foyer.

"Good afternoon," she responded, in unison with Holmes.

The man stepped fully into the room, turning to the older woman who still stood, frozen, by the front door. "You may attend to your affairs, Martha. I have matters well in hand."

The woman inclined her head. "Very well, Henry. I shall be in the Drawing Room if anyone needs me." She flicked a glance at both Holmes and Augustine, before disappearing down a long, hollow hallway.

"Charming woman," Holmes murmured, and Augustine bit back a smile.

"My mother-in-law, Martha Bellows," the man said, with a dismissive flick of the wrist. He eyed Holmes curiously, but Augustine caught the wariness in his gaze, before his expression changed. "May I ask why the World's Greatest Detective saw fit to pay me a visit?"

Holmes inclined his head in acceptance of the compliment then turned to Augustine. "May I present my colleague and friend," he said, sweeping a hand toward her with a flourish. "The delightful and utterly charming Miss Augustine Dalrymple, who has earned quite a name for herself in the field of detecting."

The man's eyes widened slightly as he took in Augustine. She stood beside the great Sherlock Holmes, looking somewhat windblown and ever-so-slightly disheveled. She nodded in greeting, wishing she'd had a chance to run a comb through her untamed locks.

"Charmed, I'm sure," the man responded, although not very convincingly.

"Well, now that you know who we are," Holmes commented, "perhaps you'll be good enough to introduce yourself."

The man took a step forward, his blue eyes darkening with anger, or an equally strong emotion. "I am Henry Folsey," he replied, tight-lipped. "Kindly do me the honor of explaining your presence in my house."

"We're here to see Beatrice," Holmes said. "It has been a few years, but as I am in the area, it would be most remiss of me not to pay her a visit."

Folsey flinched visibly, but quickly pulled himself together. "As my mother-in-law has no doubt told you, Bea is out for the day visiting friends. She's not expected back any time soon."

"We'll wait," Holmes countered, unfazed by Folsey's hostility.

Folsey hesitated, and Augustine could see that he contemplated throwing them out. But then again, the man watching him with a hawk-like expression was none other than Sherlock Holmes. Augustine could imagine Folsey bragging to the locals in the pub that the Great Man himself was a guest in his house.

She watched as the man struggled to make a decision, but in the end it was Holmes himself who made it for him.

"We'll wait in there, shall we?" he asked, indicating the room recently vacated by Folsey. Without waiting for an answer, Holmes strode by him and entered the room. Augustine gave Folsey a quick smile before following in Holmes's footsteps.

*****

It was a wait of almost two hours before the front door opened and a cheerful, female voice called out. "Henry? Henry darling? Where are you?"

Footsteps clicked on the marble floor as she moved across the foyer. Augustine heard a heavier footfall, then

Folsey's voice, speaking in hushed tones. She strained to hear their conversation and turned to Holmes, wondering if he was doing likewise. But he appeared perfectly relaxed seated on the divan, his hands laced across his waistcoat, his eyes closed, his breathing rhythmic.

"If you want to hear their conversation, dear lady, I suggest you do what most people do and press your ear against the keyhole. It is far less taxing than your method."

Augustine felt a hot flush creep up her neck, but nevertheless, she rose and stepped to the door.

"... to worry about. They'll never catch on." Folsey's voice.

"But how can you be so sure," Beatrice hissed, sounding somewhat hysterical.

"Because it's foolproof," Folsey said softly. "Now come. Say hello and let's be rid of them."

"But what shall I say. I don't know him."

"Play along. I'll help you."

Augustine beat a hasty retreat back to the divan before the door opened and Beatrice Folsey entered, a radiant smile pinned on her lovely face. "Sherlock," she exclaimed in delighted tones, and stepped forward, slender arms extended. "How lovely to see you again. It's been far too long."

"Bea," Holmes said, stepping forward and bowing. He took one gloved hand in his, touching his lips to it briefly. "You look positively radiant. Why, you haven't aged a bit. Tell me, what is your secret?"

Beatrice laughed, but the sound had an edge to it. "Clean living, of course. What else?"

Holmes inclined his head in acknowledgment. "Of course." He turned to Augustine, gesturing grandly. "I believe you're acquainted with my colleague, Miss Augustine Dalrymple?"

Beatrice's eyes widened as recognition dawned, then narrowed with suspicion. "Why are you here? I told you I would have my manservant deliver the books to the library."

"She is here at my request," Holmes said, with a smile. "I mentioned to Miss Dalrymple that I would be paying you a visit, and as she is acquainted with you through your very generous donations to the library, I invited her to join me. Knowing your generous nature I did not think you would mind."

A slight hesitation before Beatrice responded, pinning a smile on her painted, blood-red lips. "Of course not. Your friends are as welcome as you are, Mr...Sherlock."

"So, tell me, how is dear old Bernie? Still commanding the stage?"

Beatrice laughed again, glancing at Folsey, who stood woodenly by, eyes fixed on Holmes. "Oh, you know Bernie?" she said, waving a hand dismissively. "He'll never change."

Augustine glanced at the woman's gloved hands. *She must be nervous. She even forgot to remove her gloves. Sherlock must be getting to her.* She watched as his eyes remained focused on Beatrice's face, and for a moment, she felt sorry for the woman. Beatrice Folsey was about to find out just how outmatched she was.

"And Felicia and Martin? I take it they're all in good health?"

"Perfectly. I'll be sure to mention that you asked after them."

Holmes smiled. "I would be most appreciative."

There was a moment of silence, during which Beatrice glanced again at Folsey. "Should I call for some tea?"

"Oh, please don't bother," Holmes said, reaching for his hat and cape. "We have imposed on your hospitality long enough. We must be going."

Relief swept across Beatrice's face. "Not at all. It was certainly a pleasure to see you again, Sherlock. Do drop by again when you're in this part of Dorset."

"I shall, and thank you." Holmes bowed again over Beatrice's hand. "Come, my dear," he said, smiling at Augustine.

"Those people you mentioned ...?" she began as they walked to the Peugeot parked in front of the grand house.

"Fabricated," Holmes supplied, as he held the passenger door open for her.

"When I eavesdropped," Augustine said, as Holmes maneuvered the automobile through the darkening countryside, "Folsey said that we'd never catch on. He added that it was foolproof."

Holmes raised an eyebrow. "My dear lady, nothing is foolproof."

*****

"Augustine," Holmes said that evening during dinner at the manse. "Will you be kind enough to share what you've learned about your case?"

"*Our* case," she said, reaching for the boiled spuds. "Very well, but please keep in mind that this is all mere speculation on my part, as nothing is certain."

"Of course. Please, continue."

"I am throwing caution to the wind and making a wild guess. A shocking guess." She took a deep breath. "I believe that Mrs. Folsey is not who she claims to be. Oh, the resemblance is striking. Uncanny, in fact. But...based on her reaction when I mentioned the pond, and, more importantly, the entire fabricated story you conjured up about being acquainted with her, which she accepted as truth...I mean, if she were the real Beatrice, wouldn't she have been puzzled by your claim to know her? She would have no reason to pretend otherwise, would she? And, don't forget what I heard outside the door when she was talking to her husband. She said she did not know you and Mr. Folsey said to play along. Clearly, there is something they are hiding. Sherlock, none of it adds up. If she is indeed not Beatrice Folsey, then who is she? And, more importantly, where is the real Beatrice?"

"So, you are convinced that the woman we met is not her?"

"Yes. I don't know how I know. Something about the way she walks, maybe? Her smile?" Augustine dropped her fork onto her plate, burying her face in her hands. "Oh, I don't know what I'm talking about. It all sounds so preposterous, doesn't it?"

"On the contrary, my dear, that is my summation as well. Brava."

She went still, then lowered her hands, leveling a gaze at the man sitting across from her. "It is?"

He inclined his head. "Indeed. I believe, based on the trap I set for her, in which I pretended to be a somewhat close acquaintance, and based on what you have shared with me, that this woman is an imposter."

"Then...then you think the real Beatrice is in trouble?" Augustine whispered.

Holmes's face hardened. "I do believe, my dear, that this heinous charade has gone beyond that."

Augustine paled, gripping the edge of the table. "You...you mean Mr. Folsey and the imposter...?"

"Murdered her? Yes, my dear. Unfortunately, that is exactly what I think they did."

She groaned, tasting bile at the back of her throat. "Oh God, Sherlock. Where do you think she is?"

"Where, indeed?" he murmured, examining his pipe. He raised his eyes, pinning her with a scrutiny so intense she couldn't breathe. "Where would you begin to search for her?"

Augustine thought for a moment. "Well, based on my dreams, which occur on Hammersley Pond, and on the imposter's reaction when I mentioned the pond…"

He merely inclined his head.

Augustine clenched her fingers together so hard her knuckles showed white. "You…you think that the real Beatrice has been coming to me in my dreams? Showing me where she is?"

"No, Augustine. I believe that your subconscious mind has been trying to tell you what's happened to the real Mrs. Folsey. You've obviously seen her at the library and possibly around town as well, and then later, the imposter. Your subconscious must have picked up on the slight differences between the two women and was trying to tell you that something was amiss."

Augustine shook her head. "No, Sherlock. That cannot be. Why would I pick up on them and not others? Household staff? Friends of the former Beatrice?"

"Because you, my dear, are a true detective. You notice things others don't." Sherlock set his knife and fork down on his empty plate and leaned back in his chair. "Add to which, Mr. Folsey and his new wife have done their homework. She is, no doubt, a perfect match for the real Beatrice in every way. I noticed the theatrical makeup she wore."

"Is that why you made up that story about a mutual friend commanding the stage?"

Holmes smiled. "I could not resist. On further investigation I am quite convinced we will find that our imposter is a stage actress. Her gestures and mannerisms were of an actress quite used to commanding the stage."

"She wasn't all that convincing," Augustine snorted. "There was obvious fear in her eyes."

"Because she was in danger of being caught. I am sure in other company she plays her part to perfection. The proof is in the fact that she has gotten away with it." He smiled at Augustine. "Until now, of course. They have met their match in you, my dear. You have noticed what everyone else has failed to."

"But we have no proof. We could be entirely wrong about everything."

"Indeed." Holmes pushed his chair back and stood up. "We will simply have to find proof that the real Mrs. Folsey was killed."

"So we start by combing the pond?" Augustine said, rising to her feet.

"Of course. It's elementary, my dear." Holmes smiled as he adjusted his waistcoat and smoothed down his hair. "Your subconscious is a powerful ally, my dear Augustine. "I suggest you pay close attention to it from now on."

"We shall see if it serves us well," she murmured, following Holmes to the Drawing Room for a much needed glass of sherry.

*****

Holmes and Augustine watched as the local constabulary dredged Hammersley Pond. It was, no doubt, hard work, as the men frequently paused to dab their faces with the tails of their shirts.

Augustine was acutely aware that, thanks to the chemical composition of the pond, whatever lay in its watery depths remained preserved for a good many years. If Beatrice was in there, she would still be intact, her features readily recognizable.

"Are you nervous or excited?" she whispered to Holmes, shifting from foot to foot, every nerve on edge.

"Neither, of course," Holmes replied.

"How can you be so calm?" she burst out, then lowered her voice as a few of the workmen glanced at her. "I mean, what if there is no murder, no imposter, no foul play?"

Holmes merely shrugged. "There is the possibility that nothing will come of our deductions, of course..." his voice trailed away as he watched.

Augustine gritted her teeth, curling her fingers into fists to keep from strangling him. Maybe then she could dump him in the pond. At least then there'd be a body to dredge up and –

A shout from one of the men caught her attention. As one, she and Holmes moved closer to the edge, and this time she felt him tense beside her. *Aha!* So, he wasn't as blasé about this case as he appeared to be.

Augustine watched as some of the men lifted something from the murky water. At first it looked like a mound of mud. Until, slowly, an arm slid free from the muck and dropped down, dangling above the water.

The buzz of conversation ceased, leaving the crickets, the birds and the bullfrogs to fill in the gap bereft of human voices.

On firm ground, the county coroner wiped away the mud from the victim's face, revealing a visage that keenly resembled Mrs. Beatrice Folsey, of 122 Spedwell Lane.

*****

"Knowing that Beatrice has finally received justice, that her killers are where they belong ..." Augustine took a deep, cleansing breath. "I hope she can finally rest in peace now."

"I am sure of it," Holmes murmured, donning his deerstalker hat and adjusting his cape.

"It has been an honor and a privilege, sir," she said, shaking his hand, and trying desperately not to weep at his departure.

"My dear Augustine, the honor and privilege was all mine, I assure you."

She smiled. "You will go back to your retirement, I take it?"

"Perhaps," he murmured enigmatically. "We shall see. There are stirrings of war with Germany in the air, although most of Parliament denies that it will ever happen. I, on the other hand, am not so sure. I believe it to be a very real possibility."

"If it happens," Augustine asked, "will you lend your brilliant deducting skills to the war effort?"

Holmes smiled. "It so happens that I have been asked to call on the Prime Minister a week from Friday."

"Ah, so you are coming out of retirement." She smiled. "Was this case a starter, perhaps? The first course to whet your appetite as you prepare to plunge back into the world of mystery and suspense?"

"No, indeed. This, my dear, was a case with spirit." His grey eyes twinkled as he turned and strode toward his Peugeot, his plaid cape flapping in the gentle breeze.

Augustine watched as the automobile headed down the road toward the setting sun, then turned and went back inside. After all, it was time for tea.

The Esau Ladies

by Robert Perret

It felt as if the summer sun had not set upon Baker Street for a month. The air was thick and the walls perspired. Holmes had even forgone his daily plug of tobacco, instead applying a compress of the leaves to his temples. Mrs. Hudson had long since abandoned us for a rocky beach in the north. For my part, I sat propped on the windowsill, looking down at the empty street below. In the distance, I heard the clatter and hew of a traveling carnival that had set up shop upon the municipal green. While the precise words were lost upon the wind, the tenor of the barker's patter told me that this was not proving to be a successful stand. They likely counted upon their London shows to tide them over, poor fellows.

"You there!" came a voice from below. I looked down to see a boy pointing at me. His clothes were well worn and too large by half, but he didn't have the haggard guise of Holmes's irregulars. "Hey! Have you got some money, governor?"

"That is none of your concern!" I called back, bristling at the insolence.

"These coupons are good for two-for-the-price-of-one admission down the street."

"You'd like me to bring my purse down, would you?" I snarled.

"It's nothing to me either way," the boy shot back before turning on his heels and making his way up the street where he began shouting at someone else.

"Really, Watson," Holmes said from his chair. "You were a bit cross with the poor lad."

"It's this damned heat," I groused. "I've half a mind to jump in the Thames and let it take me where it will. I've had about all I can stand of this."

"That seems a bit much," Holmes said, "but some fresh air would certainly not go amiss. Let us take the lad up on his offer."

"You want to go to the carnival, Holmes?"

"While I am not so given to theatrics as you, I would welcome any break in this stifling monotony as well. The barometer suggests we've another three days at least, and I don't intend to soak into the cushions while waiting."

Minutes later we were out of doors, but it little improved our situation. If anything, the atmosphere was somehow more oppressive. Holmes seemed unaffected as he made his way up the street with spritely steps. As he went, he plucked one of the promotional bills from the ground. We quickly arrived at the carnival, a makeshift village of small tents, the paths in between which were hemmed in by placards brazenly enticing whoever might be perambulating by to relinquish his money for a viewing of acts that spanned the gamut from sublime to profane. Holmes began making his way towards a tent that offered a daily vivisection of a man who could feel no pain. I rather feared that Holmes would spoil everyone's fun as he debunked the charade, so I corralled him instead into a presentation of wonders of the modern world.

Holmes presented his coupon to the man at the opening of the tent and then looked expectantly at me. "Go on, Watson, I've put in my share."

I sighed and placed my last shilling in the barker's palm. When we stepped inside, it was, at least, inexplicably cool. We took our places upon the rickety wooden benches surrounding the stage. We had our choice of seats for there was hardly a dozen people in the audience, and I would guess the tent was made to accommodate five times that number. The show began with a trio of performers dressed in horse costumes frolicking about the ring. Holmes sighed and made a great show of lighting his clay pipe. Next came a knife-thrower, at whose act Holmes simply chuckled and murmured, "Really, Watson." Next came a strong man who snapped a variety of objects in half. Holmes's feet danced beneath his seat, and I knew the next act would likely be the last he would endure. Opposite us in the stands was a blighter who guffawed loudly at every new performance, and his friend who seemed to have some quip to fill every lull in the program. While I first found them to be grating, I had to concede that they were at least enjoying themselves.

Next came Geraldine, a bearded lady, and Holmes was up before the poor girl made it into the spotlight.

"This was your idea," I hissed at Holmes. "And what else have we to do."

Holmes turned to reply but was cut short when a man began yelling from the audience.

"Shame upon you, you callow wagtail!"

He carried on from there, but it does not bear repeating. When it reached a crescendo the man leaped at the lady, and Holmes was skipping across the benches to intervene. Before he arrived our wry opposite and his merry companion had wrestled the attacker to the ground. The smaller of the pair wrapped his arm around the assailant's neck and squeezed. The malcontent thrashed for a moment but then collapsed. I ran forward to check his pulse.

"You could have killed the man," I reproached him.

"I put him gently to sleep, sweet as a baby," the man, an American from his clumsy accent, replied.

"Learned that trick from a Tennessee gator wrestler," the other man bellowed.

"Hardly sporting with your fellow pinning the man to the ground," Holmes said.

"It was hardly sporting of him to attack a woman."

Geraldine had collapsed onto the edge of the ring, trembling.

"I don't understand," she said. "I've never seen that man before in my life."

"There, there, my dear," the smaller man knelt next to her and took her hand. "The danger has passed and we'll figure out the rest."

"We will?" she said, now greatly calmed.

"My name is Simon. Simon Honor; and I'm a detective."

"Detective?" she gasped.

I shot an inquisitive look at Holmes, who made no response.

"The greatest detective, ma'am," said the large man. "Take it from me."

"That's strange," I said. "I've never heard of you, and I take a bit of an interest in such matters."

"Mr. Honor is a front-page celebrity in the States," the large man said.

"That's over-selling it a bit, Wotner," Honor replied.

"I am familiar with your work," Holmes said, offering his hand. "Sherlock Holmes, and my partner Dr. Watson."

"There, Wotner," Honor said, shaking hands briskly. "You just bragged about my renown as a detective to the very pinnacle of the deductive arts. We'll have to leave England immediately under a cloud of shame."

"Sherlock Holmes, huh," Wotner responded. "The one that's afraid of dogs?"

"I'd like to see how you fare when being chased through unfamiliar woods by a glowing hound," I shot back.

"This is hardly the time, fellas," Honor said, helping Geraldine to her feet.

"You are certain you have never seen this man before?" Holmes demanded.

"Never! I hardly see anyone outside the circus." She blushed as she stroked her beard. "I am not always well-received."

"Fools," said Honor. "The world is full of them."

The lady's cheeks somehow found a deeper shade of crimson.

"What is the meaning of all this," came a bristling man in a gilded red coat.

"That man attacked me," Geraldine said. "These fine gentlemen leaped to my rescue."

The ringmaster, or so I took him to be, took a sneering look at each of us. "Geraldine, get back to your wagon."

"They have been so kind, Mr. Farrington."

"A bit too kind for my liking. Get now, girl!"

"I appreciate that you are protective of your performers," Honor said. "However, let me assure you..."

"You can assure me by taking your leave," Farrington said. "I don't like a bunch of foreigners sniffing around my freak. I don't know what you want from her but you aren't going to get it."

"I must object to your coarse language," Honor said.

The would-be assailant began to stir.

"And take him with you," Farrington said.

"You aren't going to summon the police?" I asked.

"What are the police going to do for someone like her? Even I can't get justice from the law."

"We shall remove ourselves immediately," Holmes said. He lifted the offender by one arm, while Wotner took the other.

As we left, I objected, "Holmes, you can't mean to let things stand?"

"The harder we pushed, the worse it was going to be for Geraldine," Honor said. "Old Farrington is going to blame her for all this ruckus. Thankfully I didn't see anybody asking for their money back or she'd really be in for it."

"Precisely," Holmes said.

"We still have this gentleman in hand. We can present him to the Yard ourselves. We shall certainly be taken seriously there."

Honor hailed a passing cab, and we shoveled the semi-conscious perpetrator in. Holmes climbed in next. When Honor tried to follow, Holmes stopped him.

"I believe we can handle things from here," Holmes said.

"Wotner and I can take him in just as well as you can," Honor objected.

"I have personal contacts within the Yard who can smooth over any irregularities with the nature of tonight's proceedings."

Wotner snorted.

"Come by Baker Street tomorrow, and I'll let you know the conclusion of the affair. I'm more than happy to lay all of the credit at your feet." Holmes produced his calling card.

"It is not a matter of credit," Honor said.

"It is a bit if you want to build a reputation over here," Wotner said.

"Baker Street tomorrow morning, then," Honor said.

"There's an odd pair," I said as we clattered away.

"But a good one to have at our backs, I think," Holmes said. "Honor has the brashness and naivete common to his countrymen, but he is truly an agent for good."

"Yes, well, I hope he doesn't mean to set up shop in London," I said.

"Watson, look!" Holmes said, pulling me towards the window.

"What is it?" Dusk had fallen and there were a handful of people mulling around listlessly in the street.

"That figure there," Holmes said.

"The religious fellow in the dark coat and hat?"

"The beard, Watson. Could it be Geraldine?"

"I don't see how," I said. "She would have had to cross town more quickly than we somehow, and then immediately return on foot. It doesn't make any sense."

"No," Holmes said. "It doesn't. Deliver this chap to the Yard with my compliments."

With no more said, Holmes opened the door and leaped from the moving carriage. I watched in disbelief as he jogged after the disappearing figure, only slowing to an unobtrusive amble when he was a short distance behind.

I turned to find our prisoner watching me with blurry, bloodstained eyes.

"Let me out of this carriage!" he demanded.

"You'll get out when we arrive at Scotland Yard."

"I didn't do anything!"

"What you said to that poor lady would have made me blush at the height of my soldiering days in Afghanistan," I said. "And that was before you lunged at her."

"Ha! Poor lady indeed."

"Just because she performs in a carnival does not make her subject to your contempt."

"I mean, she's not a lady," the man said. "She's a man."

"I think not," I replied. "There are physignomical differences that outstrip any excess follicular development. Her costume left little enough to the imagination, and as a doctor I can certify she is a lady."

"Take me word for it, doctor," the man snorted. "There is something under there for the imagination after all."

"How would you know anything about it?" I asked.

"I arranged a private liaison," he said. "Don't give me any funny looks. It was a jape, that's all."

"I find it highly unlikely that Mr. Farrington would allow any personal engagements," I said. "He lost his temper just seeing her speaking to us in a public place."

"Mr. Farrington didn't have anything to do with it. She, well he, made the arrangements himself. She, I mean, he, had been blowing me kisses and winking at me all through the performance a few nights ago. I played along, you know? Afterward, she finds me in the crowd and slips an appointment card into my pocket."

"Do you still have the card?"

"It was in my billfold when he robbed me."

"Miss Geraldine robbed you?"

"I'm not proud of it, but he took me unawares and had a knife to my throat before I knew what was happening."

"You are twice her size and seem fit enough," I said.

"Don't believe me, then. I knew no one would. That is why I didn't go to the police."

"Well, we are on our way now," I said.

"Look, Doctor?"

"Watson," I sighed.

"Doctor Watson, I'm not a bad man, but this Geraldine chap took me for everything. I'd just been paid for work I'd done in town and was headed back to my family in Derby."

"It seems to me that if you had just gone home without a detour for a private liaison, as you put it, you'd not be in this mess."

"You're right, Doctor Watson, and I'm not saying otherwise, but I can't go home now short a month's pay. We'll be turned out on the streets."

There was something in his manner that rang true but I had trouble reconciling his story with the young lady I had just met. "We'll tell all of it to the inspector and see what transpires from there," I said.

I turned my back to him to smoke and watch the sun-baked streets of London roll by. When we arrived at the yard I was recognized by the constables and we were soon sitting before Inspector Barton.

"I'm a bit confused, Doctor Watson," he said. "Are you to file a complaint against this man or for him?"

"What I witnessed was this man attacking Miss Geraldine with no immediate provocation."

"So, against, then?"

"Yet," I said, causing Barton to sigh theatrically, "I have listened to hundreds of testimonies, and I believe Mr. Carter is telling the truth. Or at least what he understands to be the truth."

Barton rubbed his head for a moment. "I'll tell you what we'll do. Mr. Carter will enjoy the hospitality of one of our waiting areas."

"A cell," Carter said. "He means a cell."

"In the meantime," Barton continued, "I shall go to interview this Miss Geraldine and see what I can make of it all."

"That's hardly fair," Carter complained.

"Such is life," Barton said.

Having made my uncertain delivery, I wound my way back to Baker Street. I had hardly put my feet up and found my place in the novel I was reading when Holmes came quickly up the stairs.

"You have deposited the roughian at the Yard?"

"Carter is his name, and he currently waits at the Yards for the results of Inspector Barton's investigation. Carter had quite the unbelievable story to tell."

"He believes Miss Geraldine to be a man who has ill-used him," Holmes replied.

My book dropped from my hands and Holmes smiled. "The other Geraldine that I followed did indeed make her way back to the carnival. I followed the figure all the way back to a modest muslin covered wagon. I heard Miss Geraldine chastise the other for being out when she had been assaulted, and a man replied. Chancing to peer through a gap in the covering I saw the second Geraldine shedding her dress."

"Holmes!"

"All that was revealed was a rail-thin man, sporting an identical beard to our beleaguered lady."

"A bearded man in a dress?" I laughed. "To what end?"

"Likely it is a feint used in her act. Perhaps it allows for a costume change, or facilitates some sort of stunt. For our purposes, what matters is that there is a second bearded lady, and he is a man. Also, it seemed the lady we met was genuinely consternated that her partner had departed during the performance."

"So, this Carter fellow was both the victim of one bearded lady and the unprovoked assailant of another."

"So it would seem."

"We must notify Inspector Barton right away!"

Holmes could not rouse himself to partake in this triviality, so I took it upon myself to brave the evening swelter and send the message from the telegraph station down the street. It would not exonerate Mr. Carter, but it would perhaps save Inspector Barton some small effort. Returning to Baker

Street once more I found Holmes engrossed in his ampules and beakers, so I returned to my book and read of an icy arctic expedition until at last slumber found me.

Mrs. Hudson had barely cleared the breakfast table when Mr. Honor and his companion Wotner came knocking.

"There's more going on here than you might think," Honor said before even being seated.

"Is that so?" Holmes said, leaning upon the mantle. "Pray, elaborate."

"After you made off with Prince Charming, we went back to check on the lady," Honor said.

"Mr. Farrington had seemed most adamant in keeping us away from the poor girl," I said.

"The man is trying to keep his thumb on a dozen acts," Honor said.

"And his eye on every coin that changes hands," Wotner added.

"It was trivial to make our way back to Geraldine's residence," Honor replied.

"None of the other carnival workers took notice of you?" Holmes asked.

"Confidence, Mr. Holmes," Honor said. "With the right attitude, you can go anywhere."

"She put on a brave face, but she was scared, Mr. Holmes."

"She took us to see the animals, or so she said," Wotner added.

"In fact, it was clear she was afraid to be discovered speaking to us."

"By Mr. Farrington?" I asked.

"I'm sure, but her more pressing concern was a brother. He lives with her, it seems, and she begged me to forget about the whole thing before it got her in worse trouble."

"Mr. Honor isn't accustomed to leaving a lady in distress," Wotner said.

"I told her I wanted to meet this brother and she began weeping. I demanded to know exactly what she thought was going to happen. She said something I couldn't quite hear and ran away."

"Well, it turns out they do their laundry in the same trough the animals drink from," Wotner continued. Upon the drying line are two of Esmeralda's dresses. Or so we thought."

"Only one was sized for a lady. The other, identical in design, is cut to wholly different proportions."

"Yes, her brother takes the guise of a bearded lady himself it seems," Holmes said. "We discovered as much last evening. This does seem to confirm the hypothesis that Esmeralda herself is a victim, rather than a conspirator, in whatever scheme is afoot."

"Alright, then," Honor said. "Tell us your news of Mr. Carter."

Holmes responded with an arched brow. "It seems you may know as much as we already."

"We left by the fairway to alleviate suspicion," Honor said. "And a good thing too. I soon discovered the hand of a young roustabout in my pocket. For a few coins and the promise not to involve the police, he was very forthcoming in fingering Felix Esquibel as the mastermind behind the carnival's little crime ring. Seems they made a habit of picking out customers with laden wallets and found ways to separate the two. The boy was employed only in simple pickpocketing. But Mr. Esquibel had designs of a grander nature."

"And among these designs, he traded upon his sister's allure?" Holmes asked.

"So it seems," Honor replied. "This Mr. Carter came to see the exhibition every night, sometimes more than once.

Her brother always has an eye on the crowd, looking for just such an opportunity."

"It should be a simple matter to expose the blackguard," Holmes said. "The matter is all but settled."

It came as no surprise to me that at this moment there was yet another knock at the door. Inspector Barton strutted into the study looking very pleased indeed.

"That fellow you brought in last night is none too pleased with you, Watson," Barton said. "I'd keep your eyes open for a few days."

"You've released him?" Holmes asked. "But why?"

"I searched the bearded lady's quarters and found Carter's wallet. Confirms that she robbed him, and you lot stopped him before he could have his vengeance, so he walks free and the woman takes his place in gaol."

"She lives with her brother, and he is the one that committed the robbery," Honor spat.

"Have you any proof? I saw no sign of a man in that wagon."

"We can show you dresses that match hers in a man's size."

Barton chuckled. "Even if that is true, she was caught red-handed, as it were. The victim clearly described her and his property was in her possession."

"It looks bad, but you've got the wrong person in gaol," Holmes said.

"If you can prove any of this before she goes before a judge I will gladly listen. Until then, the arrest, and my findings, stand."

"How long do we have?" I asked.

"Her Majesty's justice is swift," Barton said. "I wouldn't count on more than a day or two."

Honor continued to argue the point, but Barton simply tipped his hat and left.

"Is this what passes for justice in London?" Honor barked. "He isn't even corrupt; he is just lazy."

"He'll address many more cases today whilst we need only worry about this one," Holmes said. "I make no excuses for slipshod effort, but he is correct that he has a case in hand that will lead to a conviction."

"You won't let this stand will you, Mr. Holmes?" Wotner demanded.

"Of course not, but charging out the door with blood boiling is not going to exculpate Geraldine Esquibal."

"So, we drag that lousy brother into the police station and settle the matter once and for all," Honor said.

"Dragging suspects around by the collar is simply not how things are done here," Holmes said. "We'll lay a trap for the man and get him to confess his sins with Inspector Barton waiting around the corner."

"You saw him stroll out of here," Honor said. "Barton is done with this case. And what if Felix Esquibal doesn't confess? We are racing the docket here, gents."

"Mr. Honor, I can assure you that Holmes's methods are sound," I said.

"Well I'm not going to bet a woman's life on it," Honor spat as he rushed out.

Mr. Wotner seemed to struggle for a moment for an excuse and then he left as well.

"Mr. Honor is going to throw this whole situation into chaos," Holmes groused.

"If he does lay hands on the brother, Barton will have to concede the truth, or at least that the identity of the true thief is unresolved."

"And if he comes on too strong, he may just send the brother into hiding," Holmes said. "We must find the man first."

"Mr. Honor is likely making right for the carnival."

"Yes, and to try to beat him there would be futile. Even should we arrive first, he will show himself before we can get a confession. No, let us consider where else Mr. Esquibal might be."

"If he is not at the carnival he could be anywhere. We know nothing about the man."

"Save where he was last night," Holmes said.

"He was already walking when we saw him," I objected. "We have a general direction, but he might have started out a mile or more further along."

"Our first stop shall be old Sherman's then," Holmes said.

I am generally regarded as Holmes's dearest friend and truest companion, but I harbor suspicions that I am not his preferred partner in sleuthing. It was a certain mongrel by the name of Toby that my friend was after now.

Within an hour, I was trailing behind the pair as we returned to the intersection where we had first seen the bearded figure. Holmes produced a small tatter of cloth, and after siccing Toby upon it, they were single-mindedly scouring the streets. Toby stiffened when he caught the scent and began pulling at the lead. Holmes was drawn along after the dog and me after him. The trail went through dark alleys, some hardly wider than my shoulders, and across brambled gardens until the dog was at last pawing at an ill-set door. Just before I quite caught up with Holmes, the door opened and an old couple peered out. I saw Geraldine's striking eyes upon the lady and the cast of her nose upon the man, who was ironically cleanly shaven.

"Good afternoon," Holmes began. "I take it you are the parents of Felix and Geraldine?"

"Why?" returned the father. "Why not just leave us alone?"

"I'm afraid there might be a misunderstanding," Holmes replied. "We urgently need to find Felix."

"This is cruel!" the mother cried. "Shame upon you!"

"It is truly not our intention to be cruel," I interjected.

"Then why do you come here and taunt us?" she cried.

"We are not taunting you."

"Asking after our children, long disappeared," the father replied. "Despicable."

"When was the last time you saw your children?" Holmes asked.

"Felix ran away nearly ten years ago," the father replied.

"And Geraldine?" I prompted.

The mother began sobbing.

"That was the beginning of our grief. She was different, you know?" The man's shoulders slumped. "We did not want her to feel as if she were cursed, but at the same time we tried to keep her safe."

"The people here, they all knew her," mother said. "They all loved her. She could have had a happy life if she had stayed here."

I glanced around at the ramshackle tenements and despaired that this was anyone's idea of a happy life.

"When strangers would pass through, tradesmen, missionaries, and the like, she would inevitably be discovered. She didn't know enough to hide herself; she was too trusting."

"Then one awful day, Felix discovered he could charge a fee to let others look at her. A penny here, a penny there, but it was enough to damn them both."

"He must have finally displayed her to the wrong person, for one day she simply vanished," the father said. "The guilt weighed upon my son horribly, and a few weeks later he went looking for her and never returned."

"Since that time, you have never seen either of your children?" Holmes asked.

"I dream that they have died," the mother said.

"Madam, I can assure you that they are very much alive, but each in danger."

"Can it be true?" the father shouted.

"Geraldine is being held even now at Scotland Yard."

"She has been arrested? But why? And why did they not return her to us? We have filed many reports about her."

I suspected that reports of poor, missing immigrants were soon disposed of. "What matters is that she is there now, and you can see her today."

"Why should I believe you?" the mother asked. "Maybe you trick us to rob our home."

Holmes produced his calling card. "Here are all of my particulars, and my friend here is named Doctor John Watson."

"Your name is like the hero of the magazines."

"I give you my word that we intend you no harm. If you would like, one of you could remain here while the other goes to Scotland Yard."

Mother grasped Holmes's hands and gazed deeply into his eyes. "No! It has been too long, and I sense that you are a decent man, Mr. Holmes. We shall go straight away."

"Do call on us should you need any assistance," I said as we parted. "Even showing the officers Mr. Holmes's card is likely to smooth things along."

They returned inside to prepare to meet their daughter, while we began the process of retracing our steps. I hoped Holmes had the way memorized, for I would struggle to find a clear path out.

"Do you think Farrington kidnapped the pair of them?" I asked.

"Worse, I think Felix sold his sister to the carnival, although he seems to have some remorse."

"How so?"

"It appears that he is looking in upon his parents. I wouldn't be surprised if they are accustomed to finding odd sums of money shoved under their door. If the siblings were truly prisoners, he could reveal himself to them, or if he were completely heartless, he could simply avoid them."

"He has shown himself to be nothing but a blackguard until now," I said.

"Rarely is anyone so simple," Holmes replied.

Just then a shot rang out. Echoing back and forth across the winding brick passage it was impossible to tell from what direction it came.

"Stop meddling in affairs that don't concern you!" came a voice from the shadows behind us.

"This affair does concern me greatly," I replied. "Your sister is going to prison for your crimes."

"Prison will be a better life for her than the freak show," Felix replied.

"That is a fate you condemned her to," Holmes replied.

"I had to do something," Felix said, seemingly from a new place in the darkness. "She was never going to be able to fend for herself among the common people. Never find a husband or a job. She was going to be destitute the moment our dear parents passed away."

"It seems to me a shaving razor would have solved many of her problems," Holmes said.

"Don't you think we tried that? With the beard, she is a novelty. A woman with stubble is treated so much the worse."

"Has she had any say in this?" I asked.

"I have done what is best for her," Felix responded.

"Your surrender is what is best for her," Holmes said.

"Just stay away," Felix said. "I'm leaving London forever so keep out of it and everything will settle itself."

I heard his feet upon paving stones then. My first instinct was to run the fiend to ground, but when I reached the recess from which he had spoken there was no sign of him, nor any obvious means of escape. Had he run through the alley, I would have seen him. Holmes appeared beside me.

"Mr. Esquibal spent his childhood in this warren," Holmes said. "We'll never catch him here."

"You got your confession," I said. "It is too bad no one with a badge was here to hear it."

"Felix knows little of the world beyond these slums and the carnival. He must be planning a return to the Basque Country, the only place where he might expect succor. If we find the least expensive ship leaving for Spain in the next day, I imagine we can put bracelets on the man at last."

There are few detectives whom could be described as peers of Holmes, but I finally had to concede that Mr. Wotner's puffery might not be completely unwarranted when we hopped out of a cab at the port to find Mr. Honor and Mr. Esquibal on the boarding ramp of the Spanish steamer the Alfonso XIII. Honor was at the top of the ramp, a dozen Spanish sailors at his back. At the bottom of the ramp was parked a police wagon, with Inspector Barton at the fore of a squad of patrolmen. In the middle teetered Felix Esquibal, every part of his being from his beard to his frock flapping and snapping in the maritime winds. Holmes and I hurried to Barton's side.

"Mr. Holmes, it appears our American friend has beaten you on this case," Barton chuckled.

"But how?" I asked.

"He and his friend spent much of the evening sweettalking the girl from outside her cell."

"Surely a practice not condoned by the Yard?" I objected.

"They knew just which cards to play," Barton said. "Brought in roasted nuts and bottled beer for the men on guard duty. That Wotner fellow begins passing out American cigars, Kentucky tobacco I understand, and then telling the kind of stories that make idle men forget their duties. Seems he is but a humble hack in the New World, and so, of course, he has an endless quantity of ribald and grotesque adventures to relate."

"And meanwhile, Mr. Honor is making his plea to Geraldine," Holmes said.

"Just so. Wanted her to throw over her brother, reveal any stolen goods he might be hiding, that sort of thing. She wouldn't hear a word of it. He gets her talking, though, about her family and the people that will be missing her. Well, he hears something that he likes and takes off like a fox on the hunt."

"And now?" I asked.

"If the lad makes it onboard, we'll lose jurisdiction, or might as well. We can't stop her from setting sail without papers that will take too long to arrive."

"And he can't come back ashore without being arrested," Holmes said.

"Too right," Barton said. "I know you lot thought poorly of me earlier but I sincerely do my level best to see that justice is served. Now that we've got him, we won't lose him."

"And Miss Geraldine?" I asked.

"As it stands a cloud of suspicion yet hangs over her, but the worst I can see a judge pinning on her is accomplice, and there are provisions made for women with little recourse. She'll likely end up in a workhouse rather than a prison."

"She remains innocent of all wrong-doing," I protested.

"If Mr. Honor gets the boy in British cuffs, we'll see things put right," Barton said.

"There is nothing for you here!" Honor was shouting. "I have told these men everything that you have done."

Esquibel held up a purse. "This speaks louder. Just see if it doesn't."

Something flew through the air then, and moments later Felix's fortune began spilling forth, the coins tumbling down the ramp, the bills fluttering into the ocean. Already the poor that lived beneath the piers were clamoring at the water's edge, waiting for the paper to wash up.

"No!" Esquibal screamed. "Everything. That was everything."

"Even my best jackknife," Wotner called from the pier. "I hope Poseidon appreciates good steel."

Esquibal turned and fired at Wotner. As he did, Honor rushed forward and threw Felix down, pinning his shooting shoulder to the ground.

"What are you waiting for?" I asked Barton.

"It would be better if he were definitively on British soil."

Holmes and I clambered up the ramp, followed shortly by Mr. Wotner.

"Turn him over," Holmes said, and Wotner and I set to it. "Courtesy of Inspector Barton," Holmes said, brandishing a set of handcuffs. "Though I don't think he is quite aware of it yet."

To his credit, I suppose, Felix Esquibel kicked and thrashed the whole way down. Some in the crowd, to whom the spectacle must have been mystifying, began yelling that we should treat the lady more gently and so forth. Esquibel played into this by shrieking at a high pitch. I thought we might have a brawl on our hands when we reached the pier, but the police did a fine job of creating an open path to the rear of the wagon. We all climbed in with Esquibel and held on as the vehicle was buffeted by the confused crowd.

Honor seized Felix by the collar. "Listen up, you're going to do the right thing and confess to it all. You are going away for a long, long time regardless, but she can go home to your parents tonight."

"You've ruined me," Felix spat. "You've ruined her."

Honor looked as if he were about to press his argument physically when Holmes placed a halting hand in between. "As much as it may pain me, I have no small influence upon the police, and even the docket, of London. I'll make certain that the truth finds the right ears."

"I'm holding you to that, Mr. Holmes," Honor said, offering his hand. The two detectives held fast their grips for more than a moment before reaching a private understanding. "And you thought it would be nothing but warm beer and blood pudding, Wotner."

"We're still bound for Paris, aren't we?" Wotner asked. "I've heard a few things about French women that I need to see for myself."

When we were back in Baker Street, Holmes went straight away to add Mr. Honor to his index. Every once in a while, I will take a peek at the clippings Holmes has accumulated upon his American counterpart. It is a good thing for me that Wotner is no writer as there were more than a few tantalizing yarns to be had.

The Adventure of the Edinburgh Professor

by Stephen Herczeg

After all these years I can truly say that life with Sherlock Holmes never presents a dull moment. Even a simple train trip has the opportunity to turn into a case of life or death.

Such was the situation I once again found myself in as we returned from a trip to Edinburgh on the East Coast express. Though some would argue that the ten-hour journey, with multiple stops along the way, could be called anything but an express route.

The occasion had seen us journey north to visit my cousin, Dr. Patrick Watson, a renowned surgeon who emigrated to Scotland ten years previously. It was there that Holmes and I became embroiled in an investigation of an apparent haunting of a young family. The case was cleared up quickly and as with most supernatural occurrences was explained away, by Holmes, in an utmost rational solution.

We had booked a first-class sleeper, even though we did not envisage needing the beds. It gave us the comfort of knowing we had somewhere safe to store our belongings and seek refuge if the situation required.

The train itself was quite full. It was mid-January, and many Scots sought out the warmer climes of the south of England at that time of year, plus the service only ran once or twice a day, putting immense pressure on the limits of the train. We were very lucky to have retained our sleeper, as we were almost required to postpone the return trip due to the haunting.

All that aside, we managed to enjoy the first half of the journey, spending the majority of our time in the club car after a delightful luncheon. It was there that we met up with Professor Bernard Lumley. A fellow first-class traveller from Edinburgh who was travelling in the sleeper three doors down from our own.

He was a jocular fellow in his early sixties, that thoroughly enjoyed the sound of his own voice. We found that he was an emeritus professor of Eastern European anthropology at the University of Edinburgh. His work centred on the early Prussian kings and the influence of the last vestiges of Charlemagne's rule on them. He was very coy about the purpose of his journey, but it seemed to involve the transportation of a very important relic to do with his work. He was bringing it to the University College in London as they were undertaking their own studies in that same area.

Holmes was entranced and engaged with the good Professor in a thoroughly detailed conversation about Prussia and Charlemagne. I'll admit that I was completely lost and as time drew on began to grow extremely tired and quite bored. I decided I needed to stretch my legs and possibly take in some of the cool evening air to reinvigorate my senses.

I stood and bid adieu to Holmes and the professor before striding from the carriage. I found the gangway between the club car and first-class sleeper occupied by several smokers. Even though I enjoy the odd pipe and cigar, I didn't wish to partake in their second-hand smoke and pushed through into the sleeper car.

As I rounded the corner, I noticed two gentlemen further down the corridor. One was leaning over, the other seemed to be keeping watch. I ducked back and stood with my shoulder pressed to the wall listening intently.

They spoke German and the coarseness of their hushed tones precluded me from translating anything I could hear. I could however, hear the rattling of a sleeper door which seemed to indicate that they were struggling to open it. I deduced that they were either breaking into the sleeper or had forgotten their keys. My suspicious mind told me the former.

I decided to play dumb and simply stroll down the corridor to take in as many details as I could.

Upon seeing me they both straightened up and tried to look as innocent as possible. Failing dismally on all accounts.

I genially said, "Good evening," to them as I passed. Taking in the number of the sleeper, and as many details about the two men as I could. They mumbled a similar reply to me and fidgeted about until I was well past.

I noticed that they turned back to the door as I rounded the far corner.

I quickly found the guard at the far end of the next sleeper and told him what I'd seen. It was his duty to move them on, so I made a note to check back with him later.

I soon found myself in the second-class coach. Almost every seat was taken. The racks above were full to overflowing with suitcases and bags, and at either end several people milled around. These were the poor unfortunates that either didn't manage to book a seat or were left adrift when the earlier train was cancelled.

I made my way down the centre aisle, feeling a little self-conscious as I was wearing my travelling suit which was a more expensive style of dress than most of these passengers could afford.

As I moved along my eyes were drawn to a most lovely face. She was young, in her early twenties, had shortish brown hair and a rather dark and swarthy complexion. Very out of step with the lighter skin tones and reddish-brown hair of the passengers around her.

I also noticed she was reading one of my own treatises of Holmes's cases. A shimmer of pride ran through me to think that a young girl, such as this, would take the time to read my work.

It was at that moment that she looked up and caught my eye. A small smile played across her lips, before she took her attention back to the story.

I carried on and eventually found myself in the guards' car at the very rear of the train. I had a quick chat with the guard and said I was just trying to find somewhere to take in some fresh air. I noticed his straight-backed demeanour and managed to prize the name of his regiment and the rank he had held. Upon hearing of my own service, he relaxed, and we quickly swapped a few war stories and remembrances.

At one point, he even pulled out a bottle of whiskey and offered it to me. I thought better of it for a moment, but then the chill made its presence known, so I thankfully took the bottle from him and gleefully downed a short swallow.

It was as I handed the bottle back, that there was an almighty thump from the front of the train.

The carriage swayed dangerously as the driver applied the emergency brakes. I was thrown forward and the bottle slipped from my grasp and broke upon a large steel box hidden in the corner. I landed in an unceremonious heap at the guard's feet. He managed to hold on to one of the railings nearby.

Screams and shouts of dismay could be heard running up and down the carriages. I rolled over and looked up the aisle. Suitcases were strewn all over. Several people had been cast from their seats and lay atop the cases, or vice versa.

A few people had suffered small cuts and abrasions either from striking the seats nearby or from the baggage that rained down on them.

When the train finally came to a standstill, I regained my feet with the help of my new-found friend and moved forward to provide any level of assistance that I could.

Luckily, most of the injuries were light and superficial. Most of the passengers were simply in a state of shock. I told those suffering to sit still in their seats and relax themselves until more information arrived. I did not have any supplies to treat the wounds, so I told the guard to stay with the injured passengers, and I would come back with my medical bag.

I worked my way through the next carriage, attending any unfortunates that I found and telling them to remain seated and relaxed until I could return. In the back of my mind, I started to worry about whether I had enough supplies on hand.

It is my habit, especially when travelling with Holmes, to bring my medical bag, but it is only ever lightly packed with bare essentials for emergencies. This was an emergency, but the scale was probably beyond even my foresight.

I reached our sleeper and unlocked the door. On returning to the corridor, bag in hand, I began to make my way back to the second-class car when a voice called out from behind.

"Watson? Where the devil have you been?" it said.

I turned to find Holmes moving up the corridor towards me.

"I was taking some air with the guard at the back of the train, just before this calamity," I said, "There are injuries to many of the passengers, I was returning to give aid where I could."

"Good man. I wanted to check that you were uninjured then lend a hand outside. This may be a simple problem with the train, but there was a loud thump before we braked that has me puzzled," he said.

"I heard that too, I presumed we'd hit something on the track."

"From the forward compartments it sounded a lot like an explosion," said Holmes, his face becoming stern as the thought of an investigation loomed.

*****

I managed to very quickly dress the majority of wounds within the second-class carriages. They were only superficial, and my assistance was more or less comfort to the passengers rather than a medical need.

As I was finishing up with one patient, the head conductor entered the carriage. He addressed the assembled passengers and said that the train had been damaged and would require repairs before there was any chance of proceeding through to London.

He stated that the train had stopped about ten miles North of Grantham, near the small town of Hougham. Two porters had been sent to a nearby farm to procure some horses and ride on to Hougham to organise transport and accommodation.

The conductor said that all passengers would be lodged for the night or could be transferred to Grantham where they could make alternative arrangements.

A passenger raised a hand and asked, "Can we not sleep on the train?"

The conductor said that suggestion had been brought up, but that all the sleeper cars were full of first-class passengers and it was considered unfair to subject others to the inconvenience of sitting for the entire night. He added that there were also standing passengers and did not consider it appropriate that anybody sleep on the floor.

There was a general murmuring and mumbling of voices as the passengers gathered their things and prepared to leave the train.

I quickly tidied up my medical bag and made my way back towards the first-class sleeper carriage. As I stepped into the corridor, the door of the compartment near to ours opened and a man stepped out. I once again found myself face to face with one of the German gentlemen. He was as surprised as I was and quickly ducked back inside.

I made a note of the compartment number and stopped by my own to retrieve my suitcase in readiness to leave. I noticed that Holmes's case was still present, which seemed odd as he'd had much more time to pack than I.

I decided to find him first so that we could join the procession of passengers together rather than become separated.

As I reached the end of the corridor, I turned back just in time to see both Germans leaving their compartment. They looked around suspiciously then headed towards the second-class carriage. I noted they only had a small valise between them. I thought about calling out to them that the train was being evacuated but they were away before I could gain their attention. I stared after them for a moment before carrying on to seek out Holmes.

*****

As I entered the club car, I found the majority of first-class passengers milling around with their belongings. A porter was checking names and allocating people to small groups for the onward journey.

I asked what the current plan was, and he told me that they had managed to acquire two small wagons that were able to transport four passengers at a time on to Hougham. There they had managed to find accommodation in the Inn and a nearby manor house for the first-class passengers. The townsfolk had rallied and set up temporary beds in the town hall for the remaining passengers.

I gave my name and Holmes's and we were allocated to a twin room at the Inn. I noticed that the Professor was in the same place. I was a little inwardly disturbed by the prospect of spending an evening talking further about mid-sixteenth century Prussian politics but decided if there was brandy involved then I would be fine.

I pushed on further, searching for Holmes but finding nothing, until I came upon the open doorway leading down to the trackside. A chilly breeze wafted in through the doorway, so I pulled my collar up and left the train.

Darkness had well and truly set in, making it very difficult to see anybody outside. A few paraffin lanterns marked a bustle of activity further up the track. Just the sort of thing that would draw Holmes, so I pushed on through the cold to see what was happening.

A group of men milled around the train engine, pointing and waving hand held lanterns at parts of the train.

From what I could see, the driving mechanism on one of the great steel wheels, located towards the rear of the engine car, had been damaged.

From my rudimentary knowledge of trains, I realised that the pin that held the crank in place was missing. There was just a hole with buckled metal, and the crank itself was bent and broken and lying askew.

It was that crank that drove the wheels, which meant this engine was going nowhere on its own.

The Adventure of the Edinburgh Professor by Stephen Herczeg

"Damnable luck, ay, Watson," came Holmes's voice from behind me.

I turned and saw that he was smoking a cigarette and viewing the broken engine next to me.

"What would have caused something like that?" I asked.

"I can only assume we either hit a rock or tree trunk, or it was poorly maintained and broke from over use," said Holmes.

I found his explanation a little below his usual enthusiasm for solving the unknown but forgave him as this didn't appear to be anything worthy of his skills.

Then a new voice piped up from the gloom behind us. It had a much higher pitch than either of ours.

"I reckon I know what's happened." it said.

We both turned to see a young woman sitting on a tree stump in the gloom out of reach of the paraffin lamps. She stood up and stepped towards us.

It was then I realised it was the young lass I'd spied in the second-class car reading one of my pamphlets.

"And what do you think caused this?" Holmes asked, his interest now piqued. I was unsure if it was because of the attractiveness of the woman or from boredom.

"A bomb," she said.

I admit I guffawed out loud at the claim.

Holmes simply smiled and asked, "And why would you say that?"

"Two reasons," she said, "Don't you think there's an interesting smell?"

Holmes leaned in towards the wheel and sniffed.

"Oil, coal smoke," he said and sniffed again. It was then his face changed to surprise.

"That's it," she said.

"What is it, Holmes?" I asked.

Holmes turned and peered at the girl.

"Smells sweet. I'd say it's nitro-glycerine, most likely from dynamite. They still use it in Scotland. Easy to get," she said.

"And your second reason?" asked Holmes.

"This," she said and brought something out from behind her back.

Holmes reached down and grabbed one of the paraffin lamps to allow us a better look.

The object that the lass held was simply a mess of wires, metal strips and pieces of wood. It looked nothing like any type of bomb that we had ever dealt with before.

"Perhaps it's just some trackside rubbish that fell from a previous train?" I said.

She stared into my eyes with disdain. I immediately felt like retracting my statement just on the piercing derision contained in that stare.

"I think you sell the young lady short, Watson," said Holmes. He handed the lamp to me and took the object from the girl. Then proceeded to study almost every part of the mess.

After a moment he said, "Ingenious."

He looked up at the young woman and said, "Not just this device, but the fact you recognised it as such."

He began to point out parts of the contraption and explain what they did.

"These two flat panels would have been placed over two consecutive pieces of track. When the train wheel ran over both it completed an electrical circuit. The current ran down these wires that would have been inserted into a bundle of dynamite. It would have taken less than a second for detonation to occur. The fact that the main pin on the eccentric crank, which sits on the third to last wheels, was affected explains that. With the pin blown out the wheels could no longer turn; therefore, the train was disabled. By design, not accident."

He leaned in and sniffed the device.

"The same sweet smell as the train wheel. This device was definitely in contact with nitro-glycerine," he said.

He looked at the girl and handed the device back to her.

"Have you told the engineers?"

She nodded, "Yeah, they took one look at me and fobbed me off. I'm a girl. They know better."

She indicated the tree stump behind us.

"I've been sitting there, hoping you two would turn up," she said giving me a scornful look, "Thought you might at least listen."

I dropped my eyes to the ground, a little shameful of my own dismissal of her claims.

"Where did you find that?" Holmes asked nodding towards the device.

She turned her head and looked up the track.

"About seven hundred yards that way," she said, "When that bang went off, I started counting. We came to a standstill around thirty seconds after the bang. One of these trains goes about fifty miles an hour. I did the math."

"Extraordinary," I said.

"Then I walked off seven hundred steps and started looking. Found that about a minute later and hightailed it back here."

I found that I was regarding this young lady in a whole new light. Not only was she rather attractive, she was incredibly intelligent and resourceful.

It was then she held her hand out to Holmes.

"I'm Lois Cayley," she said shaking his hand and smiling.

"Sherlock Holmes," Holmes replied.

"Oh, I know who you two are," she said.

"Really?" I questioned.

"Yeah. I've read all your stories, Dr. Watson. Love them. I couldn't believe my eyes when I saw you walk through the second-class carriage."

She pulled a pamphlet out of her vest pocket and unfolded it. A small drawing of my likeness sat in the centre of the back page. I couldn't even remember sitting for the portrait but was most approving.

She looked at the drawing and said, "The picture doesn't really do you justice Doctor, but when I saw you here with Mr. Holmes, who looks exactly like his drawings, I knew it was you two."

"We are very flattered to have such a public knowledge of our appearance," said Holmes with a reproachful tone to his voice, mostly aimed at me, "But the question remains Why?"

"Why?"

"Yes, why, did someone wish to stop the train? What is their motive? Has there been or will there be a crime? If so what is it?" he said.

*****

A group of engineers appeared to take another look at the broken wheel and crank. Holmes showed them the broken device and tried to convince them that the damage was possibly due to a bomb. None of the men seemed to be imbued with any level of humour and refused to even give any credence to the notion. After several moments of interchange between Holmes, Lois, and the engineers, the three of us gave up.

Holmes said, "There's nothing more we can really achieve until we determine why someone wanted to stop this train. I think the only avenue open to us is to journey into

Hougham with the rest of the passengers and take stock of those present."

"Ask around?" I asked.

"Precisely," he said.

Holmes handed the device back to Lois and said, "Yours I believe."

She simply looked at the mangled mess of wires and metal and tossed it to one side. Its usefulness had passed.

"If you think you're ditching me to take over this investigation, then you've got another thing coming. You're first-class passengers, so I'll meet you at the Inn," she said and walked off into the gloom towards the second-class carriage.

We both watched her leave, then I remarked, "My word, what a remarkable young lady."

Holmes simply watched her leave, a small grin on his face.

"She is that," he said.

We made our way back onto the train and found it remarkably empty. The other passengers had been ferried off to the nearby town whilst we had investigated the damaged train.

We headed back towards our sleeper and as we approached our own room, I noticed the door to the cabin the Germans had occupied was slightly ajar. It shouldn't have been of any interest but being a part of Holmes's life instils a heightened level of curiosity in one's soul.

I stepped up to the doorway and knocked. There was no reply, so I pushed the door open and looked inside. It was empty, the Germans and any luggage long gone.

It was only through sheer luck that I heard a groan as I started to close the door. I pushed my way into the room and noticed the connecting door was open.

From what I had gathered so far, the connecting room was Professor Lumley's room. I ducked in and was stunned at the scene.

The room had been ransacked. The contents of drawers and cupboards were strewn across the place. The professor's suitcases were open, any remaining items tossed aside.

Another groan echoed up from the floor.

There, lying amidst the detritus of his suitcases, several items of loose clothing draped across his supine frame, was the professor himself.

I dropped to one knee and examined him. He had a nasty gash on his forehead and bruising around his chin and cheek. I was certain that the poor man had been assaulted.

"Professor?" I said, "It's John Watson. Can you hear me?"

Holmes poked his head into the room and looked around.

"What have you found, Watson?" he asked.

I looked up.

"The professor has been assaulted. My initial reaction is it was those Germans who were using the room you're standing in."

I looked back at the professor and lightly tapped him on the cheek.

"Professor? Professor?"

His eyelids fluttered slightly then opened.

"Professor, thank Lord," I said.

His face showed abject terror. He grasped my arms with his thin, scrawny fingers.

"I didn't tell them where it is. I didn't. It should still be safe."

"What is?" I asked.

He pulled himself towards me.

"You must protect Charlemagne," he said, his eyes wide in fright.

His eyes slowly shut again, he let out a final breath and relaxed his grip on my arms. I eased him back to the floor and gently tapped his cheek once more.

"Professor? Professor?" I asked.

I felt his neck, searching for a pulse or any sign of life. There was nothing. My shoulders slumped.

As I turned away, my knee caught some of the clothing and dragged them off the Professor's body.

"That explains it then," said Holmes.

I peered back and saw a large blood stain on the professor's midriff. I could see an inch-wide wound, with blood still seeping from it.

"Murder," I muttered under my breath.

I turned to Holmes and asked, "But what was he muttering about?"

Holmes simply shook his head. I turned and began another scan of the room.

"The simple answer would lead to the reason the train was stopped," said a feminine voice from behind Holmes.

I looked over Holmes's shoulder and saw Miss Cayley standing behind him. I was stunned that she could have crept up on him without notice.

Holmes pondered for a moment before posing the question.

"What was so important that the poor professor gave his life to protect it? And what was that about Charlemagne?" he asked of no-one in particular.

Miss Lois took that as a request for information and began to speak.

"Well, the professor and I were undertaking a similar journey, I presume. I am transferring from Edinburgh University to Cambridge. The word across campus was that

Professor Lumley was taking a leave of absence to undertake some study in London. He was an expert in modern anthropology, specialising in early Prussian monarchy and politics. One of the rumours that has haunted the university, since I joined at least, was the existence of some rare artefact in the anthropology department. Nobody knew what it was, but all the gossip led back to Professor Lumley," she said.

"Well, we'll never know now," I said.

"Have you found his journal?" Lois asked.

I turned back towards the comely girl.

"What?" I asked.

She pushed past Holmes and came into the professor's room. I thought it most impertinent of her at the time but was beginning to gather this was her normal attitude.

"His journal? He's a professor of history, surely he would have some form of diary or journal in his possession," she said as she began to rummage through the spilled contents littering the room.

I turned to Holmes, a questioning look on my face. He simply smiled and watched the young woman at work.

"She has a point, Watson," he said.

I spun back just as Miss Cowley stood up with a thick leather-bound volume in her hand.

"I'd say this would be it," she said handing it across to Holmes, "It's locked. I reckon you'd have a better chance of breaking it open than me."

Holmes reached into a pocket and extracted a small set of picklocks. He had the diary open within a matter of moments and flipped straight to the last entries.

All three of us crowded in to see the pages. Holmes flipped backwards and found one that had a rather detailed hand drawn diagram of an ancient crown. It had none of the delicate beauty of Queen Victoria's crown jewels but was more of a simple affair. There were eight golden panels each in a rectangular shape with a curved top. Each panel was adorned with large, somewhat gaudy jewels. I assumed that the artisans of the day did not possess the quality of implements to cut the gems to a smaller more ornate size. Four of the panels contained pictograms surrounded by jewels, the front was topped with a large golden cross and an arc of gold ran from front to back to strengthen the whole thing.

"The crown of Charlemagne," said Holmes, "Formally used to crown the kings of France and believed to have been lost during the revolution."

"It must be priceless," I said.

"That would be an understatement," said Holmes, "But the monetary value is negligible compared to the intrinsic heritage value to any of the Prussian, German, or French states that Charlemagne once ruled over."

"Do you reckon that's what the Professor was bringing to London?" asked Lois.

Holmes flipped to the last entry, read it to himself, and nodded.

"That's exactly what he was doing," he said.

"Does it say where he hid it?" Lois asked.

"No, but any person of intelligence would have left it in the safest place possible," he said, "And that would be the strong box in the guards' carriage."

"You met the professor, didn't you?" asked Lois, "He was very intelligent, just lacked a bit of common sense."

"We can check the baggage car as we go through then," he said.

*****

As we exited through the connecting sleeper and into the corridor, Holmes ducked back into our room and moments later returned cradling our guns. We had taken them with us to Edinburgh in case any rum business arose. Thankfully they weren't needed.

He handed mine to me and the weight of the cold metal in my hand brought back a flash of memories from the action I had seen in Afghanistan. I felt the phantom pain from my bullet wound again and winced.

Holmes saw my look and said, "These are just for protection. I don't envisage we will be needing them." He patted me on the shoulder and placed his own gun away. I followed suit and proceeded after him towards the rear of the train.

Lois piped up behind me.

"You don't have a spare do you?" she asked.

I shook my head.

"Damn shame," she said, "I suddenly feel a little vulnerable."

I turned to her and said, "I'm sure that's a new position for you, not something you would feel very often."

"It's a modern world, Dr. Watson, a woman has to have confidence and be prepared to survive in it."

I nodded and smiled. We hurried on after Holmes.

As we made our way through the next first-class carriage, we could hear grunts and muffled curses from ahead. Holmes slowed and eased himself against the wall leading to the gangway between cars.

I could hear the noise of several large suitcases and trunks being tossed around and finally a curse in German wafted out. The owner of the voice was evidently looking for something as he mumbled to himself, "Wo ist es? Gottverdammt." (Where is it? Goddammit)

The sound of another loud thump against a sidewall, announced another suitcase flying across the car. Holmes placed his right hand in his pocket, grasping his gun, and walked out into the gangway. We followed close behind. I had my hand on my gun as well.

"Hello there," he said, "We've just come to see about out bags. I see you're having a little trouble yourself, perhaps we can help?"

We stopped as the tall, ugly faced man, stared at us with intense hatred and pulled a knife from his pocket.

"Niemand wird dir helfen, Englander," he said and launched forward with the knife. (No-one will help you, Englander)

Holmes batted the blade away and stepped to his left. He immediately jabbed at the German's jaw with his left hand and followed through with a right punch.

Dazed, the German reeled back, before refocusing and launching forward with the blade once more. Holmes managed to grab his leading arm and brought it down on his knee. The blade dropped from his hand and skittered across the floor of the baggage car, disappearing under a discarded suitcase.

Holmes and the German squared up and began to trade blows. I pulled my gun and tried to aim at the German. I intended to wing him, but such a shot was difficult to pull off in the circumstances.

The two combatants finally parted, and just as I was about to pull the trigger, Lois stepped in front of me. I cursed under my breath and dropped my gun hand.

The young lady kept moving, and it was then I noticed she held a portable fire extinguisher. She hefted the shiny cylinder above her head and waited for the right moment.

Suddenly, the German was forced back towards her from one of Holmes's left crosses and she struck. Lois brought the extinguisher down onto the German's head with a resounding crack. He dropped like a stone and lay still.

Worried that she'd killed him, I dodged around her and knelt to check the man's vitals. I let out a sigh as I realised he still had a pulse.

Holmes said, "Good work young lady, though I would have had him eventually."

"I figured we didn't have time for macho heroics. We need to find the other one and rescue the crown," she said.

Holmes nodded in deference, "Quite so."

He turned and led the way through the second-class carriage. I sidled up to him and whispered.

"We should have tied him up," I said.

"No time, Watson, plus the young lady is right, we need to get after his friend," he replied.

*****

Just as we entered the final second-class carriage, we spied a shadowy figure moving about in the Guards' carriage.

"There," shouted Lois.

I drew my gun, as the three of us hurried our way down the aisle. Holmes managed to outpace both Lois and myself, and reached the final car first.

He suddenly turned, a horrified look on his face, and rushed back towards us.

"Back," he cried. I soon knew why.

An explosion in the guards' car rocked the carriage, throwing the three of us backwards. I landed heavily against a row of seats and struck my head. I understand that I passed out and only have the recollections of Holmes and Miss Cayley to piece the rest of my narrative together.

Holmes landed near me and was rendered unconscious also. Lois was the lucky one. She was shielded from the blast by the two of us but was thrown backwards. She landed heavily but remained relatively unscathed.

She got to her feet, her head still a little groggy, and looked towards the guards' car. The shadowy figure crept back into the burning carriage and picked a cube shaped object from within the ruins of the strong box. The figure turned and looked once towards her before darting out of the back of the wagon.

Lois picked her way past our reposing forms and hurried towards the rear. As she reached the exit, she spied the man running up a nearby pathway towards a waiting horse-drawn cart. She jumped down and gave chase, catching up with the man just as he placed the small box into the rear of the cart and jumped up onto the trap.

In the most unladylike fashion, Lois leapt onto the trap runners, grabbed the man by his lapels and pulled him bodily from the cart. They both landed amongst the dust and stones by the side of the road.

Lois regained her feet first, strode to the cart, and pulled out the metal box. She turned to the man and said, "I will return this. It's not your property. It's the property of the University and the Queen herself."

The man began to chuckle as he got to his feet.

"Oh, but there you are right and very wrong, Fraulein. True, it is not my property, but neither is it the property of your Queen. In fact, it is the property of Kaiser Wilhelm, the Emperor of Germany and of modern Prussia," he said.

"If that is the case then he should talk to the correct authorities, not send a pair of common thieves to steal it for him," she said, "I'm sure they would listen."

"You are still yet young. The power and prestige possessed by such as that crown, are not given up lightly. Your Queen, your Prime Minister, your Government, would never submit to such a request. We thought it much easier to take matters into our own hands," he said as he brushed dirt from his coat.

"You killed an old man," she said, her voice filled with vitriol.

"He would not cooperate. Damn fool. Gunther overstepped the mark, but," he held out his hands in a plea of innocence, "if the professor had complied, he would still be alive."

Lois stared at the German. Her anger simmering and ready to boil. She took a step forward.

"I will take this, and the proper authorities will deal with you," she said.

"I think not, Fraulein," the German said.

Lois stopped when she spied the gun pointed at her.

"Are you going to kill me too?" she said as her anger began to subside, and she tried to maintain her composure.

"I wish not as you are a lovely creature, but you know too much and that could embarrass the Kaiser," he said, "Now please put the Crown back onto the cart. There's a good girl."

"Don't good girl me," Lois screamed, her resolve flooding back in waves.

She hefted the box and threw it towards the German. It struck him in the chest, knocking him slightly backwards. The box continued its journey, falling to the ground with a dull thud.

The German's gun hand rose and aimed at Lois.

"Thank you, Fraulein, and Auf Wiedersehen," he said.

The sound of the gun cocking filled Lois's ears. She turned away in an attempt to avoid the bullet.

The sound of a gunshot rang out into the still night.

After a moment, Lois's eyes opened. Her brain searched through every nerve ending but failed to feel any pain. She straightened in time to see the German's stunned expression as he stared at her, his finger still poised on the trigger of the gun.

He gagged several times, trying to form words but failed. A dark stain spread out across his shirt. His hand relaxed and the gun fell to the ground, no longer a threat to anyone. The German dropped to his knees then fell face first into the dirt.

Standing behind him, smoke trailing from the barrel of his gun, was Holmes.

*****

I awoke to find Holmes kneeling over me, a concerned look on his face. As I blinked my eyes to allow them to focus on his aquiline face, I saw a smile bloom on his mouth.

"How are you, old friend?" he asked, reaching out a hand to help me into a sitting position.

I noticed Lois standing nearby holding a solid looking metal box.

"Is that?" I asked.

Lois nodded.

Holmes cocked his head and said, "Actually, we haven't checked yet."

I managed to regain my feet as Lois placed the box on a nearby seat. The strong padlock on the front proved to be no hurdle for Holmes as he quickly went to work with his picklocks.

The padlock dropped to the floor of the carriage and we all congregated around as Lois slowly opened the lid.

I think all three of us were rather relieved when we saw the circular gold shape within the box. Lois reached in and withdrew the crown. It was almost exactly like the drawing in Professor Lumley's journal.

It was a very chunky and overtly ornate piece of jewellery, but it had a certain regal look about it, and I could

The Adventure of the Edinburgh Professor by Stephen Herczeg

well imagine it sitting on the head of the once king of all of western Europe.

My thoughts were broken by Lois.

"Good Lord it's ugly," she said.

"It has a certain charm though," said Holmes.

"I believe it would have looked magnificently majestic on top of Charles the Great's head," I said in defence of the crown.

Holmes smiled and said, "I do agree with you there, Watson. Maybe not the style of crown to adorn our own Queen's head, but a ninth century warrior king? Yes, I believe so."

Lois turned it around to examine every side of the crown, before returning it to the box.

"Well, what do we do with it now?" she asked.

*****

We quickly found the chief engineer who was still surveying the damaged engine and consulting with his crew to determine a way of moving the train. After briefing him of the whole affair he located the conductor and left us to it.

As luck would have it, the next carriage to Hougham was just leaving, we sent word with them to alert the local sheriff. With nothing more to do, we settled into the club car and awaited the arrival of the authorities.

The bar had been vacated, so I fixed some drinks and we sat down to allow Holmes and Lois to run through their version of the evening's events. I pulled out my notepad and took down copious notes, surprised and alarmed by the various actions of my cohorts.

When both stories were finished, I reread and asked questions to garner extra details. I was amazed at the audacity and athleticism of the remarkable young lady. I peeked across at Holmes from time to time while she told her tale and saw a smile and a look of admiration on his face.

"This was probably not the gentle journey you had expected, my dear," said Holmes, "Where will you go to from here?"

Lois took a sip from her gin and tonic and told us how she spent two years at finishing school in Switzerland, before returning and entering University in Edinburgh.

"I'm afraid that I didn't enjoy the courses on offer, so I'm heading south to Girton college in Cambridge. I hope to finish my course over the next two years," she said.

"Admirable," said Holmes. "What is your desire for career and life?"

Lois paused for a moment, staring off into space as if to gather her thoughts.

"Adventure," she replied, "I think not the dull life of a married woman for me. My father was a soldier, he always told me to take life by the throat and wring as much out of it as possible."

"And good for you," said Holmes, "Too many a good spirited woman succumbs to a life of servitude. There needs to be more of your ilk in this world."

I thought on the mention of her father for a moment then asked, "Your father. Where did he serve?"

"He was in the Forty-second Highlanders," she said, "Sadly he died in the war with Afghanistan."

"My word," said Watson, "Captain Thomas Cayley."

She cocked her head at the name.

"Why yes," she said.

"One of the bravest men I've ever met," I said. We had crossed paths during the war. It was one of the biggest regrets of my life. I met him several days before his final campaign. So, full of life and a larger character than even his imposing frame could promote. The next time we met he was carried in on a stretcher. His flesh rent by wounds and bleeding profusely. I had neither the skill nor tools to aid him, and he passed under my care.

I related this all to Lois whose face dropped, showing a mix of sadness and admiration. She held back tears as she leant forward and took my hand in hers.

"Thank you, Doctor," she said, "He obviously made quite an impression on you in such a short time, and I can only express my gratitude that you tried to save him."

She leant back and took a long draw on her drink. I repeated her actions. I rose and fixed another round. After my little story I think we all needed it.

After a brief pause, Holmes finally spoke up.

"I think, Miss Cayley, should accompany us to London for the time being. If I understand correctly, the next semester does not start at Cambridge for at least another week," he said.

Lois nodded. Holmes pointed to the metal box.

"We need to see that the cause of all this fuss is taken on to its intended destination. I also believe that my brother should be informed of these events," he said, "And I strongly believe that Miss Cayley here should be rewarded for her part in the recovery of the crown. I will be putting that to Mycroft as well," he said.

He smiled at Lois.

"My brother works for the Government, so I am sure they will be filled with gratitude and can be convinced to convert that gratitude to some form of compensation," he said.

Lois's face lit up with that thought.

"I was only doing what I thought was right but could always manage better with extra funds," she said.

"Couldn't we all," I remarked.

The Chapel of the Holy Blood

by Chris Chan

It is often said that two heads are better than one, although this is by no means a universally shared perspective. When an acquaintance once repeated this dictum to Father Brown, the priest immediately replied that when two heads of state get together, the result often leads to war. His acquaintance retreated immediately, and from that point forward was noticeably recalcitrant to engage the good Father in any form of conversation whatsoever. Father Brown has never complained about that.

It was a dreary Thursday afternoon, and as the little priest was making his way down Baker Street, he was holding tightly to his umbrella. The weather was so blustery that had anybody bothered to look at Father Brown, they would have worried that a sudden gust of wind would send the priest flying over London. No one was seriously concerned about his welfare, however, as everybody on the street that day was completely engrossed in their own affairs, and there was so little light that a small man clad all in black and covering himself with a black umbrella was virtually invisible.

When Father Brown knocked on the door of 221B, Mrs. Hudson informed him that Sherlock Holmes was currently out and she didn't know when he'd be back, but he was more than welcome to wait in his rooms. Father Brown stood by the fire, waiting for his cassock to dry, and sustained himself with the pot of tea and the plate of Scottish shortbread that Mrs. Hudson had thoughtfully provided for him.

After about twenty minutes, the priest was shaken out of his daydreaming when a familiar voice called out to him. "My dear Father Brown! How wonderful to see you!"

"Holmes! I hope that I haven't arrived at an inconvenient time."

"Not at all. I just resolved a rather disappointing situation involving a banker absconding with funds. His initial trick of using mirrors to make it appear that the vault he'd been pilfering from was fuller than it was had at least a touch of ingeniousness to it, but his getaway plan was shamefully obvious. His disguise was positively laughable. In any case, he is now sitting uncomfortably in jail and the stolen funds have been recovered. I shall not go into any more detail. The crime simply is not that interesting. Anyway, how are you, Father? I haven't seen you since we solved the case of the two Coptic Patriarchs together."

"I'm quite well, thank you. I've been working at the Deaf School along with my usual parish duties, and my old friend Flambeau is coming for a visit next week."

"Good old Flambeau! Give him my best, will you?" Holmes had met the reformed thief Flambeau a few years earlier during the case of the Vatican cameos. Flambeau had been the chief suspect, and Holmes and Father Brown's combined efforts had managed to clear his name and prevent an international uproar.

"Where is Doctor Watson?"

"He's at a conference in Wales now. Won't be back for several hours. He'll be sorry to have missed you."

"And I'm disappointed to have missed him this visit."

The two men helped themselves to tea and shortbread. Father Brown checked his cassock and after he assured himself that it was dry, he settled down in a chair next to Holmes.

"So Father, what brings you all the way to London on this most inclement day?"

"I came to you because I needed your assistance– particularly your knowledge of chemistry."

"Indeed? Is there a matter of science that you needed to discuss?"

"There is. If it isn't too much trouble, I need you to use your famous re-agent."

"The one precipitated by haemoglobin?"

"The very same." Father Brown reached into his pockets and pulled out a rosary, a breviary, four small coins, a whistle, a compass, two sticks of chocolate, and three handkerchiefs (all of different colors) before finally pulling out a small glass jar containing traces of a dried reddish substance.

"Is that blood, Father?"

"I was hoping that you could tell me whether it is or not."

Holmes' face lit up, and he happily snatched the jar from Father Brown's hands and rushed over to his small laboratory. "I shall fill this flask with water, and I just need to take a tiny bit of this sample– as much that will cover the tip of this bodkin here. Now just one moment..." Holmes shook the flask vigorously, dropped some pale crystals into the solution, and then uncorked a bottle full of clear liquid and shook a tiny trickle of it into the flask. After about four seconds the water turned the color of strong tea.

"Is that a positive test, Holmes?"

"Well, yes... and no. The haemoglobin test is positive, but... the color of the test result isn't quite right. It isn't dark enough. Which means..." Holmes drew another tiny sample from the jar, spread it onto a glass slide, and slid it onto his microscope. "If I'm right, the red blood cells will be slightly oval... Yes, by thunder, they are!"

Father Brown's face brightened. "That means that's not human blood, then?"

"I'm afraid I can't be positive, but based on my previous experiments with animal blood like beef and chicken, I'd be willing to give fair odds that this blood came from a sheep."

"That's better. That's very much better." Father Brown smiled, walked back to his chair, and sat.

"Are you at liberty to explain where the blood came from, Father?"

"Oh, yes. The seal of the confessional is not a factor here." Leaning forward, Father Brown turned to Flambeau, who had returned to the chair next to him. "Have you ever heard of Dirus Castle?"

"I dare say I may have come across its name in the newspapers at some point, but at present I can recall nothing about it."

"Dirus Castle was for many centuries a monastery. When Henry VIII seized most of the Catholic Church's property for his own use and gave much of what was left to his powerful friends, he sent a squadron of armed men to seize the monastery, which was located on some particularly fertile farmland. The monks were known for beekeeping and other agrarian pursuits, but they were not trained fighters, and in a very short time all of the monks were slaughtered. What happened next is obscured by legend. According to the story my niece told me, the abbot was the last to be slain, but as he was dying from a mortal blow, he placed a curse on the property, claiming that every so often, the blood of the slain monks would trickle down the halls of the monastery as a reminder of this horrific crime."

Holmes arched an eyebrow. "Do you– er– believe that story, Father?"

"Oh, I'm quite convinced of the veracity of the first bit of the tale– the part where Henry VIII ordered the murder of a lot of members of the clergy and stole their land. That's well-documented, despite the current owners' attempts to hush up the violent history behind what's now called Dirus Castle. You see, the title of Lord Dirus was bestowed upon a particularly brutal fellow who raised a great deal of money and land for Henry VIII and his allies by killing anybody who opposed the King and seizing everything of value. I may say, Lord and Lady Dirus don't like people knowing that the family lands, funds, and titles derive from a massacre of unarmed monks. They prefer everybody to think that their titles derive from antiquity, and that the family's lineage dates back to the Knights of the Round Table. All tosh, of course."

"But what do you think about the curse, Father?"

The priest smiled. "I suppose that given my personal predilections, I'd prefer to think that a dying man of the cloth would choose to spend his dying moments praying for the souls of those who persecuted him rather than using his last breath calling for vengeance through sanguineous haunting. I certainly believe in miracles and the supernatural, but I can also smell a rat. And I believe that some sort of fakery is happening at Dirus Castle at the moment. You see, Holmes, I took that sample of blood from the walls of the castle."

"Are you saying that there really was blood flowing from the walls?"

"Well, not really flowing. Earlier this morning, trickles of a dark reddish substance, presumably blood, were found smeared and splattered all over the walls. I took this sample from the inside of Lord Dirus' study, which was once a room of private contemplation for the monastery known as, ironically enough, the Chapel of the Holy Blood."

"Did Lord or Lady Dirus call you in to investigate, Father?"

"Oh dear me, no. The Dirus family is decidedly antireligious. They have nothing but cold hostility for me and everybody of my faith and vocation. But my niece, Betty, is engaged to the son of Lord and Lady Dirus. A young fellow named Agro."

"Best wishes to her. What is this Agro like?"

"Holmes, I believe that in Doctor Watson's account of "The Copper Beeches" that you discussed how the character of parents can be seen in their children, and vice versa."

"I did. In the case that you refer to, I was talking about a particularly nasty and cruel boy, and I postulated that he inherited his unpleasant demeanor from one or both of his parents. Am I right in thinking that your niece's fiancé is… not such a pleasing youth as you'd hope?"

The priest made a face. Even though he couldn't see his own expression, he was quite sure that anybody watching him might conceivably concluded that he was being uncharitable. Anybody familiar with young Agro would have found Father Brown's reaction understated. Dozens of the family's former servants had surreptitiously warned away potential employees with horror stories of the tantrums that the heir to the title was prone to throwing.

Holmes smiled, "My dear Father Brown, you needn't worry about speaking ill of others. It so happens that on a recent case I interviewed a kitchen maid, and though she could provide very little in the way of information useful to my investigation, she told me a great deal about her previous employer. Lord Dirus is an angry man, a womanizer, and excessively fond of the bottle. His son follows in his footsteps, and Lady Dirus is a coldhearted, imperious woman who doesn't just work her staff to the bone, but to the marrow as well." Taking a sip of tea, Holmes redirected the topic. "How, exactly, did your niece become engaged to that fellow? If your niece's character bears any resemblance to your own, then I doubt that Betty and Agro are compatible."

"They are not."

"Will you take offense to my broaching the possibility that your niece may be... shall we say... blinded by the glamour of lands and a title?"

"Oh, no. Betty is not a golddigger. Her mother, however, has always wanted her daughter to marry "well," and Betty has always tried to appease her mother at all times. In any case, Betty has had bad luck with previous suitors. More than one of these seemingly respectable young men has proven to be a criminal, and the cycle has been going on for rather a long time. Betty has, unfortunately, developed a certain amount of anxiety about her unmarried state, and I believe that she has latched onto this relationship both to please her mother and because she has come to the deeply flawed conclusion that a bad marriage is better than no marriage at all."

"Father, have you come to me for help in breaking up this engagement?"

"No, though that would be a welcome development. I visited you today in the hopes that your test would confirm whether or not the substance on the walls of the chapel was blood or not, and if so, if that blood was human. Depending on your verdict, I was going to investigate further in the hopes of explaining why the blood was decorating the castle walls."

A delighted look spread across Holmes' face. "Would it be presumptuous if I were to offer my services?"

Father Brown immediately accepted Holmes' offer, and half an hour later the pair were on a train bound for Dirus Castle. Once the train was on its way, Holmes asked, "Explain again to me what you observed this morning, please."

"My niece invited me to elevenses at the castle, and I met her in the village and walked with her to visit her intended and his family. When we arrived, we could see at once that there were bloodstains on part of the wall of the entryway. Young Agro showed us into his father's similarly-stained study on one side of the entryway, which used to be the Chapel of the Holy Blood when the structure was a monastery, and rather gleefully told us about the legend– which I was already familiar with– and declared that the abbot's curse was at work."

"Interesting. You say that Agro seemed happy about the blood on the walls. Has he ever, to your knowledge, showed any interest in the supernatural?"

"On the contrary, as I said earlier, Holmes, the family has a reputation for being particularly antireligious. When Agro waxed lyrical about the abbot's curse and the vengeance of the slaughtered monks, his parents were standing there, gritting their teeth and glaring at Betty and myself. Neither of them had anything to say about the blood on the walls. Indeed, they wanted to ignore it altogether."

"Really?" Holmes pressed his fingertips together underneath his chin. "You would think that they would have at least been interested in talking about it. After all, such an occurrence mustn't happen every day. It would have made for some amusing conversation over elevenses."

"I agree with you. Unfortunately, our meeting was particularly unpleasant. Lord Dirus and his son made a few derogatory remarks towards my profession and my religion, and when I contradicted them and defended my faith and vocation, they both became rather annoyed and left the room. As for Lady Dirus, she never said a word to me or to Betty, despite our best efforts to ask her questions about the phenomenon going on in her home."

Holmes permitted himself the faintest trace of a grin. "Far be it from me to criticize a lady, but I rather doubt that Lady Dirus is living up to the highest standards of hostessing.

I am surprised that she didn't provide her future daughter-in-law with a warmer reception. Am I correct in theorizing that Lady Dirus is opposed to the match?"

"I should say that assessment is accurate. Betty comes a line of country squires that are rich in family history but poor in funds. I don't know the exact state of the Dirus finances, but people with substantial estates seem to be in constant need of more money to pay for the upkeep of their considerable property. In any case, they've shut up most of the castle to save on maintenance expenses. They're only using a tiny portion of the property, which is why we had our elevenses in the little dining nook right next to the chapel."

"And the landed classes of England realized a long time ago that the best and most reliable way of raising enough money to support one's estates is to marry money." Holmes' eyes glinted with amusement. "I've heard it said that when England's gentry with country estates start their families, they pray for a son to inherit the property, and they pray for a wealthy heiress for their son to marry about two decades down the line. I trust that you will take absolutely no offense when I ask, why exactly did young Agro agree to the match?"

"I regretfully but relievedly concluded a while ago that Betty was not entering into a love match. Agro is close to his parents, but one of his chief joys in life is riling them. I've made some enquiries, though I suppose that it would be ingenuous to call my questioning discreet. Apparently Agro likes to toy with his parents' nerves, and he has a reputation for courting attractive young women without a bean to their names, even getting engaged to them if it suits his fancy. Of course, none of these relationships ever come to anything."

"Wouldn't such behavior leave that pleasing youth vulnerable to the prospect of a breach of promise lawsuit? I know of at least two dozen cases where a wealthy young man has gotten engaged to a wholly unsuitable woman, and when he tries to extricate himself from the relationship, the young woman takes legal action over being jilted, and invariably receives an impressively lucrative settlement without ever having to enter a courtroom."

Father Brown sighed. "I suppose the financial risk is part of the sport for our friend Agro. When he tires of his latest lady friend, he engages in such boorish behavior that the young woman terminates the engagement. He's careful to have a friend of his as a witness at all times. That leaves him well immunized against any lawsuits. Indeed, my sources– most of them former employees of the Dirus family– make it clear that the girl is usually so relieved to be free from that singularly unpleasant young man that she would be willing to hand over her life's savings to her ex-fiancé if it meant that she would never have to see him again."

"I see. Do you think that your niece wants to escape from the relationship?"

"She hasn't said so in so many words, but if past patterns hold, the only reason why she entered the relationship in the first place was to please her mother. She's a very dutiful daughter, although perhaps it's a lot easier for her to pursue relationships with men she doesn't particularly care for than it is for her to listen to her mother complain about her marital status."

Holmes took a breath and redirected the conversation. "How exactly did you get that blood sample? Even if Lady Dirus wasn't speaking to you, I can hardly imagine that she would let you scrape off a bit of coagulated blood without protest."

"Lady Dirus walked away without so much as an "excuse me" when she finished her coffee. She did pause to give a large golden candelabra a quick dusting with her handkerchief before leaving the room. I went straight to the chapel– technically the current Lord Dirus' study, although I dare say that it was never officially decommissioned– and used the edge of a coin to remove a substantial amount of the blood. Luckily, I happened to have an old jam jar with me, though for the life of me I can't remember why I was carrying it with me in the first place. Betty was a bit nonplussed about the whole thing, but she was rather keen on the prospect of me coming to you. Betty's mother has gotten her into a number of excruciating relationships with unpleasant yet wealthy young men, but she's always been able to escape, usually with my help. Young Lord Agro may be her least pleasant and most intimidating fiancé yet, and she was enthusiastic at the prospect of you getting involved in the situation, even if it was only to analyze the blood sample. In a situation like this, she wants as many allies as possible in her corner."

"Sensible young woman."

Holmes and Father Brown continued their discussion of the case for the rest of their journey. In a little under an hour, their train reached the tiny station on the outskirts of the village closest to Castle Dirus. At the priest's suggestion, they went directly to the Purple Boar, a pub where the former second footman at the Castle had found employment after an unpleasant incident involving an irate Lord Dirus and a tantrum involving a chamber pot and a flaming log from a fireplace.

"I tell you, I wouldn't go back to work at the Castle again, not if you paid me a million pounds. *Two* million," the ex-second footman declared as he poured drinks for Father Brown and Holmes. "They're batty, every last one of them. Lord Dirus is an absolute monster. When he's not drinking up half the wine cellar, he's chasing after girls from the village or the female staff. Not very dignified for a man of his age, is it? He's careful not to do anything untoward in the presence of his wife, of course. She's an iceberg, she is, but when somebody crosses her, that porcelain façade cracks pretty fast, if you get my drift. And the son takes after the father, you know. Chases after anything in a dress, and a fuse so short a single spark would burn it up completely in a half-second, it would. Why, I'll tell you about the time…"

The second footman turned publican continued expounding upon the many personal flaws and offensive aspects of the Dirus family, and Holmes and Father Brown sat and listened quietly, and marveled at the ease at which they were being provided with information on the local nobility's personal foibles. It was a full seven minutes before the former second footman took a breath, giving Holmes the chance to ask, "Do you happen to know how many members of the staff are left at the Castle?"

"Well, when I left last month, there were only four of us left. The housekeeper and both of the gardeners had given notice the week before, after Lord Dirus had gotten good and soused and fired his shotgun through the window at them– the gardeners, that is. And when the housekeeper ran into the room to see what had happened, he fired again at her! If I'd had any sense, I'd have left myself that day, especially considering how scant my wages were. They're not so well-off as they'd like us to think, you know. Lucky for me, I got out of there soon enough, and I found a place here. Not as fancy as the Castle, but a darned sight jollier."

"Who are the four remaining employees?" Holmes asked.

"Actually, only three now. A week after I made my happy escape, my pal, Lord Dirus' valet, decided he'd taken enough verbal abuse from the old… Better watch my language in front of a priest, I suppose. Anyway, he found a place working for a retired army colonel in the next village. Due to the Dirus family being short of ready cash, and the fact that their reputation for being terrible employers is well known for miles around, they haven't been replacing their missing staff members lately. The only ones left are that dotty old butler Bassett, who's half-senile but still manages to do his job. I think the only reason the butler sticks around is because he forgets Lord Dirus' insults the moment after he shouts them, and Lord Dirus keeps him around because his memory's so bad, Lord Dirus can claim he's already paid him his salary for the month, and the poor old fellow can't remember otherwise. Then there's the cook– a real tartar, that woman. The only staff member who can hold her ground against the members of the Dirus family. If she doesn't want to prepare something, she doesn't make it, even if the family demands it. Finally, there's Agnes, the housemaid. Pretty thing, though I'm disappointed to say that I've never gotten anywhere with her."

The former second footman continued to ramble for a long time after Father Brown and Holmes had finished their beverages. Most of what he told them was a rehash of what he'd previously said, although at times he would slip in the name of an unfortunate person, usually a maid or a girl from the village, whose life had been damaged in some way due to coming into contact with the Dirus family. Eventually, the owner of the pub told the former second footman that he wasn't being paid to chat with the customers, and the mildly chagrined man turned to serving other customers.

As Father Brown and Holmes left the pub and walked through the village, Holmes turned to his friend and asked, "Do you remember the first case we investigated together?"

The priest nodded. "The sudden death of Cardinal Tosca. Of course."

"When we were following up on that note we found in the Cardinal's breviary, I told you that we needed to investigate the scene of the crime for clues. You told me that we needed to find out more about the Cardinal's character and what he truly believed him if we were ever going to find out why someone would want to kill him. In the end, we were both right. If we hadn't followed both lines of inquiry right away, we would never have proved it was murder or identified the culprit before it was too late and additional lives were lost."

"What are you saying, Holmes?"

"I mean, my friend, that we need to hurry up and investigate. Can you manage to get another invitation to Castle Dirus? If I can get a look at the bloodstains on the wall, and if you can try to gain some insight as to the family's behavior, I think that we can figure out what's going on here surprisingly quickly."

Father Brown explained that his niece had gone back to her mother in a nearby village, and that the Dirus family would never let him inside if they could help it, but that he was on friendly terms with the cook, and she would help them if they were to approach quietly by the servant's door.

When they arrived at the castle a quarter of an hour later, the cook was indeed happy to help them. Like nearly all of the other servants who had worked for the Dirus family, the cook made no pretense to any claims to loyalty to her unpleasant bosses.

Luck was on the side of the sleuths, and Father Brown and Holmes were able to make their way to the former chapel as stealthily as they possibly could without being seen by the other inhabitants of the castle. Upon reaching the chapel-turned-study, Holmes immediately whipped out a magnifying glass and began scrutinizing the bloodstains on the wall. Meanwhile, Father Brown crossed to the window, where he observed the three members of the Dirus family walking towards the house.

"Better hurry, Holmes. They're returning." After a moment the priest murmured, "I wouldn't have taken Agro for a gardener."

"What do you mean by that?" Holmes did not avert his eyes from the wall.

"He's carrying a shovel and a spade."

"Look at this, Father," Holmes pointed at the bloodstains. "Most of these droplets appear to be poured on the wall, as if someone took a bottle full of blood and gently tipped some of the contents down the sides. I don't think there's anything miraculous about this. Just a gory and unhygienic sight. However…" Holmes squinted. "Not all of these bloodstains follow the same pattern. I have made a study of the shapes blood droplets make during acts of violence. Most of the blood on these walls was gently poured. But here and there are different patterns of blood. Spattered droplets, rather like–"

Holmes was interrupted by the sound of the door clanging, and three pairs of feet came clamping towards the chapel.

"Well, that takes care of that," the gruff voice of Lord Dirus declared. "First thing tomorrow, I'm going to call that fellow and ask him to make good on his boasting and fix up a sixteenth-century document for us. Bassett? Bass-ETT? BASSETT!" Lord Dirus bellowed. "Get down here at once and make me a whiskey and soda. In the largest glass you can find, and don't feel it necessary to go heavy on the soda."

There was only one door to the former chapel, and nowhere to hide, not that Holmes and Father Brown had any intention of trying to avoid seeing the Dirus family. As father, mother, and son walked into the study, all three visibly blanched when they saw the two men standing there.

"Father Brown!" Agro blurted. "And… are you Sherlock Holmes?"

"What are you doing here?" Lady Dirus demanded.

"Investigating some very interesting bloodstains," Holmes replied smoothly. "I should like to speak to your housemaid, Agnes."

At this, all three members of the Dirus family swooned. Lady Dirus was the first to recover her composure. She clenched her jaw and pointed at Holmes and Father Brown. "You are not welcome here. Leave this instant or I shall summon the police and have you arrested for trespassing. And you will go to prison, whether you're a famous detective or a priest or not."

When asked about that moment later, Father Brown freely admitted that he had made an enormous leap, and that it would have served him right if he'd fallen flat on his face. Perhaps he was just lucky, and perhaps he had made a brilliant deduction based on meager evidence, but in any case, he came to the correct conclusion. "We'll be happy to leave, if you can produce your land grant to the Castle."

With that statement, Lord Dirus slumped to the floor, all the muscle strength seemed to have dissolved from Lady Dirus's shoulders, and young Agro crossed to the nearest decanter, tossed the stopper over his shoulder, and downed most of the contents with an enormous gulp. "What... what do you mean?" the no longer imperious Lady Dirus quavered.

"I mean, *Mrs.* Dirus," Father Brown put special stress on the title. "That I should like to see the documents that prove your ownership of this building, and your claims to nobility as well."

It is not necessary to describe the next five minutes in detail. Both Lord Dirus and Agro attempted to attack Holmes and Father Brown, but Holmes' knowledge of baritsu helped him to subdue both men. Lady Dirus lunged for Father Brown's throat, but luckily for the priest, the cook heard the commotion and hurried up to the chapel, holding a cast iron frying pan. When the cook saw Lady Dirus attempting to choke Father Brown, the tough but good-natured domestic had realized first, that she didn't care for Lady Dirus, second, that she did like Father Brown, third, that with her cooking skills she could find a better job elsewhere, and fourth, that she was holding a very heavy, blunt object.

One does not need to be a great detective to deduce what happened next.

Later that evening, after all three members of the Dirus family had been arrested, and Holmes and Father Brown were back in London, they told their story to a recently returned Watson.

"But surely an accusation of murder based on such little evidence was rather foolhardy, even for you, Holmes?" Watson remarked.

"I suppose it was, but based on the available clues, it was worth the risk in order to bring the perpetrators to justice. In any event, the nerves of that unholy family were already so badly frayed that it only took a very small tug to lead them to unravel altogether."

"Could the two of you please explain your thought processes from the beginning?"

"Of course, Watson. First of all, there was the issue of the blood on the walls of the former chapel. Let us assume that this is not some supernatural event based on a centuries-old curse– indeed, as Father Brown suspects, the narrative we have been told about the curse of the abbot is very likely highly fictionalized. If so, then why would blood be poured on the walls, blood that was probably that of a sheep, rather than human? The Dirus family would not willingly embrace such a sanguineous form of interior decoration, and it didn't appear to be a practical joke or a threat. If anything, according to Father Brown's narrative, they all seemed airily dismissive of the bloodstains and wanted us to ignore them. This odd behavior indicated that the blood caused no distress for them and did not interest them. Yet why wouldn't they want to make use of such a unique and effective conversation starter? Why did the notoriously irreverent Agro draw attention to the blood and then drop the subject?"

Holmes paused for effect and continued. "I must admit that I was at a loss until I examined the walls and discovered that there were two different patterns to the blood. There was the dribbled blood, and there was another set of stains that resembled a cast-off pattern, perhaps caused by the arterial spray that results when a person sustains a serious wound. In a moment, I realized the true purpose of the dribbled blood. It was meant to cover up blood that fallen on the wall in a violent attack, and from the amount of blood I saw that did not follow the dribbling pattern, the assault was most likely fatal."

"So far, so good," Holmes said after another dramatic pause. "But if there was an attack, there must be a victim. Who could it be? All three members of the Dirus family were accounted for, and they rarely hosted guests. Of course, the possibility of an intruder could not be dismissed, but what of the servants? We made inquiries and learned that at the moment, there were only three servants at the castle. We met the cook, she was unharmed. We heard Lord Dirus calling out to the butler, so we could eliminate him as a potential victim. That left the housemaid, Agnes. She was nowhere to be found, so she was the most likely victim. I formed a theory. The housemaid Agnes had been murdered. Perhaps she was having an affair with the notoriously lecherous Lord Dirus and Lady Dirus had bludgeoned her out of jealousy?"

"Wait a minute," Watson interjected. "How did you deduce that Lady Dirus was the killer? And that the death had been caused by bludgeoning?"

"Father Brown, why don't you expound on that that?" Holmes asked.

"Well, I formed a theory about what happened when I saw Lady Dirus polishing a candelabra with her handkerchief," the priest explained. "That's not the sort of thing that a noblewoman with a very high opinion of her own self-importance does of her own volition. She calls the maid and orders her to do a better job of cleaning. She doesn't lower herself to do a servant's work for her. That put two ideas into my head. First, that there was something on the candelabra that needed to be cleaned up right away and Lady Dirus couldn't wait for someone else to do it, and second, that either the maid wasn't to be trusted with this cleaning job, or more likely, that the maid wasn't around to do it."

"Father Brown and I had independently come to the same conclusions," Holmes continued. "For some reason, Lady Dirus had bludgeoned Agnes the housemaid with a candelabra, and her husband and son had helped her cover up the crime. The precise motive we'll address in a moment. I suspect it was young Agro who came up with the idea to take some sheep's blood– the cook was planning to make some mutton blood pudding that evening, so Agro probably crept downstairs and stole the bottle of sheep's blood from the larder. His mother's attack on poor Agnes led to stains on the wall, so what to do? They didn't have a maid to clean them up anymore. In any case, it's a time-consuming process to scrub blood out of the kind of absorbent stone used to build that part of the castle. With Father Brown and his niece coming soon, there was no time to clean it. Only one thing to do– spill a little sheep's blood to cover it all up. Father Brown just happened to take a sample from the sheep blood part by chance, though he could have easily taken some from the human blood portion, or some of both."

"But what was the motive?" Watson asked. "Are you saying that it wasn't jealousy over Agnes' affair with Lord Dirus?"

"Oh, no," Father Brown explained. "Lady Dirus was quite used to her husband's adultery, and in any case, she was sufficiently dispassionate towards her husband that any feelings of jealousy would have been completely impossible. Indeed, I don't think Agnes had an affair with Lord Dirus at all. No, there had to be another reason, only I never would have thought of it if I hadn't heard Lord Dirus talking about finding a forger to create a sixteenth-century document. I knew the history of how the family gained control of the castle through massacring a monastery, and everybody assumed that Henry VIII had given them the title and property through a royal land grant and decree. But what if for whatever reason, that never happened? If the King never signed an official document, then the Dirus family have no legal right to the castle, and they're not even really titled nobility. They've just occupied the property for centuries and called themselves "Lord" and "Lady," when in fact they're just squatters with pretensions of grandeur. I suppose that it's been a dark family secret for generations, and somehow, poor Agnes came across some document or journal or something that revealed the truth while she was cleaning up and peeking through Lord Dirus's papers. And she realized that Lord and Lady Dirus were just "Mr. and Mrs. Dirus," and when for whatever reason she confronted them... Well, you know the rest. Holmes and I caught them returning from burying the body, which they'd hidden somewhere while they were waiting for my niece and I to leave. The police found poor Agnes in the woods after only a few minutes of searching."

After a long period of quiet, Watson asked, "What will happen to the castle? Will it be returned to the Church and become a monastery again?"

"Unlikely," Father Brown sighed. "That would require the British government admitting that most of the Church of England's property and much of the aristocracy's lands came from murder, theft, and centuries of denial. More likely, the powers that be in the government will find some loyal Member of Parliament who they think deserves a promotion, and they'll give him the estate and award him and his descendants some nice, impressive-sounding title."

The three men sat in silence for a moment.

"It seems your niece's engagement is at an end," Holmes remarked to the priest.

"And a good thing, too," Father Brown replied.

The Adventure of the Philanthropic Crook

(Sherlock Holmes meets The Gray Seal)

by D.K. Latta

Jimmie Dale stared out the French windows at the windswept grass that swayed almost in rhythm with the ocean waves frothing restlessly beyond the short cliff at the end of the property. He felt as restless as Poseidon's domain appeared, which was entirely contrary to the point of his sojourn here in the Sussex countryside, so far from the bustling New York City that was his natural stomping grounds. This was meant to be a vacation, after all — though friends had chuckled at that description, wondering what an idle dilettante like him needed with a vacation. A vacation from what? they had asked good naturedly when he made it known he would be quitting the city for a time. But how could he explain that his days were often far more full, far more adventurous, and — perhaps most significantly — far more dangerous than any suspected?

The Adventure of the Philanthropic Crook by D.K. Latta

If only he could tell them — or tell anyone, in fact. But no, there were some secrets that must be kept. Especially as they were not his secrets alone.

And once again, he thought — of her!

He flung open the glass doors and let the cool sea air wash over him, rustling his hair, filling his lungs. Even here, even now, she filled his thoughts, dancing elusively before his mind's eye; her, a woman he had never truly met, but who he was convinced he loved all the same. He could only speculate about the shape of her nose, could only ponder upon the possible hue of her locks, could only idly play with possible names that might be hers.

For he knew her simply as The Tocsin. And for now, he had to content himself with that being enough. For since she had intruded herself into his life, Jimmie's existence had become one of not infrequent danger, but she had also filled it with something more, something greater: excitement, passion, and perhaps most importantly, purpose. For Jimmie had a secret life, that of the notorious criminal and underworld figure, The Gray Seal — an identify itself which was but another disguise, for in truth Jimmie used his Gray Seal alias, with the unseen aid of The Tocsin, to fight crime, not to implement it.

"Excuse me, sir."

Jimmie turned to see the elderly man standing tentatively in the inner doorway. Jason, his butler — and as faithful an aide as any man could hope for. When he had decided to take his break from the city, he had contemplated leaving Jason behind, telling the old man to take some time for himself. But he knew that Jason would interpret such an admonishment as tantamount to chastiscment, and would beg to know what he had done to incur Master Jimmie's displeasure. The old man was as much family as he was an employee, often quick to reminisce about dawdling Jimmie upon his knee when they were both a good deal younger. So instead Jimmie had brought him along, figuring the change of scenery would do them both some good.

Yet as the old man stood in the doorway, Jimmie was surprised to see an all too familiar look upon his face — one equal parts trepidation and puzzlement. An expression Jimmie had seen before, but had never in his wildest imaginings expected to see reprised in this bucolic countryside. Even before Jimmie's eyes dropped to the old man's hands, he already knew what he would espy there — though it beggared all rational belief.

The old man clutched a simple white envelope.

"I found this slipped under the front door, sir — I can't say precisely when it was delivered, save it must have been within the last hour." Jason looked down at the letter, then up again. "Is it what I think it is, sir?"

Was it? Jimmie wondered. Could it be possible? They had arrived only yesterday — Jason had not even fully unpacked their boxes. Breaking free of what seemed a momentary paralysis, Jimmie stepped forward and took the proffered letter. One glance told him all he needed to know. "Thank you, Jason." He did not directly respond to the old man's query, nor did he need to. His demeanour was all the answer the butler needed.

"Very good, sir." The old man nodded, then he backed out of the room, gently closing the door and allowing Jimmie his privacy before the younger man even needed to request it.

Jimmie stared at the envelope. It was from her! The Tocsin! And that could only mean one thing: a summons, a call to arms!

He tore open the envelope and unfolded the letter. And there at the top, in a delicate, achingly familiar hand, was the familiar opening refrain:

"Dear Philanthropic Crook…"

The Adventure of the Philanthropic Crook by D.K. Latta

*****

Since my friend, Sherlock Holmes, had retired to the Sussex countryside, exchanging the often rambunctious existence of a consulting detective for the more sedate reality of that of a rural bee keeper, I must confess that I sometimes felt retirement had been imposed upon me as well. I continued with my medical practice, of course. And being a few years older than Holmes, one might well think I would find it agreeable to settle into a less perilous life style. But I would be a liar if I did not acknowledge that, from time to time, I felt a restless stirring of the blood; a desire to foray out into the fog-draped night at my friend's side, part ally, part Boswell, continuing the activities for which he, and to a lesser degree, myself, had become so celebrated. A stirring that, naturally, mostly went unanswered.

We did not fully lose touch after Holmes' relocation. Although it was rare to see him wandering the narrow, crooked streets of London in those years, I made the trip out to the chalk cliffs of the South Downs to spend an occasional weekend visiting with my erstwhile housemate. Such visits were invariably pleasant and agreeable, but perhaps served to remind us both, even if unspoken by either, of how much our relationship had been cemented by the baffling mysteries that invariably deposited themselves upon the doorstep of our former abode at 221B Baker Street. With a case to excite Holmes and to befuddle me, we were bound as closely as

The Adventure of the Philanthropic Crook by D.K. Latta

brothers; without such a dilemma we were, perhaps, more akin to amiable cousins.

I state this all forthrightly so as to acknowledge that we both were perhaps subconsciously primed for something dramatic and exciting to occur that day Harold Stackhurst dropped by Holmes' country estate in the company of his comely niece, Matilda. Even so, neither of us could possibly have predetermined the curious events that would ensue.

It was just a few years prior to the commencement of the Great War — I am reluctant to be too precise about the date so as to provide some cover for those only peripherally involved, and who might not wish to be publicly associated with events of such lurid sensationalism. Stackhurst operated The Gables, a respected coaching establishment in the area, helping to prepare young fellows for careers both varied and important. And he and Holmes had become friends. I dare say another man might have been a bit jealous of their camaraderie, but in truth I was genuinely pleased that my notoriously solitary friend was not spending all his latter days communing solely with those of a strictly insect disposition. And Stackhurst was a standfast and amiable fellow.

As Holmes' housekeeper went to fetch an extra couple of tea cups for the two newcomers, I prodded Stackhurst about any interesting changes in the area — Holmes far less likely to concern himself with village gossip. "There's that stately old place out on the cliffs," I remarked, having noted the house from the road as I passed by. "I seem to recall a middle-aged couple lived there last time I was here, but have they sold it? I spied a strapping young man walking the grounds this time."

"The Ferguson place, you mean?" asked Stackhurst, giving a thankful nod to the housekeeper as he accepted a cup of tea. "No, they've just rented the place out while they're on a tour of the Continent. It's been occupied for the last week by a

The Adventure of the Philanthropic Crook by D.K. Latta

young man named Jimmie Dale and his butler. Apparently, he's living off his family's money, and was looking to partake of a bit of country air."

"Dale, you say?" spoke up Holmes, looking a bit thoughtful.

"You know him?" I asked.

Holmes shook his head. "Something about the name is familiar, though. But I'm afraid my memory isn't as sharp as it used to be."

Stackhurst and I exchanged an amused glance. For all his self-deprecation, Holmes' mind was still a good deal sharper than most fellows half his age.

"Do you recall the family business?" Holmes prodded.

"Not sure that I do," Stackhurst admitted. "I seem to recall it had something to do with banking — or maybe security?"

"Of course!" Holmes snapped his long, nimble fingers. "Dale safes and strong boxes!"

"By Jove, that's it," laughed Stackhurst. "Fancy you knowing that, Holmes."

"Tut tut," the erstwhile detective chided. "In my business — my former business — knowing the make and model of safes and locks could be most instructive in solving a conundrum or two."

Doubtless Stackhurst assumed Holmes meant in solving a burglary. I did not disabuse him of that assumption by adding that Holmes had also had occasion to pick a lock and break into a safe himself during his investigations.

"The Dale company makes some of the best. No wonder the lad has the financial wherewithal to lead an idle life. Although it seems rather a shame for him to spring from such clever and imaginative stock only to fritter away his own potential so. Young people, eh?" He tsked.

Stackhurst, the school teacher, felt compelled to defend those not yet sporting grey hairs as did we three. "I daresay this generation is no worse than any other — comprised of equal parts idlers and doers, sinners and saints." It was at the speaking of those words that Stackhurst seemed to lose his train of thought and fell abruptly silent. And it was only then that I recognized there had been some weight pressing down upon him that he had been trying valiantly to disguise. But if I was slow to perceive it, Holmes was, as always, well ahead of me.

"Oh, come come, Stackhurst," he finally said, exasperated. "We've made our small talk, we've dance around whatever's the matter. Don't you think it's time you came out with it?"

"Holmes?" I queried, surprised.

"My word, Watson, you have become rather obtuse in recent years, haven't you? Stackhurst has been on edge since he arrived, while his niece here — Matilda, was it?" Holmes said, directing this at the young woman. "Matilda has said not a word. Odd behaviour for someone paying a social call wouldn't you say?"

I had attributed her demureness to simple social propriety, allowing the three older members of our impromptu tea party to lead the conversation. But as I saw Stackhurst and his niece exchange a glance I knew that Holmes, as usual, was correct.

"You're right, of course, Holmes," said Stackhurst, forcing a wry smile. "I'm afraid we did arrive with an ulterior agenda. But I wasn't sure how to broach the matter, not wanting to presume upon our friendship, especially as I know you are officially retired."

"Then the matter is a criminal one?" I suggested and, I'll admit, not without a slight racing of my pulse, much as a racing hound retired to a farm might feel an involuntary tremor on catching a possible glimpse of a rabbit.

"To be honest, Doctor, I'm not quite sure what it is yet. But I — well, we," he said, glancing at his niece, "are concerned about recent events. I know you're not one for gossip, Holmes, so I'm assuming you've heard nothing of the Skulker?"

"The Skulker?" I said before Holmes could respond. "Now there's an ominous appellation if ever there was one."

"Ominous, indeed," agreed Stackhurst. "I stranger has been seen lurking about at night — a disquieting figure, though he's only been glimpsed by moonlight. Garbed rather shabbily, with a broad-brimmed, sloping hat that conceals his features, and bent over somewhat as though possibly a hunchback. Some locals have even started referring to him as The Bat because he flitters about in the darkness and seems to wear a long coat, or possibly cloak, that evokes wings."

"And who is this fellow?" asked Holmes.

"No one knows."

"How is that possible?" I demanded. "He sounds like he cuts quite a distinctive figure, and this is hardly central London, teeming with anonymous millions. Surely someone must know him, or lets him a room in the area."

Stackhurst shook his head. "He has been seen at night, scurrying across a field, or darting around a corner — but is non-existent during the day."

"Curious, indeed," Holmes conceded, and I could barely repress a smile — most inappropriate given Stackhurst's obvious discomfort — on recognizing a tone to my old friend's voice I hadn't heard for a number of years. "But how does this impact upon you or your niece? A man is allowed his nocturnal perambulations, after all — even an eccentric or ugly man."

"Because, Mr. Holmes," said Matilda, speaking for the first time, "his nocturnal perambulations, as you put it, brought him to my very window just last night."

"Good Lord," I ejaculated. "Are you sure?"

"It's not something I am likely to forget, nor an image I would be prone to dream of if that was to be your next question."

"Your room is upon the ground floor?" Holmes asked, not one to be swayed by emotion or melodrama.

"Yes."

"And about what time was this?"

"I would guess around 11:30."

"And was the light on or off in your room?"

"I had just doused the candle not more than three or four minutes before the face appeared."

Holmes' face was impassive, his long fingers tented before his lips. Although he affected an air of nonchalance, I could tell he was taking the matter quite seriously. "And for how long has this "Bat" been seen about the countryside, Stackhurst?"

"About a week as near as anyone can figure. At least no one can recall noticing him any earlier than that. Is that significant?"

"I have no idea — not at the moment. What does puzzle me is the timing of the dousing of the bedroom candle. If the room had been dark, we could surmise a tramp, perhaps looking for an empty ground floor room he could break into, in order to steal any loose odds and ends. If the room was lit, we could infer — forgive my bluntness, madam — a peeping tom. Both troubling motivations, but fairly mundane ones. But this "Bat" must surely have known the room was occupied, even as he peered into darkness." Holmes was silent for a moment longer, as if forgetting the rest of us were even in the room. Then he stirred and shot a look at his two guests. "You said you were concerned about recent "events" — plural. I'm assuming something else has been bothering one or the other of you, something not explicitly connected to the Bat, but contributing to an overall sense of unease. Pray tell the rest of it."

Stackhurst and his niece exchanged glances. It fell to the latter to speak. "It's Mister Thomas Leyton, a young man who has done me the courtesy of asking me to marry him."

"Hardly sinister, I would think, then," I said cheerfully.

"I am not well-versed in the more romantic side of human relations," Holmes said, somewhat understating the situation I thought wryly. "But describing his proposal as "courteous" does not suggest you regard his attentions with excessive passion."

A slight smile quirked her lips, and I thought how pretty she would be if this pall of consternation could be fully lifted from her. "Don't misunderstand, Mr. Holmes. Thomas is a handsome man, with good prospects, and a pleasant enough disposition. He arrived at the school to take on a position as an instructor about three months ago. He is quite an ambitious young man," she said, as if perhaps a less flattering adjective had come to mind first. "He'd barely been at the school a couple of weeks before he was approaching my uncle about a promotion, even sounding him out about the possibility of becoming a co-owner of the school."

"Does he come from money?" I asked, surprised a young man as she described had such capital at hand.

"That is not entirely clear," she said, and I understood there was more still to tell. "My uncle expressed no interest in

The Adventure of the Philanthropic Crook by D.K. Latta

acquiring a partner, and soon after Thomas began courting me. I was quite flattered, naturally, and it seemed an enticing pairing. I have grown rather comfortable with this life since coming to live with my uncle. And so finding a potential husband interested in not just the educational profession, but in settling permanently in the area — as his inquiries about acquiring some ownership in my uncle's coaching establishment indicated — is appealing."

"But-?" prodded Holmes.

It was Stackhurst who responded: "As Matilda said, he's a pleasant enough chap. But there is something about him — a lean and hungry look, if you will, to quote Shakespeare. And he keeps some odd company. About a month ago two men arrived to join him — he lives off the grounds in a house he bought in the village. He says they are his brothers, but there is something, well, thuggish about them."

"Arrived from where?"

"New York, I believe — all three Leytons are American."

"And now there has been the robbery," Matilda said.

Holmes' expression barely changed, but to one long familiar with his moods, it was as if he sat bolt upright.

"Thomas showed me a ring — a magnificent diamond in a gold band. When Dr. Watson asked me before if he came from money, and I said it was unclear, that is what I was thinking of. For the ring is clearly quite valuable. He said it is a family heirloom and would be mine if I agreed to be his wife. And last night it was apparently stolen."

"I realize this must all seem like a bunch of nonsense to you, Holmes," Stackhurst confessed. "A bunch of random incidents, some not even particularly sinister, but"

"When I was employed as a detective," Holmes interrupted, "my bread and butter was random incidents and peculiar circumstances. A secretive lodger, a curious personal ad, an illogical utterance, and many other incidents that, at first, hardly pointed to a definitively criminal outcome. If they had, potential clients could simply have gone to the police and Watson and I would have spent many a dull evening staring at our fireplace." He tapped his fingertips together. "So just to recapitulate: we have Thomas Leyton, a suitor of pleasant disposition if, perhaps, a touch overly ambitious, who presents as being of modest means except he seems to have access to capital and valuable heirlooms; four weeks ago he is joined by two companions he names as brothers but you, Stackhurst, are unconvinced; a week ago an unknown and sinister figure begins to be seen lurking about at night; also a week ago, one Jimmie Dale begins his vacation in the area—"

"Dale?" started Stackhurst. "What on earth has he to do with anything?"

"Perhaps nothing. But when drawing threads between random factors, it is worth noting that the Dale company is based in New York — and the Leytons are from New York; so the population of New Yorkers in this area has literally quadrupled in just three months. And finally, we get to last night, when a diamond ring is stolen from Miss Matilda's suitor's house in the village and this Bat fellow is seen peering in Miss Matilda's window. How, why, or even if any of these incidents are connected is, as yet, unknown." Holmes was silent for a long moment, staring once more at nothing. Then he looked at Stackhurst. "Would it be agreeable to you if I paid a call upon you later? Perhaps I could even meet this Thomas Leyton fellow — if only to see about this missing ring matter?"

Stackhurst let out a sigh, as if he had been holding his breath, and a crooked grin turned his lips. "I can do you better than that, possibly. Tonight I'm hosting a gathering at the school for anyone who wishes to come — we do it every year, as a sort of good will gesture to the community. Leyton should be there. Why, that Jimmie Dale fellow might even make an appearance if he still interests you."

"Splendid," said Holmes. "We will attend. Oh, forgive me, Watson. I should not have spoken for you. Perhaps you are finding this whole matter rather dull and tedious." He said this last with a sly smirk — the rascal.

"I would be delighted to attend," I said, feeling perhaps inopportunely buoyant. "It feels a bit like old times, doesn't it?"

"There's just one final matter," Holmes said suddenly serious, turning back to Stackhurst and his niece. "What is it you haven't told me?"

The two stared at him, surprised.

"One piece of the puzzle that is so irrelevant, or so obscure, you have not thought about mentioning it. Come, come," he said, snapping his fingers abruptly. "Don't think about it, or it will slip away again. Just the first thing that comes into your mind."

"I don't—?" Stackhurst looked perplexed.

"Well," Matilda hesitated, glancing at her uncle, "I suppose there was that peculiar stamp I saw on my window this morning — I don't recall it having been there before. But I hardly see how it could have any relevance—"

"A stamp you say?" said Holmes. "Of what kind?"

"It's just a little grey, diamond-shaped, sticker, of the kind you might use to close an envelope."

"Good Lord," I gasped. "You mean — a Gray Seal?"

Holmes settled back into his chair, a smug, self-satisfied smile on his lips.

After the Stackhursts' had departed with our assurances we would see them in the evening, Holmes turned to me with a decided twinkle in his eyes. "All right, Watson — out with it. Clearly you have information I lack," he said this with more than a hint of ironic amusement. "What does this gray stamp convey to you?"

"You mean you honestly have heard nothing of The Gray Seal, Holmes?" I asked, momentarily incredulous. But then I realized that when Holmes had retired to the life of a bee keeper, he truly had left the study of crime behind him. "It's the name — and the calling card — of a notorious criminal, a masked man who has eluded the New York police for months. I'm dumbstruck to think he might for some reason be operating here in the South Downs. But if he is, you've got your work cut out for you. The man's a veritable devil, by all reports."

"And how do you come to know of him?"

"A magazine editor approached me a few months back. Knowing of my success chronicling your investigations in years past, and aware that no further such stories would be forthcoming in that field, he suggested I try my hand at writing fictionalized tales of this Gray Seal fellow. I looked into the matter a bit, but decided it really wasn't my cup of tea, that I wasn't interested in romanticizing such a scoundrel." I then related to Holmes a condensed version of the news reports I had read while researching the Gray Seal. I described how he was a master safe cracker, that no lock was secure from his almost preternaturally deft fingers. I told Holmes how he was so avidly wanted by the police they apparently had an unofficial slogan: "The Gray Seal, Dead or Alive — but the Gray Seal!" I explained how he was as elusive as a fish, and had yet to be caught by the police or his enemies within the New York underworld itself.

The Adventure of the Philanthropic Crook by D.K. Latta

Holmes settled back in his chair, his eyes taking on a glazed, contemplative look I recognized from so many evenings past. For a long time he said nothing, then he surprised me with a little chuckle. "Interesting, Watson — very interesting," he said at long last. "An expert at safe cracking, you say? And he is believed to be hated as much by his fellows among the criminal class as he is by the stalwarts of law enforcement?"

"Yes — apparently he has a habit of interfering in others' crimes and leaving them to take the rap."

"While also, on more than one occasion, exonerating those wrongly accused, hmmm? A most ill-fortuned criminal it is who sees his allies incarcerated, the innocent vindicated, and often seems to escape in the end without acquiring his intended booty. It makes one think, doesn't it?" Holmes' voice drifted off, and I knew then he was not truly talking to me, but was using me as a sounding board while he moved pieces around in his head, trying to get a sense of that chess board only he could see.

"The only thing I think is: what could The Gray Seal possibly have to do with a nocturnal creeper and a missing family heirloom?" I said.

I suspected that night might prove more tumultuous than I had anticipated when I first packed my bags for a lazy weekend visit with my old friend.

*****

Jimmie Dale scanned the large room from over the lip of his wine glass. Amid the murmur of voices there were a couple of score of people milling about, partaking of complimentary wine and canapés, enjoying the hospitality of The Gables, the prestigious coaching establishment. It was quite a striking room, the floor of gleaming hardwood, the

The Adventure of the Philanthropic Crook by D.K. Latta

curtains framed by long scarlet drapes, the light supplied by elegant candelabras — gas pipes having not yet made their way out to the institute.

This was the first time Jimmie had had a chance to observe The Gables from the inside — though he had seen the outside quite a bit these past few nights; ever since he had received the enigmatic Tocsin's initial missive a week ago, advising him to keep an eye on the place and certain of its inhabitants. He had chosen to follow her instructions in the guise of Larry the Bat — an alter ego he normally employed when skulking about the New York Bowery, adopting the mien of a low level crook and drug fiend. Employing Larry the Bat here was not quite as satisfactory as it was in New York where the deliberately shady character was meant to blend in with his typically shady surroundings; among these genteel and bucolic environs, Larry rather stood out like a proverbial sore thumb, and Jimmie had been privately amused to hear the village gossip about a mysterious and sinister Skulker. But it was far better that the unidentifiable Larry be spotted making nocturnal rounds than that Jimmie Dale, wealthy vacationer, be recognized by moonlight, inviting questions he was not prepared to answer. And so following The Tocsin's directions he had kept an eye upon young Matilda Stackhurst and her would-be fiancee, Thomas Leyton — even leaving one of his trademark gray seal stickers in the hopes it might scare away those with sinister intentions.

Such a hope, though, proved fruitless, as just this afternoon he had received another mysterious message from The Tocsin with the dramatic proclamation "Tonight!" and further instructions as to what Jimmie was required to do, and why. It was a sinister plan he was attempting to foil, one of Machiavellian cunning and repugnance. He still did not know how The Tocsin was privy to all the underworld secrets she had, but in the months that she had been sending him letters, in the months that he had thwarted the schemes of evil men under the illusion that The Gray Seal himself was a master criminal, she had rarely steered him wrong. It was this brilliance she possessed, this unfaltering courage she displayed, and this trueness of heart leading her to risk so much to see justice was served that made Jimmie love her even as he had never laid eyes on her. And she was cunning, there was no denying that. Indeed, after initially being surprised that she had tracked him down here, and that there were local doings that required The Gray Seal's intervention, he wondered if it was really such a coincidence after all. He began to wonder if this very idea of taking a vacation in the Sussex Downs was something she had subtly suggested to him in her messages back in New York — leading him to think it was his idea, when this was just more of her ineffable planning.

His eyes narrowed as he espied a dark-haired young man across the room; handsome, dapper, but with a look in his eyes that made Jimmie think of a shark he had seen once in an aquarium. Thomas Leyton was staring across the room at the lovely Matilda Stackhurst, the girl chatting amiably with a couple of the school's instructors. At Leyton's side were two broad-shouldered, beetle-browed men who Jimmie knew he claimed as his brothers — but evinced little of a family resemblance. Still with his eyes on Matilda, Thomas whispered something to his brothers, who both nodded, and then quietly slipped out the door.

Jimmie placed his glass on the nearest table and turned to find the most convenient exit — and instead found himself

The Adventure of the Philanthropic Crook by D.K. Latta

facing two elderly men. One was robust and broad-shouldered, his moustache streaked with a few lingering dark hairs otherwise absent from the snow white mantle upon his head. The second man was tall and gangly, with a narrow skull and sharp, aquiline features that put Jimmie in mind of a bird of prey. Despite their advanced years, both men appeared spry and with sharp, intelligent eyes.

"Ah, Mr. Dale, isn't?" asked the bird of prey, a sardonic twist to his lips.

"Um, yes," he said, trying to peer past them, to keep an eye on Thomas Leyton. "And you are—?"

"Oh, this is my friend, John Watson, and my name is Sherlock Holmes."

Jimmie started, almost as if the man had identified himself as Santa Claus. "Like the famous detective?"

Holmes chuckled. "Quite like him, yes. In fact, I am him, for my sins. Retired, of course. I wanted to introduce myself and say how much I appreciate your involvement with crime."

Jimmie was sure the blood must have drained from his face, and his only hope was that they were far enough away from the nearest candelabra that it wasn't obvious. He had heard of Sherlock Holmes, of course, but how on earth could the old man know anything about his secret life?

"Your family's involvement, of course I mean." There was a twinkle in Holmes' eyes as he stared intently at Jimmie: "Your family is the Dales who make all those wonderful safes and strong boxes, correct?"

Jimmie barely kept from releasing an audible sigh. "Oh, yes — yes, of course. That. Well, I'm glad you — you enjoy them," he said lamely. "But if you'll excuse me I have someone I have to catch up with. Perhaps we'll meet again later." And without waiting for a response, Jimmie sidled quickly past the two men and hurried toward an exit. Pausing at the threshold, Jimmie glanced back. The man identified as Watson was moving toward one of the refreshment tables, but Holmes was still watching Jimmie, a sinister, inscrutable smile upon his lips.

Once out of sight Jimmie raced down a dark hall, and flung himself through the first door that led to the outside grounds. He thought he had been prepared for the night's events, but meeting the legendary British detective had taken him completely by surprise — and he suspected even The Tocsin hadn't anticipated the old man's appearance as she'd made no allusion to its possibility in her messages. If it was his life alone that was at stake, Jimmie might well have aborted the matter entirely. But to do so would be to leave others to suffer an unjust fate, and to allow for an evil to plant seeds that could grow sinister fruit in the years to come. No! Whatever the risk Holmes presented, Jimmie knew he had to continue as The Tocsin had planned it.

Racing across the dark lawn Jimmie drew a silk mask from his pocket, and soft kid gloves, donning them as he went. Beneath his jacket was his trusty girdle, where he kept his various pick-locks and other necessary tools employed by The Gray Seal.

Wheeling about a corner of the building, onto the side where some of the residential rooms were located, Jimmie bounded toward the window that showed upon Matilda Stackhurst's room. A light flickered through the pane, despite the young woman herself still being in the main hall with the rest of the guests.

Jimmie ducked beneath the window, then slowly raised his head to peer inside as he had done on previous nights when disguised as Larry the Bat. And tonight he witnessed what he had been so determined to prevent — if only Holmes and that Watson fellow hadn't delayed him! Skulking about the young woman's chambers were the two hulking figures of Thomas Leyton's so-called brothers; one of them crouched before something on the lower platform of a bookshelf.

Hands moving as though with a life of their own, Jimmie carefully drew a pick-lock from his girdle and without needing to take his eyes from the two men, almost effortlessly jimmied the latch of the window. Praying that Matilda kept the hinges oiled, Jimmie gently pushed in the window. It was a mild night and with little breeze, so the two men did not instantly detect the intrusion, even when the candle flickered momentarily. Jimmie slipped over the sill. He hesitated. Whatever had fortuitously possessed him to pack his Gray Seal accoutrements for this trip had not extended to the thought of bringing his gun on his vacation — not that Jimmie ever did more than fire warning shots. Still, he held one hand as though he was armed — hoping that in the dim light it might fool them. He cleared his throat.

The two men whirled about, the crouching one rising so that Jimmie could glimpse the small, open safe at his feet.

"What the—?" grunted one of them.

"Steady on, boys," Jimmie said, affecting a menacing snarl. "The Gray Seal don't take kindly to small fry muscling in on his operations."

"Your—?" echoed the one. "But — huh? The Gray Seal?!?"

Quite the conversationalist, Jimmie thought wryly. Then his eyes darted to a small box the other man held in his thick hand. "I'll take that if you don't mind." He grabbed for it but the other was quicker and simply tossed it into the safe.

The Adventure of the Philanthropic Crook by D.K. Latta

Then he made to kick the door of the safe closed. "No!" Jimmie shouted, leaping forward, elbowing the first man out of the way. Jimmie managed to intrude his foot between the safe and its door, but that opened him up to a right cross from the second thug. Jimmie reeled back, but then retaliated with a savage uppercut. Just then arms snaked around him from behind, the first man having recovered. As the second man came at him, Jimmie took advantage of the grip and flung up his legs, kicking the on-rushing attacker. But Jimmie's grin sagged into a look of anguish as his blow sent the man staggering back into the bookshelf — and knocked the safe door closed, where it made an audible click. Jimmie flung back his head, butting the man pinning him, loosening the other's grip; Jimmie rammed both elbows back into a stomach less solid than it needed to be. As the man fell away, the other man he had kicked scrambled to his feet and came at Jimmie — but only to knock Jimmie aside as he clambered out the open window. "Come on, come on," he shouted to his partner. "The job's done — we don't have to mess with The Gray Seal!" Jimmie watched as both men tumbled out the window and raced away into the darkness. He resisted the urge to pursue.

Instead he whirled and dropped before the little safe, cursing his own ineptitude. Because of his clumsiness, was it possible everything was lost?

No! he told himself. Stay calm. There might still be time. Knuckling sweat from his upper lip he examined the lock, then deftly began rolling the dial, feeling the vibration of the tumblers through his fingertips. He had been raised around locks and had cracked his first safe, for fun, when he was twelve. And this wasn't even a particularly good make. Calm down, he reassured himself. Calm down — and this can still be done.

He stiffened, hearing agitated voices advancing down the hall. Had his fight with the men been heard? But no, he

The Adventure of the Philanthropic Crook by D.K. Latta

realized. This is merely what The Tocsin had predicted — what she had warned him about.

He had only seconds. Was there time?

Suddenly the safe let out a satisfied click! and the door swung open. Jimmie grabbed up the little box and flipped open its lid, revealing a dazzling diamond ensconced in a gold ring. He closed the safe and whirled toward the window — but already voices were outside in the hall, already the door was yawning open, a brighter light washing into the room. Jimmie flung himself behind the door even as it swung wide and he heard a trample of feet thunder into the room. The door bumped repeatedly against him as bodies pressed on the other side. Desperately he tore off his mask and gloves, shoving them in his jacket pocket, then likewise slipped the ring and its box into another pocket. Carefully he slipped out from behind the door, merging with the crowd of a dozen people milling about the room.

"This is insane, Thomas," Matilda was saying, practically begging, her face moving in and out of his sight near the front of the crowd. "I don't understand how you can believe such a thing."

"I don't want to believe it," snapped Thomas. "Dear God — I loved you. But how should I react when an anonymous note tells me you were the one who stole my mother's ring? The ring I would have given you freely the moment you consented to be my wife?"

"Uncle—?" Matilda turned toward Harold Stackhurst who was looking completely at a loss.

The Adventure of the Philanthropic Crook by D.K. Latta

It was clear to Jimmie what had occurred — Thomas Leyton had accused Matilda of stealing the missing ring, choosing as public a spectacle as he could for his accusation. Jimmie scanned the crowd — and froze, seeing the hawk-faced Sherlock Holmes looking, not at the man and woman arguing, but at Jimmie himself; and he was staring with a puzzled expression. Suddenly Jimmie was acutely aware that his face must look flushed from the fight, his hair damp with sweat.

"If you are innocent," sneered Thomas, "prove it — simply open the safe."

Matilda glared at him, then stamped her foot. "Very well, if my word is not enough for you." She turned and primly knelt before the safe. She twirled the dial left, then right, then left. There was a click, and the door swung open. She stood erect and crossed her arms over her bosom. "As I said…"

Thomas gawked, and despite everything Jimmie couldn't entirely suppress a smile seeing the blackguard's genuine expression of surprise. He brusquely shoved Matilda aside (with cries of "Steady on" and "None of that" from the more gallant of the on-lookers) and started rummaging through the little safe — but, of course, to no avail. He straightened, looking a bit ashen, and then glanced about the crowd. "I — I don't know what to say. I guess I've made a terrible mistake."

Jimmie frowned. Matilda had been saved from a false accusation — which was part of The Tocsin's plan. But there was also the matter of seeing that the guilty party was exposed. And that he was in danger of failing to accomplish. He tried shouldering his way through the cluster of on-lookers. "Let me search him," Jimmie said abruptly. "How do we know the ring was even stolen?" Jimmie was struggling to push through those in front of him.

Thomas glared at him — having no idea who this young man was, or why the ring was not in the safe where his henchmen had been instructed to secret it, but he knew something was up. "I'll not be manhandled by you, sir. Good God, to accuse me—" he stammered, ignoring his own accusation against Matilda moments ago.

Jimmie continued to try and push forward, though aware others — even Harold Stackhurst — were looking at him oddly, clearly wondering why he was so eager to insert himself into these dramatics. He realized if he pressed it, he might expose himself to greater scrutiny.

Suddenly Holmes was in front of him, reaching out to hold him back. "Steady on, dear boy," he said, not unkindly. "Your enthusiasm is laudable, but a tad inappropriate." Then he whirled about. "However, I dare say my interest is not. As most of you know, I am Sherlock Holmes — and I'd like to think I have something of a decent reputation. Therefore, if Mr. Leyton will permit me, I'm sure we can all put these reckless accusations behind us." He stopped before Leyton, head cocked quizzically. Leyton looked unsurely about, but undoubtedly realized it would be hard to refuse the celebrated detective. Grudgingly, he nodded. Holmes reached out and began patting him down. Then as Holmes reached one of the jacket pockets he stopped, affecting a look of puzzlement. "What's this?" he asked loudly, his long fingers slipping into the pocket and coming out — holding a little box. Everyone in the room gasped, including Leyton. Including Jimmie. Holmes opened the lid of the box and in the candle light the ring twinkled for all to see.

"You — you cad!" sneered Stackhurst. "You damnable bounder!"

"But — why, Thomas?" demanded Matilda. "Why would you accuse me of such a thing?"

Holmes spoke up. "I'm afraid, my dear, you were just a pawn — a pawn in a most insidious scheme. You see I think once the authorities look into matters, they will discover that Mr. Leyton here is part of a New York based criminal organization. An organization looking to expand its power and influence into the very halls of power. Imagine such a group controlling an establishment such as this. At best they would be able to inveigle themselves with the next generation of lawyers, and engineers, and politicians — and at worst, actually shape the minds of these students, corrupt their thinking while still at an influenceable age. Their initial plan was simply to buy their way into ownership of The Gables. But when Stackhurst here turned Leyton down, their next plan was more insidious: to frame you as a thief, of your own fiancee to boot, destroying Stackhurst's reputation by association, and so forcing him into a position where he would have no choice but to sell." Holmes looked distastefully at Leyton. "No doubt if they had succeeded with this little experiment, they would have attempted similar enterprises with more and even bigger schools in the future."

Jimmie stared, amazed. What Holmes had deduced was pretty much what The Tocsin had explained to him in her messages. But what she had gleaned from her underworld contacts, Holmes had arrived at with his astonishing deductive prowess.

But that did not explain the ring Holmes had found on Leyton. Jimmie patted his pocket and discovered, to his astonishment, that the ring was not there! But how? he wondered. Then he recalled Holmes reaching out to him, preventing him from approaching Leyton. Holmes must have picked his pocket, then slipped the ring into Leyton's pocket while pretending to search him.

But why would Holmes do that? Unless — unless he somehow had inferred the role Jimmie played in the night's proceedings. But was that possible? And how much did the great detective surmise about Jimmie's activities?

Slipping out the back of the crowd, Jimmie disappeared into the darkness.

*****

After the previous night's rather dramatic events, the next morning Sherlock Holmes rose uncharacteristically early and, while we were enjoying a light breakfast, Harold Stackhurst paid us a visit. He was eager to inform us that a local constable had gone by Thomas Leyton's place only to find he and his so-called brothers had absconded. However, the three men were subsequently discovered at the local train station and were currently being detained under the charge of making a false complaint, while efforts were being expended to look into their backgrounds. Unsurprisingly, there had emerged questions as to whether Leyton's academic credentials had been falsified entirely.

Stackhurst was still a bit shaken by events, perhaps acutely aware of just how close he and his niece had become to be being drawn into a spider's web of which they had had no knowledge. Yet he was looking chipper, and assured us Matilda had taken the news of her erstwhile suitor's duplicity with relative élan.

Once he had departed, Holmes suggested we enjoy the morning and take a walk around the countryside. It was a pleasant day, the sky without a hint of cloud, and with a gentle breeze rolling in off the water.

"It was a horrible trick to play on that young woman," I remarked to Holmes as we strolled. Then, as I thought about the previous night's revelations, I said, "I suppose you must think me a bit of a fool for going on about that Gray Seal fellow. Clearly that stamp Matilda found had nothing to do with anything."

"I'd never think you were a fool for that, Watson," Holmes said drily, watching cawing seagulls swoop over the water's crests.

"Good of you to say. But, say now, Holmes — I just thought of something else. How did that mysterious skulking fellow fit into it? Was he one of the Leyton boys in disguise? If so, I can't see what they hoped to accomplish, or why they were spying upon the girl. Or was he just some tramp with no involvement in the matter at all?"

"Perhaps, perhaps," Holmes muttered, not really answering my query. "Why, look, it's young Mister Dale."

I realized that Holmes' wanderings had brought us to the house being rented by the young dilettante. And though he acted as if it was happenstance, I had a suspicion there had been intention guiding his steps. A rented touring car was parked out front and the young man was in the process of securing suitcases in the boot.

"It looks like he's leaving," I muttered to Holmes.

"Hallo, Mr. Dale!" Holmes called, striding briskly up to the man.

Jimmie Dale looked up and his face seemed to take on a guarded expression, as though our visit was not entirely agreeable to him. "Ah — Mr. Holmes. Dr. Watson. Good morning."

Holmes folded his hands behind him and adopted an unusually jovial disposition, in a way that was not fully in character for him. "Quite the contretemps last night, wouldn't you agree? Who knows what might have resulted from it if you and I had not been there to play our respective parts."

Dale's eyes narrowed. "Me? I contributed nothing of note."

"Did you not?" Holmes said good-naturedly. "It was your notion to search Thomas Leyton, was it not? Which produced the incriminating ring, after all."

"Oh, yes — that," Dale said.

The two men stared at each other for a moment in silence, Holmes with an insouciant smile upon his lips, Dale looking a tad more tense and guarded. Then Holmes shrugged and glanced at the suitcases. "You're on your way, I see?"

"Yes. Last night's events rather reminded me that the world carries on regardless, and there's a fine line between a vacation and a dereliction."

"Yes, I see," Holmes responded, though I certainly did not. "When I was a younger man I suppose I felt a similar way. Well," Holmes straightened and smiled slyly at the young man, "in a manner of speaking, one could suggest that rather Seals the deal — wouldn't you agree, Mr. Dale?"

Dale looked at him a moment, then slowly smiled, too. "In a manner of speaking, yes — I'm off to the Gray skies of New York."

Holmes tipped his head at the young man. "Good-bye, Mr. Dale."

Dale returned the gesture. "Good-bye, Mr. Holmes." Then he nodded at me as if an afterthought.

As we resumed our stroll, I said to Holmes, "What was that all about? I feel like you and he were having a conversation but I only heard every other word of it."

Holmes looked at me, smiled, and then launched into a lecture about bee honey — ignoring my question entirely.

The Wet-Nosed Irregular

by Harry DeMaio

I was sitting at the desk I share with another writer when our office boy came whistling his way in my direction. "Cable for you, Miss Spencer!" He dropped the flimsy in front of me without breaking stride and proceeded with a stack of copy toward the office of the Features Editor, George Howard, my boss here at The Strand Magazine.

I was between assignments and not expecting any communications. In fact, I was a bit desperate to get my literary teeth into anything to break up the boredom. Who was contacting me? I fully expected it to be some kind of advertising circular made up to look like a telegram. I cut the envelope and stared at the terse message. "In response to your request, you may join me at my cottage in the South Downs, Sussex on Thursday. Tell me your travel plans, and I will arrange transit from the station to my home. —Sherlock Holmes."

Dumbstruck! I giggled to myself. I had totally forgotten that I had sent a missive to the now retired master detective requesting an interview. I was going to meet the great Sherlock Holmes.

I flounced into my editor's office waving the cable in front of me. He looked up and said, "Ah yes, Spencer, I was just going to call for you. There is a new ladies' emporium opening this Thursday that I want you to cover."

"Sorry, Mr. Howard, but I have an important previous engagement."

He frowned and said, "This had better be good!"

"Oh, it's better than good. It's splendid! Do you recall about a month ago, I told you I had sent a letter to Sherlock Holmes requesting an interview to reminisce with him about his days as England's only consulting detective?"

"Yes, and do you recall I told you it was hare-brained waste of time? He is now a very private beekeeper. He hates the press, has little use for women and will probably not even respond."

"I remember your encouragement only too well. As the weeks passed, I came to agree with you. Until this afternoon." I laid the cable very carefully on his desk.

He picked it up, stared at it and said, "Well, I'll be damned."

"Oh, I sincerely hope not."

"Are you sure someone is not having you on?"

"I'll find out as soon as I answer him with my travel plans unless of course, the ladies' emporium takes precedence. And don't you dare give my Holmes interview to another reporter. "

He responded to me, "All right. Go to it. I hope you get something useful out of it. The magazine will pay for your expenses."

And so it began. I immediately replied to Holmes's wire stating that I would be delighted to join him, giving him the particulars of my train ride from Victoria Station. He did indeed respond, telling me he would arrange to have me picked up by a local lad who provided automobile service from the local station.

After a relatively short ride to Brighton, I changed to a local that let me off at a railway request stop. Sure enough, sitting in his rig was a tall young man dressed in farm clothes and a flat cap. His tanned skin spoke to his outdoor occupations. Sussex is famous for its sunny days and this was no exception.

"Miz Spencer?" He lifted his cap and reached for my small bag. I anticipated returning to London in the evening, so I came armed only with the tools of my trade. I nodded and climbed up on the front seat of the jalopy with his help. "My name is Joel. Welcome to South Downs. Don't get much business from Mister 'Olmes. He's a bit of a recluse. Are you just visiting for the day?"

"Yes, Joel. I have made a request stop at this station for five-thirty this evening, and then I'll be heading back to London."

"Never been to London. Only been to Brighton once or twice. Are you a nurse? Is Mister 'Olmes ill?"

"I think he's well. No, I'm a writer for the Strand Magazine, and I'm here to get his help with a story I'm working on."

"A bit like that Doctor Watson who comes along every now and again. He hasn't been by lately. I unnerstand he and Mr. 'Olmes were quite the thing fightin' crime. Do you know the doctor?"

"I met him once — a lovely man."

"Mr. 'Olmes keeps bees. I've had some of their honey. It's wonderful stuff. Make sure he gives you some. He makes mead, too. Very powerful."

This small talk continued until we suddenly emerged over a hill from which you could spy the sea in the distance. A building somewhere between a cottage and a full-scale farm house broke the continuity of the landscape. Several smaller white structures *(beehives?)* dotted the view along with a few large trees and small copses or thickets. As we drove up a gravel road which turned into a narrow path, I arranged for

Joel to pick me up in time to make my train connection. About four-thirty. It was now noon.

As we stopped in front of the cottage door draped in English Ivy, a tall, slim figure emerged. He was hatless and wore a set of vintage tweeds that fit him well. His face was tanned and his eyes, surrounded by crow's feet, were bright and sharp. His hair was grey bordering on white, but his brows were still an intense black. His clean-shaven face retained the sharp-etched features for which he was famous. No doubt in my mind. This was Sherlock Holmes.

I am tall for a woman and my boots had modest heels, but he towered over me. I handed him my card and as he perused it, I waved good-bye to Joel. "See you at four-thirty, Miss."

When I turned back, Holmes had re-entered the door and stood aside to let me pass. We came upon a small anteroom in which a table had been set up with sandwiches, a tea service, a plate of scones, clotted cream and of course, honey. He waved me to a seat and as he passed, took my bag and placed it on a sideboard. A young woman entered from what must have been the kitchen and asked if anything was wanted. Holmes looked at me, saw I was satisfied and gently waved her away. Clearly, this was not Mrs. Hudson.

I looked quizzically at the great detective and sensing my interest, he said, "That is Marion. She lives on a nearby farm with her parents and brother and tends to my housework needs several times a week. She also comes by on special occasions such as your visit. Please, Miss Elizabeth Spencer of the Strand Magazine Features Department, have some luncheon and then we can repair to my sitting room and have our discussion."

The sandwiches and tea were lovely. but the honey covered scones were exquisite. I told him so and he graciously offered me a jar to take with me. We retired to the sitting room. It was simplicity itself. A fireplace whose warmth wasn't necessary on this summer's day. A sofa, two leather chairs with side tables, several smaller chairs and a large table centered in the room. A few pictures on the walls and a pair of French Doors that led out into a small furnished garden.

"Is this where you work and correspond?"

"No, I have a large desk in my bedroom which I shamefacedly admit is covered with papers and other paraphernalia. I shall not admit you to that sanctum. But tell me, Miss Spencer, what can I do for you? Your letter outlined a project that piqued my interest. I am constantly being bombarded with queries about my relationships with Watson; Scotland Yard Inspectors; Irene Adler; Professor Moriarty; Sebastian Moran; my brother Mycroft and others. I do not remember being asked about other professional detectives. At least not recently."

"Mr. Holmes, first let me thank you for agreeing to see me. I honestly didn't expect you would reply or if you did, you would actually give me some of your time. I'm honored. There is no doubt that you are the consulting detective nonpareil."

"I am the only consulting detective."

"But a paragon, nonetheless. I want to hear your assessment of some of the other professional sleuths with whom you've had dealings. I'm not seeking to denigrate any of them, but I would like to hear anecdotal evidence of what it was like to work with them. The detection profession is of particular interest to me."

"As it is to many people. I'm sorry, but I am not going to submit others to my professional opinions, evaluations and rankings. In the past, I have come to regret my comments about the Police, Home Office, and the Military. Comparisons are usually odious."

There was a lengthy pause. Then he turned to me with a sly smile and said, "However, I do not wish your journey to come to naught, so I will violate my rule and make a single exception. May I present one of England's most outstanding detectives."

He walked back to the anteroom, retrieved my bag from the sideboard and handed it to me, clearly implying I should start taking notes.

He then pointed to a large, watercolour painting on the wall. In a simple frame sat an image of an ungainly, long-haired, lop-eared canine, breed indeterminate, brown and white in colour. I gaped.

"Are you serious, Mr. Holmes?"

"Never more so, my dear Miss Spencer. Behold Toby! A truly extraordinary animal and flawless sleuth. Are you familiar with Watson's hyper-emotional tale called *The Sign of the Four*?"

"Yes and No! Unfortunately for The Strand Magazine, that story was published by Lippincott's. But I did read it. Please don't tell my employer."

"Then you must remember Toby's almost miraculous ability to track a creosote spill to a distant wharf. That was only one of his many feats of detection. Unfortunately, he has now passed on to wherever canine spirits go to their well-deserved rest. A wonderful dog!"

I was fascinated not only at the prospect of Toby himself but at Holmes' enthusiastic affection and respect for him. I decided I may have something truly unique to tell my readers. I pressed on.

"How did you and Toby first meet?"

"That's a story in itself. You are familiar with the Baker Street Irregulars?"

"The group of indigent children whom you employed for a variety of intelligence assignments?"

"They were far more versatile than simple spies. A fundamental principle of detection, my dear Miss Spencer, is that no one notices raggedy kids. They could slip in and out of any location or situation and no one would even remember they were there. Somewhat akin to the way aristocracy regards the servant class when they are not making demands of them. But before we go any further, take a moment to tell me about yourself. It will help me tailor my thoughts and remarks toward your background and interests. Would you care for a glass of mead to help the discussion along?"

"Thank you. That would be lovely. Well, I have been a Features writer at The Strand for several years. I am usually allocated meager space for interviews, unusual events, and unfortunately, prosaic public commentary. I assure you that this interview will occupy a significantly more important position in our pages. The name Sherlock Holmes is reader magic. After finishing training at a none too prestigious university *(I am, after all, a woman.)* I began writing freelance offerings while supporting myself as a nanny, then as a companion to an older and thank heaven, wealthy woman. It was she who encouraged me to continue writing and sharpening my skills.

It turns out she has a more than passing acquaintance with the Publisher of The Strand Magazine. When several of my articles were picked up by lesser publications, she thought it was time she could recommend me to him. I would not disgrace her. The Strand took me up on a trial basis and last year, the job became permanent or as permanent as anything can be in the publishing business. I still live with her and she has become a virtual aunt to me. It was she who encouraged me to approach you."

"Does this woman have a name?"

"Isadora Klein. Have you heard of her?"

There was a short pause. He smiled. "The name is familiar. I occasionally wondered what became of her. Please convey my regards. Now, shall we return to Toby?"

"Oh, yes! You were mentioning the Baker Street Irregulars. How are they connected?"

"Very directly. After a particularly complicated and intense case involving smugglers, the leader of the ragged group, Wiggins, a highly intelligent but marginally educated young man came to me and said, "Beggin yer pardon, Mr. 'Olmes but me and the fellows *(there was also a girl, but she dressed as a boy.)* would like to make a sergestion. *(Holmes had slipped into a very good version of a cockney street urchin accent.)* We think you need another member of the group. This last job was a bit of a trial and we know someone who would have made short work of the whole thing. Name's Toby. He's a dorg."

"A dog?"

"Not just any dorg, Mr. 'Olmes. He's a ruddy genius dorg. We've used him several times without your knowing it. No extra charge! A good beefy bone and he's in heaven. He's got a nose that can sniff its way to a target in a crowd of stinkin' sweaty longshoremen or a parade of perfumed tarts. But it's not just his nose. He's smart. Smarter than the average copper or thug. In fact, he made a monkey out of your friend Lestrade, just last week. Found a gun the Peelers and the Yard had been searchin' for fer weeks. You need to meet Toby."

"I agreed. I needed to meet Toby."

"Without telling Watson, who was re-establishing his medical practice, I joined Wiggins and several of his chums. We proceeded to a group of row houses in deep, darkest Lambeth where an eccentric naturalist named Mr. Sherman had established a veritable menagerie in his home at #3 Pinchin Lane. Sherman opened his window, ready to do battle with the police, do-gooders and other oppressors. "Get you gone, you brigands. I'll not tell you twice."

Wiggins shouted, "It's awright, Mr. Sherman. It's me, Wiggins and me pals. We have someone we want you to meet. Mr. Sherlock Holmes."

"The name and fame of Sherlock Holmes had reached even the packed precincts of Lambeth and Mr. Sherman was taken aback."

"Are ye tryin' to fool an old man, Wiggins? What would Sherlock Holmes want with the likes of me?"

"Well, ya see. It's not exactly you he wants to meet. It's Toby."

"Aha! I shoulda known. I can see where Toby might be of interest to the Great Detective. Well, Toby doesn't exactly live here. He and his missus and their two pups live over there in #7. Toby and I have an arrangement. I provide them with food and drink, and he protects my home and my animals. I'm a naturalist, Mr. Holmes. I have creatures here that the London Zoo would love to get their paws on. I'm constantly fighting them off."

He closed the window and reappeared at his front door. "Let's go meet Toby."

"I hadn't said a word yet. Wiggins had done all the talking. I don't know what or whom I was about to meet. Sherman was clearly an eccentric and my confidence in Toby's capabilities was not particularly high in spite of Wiggins' enthusiasm."

"#7 Pinchin Lane had seen far better days. It had no human occupants at the moment and Toby and his family occupied the lower level. Sherman and Wiggins walked in and amid the yelps of the puppies and the concerned look of their mother whose name I found out was Celeste, we made our way to the 'dog of the moment'."

"The dog ignored me and walked over to Sherman and Wiggins waiting to be stroked. Wiggins gave him a bone he had kept in reserve and Toby dragged it over and laid it in front of Celeste. She in turn bit off pieces of meat and presented them to the puppies. A scene of canine domesticity."

"I turned to Wiggins and said, "I am impressed with the care and affection he has for his family but, as yet I have no evidence that he can assist in any of my detection requirements."

"We're prepared for that, Mr. 'Olmes. The lads and I have come up with a test to prove Toby's habilities. Mrs. 'Udson gave us one of your scarves. Now, you take a short cab ride somewhere here in Lambeth. Don't tell us where. We'll wait here for ten minutes and then we'll see if Toby can find yer."

"I shrugged. Mr. Sherman looked noncommittal. In #7, Celeste and the puppies were working their way through the bone. I agreed and Wiggins shouted down a growler whose driver wouldn't stop until he saw there was one gentleman, me, in the group."

"I arrived at the Lambeth Palace and took a seat on a park bench. Back at Pinchin Lane Wiggins put the scarf under Toby's nose. "Here, Toby, Good Boy. Go find Mr. 'Olmes!"

Wiggins later told me "He whined and then sniffed the air. The odors in the street were enough to make yer sick. How he could pick out your smell were a mystery to me. Suddenly, he lurched forward and headed down the lane in a hurry. The lads and I followed. Sherman said he was too old to go chasing around Lambeth and stayed back."

"Suffice it to say, Miss Spencer, that within twenty minutes, I had a slobbering dog with his front paws on my lap in the Palace Park. I hailed another cab whose driver was not pleased with the prospect of three ragamuffins and a dog entering his vehicle. His horse seemed fascinated. We returned to Pinchin Lane where Sherman was watching from his window. I asked the cabbie to wait as we stepped down into the street. Toby ran to Sherman, wagging his tail and then back to Wiggins, fully expecting another delicious bone, which the Irregular's chief produced from a sack he had been carrying. The dog took it in his mouth and headed back to #7."

"I looked at the old man and said, 'Mr. Sherman! Toby is clearly an exceptional dog. I will make you a proposition. I will provide a weekly stipend of five shillings for him and his family provided I may have his services on demand.'"

"Sherman readily agreed. Wiggins and his cohorts were wearing silly grins as I handed each one of them a half sovereign. It was well worth it as subsequent history would prove. How do you like the mead?"

"It's my first taste of the liquor. It's quite delicious. Thank you!"

"This is the semi-sweet variety. I shall add a bottle to your jar of honey. Now, is there more you would like to know about my canine sleuth?"

"Oh yes! This is fascinating. Where did the painting come from?"

"It was a gift from Watson. I should say 'the Watsons.' Since you are familiar with his narrative called *The Sign of the Four*, you will remember that during that adventure he first met Mary Morstan who was to become his wife. They both felt that Toby played an important part in bringing about their eventual marriage. In fact, he was a guest at their nuptial dinner. Sherman had even given him a bath. They had this painting prepared and they presented it to me as a sort of wedding gift in reverse. I think it was to assuage the guilt Watson felt at our separation. We still kept up our relationship and engaged in some cases together, but it was not quite the same. Don't misunderstand. Miss Morstan was a lovely woman and I truly liked her. Her untimely passing was a major blow to Watson. I too, felt a great sadness. However, Watson and I never fully reestablished our partnership after her death. Anyway, the portrait of Toby is one of my treasured belongings. If you will wait here for just a moment."

He rose and headed off to what I assumed was his bedroom and closed the door. I took the opportunity to review my notes and prepare several more questions I wanted to ask him. I also finished the glass of mead. He returned carrying a stiff piece of paper and placed it in front of me. It was a colour print of Toby's portrait.

"Perhaps you will find this useful for your article. I had several copies made over time. More mead?"

I nodded. I must be careful. The alcohol was beginning to affect me. I was becoming increasingly and indeed pleasantly surprised at his solicitous generosity to me. It was a characteristic I was not prepared for. Given his reputation, I had anticipated a sourness bordering on hostility. I was still amazed that he had agreed to meet with me at all. I hoped I was not impressing him as yet another air-headed female reporter. I was trying my best to exude maturity, interest and intelligence. Since he had not ejected me from his presence, I hoped I was succeeding. I think Isadora Klein would approve. I must investigate that situation further. I certainly hoped my editor would approve.

He asked, "Do you mind if I smoke my pipe?"

"Certainly not!"

"Would you care for a cigarette?"

"I don't smoke, thank you."

He rose once again and returned to his bedroom, this time, no doubt to prepare his pipe. Meanwhile, I heard the clattering of dishes in what must have been the kitchen. Marion appeared, carrying a string bag. In it was large jar of golden honey and a substantial bottle of mead. "Mr. Holmes asked me to give this to you."

"Why, thank you, Marion that is most generous."

"You're a reporter for a magazine, Miss?"

"Yes, The Strand."

"That must be ever so interesting and exciting. I wish I could do something like that. It's pretty boring out here on the farm although serving Mr. Holmes is a fine thing. He is a wonderful gentleman and so skilled. He has those bees of his working full time. He supplies us all with great scads of honey and sometimes a little mead as well." She giggled. "He writes too, you know. Mostly about bees. I understand he was a great detective."

"He still is, Marion. I'm interviewing him for an article about great detectives. He is no doubt the greatest."

She looked down at the picture I had before me and then at the portrait on the wall. "Is he tellin' you about Toby?"

"Yes, he is."

"I love doggies. I wish I had known Toby."

"So do I."

The door to his bedroom opened and Holmes returned, preceded by a cloud of smoke. Marion curtseyed and returned to the kitchen.

"I hope this doesn't annoy you. It certainly did Toby as well as Watson and Mrs. Hudson. The dog used to sneeze when I had my pipe in full fire. But it never impaired his sense of smell. He was a true virtuoso. Do you like dogs, Miss Spencer?"

"I adore them. I had a spaniel when I was a little girl. Mr. Chips! He was the sweetest, funniest animal. I cried for weeks when he died."

"It seems Mother Nature has her priorities all wrong. The best creatures seem to have the shortest life spans while the foulest live far too long." He frowned and then asked, "Do you have a dog now?"

"Unfortunately, no! Isadora has an unnatural fear of animals. An admirer once gave her a kitten and, in an hour, she had given it away."

Once again, that enigmatic smile crossed his face. "I once thought about taking Toby in at Baker Street but that would have involved bringing his mate Celeste and their two puppies. Mrs. Hudson would never have stood for that. Besides, I think they were happy at Pinchin Lane and Mr. Sherman would probably have been upset."

"I have since thought about getting a hound, but I think I will content myself with my Anthophilic associates. Bees are wonderful creatures. Socially organized, energetic and highly productive. I have written several small monographs on the subject. I will give you one to take with you. But let us return to the subject at hand, Toby. What more can I tell you?"

"Another adventure or two, if you please."

"Are you familiar with opium dens, Miss Spencer?"

"Certainly not. Oh, I know what they are, but I have never been a habituée."

"I suspected as much. As you probably know from Watson's writings, I have occasionally used cocaine to enliven my ennui and soothe my spirits. I have also experimented with opium on several occasions at a Limehouse emporium run by a very interesting Chinese, Ah Sing. It was he who triggered a rather strange process eventually involving Toby, Watson, Scotland Yard, and me. He, of course, knew who I was and approached me at my Baker Street residence. After Billy, our page, presented his card, I told him to bring Ah Sing up. Watson was not there at the time. He was a rather diminutive man with Oriental features and a short pigtail dressed in English tweeds, an extraordinary combination. I bade him welcome and invited him to be seated. 'What may I do for you, sir?'"

He replied in unaccented Mayfair English. "Mr. Holmes, your fame as a consulting detective precedes you and I have need of such a skilled practitioner."

"Your fame precedes you as well, Ah Sing. I have been to your establishment."

"Establishments, Mr. Holmes. I have several but it is my Limehouse enterprise about which I wish your assistance. It will come as no surprise that there is a substantial feeling of prejudice in London, indeed in England, against members of my race. I, for one, am constantly accused of engaging in unlawful activities such as kidnapping, white slavery, shanghaiing sailors and the like. I have done none of these things."

"British law is vague about the legality of opium sale and use but this has not stopped my persecutors. Primary among them is Bishop Charles Montague, a member of the parliamentary Lords Spiritual. He has been promoting a law to make opium use illegal. Now, however, a new problem has arisen. His daughter has disappeared, and he has accused me of taking revenge against him by spiriting her away. This is sheer nonsense, but it will only subside when she is found and restored to him. Thus far, the Police have refused to act citing lack of evidence. I want you to find her."

"If I take you on as a formal client, I doubt I will get much cooperation from His Lordship. Let me contact Scotland Yard and through them approach the Bishop with an offer to help find his daughter. I do not think he will refuse. He will no doubt accuse you, but I will attempt to convince him that our first priority is locating and restoring the girl. What is her name?"

"Lucinda. She is seventeen. I subscribe to your strategy, Mr. Holmes and I shall be most grateful for your efforts and hopefully, success. Thank you."

"I contacted Gregson at the Yard and the two of us called on Bishop Montague, a recent widower. It was as I surmised. He was full of holy bluster, calling for the fires of Hell to envelop Ah Sing. After we calmed him and were given a picture of the young lady, we asked to see her maid. At first, she was reluctant to share any information with us, but it turned out Lucinda had been seeing a young man against her father's wishes. This gave us a prime strategy. *Cherchez l'homme!*"

"His name was Geoffrey Wright, a law clerk and therefore a commoner, unfit for a Bishop's daughter, and it seemed that he too had disappeared. She had departed with a healthy supply of baggage, hardly a kidnapping scenario. We asked the maid for several articles of Lucinda's remaining clothing with the promise of returning them shortly. Puzzled, she complied. We sought Geoffrey Wright's place of employment and made a similar request. He had left behind a scarf. We were now ready to seek out the runaways. All that was needed was our genius dog, Toby."

"This was to be a first for him. We were going to ask him to follow two different scents at the same time. We were not sure he could do it. Wright had been reluctant to cut his ties with his employer so he pled an illness in his family and gave a post office address where he could be reached. Gregson, using the power of Scotland Yard, ferreted out his actual forwarding address and we arrived at a block of rowhouses in Chelsea, one of which contained our targets. The house in this upper-class district was no doubt being paid for by the Bishop's daughter."

"I passed the clothing to Toby who at first seemed confused but then settled down and paced back and forth until the front door opened to the house in question. The dog raced up the steps, bowling over a maid who was coming out with her marketing basket. He shot past her up a staircase with Gregson, Watson and I in hot pursuit. He barked and scratched at the door of a second-floor apartment. A frightened young woman opened the door a crack, screamed,

'Geoffrey!!' and attempted to close it again. The dog was having none of it. He had found his runaways."

"I am not sure what became of the two of them. I can't imagine the Bishop being particularly forgiving when he had to admit that Ah Sing was not responsible for his daughter's disappearance. It certainly did not discourage him from pushing anti-opium legislation. He did send a substantial cheque to my attention in thanks for bringing Lucinda back. A few days later a large bag of gold sovereigns arrived at my door with a Chinese inscription of gratitude. I shared both with Mr. Sherman stipulating a large share for Toby, his mate and his pups."

"You mentioned that in addition to his remarkable sense of smell, Toby was also a highly intelligent animal. Can you elucidate on that?"

"Oh indeed! I shall give you a cogent example. You have heard of my brother Mycroft? He is in some respects, a highly sophisticated hermit. He seldom moves outside of a closed perimeter bound by his apartment in Pall Mall, the Diogenes Club and his offices in Whitehall. His function within the government is deliberately not well articulated. Some say he *is* the government. Regardless, he occasionally calls on my assistance in pursuing an issue since he himself is notoriously lethargic."

"One such event involved a set of plans for a new field cannon. The documents themselves seemed to be complete and intact but the minister from the War Office who was in charge of their development and safekeeping had gone missing. Mycroft summoned me and much to his chagrin, I brought Toby. We met in his office since the Diogenes Club of which he is co-founder, will not countenance animals of any kind. His own apartment was also considered taboo to canines. Several members of the War Office and Munitions

Staffs, the Security Service and Scotland Yard were also in attendance."

"By this time, my use of the dog had created an atmosphere of ridicule from some members of the Police. 'Sherlock Holmes has taken leave of his professional senses.' Nevertheless, I took the task in hand. I asked the minister's assistant to provide me with any article of clothing that worthy may have left behind in his office. He brought in a hat and scarf. I presented these to Toby for his consideration and then said, "Toby, search!" Instead of heading for the door, he ran over to Mycroft's desk and began sniffing a stack of documents neatly piled near the edge."

"Here, here, dog. Don't touch those. Sherlock, those are the secret papers for the new weapon. Keep him away from them."

"Instead I lifted the stack and put each one in front of Toby's nose. He smelled one after the other, barked and wagged his tail. He had scored a hit. Except for one. The plans themselves. He turned his head, whined and seemed disinterested. No amount of coaxing could convince him to recognize the scent on the plans even though they had been found in the minister's safe. I turned and said, 'Gentlemen, I believe we have a deeper problem on our hands than a missing bureaucrat. These plans are forgeries substituted for the originals by a person or persons with access to the minister's safe.'"

"At that point, the minister's assistant began to sidle toward the door. He got no further than Inspector Gregson who seized him from behind and put on a pair of cuffs. It turned out that he had been paid by a foreign government to effect the switch and also to drug the minister who was found bound and gagged in a cellar under the War Office. His finder was Toby."

"Was Toby declared a hero?" I asked.

"Certainly not. That would have required admission on their part that a dog was smarter than they were. Mycroft and I didn't speak for several months."

"What other wonders did Toby perform? You make him sound almost infallible."

"Oh, he was hardly that. Like myself, he had his failures. I remember sharing his howls of frustration sitting on a platform at Paddington station as a train pulled out, carrying a particularly elusive thief we had been pursuing. Scotland Yard ultimately tracked him down but that gave little satisfaction to the dog or me."

"Speaking of elusive, Toby had a unique talent for avoiding detection or capture. Once, Gregson, Watson, Toby and I were engaged in surveillance of an estate belonging to a well-known but as yet unimprisoned embezzler and blackmailer. We were hoping to lure him out of his house so we could gain access to his personal files. We sent Toby up to the building entrance where he set up a deafening howling, barking and general disturbance. The butler and gamekeeper rushed out of the door and set off after the dog. They chased him into the stables and slammed the doors on him. The owner came out and said, 'Leave the dog. I'll deal with him later. Or maybe the horses will. Let's find out who set him off and don't hesitate to shoot them. Follow me.'"

"Watson, armed with his service revolver, Gregson with the truncheon he still kept from his patrol days and I with an improvised cosh, waited silently for our would-be assassins. As they hastened up the driveway, Watson stepped from behind a tree and fired at the gamekeeper's knee. As he fell over. Gregson seized the owner, struck his shotgun from his arms and cuffed him. The butler quietly surrendered his weapon and gave up. While the Scotland Yard Inspector was issuing charges of attempted murder against the trio, I ran back toward the stables to rescue our canine companion. I had moved only a few yards when I felt a bump and a wet tongue on my face. Toby!! The stable doors were still shut. and the horses were raising a racket but the dog had somehow escaped and was running back to assist. We never did find out how he had gotten back out. Some things he never shared.

"If it is not too sensitive a subject, could you share with me and my readers how Toby died?"

Holmes paused for a moment and I feared he was going to refuse my request. Then he sighed, "Toby passed on like the brave and wonderful animal that he was. He was defending me."

I thought I detected a catch in his voice. He shook his head. "It happened in Park Lane of all places. I had received a call from Gregson to assist in what looked like a violent kidnapping or worse. You may remember the case of Lady Chesterfield - a dowager who lived with her nephew in an opulent, multi-storey town house. She had gone missing or so the servants had reported. The nephew was out of town at the time, supposedly at a reunion in Oxford."

"Several of the rooms including the lady's bedroom were in serious disarray and according to her maid, more than a few of her most valuable pieces of jewelry were gone. She had just returned from a house party and had not yet put them away. She told the maid she was exhausted, and her services would not be required for the rest of the evening."

"About one AM, the butler thought he heard a series of noises and a scream. He got up, ran into the hall and saw the door to the lady's suite was open. There were signs of a struggle, but her ladyship was gone. The lady's maid and a footman immediately started a search while the butler summoned Scotland Yard. Very early next morning, Inspector Gregson called and asked for my assistance. Given the nature of the supposed crime, I decided to call Watson and had

Wiggins bring over Toby. If there was a missing person, the dog was an expert."

"Our opening supposition was that a burglar had been surprised by Lady Chesterfield and he attacked her. But if so, was she dead? Where was the body? Toby found her under a pile of coal in the basement, shot twice."

"The nephew had returned and was suitably upset. He said he had just gotten back from Oxford. A call to the Inn where the event had taken place confirmed that he had not registered or signed in for the festivities. The inspector asked him where he had really been, and he had no satisfactory answer. He broke from the room and headed up the stairs with all of us in pursuit. He pushed a large urn down on us just missing Watson. I rushed up toward him. Toby was ahead of me. Gregson had taken up the rear. The sniveling nephew stood on a landing at the head of the staircase, shouting and waving a pistol. He fired one shot at me and missed but that was enough for Toby. He sprung at the man and the two of them fell through a large floor-to-ceiling plate glass window into the courtyard two stories below. When we reached them, both of them were dead."

Sherlock Holmes paused and shook his head. "Watson found a large blanket and we wrapped the dog's body in it. We left the culprit's body for Scotland Yard to handle. It seems he had been gambling, lost heavily and set about stealing his aunt's jewelry to pay off his debts.' Gregson gave us one of the police wagons to take Toby home."

"When we reached Mr. Sherman's home, he wiped aside his tears and taking the dog's body carried it to #7 where he laid it in front of Celeste. She sniffed at it, whined and laid down next to it. The puppies scampered around puzzled that their sire was not responding. Later in the morning, Wiggins had performed one of those magic tricks that only he could carry off and gathered all the Irregulars in the small yard behind #7. Each took turns digging the grave for their former companion. Watson, Mr. Sherman and I joined in. We gently placed his body in the hole and covered it up. Celeste laid down next to the grave and whimpered. The puppies crawled on top of her. One of the urchins had managed to liberate some flowers and laid them on the grave. No one said anything. No eulogies seemed appropriate. We all just looked and finally turned away. When we had completed the burial, I took Mr. Sherman aside and assured him of my continued support for Celeste and the puppies. He started to cry again."

"Celeste died two months later. She was an older dog, probably older than Toby. Sherman, the Irregulars and I buried her next to him. I arranged to have the puppies adopted. A part of my life had come to an end."

Just then, Marion stuck her head in the door and said, "Excuse me, Mr. Holmes. Miss, Joel is here to take you to the station. I nodded my head. A tear had formed in the corner of my eye.

"Thank you so much, Mr. Holmes. It was far more than I had a right to expect."

"It was my pleasure, Miss Spencer. Do have a safe journey home. I look forward to seeing your article. I hope your editor will give it the fine treatment I'm sure it will deserve."

I picked up my notes, his monograph on bees and the picture of Toby and put them in my case. I safely stowed the honey and mead and lifted the string bag. I'm not sure what came over me, probably mead-induced, but I stood on tip toe and kissed his cheek. He didn't flinch or react. He simply held out his hand and shook mine. On the way back on the train, I tried to organize my thoughts and my notes but all I kept doing was looking at the colour print of an ungainly, long-haired, lop-eared canine, breed indeterminate, brown and white.

*****

After several days of soul searching, writing and re-writing, I submitted my story to my editor. To my surprise and relief, he accepted it enthusiastically. It ran for three-pages in the front of the issue complete with Toby's picture which now sits framed on my desk. I didn't show the article to Isadora. She wouldn't have appreciated it. I did, however, send several copies to South Downs, Sussex. Two weeks later, I received another wire. This time it said, "Congratulations and thank you for the copies of your article. S.H."

I had titled the piece — *Sherlock Holmes and the Wet-Nosed Irregular.*

The Stanforth Mystery
or
The Adventure of the Felonious Fiancé

by Paul Hiscock

The man in the corner seemed most irritable when Miss Polly Burton of the *Evening Observer* arrived at the A.B.C. Shop that Saturday afternoon. His brow was furrowed behind his bone-rimmed spectacles and, as she entered, he slammed a magazine down on the marble-topped table in obvious disgust. As he saw her approaching, he picked it up once more and handed it to her.

"Have you seen this ridiculous concoction?" he asked.

Polly took the proffered publication and saw that the cover featured a familiar illustration of the street just around the corner from where they sat.

"What is wrong with the *Strand Magazine*?" she asked. "I find it quite entertaining."

"Some of the puzzles are mildly distracting. Indeed, I have been known to send them a few small contributions of my own devising. However, it is the first article in this issue to which I take exception."

Polly opened the magazine and saw that he was referring to the latest account by Doctor John Watson of his adventures with that most famous of detectives, Mr. Sherlock Holmes.

*****

The Adventure of the Felonious Fiancé

by Doctor John Watson

I was preparing to leave my practice after a busy day and was looking forward to a quiet supper at home when I received a message from Sherlock Holmes requesting that, if I could spare the time, I should join him at a house in Arlington Street as soon as possible. The prospect of a new adventure caused me to put aside all thoughts of food and comfort and I hurried to the address I had been given immediately.

It had started snowing, as it had intermittently for the past few days. I found it difficult to hail a cab, and once I succeeded, the journey down Bond Street was exceptionally slow. I was therefore surprised to find that Holmes was waiting for me outside the house.

"Watson," he exclaimed, "I was about to give up hope. I imagine our client will be getting anxious."

Then, without further comment or explanation as to why we were there, he walked up the steps and rapped sharply on the door three times.

The reception we received was less than effusive. The butler barely opened the door and demanded what business we had there through the gap.

"I am Mr. Sherlock Holmes and this is my colleague Doctor Watson. Miss Stanforth requested that we call upon her."

The butler immediately opened the door fully.

"My humble apologies, gentlemen, for the uncivil welcome. I have been fending off unwanted intrusions by the press and other gawkers all day and I feared that you were more of the same, come to revel in the misfortunes of the household."

*****

"The murder of Sir Maurice Stanforth," said Polly. "I remember this case, but I am surprised it interests you. The police solved it quite quickly, didn't they?"

"The police made a promising start," said the man in the corner, "but their blind trust in the deductive prowess of Sherlock Holmes cut short any true investigation."

While she had been reading, he had taken out the piece of string that he habitually fiddled with and tied his first knot.

"No, despite what Doctor Watson may claim in his account, the Stanforth case should be included in the annals of unsolved crimes." Then he chuckled softly, his customary good humour clearly restored. "At least, those unsolved by the great detectives of London, because the full solution is quite evident to me."

Polly waited for him to say more about the case, but he just gestured towards the magazine and so she continued reading.

*****

The butler ushered us inside and out of the snow, then escorted us to the drawing room where a young woman awaited us. I cannot describe her appearance in great detail as she was dressed in mourning black, including a veil that concealed her face. However, her attire proved no obstacle to Holmes's deductive skills.

"Miss Stanforth, our deepest condolences upon the death of your uncle."

The woman nodded in response and raised a handkerchief to her eye, but said nothing.

"It has been two days," I said. "Have the police not yet caught the blaggard responsible?"

Like every newspaper reader in London, I knew that Sir Maurice Stanforth had interrupted a burglar in the night and had been murdered to facilitate the criminal's escape. Sir Maurice was a well known figure in London society, and his murder had received extensive coverage because many notable figures, including a minor member of the royal family, had been at his house for dinner just hours before his death.

Miss Stanforth started sobbing.

"I believe, Watson, that the case has been solved to the satisfaction of the police. You must have noticed that they are no longer present, not even a constable at the door. Even the most dull-witted inspector would not leave such a high profile crime scene unattended unless he was certain that he had all the evidence necessary to make his case. However, Miss Stanforth, you show none of the signs of relief that might be expected at the apprehension of the man who invaded your home and murdered your uncle. Indeed, it is clear from your demeanour that these developments have caused you additional distress. The obvious conclusion is that the police have not arrested a stranger, but someone known to you, who you care about deeply. Finally, although I do not believe any announcement of your impending nuptials has been made, I note that you are wearing an engagement ring on the third finger of your left hand. I posit that you have *chosen to wear it now as a gesture of support for the man you love, because he is the man who now stands accused."*

"Mr. Holmes," she said. "You are correct in every respect. I beg you, please help us."

*****

Polly paused to examine an illustration of the scene, which depicted Miss Stanforth in her mourning clothes, just as Doctor Watson described.

"You are wondering how Mr. Holmes makes such amazing deductions from the appearance of his clients," the man in the corner said quietly, seemingly reading her mind with his customary accuracy.

"It is a simple parlour trick that would be more appropriately employed in one of the music halls near here. I could tell you a dozen trivial facts about every person in this room, but it would be a waste of my talents and your time. Besides, if you are trying to replicate his observations, you will not get very far with Mr. Paget's crude illustrations."

He took out his pocket book and, once he had moved his glass of milk to one side, took out a photograph and pushed it across the table to Polly.

"That is Miss Emilia Stanforth," he said.

Polly thought she could be best described as plain, not nearly as pretty as she had previously imagined from the reports in the society pages. However, the diamond pendant and matching earrings that she wore were not plain — certainly enough to make a potential suitor look twice.

"And here is the whole family in question," said the man in the corner, taking out another photograph. This one depicted Miss Stanforth surrounded by three men.

"In the middle is the unfortunate Sir Maurice and to either side his sons, Edward and Henry."

All three men were tall and well built, with very similar looks. However, the one on the left, Henry, had been caught with a sour expression on his face that spoiled the photograph slightly. Emilia, by comparison, was small and the picture made her look more delicate, almost doll-like.

"Do you wish to make any deductions?"

"I wouldn't know where to start," said Polly.

"Very wise. I have always found it best to listen to all the facts before jumping to conclusions."

*****

"Tell us everything that happened," said Holmes, "starting with the evening before your uncle died."

"Surely you know about the dinner already," said Miss Stanforth. "The newspapers reported on it extensively."

"I am inclined not to put too much trust in the accuracy of the press. Besides, they were most interested in Sir Maurice's guests, whilst I am more concerned with the activities of the household."

"Very well. I spent the afternoon in my room preparing for the dinner. The only person I saw was my maid, until Uncle Maurice summoned me to his study. Cousin Henry was leaving just as I arrived. He looked unhappy and said something unkind; I can't remember what it was now. I just remember being grateful that he chose not to pay more attention to me on that occasion."

Miss Stanton looked scared as she told us this, and I wondered what happened when her cousin chose to give her his full attention.

"Is your cousin here now?" I asked.

"No, he's at his club. He spends most of his time there. I doubt he will be home tonight, especially with his brother having come down from York for the inquest. Edward does not approve of Henry's lifestyle."

"Returning to the evening in question," said Holmes. "Your uncle summoned you before dinner. Was this out of the ordinary?"

"No, Mr. Holmes, it was part of his ritual before every social occasion. He would call me to his study, open his safe and take out his diamond necklace, which he would fasten around my neck. He would then look at me and every time he would say, 'You look so much like her.'"

"Who did he think you looked like?" I asked.

"His wife. The diamonds were hers, but she died before I came to live with him. I think he loved her very much."

She paused for a moment and wiped a tear from her eye before continuing.

"Uncle Maurice then escorted me to dinner. He would always wait until all the guests had arrived and then parade me into the room. I found it quite embarrassing, but it was a small price to pay for his kindness in caring for me."

I suspected that Miss Stanforth actually enjoyed the attention on these occasions, as she went on to relate the details of the dinner with much enthusiasm. Her recollections would be of great interest to the society gossips, and I must admit they fascinated me at the time. However, the private affairs of Sir Maurice's guests are unrelated to his murder and so I will not subject those innocent people to undue scrutiny by publishing their business here.

However, I realised that among the personages she had described, one person had been omitted.

"What about your fiancé?" I asked. "Was he not at the dinner?"

"No," said Miss Stanforth, "he was not invited. My uncle disapproved of James and would not approve the match. I asked him again after dinner that night, when I went to return the diamonds, but he refused me once more. I regret that I spoke to him quite harshly and that those were the last words I ever spoke to him."

Holmes had remained silent throughout her account, but now he asked, "When did your fiancé come to the house?"

Miss Stanforth looked at him in surprise. "How did you know he was there?" she asked.

"The police are, sadly, not very imaginative. I doubt they would have identified him as a suspect unless he was present around the time of the murder."

"You are, of course, right, Mr. Holmes. James was at the house that night. He was passing and noticed that a window had been broken. He came closer to look and heard a loud crash. Fearing for our safety, he entered the house to investigate. A few moments later, a man came running from my uncle's study and knocked him over."

"Did he recognise the man?" I asked.

"No, he was dressed in dark clothes and had a mask over his face."

"Did your fiancé not pursue this man?"

"No, by the time James regained his feet, he decided that the intruder would have already escaped through the broken window. He decided it was more important to check on us. That is how he came to be the one who found my uncle's body in the study. The rest of the household was roused by the commotion, and by the time I reached the study, there was already a crowd around the door.

"Hughes, the butler, took charge. He shooed away the other staff and fetched drinks for James, Henry, and myself to calm our nerves while we waited for the police in here.

Hughes also fetched a bandage so that I could dress James's wounds, as he had cut himself coming through the window."

"Did you know at that point that your necklace had been stolen?" asked Holmes.

"No, when the police asked if anything was missing, Hughes opened the safe. That was when we realised the jewellery was gone."

"And you are certain that they had been in there?"

"Yes, both Hughes and I watched Uncle Maurice lock them away after dinner. The thief must have made Uncle Maurice get them out before killing him."

"That is one possibility," said Holmes. "What did the police say?"

"Very little. They were mainly concerned with trying to catch the murderer before he got too far. I had thought it would be easy for them to track him in the snow, but they did not find his footprints by the window. He must have left by the door instead, but too many people had already passed that way and they could not pick up a trail."

"I still do not see why they have arrested your fiancé," I said.

"I am sure," said Holmes, "that the police realised that you lied to them. What sort of man would go for a walk at night in the snow? Only a man setting out with a purpose. He clearly planned to visit your house that night. Furthermore, he intended his visit to be clandestine in nature. Watson, did you see where the window had been broken when you arrived?"

I confessed that, being more concerned with getting out of the snow, I had not noticed it.

"Do not reprove yourself, Watson. You did not see it because it was not visible from the street where we met. I took the chance, while I waited for you to arrive, to survey the property and spotted where the pane had been boarded up, at the rear of the house. Miss Stanforth, if you want our help, you need to tell us the truth. Your fiancé always intended to creep into the house through one of the rear windows, did he not?"

"Yes, Mr. Holmes, it is true," she said and started sobbing, "but it was really the thief that broke the window, not him. He didn't need to because I had left the French doors unlocked. You see, we were planning to elope that night."

"You can see how this would look bad to the police," I said. "Why did you hide the truth?"

"It was selfish, but since my uncle was dead and could no longer object to our engagement, I hoped that we might marry after all. Admitting our thwarted plan would have just tarnished my reputation for no good reason."

"It was clumsy and has potentially caused you more trouble than admitting the truth immediately," said Holmes.

"I realise that now. I should have admitted it at the inquest this morning, but I gave my evidence before the officers and did not realise what they suspected until it was too late."

*****

"Were you at the inquest?" Polly asked the man in the corner.

"Naturally. You know that I make a point of attending the proceedings of any case that catches my interest."

He fiddled with his piece of string as he spoke, adding a new knot for each point of interest.

"It was evident from the outset that the story of the thief in the night was complete nonsense. Miss Stanforth told Mr. Holmes that they had not found any trail left by the murderer outside the window when he fled. What she failed to mention was that he had left no mark upon his arrival either. The only prints were those left by the fiancé, Mr. Clarke, when he arrived.

"Then there were his injuries. The officer's description of his wounds and the bloody marks on the glass did not tell us any more than the footprints and Mr. Clarke's own account. Yet the presence of blood makes a man look guilty, does it not? The jury certainly thought so. I could see it on their faces.

"How easy it was for them to conclude that when Mr. Clarke broke into the house he met, not with his fiancée but with her uncle. Then, when his request for Miss Stanforth's hand was refused once again, no prospect of getting hold of he murdered Sir Maurice in a fit of passion.

"Next there was the matter of the safe. What type of burglar closes and locks a safe once they have removed the contents? The murder was noisy and the household already disturbed. He would not have delayed to undertake such an unnecessary task before making his escape.

"The police realised this. They may not be capable of solving great mysteries, but they understand the minds of petty criminals well enough. The only reason to close the safe was to delay the discovery that the jewellery had been taken."

"They thought the necklace was still in the house," realised Polly.

"That is what they eventually decided. The inspector in charge, an officer named Newcomen, suggested that Mr. Clarke hid it in the first instance and then removed it from the house later. It was certainly possible for someone to have done this, since the police spent the whole night searching for the mysterious intruder. They did not conduct a search of the house until the middle of the morning, by which time it was far too late.

"The Inspector was clearly frustrated by this, but he seemed to think that the necklace would still be recovered and seal his case against Miss Stanforth's fiancé. So, after the coroner recorded a verdict of 'Wilful murder against some person or persons unknown', Newcomen immediately instructed his men to arrest Mr. Clarke."

"You never believed he was guilty though?"

"No, and neither did Sherlock Holmes."

Polly took this as her cue to return to Doctor Watson's account of the case and started reading once again.

*****

"It cannot be undone now," said Holmes, "and your fiancé would probably have come under suspicion anyway. If you would permit it, I would like to view the murder scene now."

"I will ask Hughes to let you in," said Miss Stanforth. "The room has been kept locked ever since that night."

*****

Hughes was apologetic when he opened the study door for us.

"I am sorry that you should see the room like this, gentlemen. The police told us not to touch anything, but it is in considerable disarray."

His definition of disarray and mine clearly differed wildly. Apart from the overturned chair and the blood on the floor, I could see very little out of place. Our rooms in Baker Street had regularly been in worse condition, much to the dismay of Mrs. Hudson.

"Sir Maurice was killed with a paperweight?" asked Holmes.

"That is correct, Mr. Holmes. A big old thing that he kept on his desk, but how do you know? The police took it away when they removed the body."

"You can see the indentation in the papers and the leather of the desk here," said Holmes. "It is a weapon of opportunity, which certainly supports that the intention was robbery, not murder."

"Sir Maurice never slept well," said Hughes. "He would often come down here to work in the night."

"Did you know he was in here that night?"

"No, I thought everyone was in bed until I heard the crash. You don't think that was the sound of him being murdered?"

Holmes looked around the room. "It might have been," he said, "but I suspect it was probably that."

He pointed to a large crystal decanter which had been knocked off its table in the corner of the room and smashed on the floor.

"That would certainly have made quite a racket," I said.

"Yes," replied Holmes, "but look closer. There are no signs of the struggle anywhere near it. Why did the thief go over there and make such a mess?"

He left the question hanging and returned to his interrogation of Hughes.

"Who was here when you reached the study that night?" Holmes asked.

"Just Mr. Clarke and Sir Maurice, of course, but he was already dead."

"Who arrived next?"

"I think it was the maid, Milly, then Miss Stanforth, then the rest of the household, but I'm not sure in what order. I do remember that Master Henry was the last to arrive. No doubt he was sleeping deeply after an evening at his club."

"Henry Stanforth spends a lot of time at his club then?" asked Holmes.

"Yes, sir."

It was clear that Hughes did not approve of the young man's activities and I could imagine why. The types of club frequented by young men like Henry Stanforth were notorious for drinking and gambling in excess.

"Is he lucky or unlucky at cards?" I asked.

"It is not for me to say, sir."

"Never mind unlucky," said a voice from the doorway. "He is damned foolish and wastes money like it means nothing. Father was too soft on him, but he will not find me so accommodating."

Holmes turned to face the newcomer. "You must be Mr. Edward Stanforth, his older brother."

"That is right, and I believe you are the famous Sherlock Holmes and Doctor Watson. I recognise you from your pictures in the Strand. What brings you to share in our tragedy?"

"Your cousin, Emilia, summoned us," said Holmes.

"To help Mr. Clarke, yes? I heard he had been arrested while I was with my lawyers. Of course, she believes he is innocent."

"Do you share her opinion?" asked Holmes.

"I am not sure. I barely know the man, although he seemed a decent sort. I was never sure why my father opposed their relationship. I think he just liked having a woman in the house again and wasn't ready to give her up.

Still, if he is a murderer, perhaps my father has been proved right, although he paid the price for it."

"Can you tell us anything more?" I asked.

"There's not much to say. I haven't lived here in years and was at home in York when the tragedy happened. I don't think I can be of any help to you. I'll pay your bill of course, however this turns out, but if you will excuse me now, I must go and check on my cousin."

Then he left, without waiting to hear if we had any other questions.

*****

When Polly turned the page, the man in the corner put down his string and took out his pocket book again. Polly put down the magazine and waited to hear what he had to say next.

"I suppose you are wondering about Henry Stanforth. His family might have been diplomatic about his excesses, but the society columns were far less discreet."

He took out some clippings and placed them on the table.

"You will see that Langdale Pike had quite a lot to say about him. Henry Stanforth was involved in a number of gambling disputes that became public, and no doubt many more that he managed to keep quiet. It is all quite salacious, but Pike's sources are impeccable and he is rarely incorrect.

"You will note that, in every instance, young Mr. Stanforth was on the losing side of the wager. It was quite obvious to me that he must have sizeable debts and men in such a position have often been known to resort to desperate measures."

The Stanforth Mystery or The Adventure of the Felonious Fiancé by Paul Hiscock

*****

"A fiancé murdering for love may be understood, if not forgiven," said Holmes, once we were outside in the snow and alone. "However, the truth of this case is far more unsavoury. I have no doubt that the police have arrested the wrong man, but persuading them of their mistake may prove difficult. It is certainly simpler to believe that Mr. Clarke simply lied about his encounter with the thief in the hallway."

"Holmes, you cannot be suggesting that there was a burglar in the house after all? Surely it would have been impossible for anyone to both sneak in and then escape again without leaving a trace in weather like this?"

"Of course not, Watson. It is obvious that our murderer never climbed through that window, but was present in the house the entire time."

*****

As Holmes predicted, Inspector Newcomen was loath to consider an alternative suspect, but he clearly feared the damage to his reputation if Holmes proved him to have been wrong. He became more eager when Holmes suggested that we might manage to recover the missing necklace. Finally, he magnanimously agreed to accompany us and keep an 'open mind' until we had confronted our suspect.

*****

The St. James's Club was not the type of establishment that I would normally frequent and neither were they eager to welcome us there. However, when the Inspector suggested that he might be inclined to open an enquiry into their activities, they acquiesced and let us meet with Henry Stanforth in the visitors' room.

When he arrived, he was clearly drunk, and it had made him belligerent.

"What do you want from me?" he said. "Whatever it is, you will be disappointed. I have no money left, and with my brother holding the purse-strings, no prospect of getting hold of any more."

"You can still give us the truth," said Holmes, "and, in doing so, save a young man's life."

"Why should I care about him? He has no money to pay my debts."

"If you will not confess to save a man's life, why not for the satisfaction of telling the Inspector here how cleverly you fooled him and his men? Or should I just tell him everything myself and deny you the satisfaction?"

Another man might still have tried to bluff his way out of such a predicament, but Henry Stanforth was both drunk and a poor gambler. He folded instantly in the face of Holmes's goading.

"I fooled you completely, didn't I, Inspector? You never suspected I was the masked burglar."

The Inspector bristled at this, but it was Holmes who responded.

"He detected your ruse with the window, although you might have succeeded with that if the snow had continued to fall that night. However, smashing the decanter was cleverer. You wanted to wake someone so that they could catch a glance of you in your disguise and testify that a stranger had indeed invaded the house. Then, instead of fleeing the building, as everyone was meant to suppose, you simply changed your clothes ready to join the rest of the household in investigating the disturbance."

"But why did you do it?" I asked. "By all accounts you had a comfortable life with Sir Maurice, but by your own admission, his death has left you destitute?"

"It was never meant to be murder. I only meant to steal a little to settle some bills with the type of gentlemen who do not like to be told 'no'. But then father stumbled in, and of course, close up, he saw straight through my disguise. He would have turned me in, or worse cut me off, so I really didn't have a choice."

I still could not understand how a man, no matter how drunk, could confess to murder so easily, but Inspector Newcomen was quick to seize upon it, no doubt already imagining the plaudits he would receive for his fine detective work.

"If you will come with me, sir, I believe we should discuss this further at the station."

"Just let me get my hat. After all, I am not some commoner and there are certain standards that a gentleman must maintain."

He did not wait for a response, but leapt up and rushed out of the room.

The Inspector and I were dumbfounded, but Holmes was horrified.

"Quick, man," he shouted at the Inspector. "Do you not comprehend what he intends?"

Holmes leapt out of his chair and set off in pursuit, but he was too late. Even as he opened the door to the visitors' room, we heard the shot of a pistol.

We followed Holmes out into the hall and there we found the body of Mr. Henry Stanforth. In his hand he held an antique duelling pistol and there was a gaping wound in the side of his head.

"Where do you think he acquired the gun?" I asked as I looked around the hall.

"He had obviously planned this already," said Holmes. "No doubt it was his cowardly way of escaping his debts. We just gave him the final push to go through with it."

"Never mind the gun," said Inspector Newcomen, who was obviously quite distraught. "What happened to the necklace?"

"I doubt we will ever know," said Holmes. It was almost certainly used to pay off one of his creditors, but whoever has it will never be foolish enough to reveal it now."

*****

Polly closed the magazine and laid it down on the table.

"It would have been better if the murderer had stood trial," she said, "but his death is a justice of sorts."

"He was a fool. There was no evidence against him, just a lot of theorising and guess work. He was blinded by Sherlock Holmes's reputation, as so many are. Had he held his ground, he could almost certainly have got away with it."

"Either way, it is not much of a mystery. Mr. Holmes had the case all solved."

The man in the corner stared at her over his glasses with his watery blue eyes.

"No mystery, you say. What about the diamond necklace? Where is that now?"

"I admit that is a small mystery, but hardly a great failing on the part of Mr. Holmes."

"So, like everyone else, you have fallen for Doctor Watson's account. No, my dear. Mr. Holmes was simply wrong. Henry Stanforth never had the necklace at all."

He started to unravel the knots that he had meticulously tied in his piece of string.

"Firstly, there is the matter of the locked safe. We are agreed that it was closed to delay detection of the theft, but that makes no sense. Henry Stanforth's plan was to make sure everyone realised a burglary had taken place. Closing the safe after removing the necklace just served to undermine his own efforts.

"Secondly, there is the matter of his debts. Clearly when he devised his plan, he thought that the three diamonds in the necklace would be enough to keep his creditors at bay for a while. Looking at them, you can see why."

He pushed the family portrait back towards her.

"You can see Miss Stanforth wearing it in this photograph. It is an impressive piece and certainly very valuable. Yet when Sherlock Holmes confronted Henry Stanforth it seemed that his debts were greater than ever.

"The conclusion is obvious. There is one person who had the means, motive and opportunity to commit this crime, Miss Emilia Stanforth herself. She told Sherlock Holmes that she was planning to elope that night. Of course, she would have wanted some way to finance her new life with Mr. Clarke. We know that she watched her uncle open the safe to remove and replace the necklace every time that he held a dinner party. It would have been simple for her to memorise the combination to the lock.

"No, the necklace was not taken when Sir Maurice was murdered at all. She had already removed it from the safe and hidden it hours before."

"Why didn't she just produce it when her fiancé was accused then?" asked Polly.

"Do you think that would have done any good? The police would have simply concluded that they were in league with one another and sent Mr. Clarke to the gallows even faster."

"It is a good theory," Polly said, "but like Mr. Holmes's deductions, it is just a theory, and unlike her drunken cousin, I do not imagine Miss Stanforth will be confessing to her crime."

The man in the corner smiled and untied the last knot in his piece of string.

"She does not need to confess. The evidence is there for all to see."

He pushed the original portrait of Miss Stanforth back across the marble table.

"I will admit I slightly misled you. This is not a photograph of Miss Stanforth. Rather it is of Mrs. Emilia Clarke, together with her new husband, Mr. James Clarke."

He picked up the picture and unfolded the paper to reveal a man in the other half of the image.

"It was a risk to reset the diamonds into a pendant and earrings. If it had been me, I would have disposed of the whole thing, but they had sentimental value to her and, once her cousin had approved the match, there was no need for her to elope and sell them."

"Are you going to tell Mr. Holmes that he was wrong?" Polly asked.

The man in the corner picked up his papers and folded them back into his pocket-book.

"You know my position on that. Yet, in this one instance, I did consider revealing the truth and exposing Sherlock Holmes's failure."

He savoured that thought for a moment, before putting his pocket-book and piece of string away, and standing up to leave.

"I was tempted," he said, "but that would not have been fair to Mrs. Clarke. She deserves to enjoy her victory. She managed to deceive the great detective or, just possibly, she appealed to his sense of protectiveness in order to manipulate him into covering up her crime. Either way, it is an impressive feat, and I commend her for it."

The Inner Temple Intruder

by David Marcum

Holmes had lost interest in the conversation some minutes before, as a new thought occurred to him. He was sitting at his chemical table in the corner, hunched over a fifteenth-century palimpsest, and delicately brushing some clear liquid across one of the words in the ancient text, hoping for some clue as to which direction that he should next carry out his investigation.

He wasn't in pursuit of some criminal. Rather, he was partaking in his own peculiar form of relaxation, in which he found various esoteric topics to study, some puzzle of history or chemistry, with the same intensity that he brought to his professional pursuits. In our early days in Baker Street, when funds were more limited, he would often select some abstract chemical question, working through a series of sequential experiments, either to reproduce a long-established principle, or to steer off in some new direction of his own choosing. He would sit there for days, barely thinking to eat or drink, nodding occasionally and sometimes grumbling, and always making meticulous notes in a small book in which he carefully recorded his experiments.

"We must be able to reproduce it, Watson," he'd explained once. "As the lawyers say: If it isn't in writing, it doesn't exist. When a question of chemistry enters the realm of my investigations, what I'm able to show through my experiments becomes evidence, and it does no one any good for me to simply say that such-and-such occurred without reproducible proof."

Often to me this was no more than a beaker shifting from dark to clear, or litmus paper turning either blue or red, but he would be pleased, possibly telling me that a man's life hung on what he had just showed me. As a doctor, I'd had my share of the study of chemistry, but in many of Holmes's cases, I'd simply have to accept his word on the matter. Fortunately for a great many falsely accused men and women who had been proven innocent by his efforts, and also for those victims who required and received justice, his word had become widely respected and accepted.

But it wasn't only chemistry which he found to distract his ever-racing mind. In a practice that I believe began during those years when he lived beside the British Museum, when time was more plentiful than clients, he would pick a subject and immerse himself in it. Once, not long after we had met and agreed to share rooms, he'd made reference to not being aware that the earth circled the sun — and in fact he professed to be indifferent to the fact. "If we went round the moon," he'd cried, "it would not make a pennyworth of difference to me or to my work!" However, I soon realized that this hyperbolic statement was more to make a point than true gospel. Along those lines, in that same conversation he had likened his mind to a "brain-attic", stating that "the skilful workman is very careful indeed as to what he takes into his brain-attic. He will have nothing but the tools which may help him in doing his work, but of these he has a large assortment, and all in the most perfect order. It is a mistake to think that that little room has elastic walls and can distend to any extent. Depend upon it, there comes a time when for every addition of knowledge you forget something that you knew before. It is of the highest importance, therefore, not to have useless facts elbowing out the useful ones."

At the time of that conversation in early 1881, I was still in a raw and uncertain state, recovering from my wounds at Maiwand, little more than half-a-year before, and wondering whether the fine Baker Street rooms in which I'd found myself were worth it, considering that I was living with someone who could argue such foolishness. Soon after, I'd even made a list of Holmes's limits, as I weighed the balance of staying or finding new rooms — and with it a new and more reasonable flatmate. However, as I came to know Holmes better, I realized that he was given to statements such as those when in a certain mood, almost intending to provoke some sort of dynamic conversation — and dare I say, he also chose to be confrontational, in order to bleed off some of his nervous tension.

Over the years, I'd seen him plunge into any number of researches in order to avoid those black moods which might leave him in the dumps without opening his mouth for days on end. It had been a successful course of treatment, as he had learned to find a way to keep his mind occupied when not involved in clients' business. These distractions had included researches into miracle plays and mediæval pottery, Buddhism of Ceylon and warships of the future, bees and violins, tobacco ash and Cotard's Delusion. Later in that year of 1895, he would become interested in the Polyphonic Motets of Lassus. But right now, on the morning of which I speak, he was consumed with researches into early English Charters.

The previous November, he'd come across a palimpsest in a junk shop in Portsmouth Street, and simply for the exercise he'd bought it and attempted to learn all that he could from it. His original examination had revealed nothing more exciting than an Abbey's accounts dating from the second half of the fifteenth century. But he kept at it here and there, and gradually some reference within it had awakened his now-great interest in Charters. He was quite busy professionally by then, so his research was never allowed to become terribly time-consuming — and yet, he would always find a few spare minutes. That's what surprised me when he leaned back just then, stretched, and stated, "I have no choice. The answer lies in Oxford."

I glanced over at our visitor to see his reaction to this statement, which had nothing to do with the conversation that we'd been carrying on while Holmes was immersed in his studies. However, young Thorndyke had known Holmes for far too long to be surprised.

The young doctor had dropped by after lunch in order to learn what had happened following the arrest the previous day of The Kinlochard Strangler. Holmes's examination of the hotel records in that remote region had found a common link with a commercial traveler who stayed there during the time of each killing, although he'd always checked out and was seen to depart several days before the murders, previously removing him from suspicion. Holmes had proven that the man spent the time after he left the hotel camping nearby while stalking his next victims. Then he would hike overland to catch a train elsewhere, returning to his cozy London home and his unsuspecting wife until the urge to kill again overtook him. I doubt that I'll ever meet such a cold killer as was revealed when Gerald Pateley was confronted and so masterfully unmasked.

John Thorndyke had listened avidly as I related the details of the case, as was his way. He'd always been a sponge for knowledge. He had taken his medical degree the year before, but then found himself at loose ends. He began his residency at St. Margaret's Hospital, and like so many young doctors, he also accepted work as a *locum tenens* on a regular basis, gaining valuable experience. Yet at the same time, he appeared to feel a certain amount of frustration as he watched as the months slipped by without something more meaningful occurring to advance and secure his future. In many ways, Thorndyke was like Holmes — his mind was always hungry for knowledge. Now approaching his twenty-fifth birthday, he'd found a comfortable routine between his residency, his *locum* duties, and occasionally assisting in the occasional investigation, as he had done when he was younger, before Holmes and I took him under our collective wings to shepherd him toward an education and a better future.

He was still always enthusiastic and willing to assist in any of Holmes's cases when called, and he'd been invaluable in the capture of Pateley. The man's hidden madness had been of great clinical interest to Thorndyke, and he'd asked some very elucidating questions when joining us in the interview at Scotland Yard the previous day. Now, however, we had discussed all that we could along those lines, while Holmes had seemingly ignored us, and talk had drifted to Thorndyke's return to the normality of his routine, like a train running on the same rails day after day. I sensed a tiny thread of despair in his tone.

Holmes took hold of the palimpsest and moved a few feet from the corner to his armchair, dropping into it. "The Old English word *murdrum* appears no less than four times, and given that it means 'hidden' or 'occult' — "

He seemed prepared to pontificate, but he was interrupted by the ringing of our bell. Thorndyke and Holmes both evinced the same expression of interest, resembling hounds hearing the first distant sounds of the hunt. I smiled inwardly — I daresay that I showed something of the same on my own features.

In a few moments, we heard the steady tread of a heavy-set man climbing the stairs. Obviously, Mrs. Hudson had determined there was no need to ascend with him in order to provide an introduction. I knew that she would accompany strangers — but not always. And sometimes she would climb upstairs with those who knew the way as well as they did the steps of their own home — men such as Inspectors Gregson and Lestrade, for instance. On other occasions, she would come up with a visitor to recover dirty dishes from a recent meal, or to see if we wished to share refreshments with our visitors. Or she might simply make tea or coffee unasked, carrying it up a few minutes after the guest arrived. I've never quite understood her system for deciding what to do and when — or whether there is any system at all.

In this case, I suspected that I knew who was arriving, and I was proven correct when he opened the door. It was old Kirbishaw, the lawyer. Gripped in his hand was a rolled document, tied with a red ribbon.

We three stood as the stout man entered, puffing a bit from the climb. He left the door behind him open, stating, "Your landlady indicated that she will be up in a moment with tea." Then he stepped toward us.

Thorndyke looked as if he was unsure whether to leave, rather than intrude on some new confidential business, but Holmes waved away his concern. "Dr. John Thorndyke, meet Ian Kirbishaw, of the Inner Temple. I believe that he's come bearing gifts."

The old man wheezed and laughed, waving the rolled document. I could see that it was about two feet in length from end to end. It was clearly a parchment, and what showed along its tea-colored length indicated great age.

"I do, Holmes, direct from the Temple Library. The fossils there didn't think that it existed, but your description gave one bright lad a different idea of where to look. It's been lost there for a century or more — or so they theorize." He handed it to Holmes. "This is going to make a few people who think that they're rich now rather queasy, I expect."

"Perfectly timed," said Holmes, untying the red ribbon and unrolling it. He held it up to the light, coming in through the window behind him, and began to mutter to himself. I half-expected him to ignore our new guest as he had Thorndyke and me for the last hour and move back to his chemical table, temporarily re-designated as an area to study ancient documents. (He had long since been chased from the more spacious dining table.) However, Mrs. Hudson's arrival just then seemed to break his concentration, and he tossed the sheet onto a stack of others and joined us for tea.

Holmes gave a recounting of some of his latest researches, concluding with his statement once again that he would need to travel to Oxford in order to see what could be located within the records of the various colleges, as well as the Bodleian. Kirbishaw, who had been interested in this affair since Holmes had drawn him in a month earlier, nodded. "I wish that I could go with you. Nothing beats finding a string and following it to the other end. I was rather good at that sort of thing in my day, you know. It was of invaluable assistance in the Molesey Case, back in '66, and then when one of the distant heirs tried to reopen *Jarndyce and Jarndyce*, I was able to show that he didn't have the legal standing to bring a suit."

Holmes nodded, but I could see that he was losing interest. However, Thorndyke had perked up considerably when these cases were mentioned, as if the very names of them were somehow intriguing.

Kirbishaw didn't notice the young doctor's interest. Rather, he saw Holmes's expression and, despite the old lawyer's rather comical countenance, he was quite shrewd enough to realize that discussion of old legal affairs from three decades before was not satisfactory conversational bait. Instead, he tossed out a new and shinier lure.

"I'd love to go with you," he stated, "but I'm afraid to leave my rooms empty for too long. Someone's been trying to get in them, you see."

As expected, this awakened Holmes's interest. "What for?" he asked with a smile. "Have you taken possession of some jewel for a client?" He wagged a finger. "Those are the devil's pet bait, Kirbishaw. You know better."

The old man shook his head. "Nothing like that. You're aware that my chambers only have old files and case-notes, none of which would inspire anyone to mischief. Clearly whomever has tried to get in has made a mistake."

"Was it just the once, or have there been repeated attempts?"

"Three times that I know about. I'm a very light sleeper — if I sleep at all. A week ago to the day, at about three in the morning, I was in the sitting room, without any lights, where I often find myself when insomnia plagues me. I heard scratching at the front door. I took up a poker and crept there, intending to unlock the door and confront whomever was foolish enough to try and break in. But I had some trouble with the lock, and by the time I had the door open, the intruder had fled down the stairs and out the front door into the Temple.

"Two days later, I had been up to the Old Bailey — it was about two o'clock in the afternoon — and when I returned, my clerk, Ableson, informed me that I'd had a visitor — an American — who was going to wait, but had apparently left, as he was no longer about when Ableson had returned from a short errand upstairs. I nodded, thinking nothing of it, and went to the closet to hang my coat and hat. I was completely flummoxed when I opened the door to confront a man, standing there in the dark. He seemed as surprised as I, and he dashed past me and out the front door before I could think to stop him or call for help."

"Did you see enough to identify him?"

"I did not. It was over in an instant, and when he barreled out of the closet, I took a step back to avoid him, further reducing my chance to see his face. He was about six feet in height, heavy-set, and had brown hair. Abelson confirmed that this was the same visitor who had vanished, and added that he was an American in a suit of British cut, and that he was approximately fifty years of age. He hadn't stated the nature of his business, and had refused to leave his name, simply saying that he needed to ask me about a former lawsuit — without naming which one."

"Hmm. It might be the same fellow who was there earlier. You said three attempts. What about the latest?"

"Last night. Again, someone — and I have to assume that it's this mysterious American — was trying to quietly open the door. This time I was ready, having left the key in the lock and practiced opening it silently ahead of time. I was able to swing the door open, to the man's complete surprise. He was bent forward when the door pulled away from him. His lock-pick, still in the door, was jerked from his hand. I growled and raised the poker, thinking to subdue him until the police could be summoned, but he dropped away to the left and rolled just outside my view. I heard him scramble up as he once again got away."

Kirbishaw reached into his waistcoat pocket and pulled out a curious little object. As he leaned forward to hand it to Holmes, I recognized it as a variation of the type of lock pick that I'd seen any number of times in association with Holmes's investigations. My friend gave it a cursory glance. "A smoker's companion," he said, before tossing it to Thorndyke, who studied it more closely.

Thorndyke then made as if to return it to Kirbishaw. "You keep it, my lad," replied the lawyer. "I have no need for it."

"Did you intend to hit this man with the poker?" I asked. "You could have killed him, Kirbishaw."

"It seemed to be a reasonable response, there in the dark," he replied rather sheepishly. "I suppose that in hindsight, I'm rather glad that I didn't do him an injury. There are more appropriate ways to deal with this matter, should it happen again — and should I be able to catch him."

"Do you have anyone to assist you?" asked Thorndyke, speaking for the first time since Kirbishaw had arrived. "What about this Ableson chap?"

"I would ask him to stay and help," replied the old lawyer, "but he is married with three small children. In fact, he's offered several times to help set a trap, but I've sent him home. He needs to be with his family."

"And you have no idea what this man is seeking?" asked Holmes.

"None at all. You've been to my chambers. You know my practice. There's nothing there but dry documents that shall have to be carted off, not long after the same is done to me. I don't have the energy to sort them, and I doubt that anyone will spend the effort to do so once I'm gone."

I half-expected that Holmes would himself offer to follow up on the matter, but he surprised me. "This will need to be settled at some point," he said. "I would help, but I must follow up this lead to Oxford while it's fresh. The information you've provided today will rock several wealthy families, and they already know now that I'm looking into the affair. I have to get to Oxford before they do, and more importantly before they can start destroying the ancient charters and records that nullify many of their fortunes in favor of other claims." He waved toward Thorndyke. "What do you have on at present, Doctor?"

Thorndyke looked rather surprised, and I was reminded of the same young fellow years before, sitting in the same place, who had showed a similar expression when Holmes asked a question about his family that ended up revealing far more than the boy had intended to share. It was the start of a long road that led through Thorndyke's education, and now back to this moment in the Baker Street sitting room.

"Why, nothing out of the ordinary. My duties at St. Margaret's, and the occasional *locum* work."

"Excellent," replied Holmes. Back to Kirbishaw. "Your clerk is in the chambers during the day. I expect that he's there now?"

"He is. That's how I felt comfortable in coming around to visit you."

"Dr. Thorndyke's days are filled with his regular duties, but I propose that he stay in your rooms in King's Bench Walk, Kirbishaw, for the next few weeks, to see if he can do something about tracking down this mysterious visitor. What do you say?"

The old man nodded and turned his attention to Thorndyke. "It suits me. But perhaps the young fellow has some objection?"

Thorndyke shook his head, and his enthusiastic acceptance of the idea reminded me that, even though he was but twenty-four years old, there was something of the adventurous boy still quite apparent. "I would be very glad to help, sir."

"Splendid!" cried Kirbishaw. "Then, Holmes, I have no doubts that by the time you've returned from this charter business, the young doctor and I will have a story to tell you!"

*****

Kirbishaw and Thorndyke made their arrangements, and by the time they left, they already seemed as thick as thieves. As the door shut behind them, I could hear Thorndyke asking about the matter of *Jarndyce and Jarndyce*, about which he'd apparently read already. I was prepared to comment concerning Holmes's good idea, which would both assist Kirbishaw and provide Thorndyke with a needed distraction from his current routine, but he had already shifted back to the chemical table, poring over the parchment and occasionally making a note on the pad beside him.

Within a few days, we had shifted west and were residing in furnished lodgings close to the Library. Holmes spent his days involved in complicated research, sometimes alone, and sometimes with the assistance of several of the locals. I filled my days taking walks through the countryside, wishing that we had chosen to travel there just a month or so later when spring would have fully arrived. Afternoons usually found me visiting the various colleges or spending some time in The Eagle and Child and sharing a pint with the natives.

During the course of our stay, we met several of the local residents, some of whom were associated with the school. One such conscripted Holmes into solving a pretty little puzzle regarding a stolen academic test. It was a nice distraction, but I could see that my friend was anxious to return to his work.

Holmes's research progressed steadily, resulting in an informal gathering in the Bodleian in one of the rooms set aside for our use. There, he presented his findings to the families involved. Before the matter was finally settled the following year, his conclusions would progress through the courts, and on to Parliament and the throne itself, before an equitable solution was reached — and all without the general public having any hint as to what had occurred.

Our business done, we returned to London, with Holmes expressing satisfaction at being back in the center of those five-millions of people with his webs stretching throughout, allowing him to be instantly responsive to every little rumour or suspicion of unsolved crime. I, on the other hand, had grown rather affectionate toward the little routine that I'd constructed while rusticating away from the capital, although I quickly fell back into my former patterns.

I admit that I hadn't given Thorndyke or Kirbishaw much thought while I was gone. It seemed as if Holmes hadn't taken the matter too seriously either, as he'd handed it off to our young friend in favor of pursuing the question of the charters. Granted, his researches led to results so striking that they may be the subject of one of my future narratives, but he hadn't seemed to show more than a passing interest at the time.

This was proven wrong three or four days after our return, when Thorndyke dropped by one morning, holding the door for a departing seamstress who had sought Holmes's advice regarding damp footprints that she discovered each morning in the place where she worked, leading in one direction only — from a side room to a drain in the center of the floor. As the young doctor settled into the basket chair and crossed his long legs, I was surprised when he said, "Your advice helped."

"Advice?" I asked. "What advice?"

"Thorndyke sent a wire while we were in Oxford," Holmes replied. "I was able to suggest a course of action."

"Clearly I need to catch up," I said, and waved a hand to Thorndyke, indicating that he should proceed.

"Mr. Kirbishaw and I made arrangements a couple of weeks ago, after we left here. I retrieved some clothes and what I would need to stay in his rooms in King's Bench Walk.

Then, later that afternoon, I presented myself there and got situated. Have you both been there before?"

Holmes nodded, but I shook my head, having only a general idea of the location of the lawyer's residence, but nothing specific. "It's at Number 5, Doctor," explained Thorndyke. "One of a row of very handsome red-brick buildings on the eastern side of the Inner Temple, stretching down toward the river. It's a fascinating area — some with designs by Christopher Wren himself!

"Mr. Kirbishaw's rooms, Number 5A, are entered from the first floor. They look out over the Temple. His apartment covers three floors — a very comfortable wood-paneled sitting room and small office for Mr. Ableson on the first floor, Mr. Kirbishaw's office rooms on the second, and bedrooms on the third. The front entrance to the apartment consists of a rather thin baize-covered door which wouldn't seem to be much of a hindrance for anyone trying to get in. The lock is equivalent — an old clumsy thing that has been there a century if it's been there a day.

"The first floor is rather tidy, and there's a gas ring at the fireplace to make tea. But upstairs, in Mr. Kirbishaw's work space, it seems as if a paper cyclone has hit. Documents are stacked shoulder-high in places, and all that supports them are flying buttresses of other similarly tall stacks leaning at cross-angles. The floor is covered in loose papers, and it's a wonder that the old fellow hasn't slipped and broken his neck a dozen times. I had a word about it with Ableson, who seems a decent enough chap, though a little distracted, and he said that he'd long ago given up trying to impose any order on the old man. 'He knows right where something is,' said the clerk, shaking his head. 'If I tried to sort any of it on my own, decades of associated institutional knowledge in Mr. Kirbishaw's head would be erased like that — rendered meaningless.' And he snapped sharply to emphasize his point.

"It was explained to Ableson that I was going to stay there for a while, putting up in one of the spare bedrooms on the third floor, and function as something of a watchdog during the night. My duties at St. Margaret's out in Epping end each day in plenty of time for me to make my way to the Temple before Ableson departs. We quickly settled into a routine, and Mr. Kirbishaw went out of his way to make me feel right at home. Each evening our discussions have been more enlightening than I can say, as he relates to me various tales of jurisprudence that he has accumulated over the past half-century — both his own cases, and those others that have become well-known within the legal community, but have never come to my own attention.

"Each night we would put out the lights, and he would go to his bedroom. I, however, in spite of having a room of my own assigned for my use, would make myself comfortable in the sitting room, prepared to react if the intruder happened to return. However, night after night, nothing happened.

"It was then that I asked Mr. Holmes's advice, Doctor. Of course, it's possible that the man, whomever he is, has given up, and that would certainly be best for Mr. Kirbishaw. And yet, the continued uncertainty would be a terrible thing. Mr. Holmes advised me to convince Mr. Kirbishaw to take a short holiday, giving the impression that the premises are empty. He said that this ploy has been of use to you both once or twice in the past. Mr. Kirbishaw agreed to vacate temporarily to Dungeness to visit a nephew. He left yesterday with a great deal of public performance, saying goodbye to the neighbors, loading far too much luggage in a cab, and making several unnecessary trips out and back inside again before he was finally gone. I, on the other hand, took care to not be seen, and in fact I've been rather discrete over the last few days in my comings and goings, so as to make it seem as if I were no longer staying there — if my presence had actually been noticed at all.

"Late yesterday afternoon, Ableson locked up at the usual time, and 5A was apparently deserted. I located myself out in the shadows of the first-floor hall, toward the back of the building, with the permission of one of the neighbors, and waited for dark.

"I didn't know how long that I might have to wait, or if anyone would come at all. After all, it was possible that the thwarted intruder might have given up long ago and moved on, choosing to abandon whatever had motivated him. But I hoped that he was still intent on breaking in, for whatever reason, and that I could catch him.

"My initial thought had been to let him achieve entry, but I realized that might cause all sorts of difficulties. I didn't want Mr. Kirbishaw's fine baize-covered door to be damaged. And if the man did get inside, how would he know what to find in that mare's nest that Mr. Kirbishaw called an office? In searching for it, whatever it was, he was liable to do the very damage to that curious filing system that Ableson feared and avoided. So, I came up with a different strategy.

"The previous day, I had installed a small pipe, with an inner diameter not more than a quarter-inch and no larger than a pencil, on the floor at the bottom of the door frame, on the hinged side. It was only four or five inches from inside the room to out. I used a couple of brackets to bolt it to the floor, and painted the whole thing black, making sure that it wasn't scratched or scuffed, so that nothing would reflect from its dark surface. Then, when the building had become quiet for the night, I ran a waxed and blackened string through the small pipe and down the hall, along the wall to the spot in the alcove where I planned to hide. Back inside the sitting room, I attached the end of the string to a tall coat stand, placed in the middle of the room, upon which I hung a number of metal cook-pots. When the string was tugged, it would pull over the coat stand, setting up a hellish clatter.

"As night fell, I settled into my spot, fairly certain that I was wasting my time. If not, I knew that I had a long wait, as Mr. Kirbishaw had indicated that the two previous attempts hadn't been made any earlier than three a.m.

"In the dim light, I could see time pass on my watch, and I recalled with almost fondness waiting for this same intruder while sitting in the plush armchair before the fireplace in the sitting room, a small brandy beside me. Those hours had actually been quite useful, as they gave me a chance to think and ponder my future. Some of the cases that Mr. Kirbishaw had related had seemed to have quite a medical aspect, as well as a legal one, and I've wondered if there might be some way to combine the two professions, beyond the typical forensic associations. All that would have made those late-night contemplations better would have been a good Trichinopoly cigar.

"I had settled into something of a reverie, expecting nothing until morning, when I perceived that the intruder had arrived and was barely visible, kneeling on the floor outside the door to 5A, working on the lock. He must have fashioned a new pick in the meantime, since I still have the one that Mr. Kirbishaw found there earlier when he yanked open the door.

"With my breath held, I slowly found the string on the floor beside me and gently lifted it. Then, taking up the slack, I started to slowly pull it toward me, as if I were gently reeling in a fish who was barely on the hook. Even knowing what to expect, I was taken by surprise. A muted clank or two sounded from behind the door as a couple of the pots knocked together when the coat stand started to tip. Then, as its equilibrium shifted, I no longer had to pull on the string, and with a sudden crash that seemed to echo throughout the entire building, it fell!

"The intruder was up and dashing away like a sprinter when the gun has fired. And I was up and after him, though not intending to actually run him down. I didn't intend to be seen — I was wearing my darkest clothes. I heard him thunder down the stairs and was in time to see the front door as it banged open when he passed through at a dead run. He veered right, up the hill toward Mitre Court. I had planned for this — in fact, I'd planned for all the routes — and had borrowed some of the Irregulars for just such an eventuality. I knew that if my plan worked, the intruder would be spooked and try to escape very quickly. I might or might not lose him on my own, but placing the lads in his path, to follow along behind him unseen, would insure that even if I personally lost sight of him, they would not.

"I reached Fleet Street and stood to catch my breath. I had no idea which way to turn, so instead, according to plan, I simply waited, listening to London at night as my racing heart slowed to normal. I walked up and down a ways, but never going too far. It was clear night, and when I turned east, St. Paul's was striking against the night sky. Just to the south I could hear the river traffic, and once a horse screamed unexpectedly several streets over. I was concerned for a moment that it might have something to do with my fugitive, but it wasn't heard again, and apparently had no relevance.

"While I waited, a constable passed on his beat three different times. On the first occasion, he approached with suspicion, but then he remembered me from the old days, and asked if I was helping you on one of your cases. I left him with the impression that I was, and so he moved along, after mentioning that he was available if needed. The other two times that he passed, he simply touched a finger to his helmet and nodded. Not long after, young Nathan Wilkes appeared out of the darkness to tell me that the intruder had gone to ground at 49 Nevill's Court, not far up Fetter Lane, where it opens opposite Bream's Buildings."

And with that, Thorndyke sat back, looking at one or the other of us. Finally, seeing that Holmes was still pondering the narrative, I said, "Well? What happened then?"

"I wasn't sure what to do next," admitted Thorndyke. "It was too late to start knocking up the neighbors, asking who lived there. I left the lads in place to follow the man should he leave, and then went back to Kirbishaw's, and to bed — the first time since I've been keeping watch that I wasn't up most of the night, and slept in a real bed instead of a chair. Then this morning I took a turn back around that way— after having begged off from my duties at the hospital — and determined that the fellow is still in residence. I was able to question the neighbors and confirmed that he's an American by the name of Abraham Harden. He's been staying there in a rented room for most of a month. He has no debts, lives quietly, and doesn't receive visitors. I didn't want to talk directly to his landlady, a Mrs. Frobisher, but the neighbors all seem to find him tolerable, if not memorable. The flower girl says that he has bought from her on a few occasions — a flower for his lapel — and has overpaid. He doesn't seem to frequent any of the nearby pubs, and he usually takes his dinner in a small restaurant around the corner in Great New Street. He orders the same thing every night — whatever soup the cook has concocted, a hunk of bread, and some sort of crumble to finish up. With it he takes one pint of cider, no more. Sometimes he goes away for several hours, usually in the afternoon . . . ."

He fell silent, perhaps thinking as I did that such information, while painting a picture, didn't really add anything to explain Mr. Harden's curious motivations. Holmes, who hadn't spoken, stood then and walked around to his scrapbooks, bulging on shelves mounted to the wall to the left of the fireplace. Pulling one loose — carefully, as we had each learned a difficult lesson when retrieving volumes too quickly – he carried it to the dining table and opened it, flipping slowly from page to page, some loose and some bound, until he found the clipping that he sought. He read through it quickly, and then shook his head.

"I thought that I recognized the name Harden, but this refers to a different man —an American millionaire who has been in London for the past month or so on business. Still, two Americans with the same last name— there might be a connection."

He dropped the clipping on the commonplace book and turned our way. "This is your case, Thorndyke. So far, you've made a most satisfactory and workmanlike job of it. What do you recommend?"

His comment made Thorndyke fill out and rise a little bit somehow, as if the praise were equivalent to hydrogen being pumped into a lighter-than-air balloon. Holmes's query was sincere, and he waited patiently while Thorndyke shifted his thoughts to an honest consideration of the matter. "There's really no question," he said quickly. "I would have done it myself, but didn't want to muff it. We should interview him."

"Indeed," replied Holmes. "Watson? Are you free?"

I acknowledged that I was, and we set off for Fetter Lane.

London was bustling under the bright morning sunlight, and there was a faint scent on the breeze from the south, something rather fruit-like, that seemed to permeate the early spring air. I would have expected to smell the tidal Thames instead, but this warmish current seemed to be wafting blossom-like odors from much farther away.

We had our cab drop us off where Fetter Lane and Fleet Street meet, directly across from the low entrance to Mitre Court. Holmes wanted to get the lay of the land, so we started up Fetter Lane until we came to Nevill's Court on our right. Entering it was like finding a brightly colored bird's egg tucked in a mud-brown nest. We left the dingy sameness of that busy thoroughfare running between Fleet Street and the Holborn, and so into a narrow area filled with well-tended shrubs and flowers. Although spring had yet to find London proper, it appeared to have already taken hold here. Lupins, snapdragons, foxgloves, nasturtiums, and hollyhocks filled the space with a spectrum of renewal.

Thorndyke led us to No. 49, a well-kept and tidy place. Before we could knock, however, a boy of ten or twelve stepped from out of a nearby doorway. I recognized him as Nathan Wilkes, one of Holmes's Irregulars — the son of one of the original group that Holmes had first recruited back in the mid-1870's, when he began his practice while still residing in Montague Street.

"He ain't there," said the lad. "He's around the corner, in Great New Street, eating something. At Mrs. Michelmore's."

"I know the place," said Holmes. "Have *you* eaten?" The boy shook his head and Holmes flipped him a coin. Nathan grabbed it effortlessly and, taking that as a dismissal, nodded, smiled, and scampered past us.

Three minutes later, we were at a small coffee shop, and it was obvious to all that the man in question was certainly the chap seated at a small table along the walk, outside the front door. His empty plate was pushed aside, the stub of a cigarette mashed out in the stain of an egg yolk, and he was reading a newspaper and drinking a cup of strong tea. He noticed our approach and looked up with suspicion. By unspoken agreement, we three spread evenly around the table, so that he would be blocked should he bolt in any direction.

Thorndyke spoke. "I believe that you lost this." And he pulled from his pocket the lock pick that the man had abandoned when disturbed by Kirbishaw, last seen by Holmes and me weeks ago in our sitting room.

The man, known to us as Abraham Harden, tensed, and I thought then that he would certainly try to flee. But he seemed to give it up as a bad idea and sank back into his chair. He picked up his cup and drained the tea before gesturing that we should sit down.

"I've seen you about," he said to Thorndyke in a rather odd accent. I could hear a trace of the Americas in it, but there was something more that I couldn't identify. "I've seen you, going in and out of the lawyer's office. Do you work for him?"

Thorndyke shook his head. "I've been doing a favor for a friend, keeping watch at night. He was rather concerned that you kept trying to break in."

Harden looked sheepish. "I'm sorry about that. I didn't know quite what else to do. Now that you're on to me, I guess my chances are all gone."

Holmes interrupted. "You've made the mistake of assuming that we know why you've been trying to gain entry. I assure you that we have no idea, and that we're here to find out."

Harden seemed to consider his options and, finding none better, he ordered tea for the rest of us, playing the gracious host, and began to relate his story.

"I'm from Virginia originally, although I haven't been there since I was a lad. My family were tobacco farmers — some of us still are. But my father died when I was very small, and I haven't had much to do with them ever since.

"Back in the 1830's, before I was born, both my father and his brother inherited a substantial tobacco farm from their father, who'd had it from his father before him. They got along well at first, and made more money than they could ever spend. But then they met a woman, and they both loved her. However, my uncle, a man named John Vincent Harden, had a streak of cruelty and greed about him that she spotted early on, and so she chose my father instead. After the marriage, things seemed to go on as they had — at least for a while. I was born in 1837, and they continued to have more and more success. But gradually a sourness arose between them — all beginning on my uncle's side, according to my poor mother.

"It was in early July 1841, and we had gone over to Washington to transact some business. The heat, or so I'm told, was unbearable, and it began to wear on everyone's nerves. However, my father and uncle both needed to get along, as they had several important meetings to conduct, including one with President Tyler, himself an important Virginia businessman. It was he who invited us to the July Fourth fireworks that night, across the street from the White House, in Lafayette Park.

"My mother and I attended as well, and the press of the crowd became miserable. I remember some of it, but as I was only four years old then, and far too small to see above the crowds, mostly what I recall is rarely being held up in someone's arms to see an occasional shooting rocket, but more often standing on the ground and being able to see nothing. I have some memory that it was there that the argument between my father and uncle escalated. My mother said it had to do with something my father said, about my uncle paying a bit too much attention to her. In any case, in the middle of the crowd, they began to trade blows, even as the fireworks began.

"My mother told me that the crowd wanted no part of it, and the two men were pushed and prodded until they were ejected into the open space at the back of the crowd. This gave them room to fight that much harder. She had followed, pulling me with her and attempting to stop them. Who knows how it would have turned out, but it was then that the accident happened.

"Someone setting off the fireworks accidentally directed a volley into the crowd. Quite a few were injured. My father, hearing the screams and explosions, turned to see what happened, and Uncle John used the opportunity to hit him across the back of the neck — hard. My father went down, and my uncle then jumped on him, landing with his knee across my father's spine. My mother said the crack was as loud as one of the fireworks still going off overhead. My father did nothing more than grunt — likely already dead by then. Uncle John rose, a wild look in his eyes, and turned our way. My mother was terrified — she didn't know if he would kill us too, or instead pretend that nothing had happened. But she was afraid that if he did that, if he tried to act as if he were innocent, it would only be the beginning of an attempt on his part to win the new widow as his own. In any case, she took my hand and fled.

"The newspapers of the time reported that twelve were injured by the fireworks accident, and two were killed — my father being one of them. Somehow my uncle convinced the authorities that it was the accident that caused my father's death, and not his own actions. I suppose that money can buy anything — even a form of justice that benefits a murderer. And the only person who could tell the truth about what he had done was my mother.

"I don't know what had happened before all this to make my mother fear him so, but fear my uncle she certainly did, and only more afterwards. Rather than staying and telling the authorities, or trying to have him arrested, we simply vanished, and we never went home again. She walked away from any claim to my father's half of the fortune. We settled with some of her relatives in upstate New York, and I took their name for the longest time. Every once in a while, we'd have a hint that my uncle's agents were sniffing around, trying to find us, but they never did.

"My mother gradually told me this story when I was a bit older, but she sickened and died when I was twelve, and I suspect that there was more she would have shared if she'd had time. For so long, simply based on what I did know, I burned for revenge. But gradually some good sense took hold, and I saw that obsessing about it would accomplish nothing. Still, I could hope that someday the time would be right for true justice.

"I wandered during the following years. I joined the Union Army in '61, and served throughout the War before mustering out. Afterwards, I went out west for a while, and then up into Canada. I ended up serving on a cargo ship that sailed the world. It seemed a good life, but then, about a month ago, we made port in London, and I saw in a newspaper that my uncle, John Vincent Harden himself, was here.

"I hadn't thought of him much in years, and had no idea if I'd crossed his mind. But I decided to stay ashore as my ship left and see what I might discover about him. I went around to where he's staying, at the Langham. I sent up a note, and was welcomed with what can only be called hostility. I didn't accuse him of anything — but I didn't have to. I could tell that he was aware that I knew the truth about what he had done so long ago. We didn't talk more than five minutes. He asked about my mother, and seemed surprised that she had died. It was then that I felt my temper start to overtake me, and I knew that if we kept talking, I'd eventually say too much. As of that point, he simply knew that I existed, but had no idea where to find me, should he wish to eliminate another who still had a claim on half his vast fortune. He tried to ask a few questions, but I could see his purpose and quickly excused myself, slipping away before he had a chance to set someone on my trail.

"I started to watch the Langham from a distance, and in a day or so my uncle left in the morning, no doubt for some meeting. I have to admit that I found a way to get into his rooms — and I won't rat on anyone else, so don't ask me how. There, I searched through his papers, although I thought it very unlikely that he would have anything with him, especially after all these decades, that would mention my father, or be incriminating in any way. Still, I had to look.

"I did find a letter from a London lawyer, Mr. Kirbishaw, something of a receipt, indicating that he'd taken possession of a number of sensitive documents and would keep them in trust until otherwise instructed. This was apparently in relation to my uncle's plan to move to London permanently. Although the chances were slim, I thought that there might be a possibility that something in these related to my father, and that if my uncle were here in London to stay, he would have brought his precious papers with him, and that these were the very ones left with the lawyer, until my uncle could find more permanent lodgings in which to keep them, or make arrangements with a bank.

"So, having already burgled my uncle's rooms, I decided to see what I could at the lawyer's office. I slipped in one night a few weeks ago, but when I tried to open the door, someone was still inside, likely working very late. A few days later, I made an appointment, without giving my name or reason, as I didn't want it mentioned to my uncle beforehand, should the lawyer wish to ask some question about why I wanted to meet. I thought that I'd settle on that when I got there, on what to say. But when I was left alone in the waiting room, I decided instead, without much consideration, that I'd try to hide and search the place that night. However, that plan was soon ruined when an old man opened the very closet in which I'd hidden.

"I waited a few days and tried the door again at night, but once again someone heard me. In the meantime, I tried another time when my uncle left the Langham, and searched his rooms again, but didn't find anything else. My only chance — slim as it was — lay in the papers that had been left with the lawyer. I went again last night, and this time something caused a great crash in the lawyer's office when I worked on the lock. I got away, but I think I understand now that it was a trap — a chance for you gentlemen to follow me here."

He stopped speaking and took a long sip of his now-cooled tea. I thought of his curious and convoluted story, and glanced at my companions to see their reactions, but they gave no obvious hints as to what they thought, one way or the other.

The man set down his cup, smiled, looked from one to the other of us, and said in a friendly way, "I'm embarrassed, but what else could I do? I don't have the resources to challenge such a powerful man. He's profited from what he did so many years ago, and if there's a chance that I might right this old wrong . . . ." He looked at Thorndyke. "You said that you were doing a favor for your friend, the old lawyer. That you've been watching the place. If I return with you to his office, and tell my story, do you think he'll be able to help me, Mr. . . . ?"

Thorndyke shook his head and replied in a non-committal tone, "My name is Thorndyke. Mr. Kirbishaw isn't available this morning, although I'm sure that he would prefer to speak with you as soon as he has a chance. We can certainly relay a message to him, and have his reply sent to your rooms — in Nevill's Court, I believe?"

Harden's lips tightened, but he tried to maintain his friendly open manner. "So, you followed me all the way last night, then. I thought that someone was behind me, but I took the long way and believed that I'd thrown you off. Well," he said, pushing back his chair and standing, "if you'll please tell the lawyer that I'd like to meet with him, in the proper way this time, I'll wait to hear when it's convenient. And now, gentlemen, if you'll excuse me, I'll return to my rooms — in Nevill's Court, as you say." With that, he turned and walked boldly up the street. A woman who had been waiting nearby stepped forward, laying the man's bill in front of Holmes. Thorndyke laughed.

Holmes raised two fingers to his lips, giving a shrill whistle. Almost immediately, young Nathan Wilkes was at his side, some crumbs still sticking to his mouth. "Is everyone still in place?" he asked. The boy nodded. "Good. Follow him wherever he goes. He may bolt from the rooms, now that he knows that we are aware of them, but it may be in his interest to stay." He fished in his pocket and gave the boy a handful of coins, and then a few more on the table to cover Harden's breakfast. "Send messages the usual way." Wilkes nodded and scampered away without any other instructions necessary.

Holmes looked at us. "Do you believe him?" Both Thorndyke and I shook our head. "Why not?"

"His hands," I said. "He showed no evidence of actually having worked on a ship."

Holmes nodded and looked toward Thorndyke. "What the doctor noticed," he said, "and something more subtle. The fact that he would tell that complicated story so easily to three strangers — as if he'd rehearsed it, if needed."

"I agree," said Holmes. "And I would add that his curious accent doesn't quite jibe with his reported biography. I would say that he was born and raised in the American South, one of the Carolina's perhaps, and that he has lived in England for quite a while, instead of simply arriving here a few weeks ago after working for a long spell on a cargo ship. There's more to this Abraham Harden, should that be his real name, than he's telling."

He stood. "Our next stop, Master Thorndyke?"

The young doctor rose as well. "Why, the Langham, of course — with a stop by the post office to wire Mr. Kirbishaw to come home."

It seemed to take longer to find a cab, after we had walked north to High Holborn, than it did to actually journey west to the Langham. Along the way, we discussed the recent legal misfortunes of Oscar Wilde, and this veered into a general discussion of the premiere of one of his plays a couple of months earlier. Thorndyke indicated that he thought Wilde would soon be freed, but I wasn't so certain.

Holmes's card, sent to the tobacco millionaire's rooms, gained us quick access, and in short order we were seated in the well-appointed rooms with the man in question.

After refusing his offer of refreshments, Holmes indicated that Thorndyke should explain why we were there. He did so succinctly, relating Kirbishaw's original story, and then his own experiences, before concluding with the tale narrated by Abraham Harden not an hour before.

The old man, a lean and gristly-looking creature, browned by the excessive use of the tobacco which has so well-funded his life, was outraged.

"I'm disappointed in you, Mr. Holmes," he wheezed. "I've heard of you, of course, and I thought that you were on the side of the angels. How could you be representing this man?"

"You misunderstand, Mr. Harden," replied Holmes. "We aren't here to press his claim. Rather, we have become involved because of his attempts to see the papers that you've entrusted to Mr. Kirbishaw, who is a friend of ours. We didn't know anything of this man's identity or his story until he chose to share it with us. He has indicated that he wishes to meet with Kirbishaw about it, although an appointment has yet to be arranged, but in the meantime, we came here to get your side of the story."

"Well, I'm not sure that I owe you anything, but I can tell you that my side is that this man is a fraud! He did visit here, as you said, but he didn't simply stay for a few minutes and then leave. No, he started accusing me of murdering my dear brother, and then hinting that I had stolen half of the business — half that was now owed to him! He threatened to take his case to the public, with dark hints that he had 'proof'. I suspect that instead, he has nothing but a story, and that he's been trying to get at my papers to find something that he can use to bolster his claim."

"But," said Holmes, "if there's no truth to the matter — if it's a story that he fabricated, as you say — then he would *know* that there was no truth to it, so what could he hope to find in your papers?"

"You say that he broke in here first, and read my letters? The letter from Kirbishaw?" He rose and stepped to the desk, rustling through a stack of sheets until he found what he sought. He handed it wordlessly to Holmes, who read it, smiled, and then passed it to me. When I was done, I reached across and gave it to Thorndyke.

It was something of a receipt, as described, but not simply for unspecified personal papers. Instead, Harden had left a number of more valuable documents with Kirbishaw, including a number of bearer deeds.

"I'm moving to London," said the millionaire. "Going to finish up here. My wife is long dead, and we had no children. I've nearly finished the process of selling out the business, and there's nothing left for me in Virginia. Kirbishaw was highly recommended to me by a friend from New York — one of the Vanderbilts — and he's helping make arrangements. Until my funds are all established, I have a line of credit, and Kirbishaw is using the bearer bonds to fund a property purchase, and the subsequent renovations. That is what this man wants to steal."

Holmes pulled his lip for a moment, as he was wont to do at times when in deep thought. Then, he nodded. "I begin to have a sense of what might be going on. We'll discuss this further with Mr. Kirbishaw, and in the meantime, I'll continue to have this man — your erstwhile long-lost nephew — watched and followed to find out more of what he's up to. I hope to have an answer in a few days."

The old man, still standing by the desk, seemed to be on the verge of speaking, and asking for a further detailed explanation. Then, perhaps realizing that he wouldn't get it, he shrugged and said, "I put myself in your hands, Mr. Holmes, and that of your friends. I know that his story is a lie, a dirty attempt to blackmail me, and it's easily proven. My brother did die, but it was accidental. By that point, he'd already sold out his shares of the company to me, so there was nothing to steal. All of that is well-documented, even if I can't lay my hands on it right this minute. His widow, to whom I never directed an improper thought, did not flee and disappear with my nephew. Rather, she moved back to New England, near Boston.

"She died a few years later, and even though I offered to raise my nephew, he chose to stay with her people. He joined the Union Army at the outbreak of the war against the secession, and as I was in Virginia, I lost touch with him. I never heard from him again after that. I wondered, and had inquiries made to see if he'd died, but he wasn't on any casualty lists. It was as if he simply chose to cease having dealings with me.

"I wondered about it, of course, but I thought that perhaps something had happened during the war that changed him, or made him resent Southerners. That wasn't unusual. If he'd ever reached out to me, I would have gladly welcomed him. But then, this man — here in London after all these years — to appear and accuse me of such perfidy —!"

"So, you don't think this actually is your nephew?" asked Thorndyke.

"No, but yet, how can I say?" said the old man. "The last I saw of him was sometime in the 1850's, when he was still in his teens. The man who was here the other day certainly didn't favor my brother, but he could have taken after his mother's side — they were all more heavy-set than the Hardens."

"Thank you for sharing that," said Holmes. "The additional information should prove useful in our investigations. You have my card? Let us know if you hear anything else, and I believe that we should have some news for you shortly."

Outside, Holmes had a cab hailed for us, and soon we were meandering through side-streets as our canny driver avoided the throngs clogging the busy mid-day streets. At Mitre Court along Fleet Street, Holmes dismissed him, and we walked down through the passage toward Kirbishaw's rooms.

I glanced around the court as we passed through, recalling the story told to us by Jabez Wilson, not quite five years earlier, about the day he'd been brought here to see about obtaining a vacated position within the spurious Red-Headed League. When I wrote up and published the narrative the following spring, I'd been advised by my literary agent that it might be wise to disguise certain aspects of the stories with invented names — particularly the location of the building where the red-headed men had gathered, in case other nearby tenants complained. Thus, "Mitre Court" had been adjusted — rather cleverly, I thought — to "Pope's Court". Yet, a month or so after publication in *The Strand*, I'd received a note from Jabez Wilson, asking why I hadn't altered his name, rather than making him the laughing stock of his neighbors. I admit that I hadn't thought of it, and when I discussed the matter with my agent friend, he indicated that it hadn't occurred to him either, as the matter was one of public record, and Mr.

Wilson's name had been well-reported in the press at the time, following Holmes's prevention of the attempted crime. I tended to agree, but I have become more careful since then, on a limited basis, about how and when I choose to obfuscate those individuals whose problems end up in these case-notes, if publication is contemplated.

As we exited the southern end of the court, the last noise drifting in from Fleet Street at our backs vanished, and we found ourselves in a pleasantly quiet spot, with the view opening widely before us as we walked down the gentle slope into the Inner Temple. Progressing beyond the buildings immediately on either side of us broadened our perspective further, and then we bore to our left, along a most attractive row of matching red-brick structures. One, reached by six low steps, had a well-styled arch around the small area before the front door. Stepping closer, we could see the countless names painted up and down the doorpost, listing the tenants. A few looked rather recent, but most had been there for many years, as evidenced by their faded appearance. Kirbishaw's, on the right, was one of the most aged-looking of them all.

We passed through the double doors, set about ten feet back into the recess, and so on through the ground-floor entryway until we reached a set of black carpeted steps, winding up and turning to the left out of sight. The white walls and ceiling were a stark contrast with the dark rugs, and made for a most attractive and functional space. Upstairs, we turned toward the front of the building, where we encountered the baize door which we had heard described. I was surprised that there was no outer oak door like on the other chambers, but Thorndyke mentioned that he'd heard from Kirbishaw that it was damaged years ago, and he'd never had it replaced. "But it needs to be," he added. Then, with a knock, we were led into Kirbishaw's office.

It was a spacious room with a wide hearth, faced by several comfortable chairs. A sofa and some tables completed the furnishings, and there were three windows which gave a marvelous view of the Inner Temple, where various stately individuals could be seen pursuing their own business.

Mr. Abelson came out and we were introduced. He stated that he'd had a message from Kirbishaw that he'd be back by early afternoon. Thorndyke suggested that we find some lunch, and Abelson set about sending out for something to be delivered from nearby. We were just finishing when the old lawyer made his appearance.

"Had something to eat, I see? Good, good. No, thank you. I ate earlier."

We complimented him on the rooms, and he nodded proudly. "I'm very fortunate. I came here myself in '54, reading for the law under old Mathiason. He had the lease then, and had it set up so that it was in the name of the firm, and not himself. When he passed, I took over the practice and the lease. I still have it set that way, although it isn't likely at this stage that I'll find anyone to take it over from me when I'm gone."

He was amazed to hear what had happened the night before, although he looked with almost fatherly pride at Thorndyke when hearing the trap that had been set with a coat rack, a string, and some pots. After he'd heard what both the alleged nephew and the tobacco millionaire had told us, he confirmed that he was keeping some rather valuable documents. "They're very secure," he said. "I have a very good safe. Well, I suppose that explains everything," he added, as if the matter were concluded.

"Not quite," responded Holmes. "We have an idea what he was initially after — trying to get something out of Mr. Harden in connection with the events of 1841. And then he learned what was here in your office and seems to have become more ambitious, as well as adding a felony or two to his repertoire. He may very well be done now that we've shined a light on him, but I suspect that there's more to this, and I intend to find out the rest of the story."

It was decided that Thorndyke would continue to reside at 5A King's Bench Walk for the time being, in the unlikely event that any new assault was planned, and that Holmes would conduct further investigations using his own specialized resources. And thus, we parted for that day.

It came as no surprise later that night when Nathan Wilkes reported that immediately after parting from us at Mrs. Michelmore's restaurant, he had returned to the rooms, gathered his bags, and vanished. But in spite of his efforts to move with caution, the lads had no difficulty in tracing him to a pawn shop in Hampstead, with the owner's name, Walter Spaeth, listed prominently on the doorway. That, apparently, was his residence.

For a time, I heard nothing more of the matter. As was the case with Holmes's investigations, others came and went, and they were all intertwined. He would let some simmer until an essential fact presented itself, or when someone involved in the case did something to set things in motion once again. I knew that he was receiving reports from the Irregulars, and that information was coming to him from America as well. He'd visited the Langham twice that I knew about to confer with the tobacco millionaire, and he seemed to be satisfied with how the case was progressing.

Finally, on Saturday, April 13th — although my notes are smudged, giving the "*1*" in "*13*" the look of a "*2*" — he was nearly ready to act. And then we had an urgent visitor. A young lady named Violet Smith had arrived with a great deal of determination to tell her story, and it was evident that nothing short of force could get her out of the room until she had done so. With a resigned air and a somewhat weary smile,

Holmes begged the beautiful intruder to take a seat in the basket chair reserved for our visitors and then to inform us of what it was that was troubling her.

The upshot of it was that Holmes, who felt that the Harden matter was coming to a head, listened and felt that there was something to the girl's story. However, he couldn't get away from London, so he sent me to watch over her when she returned to Charlington on Monday. Following my report, he went down the next afternoon, whereupon he received a cut lip and a discoloured lump upon his forehead — although he assured me that the other fellow looked much worse.

Holmes's own appearance worsened through the night as his bruises spread, and he presented a gruesome appearance on that Wednesday morning when, after opening a newly delivered telegram, he announced that he was prepared to bring the Harden business to a close.

He sent several messages, explaining that the intended recipients had been alerted to expect his summons. Then, retrieving our hats and coats, we found a cab and set forth to Hampstead. After the long climb, we found ourselves in the High Street, opposite Oriel Place. There we sat until a four-wheeler arrived, with our old friend Inspector MacDonald and two constables, one a stranger and one, Avery Mills, that was known to me. The inspector spotted us and, having directed the constables up the street and around a corner, crossed in our direction, even as another cab arrived as well, a growler containing Thorndyke, Kirbishaw, and Mr. Harden.

Holmes looked north and then waved a hand. Soon one of his Irregulars had appeared from within the crowds passing along the pavement. It was young Peavy, who would later be one of the railway-men that served so heroically twenty years later during the St. Bede's Junction rail crash.

He related that the man who had called himself Abraham Harden was to be found in the small pawnshop visible just down the alleyway. Harden clearly wished to ask questions, in the manner of such men who have made fortunes and cannot stand to be left outside of any decisions. Yet he seemed to realize that this was Holmes's show.

Holmes led us to the shop's door and so inside. A surly fellow in his early twenties was leaning on the counter, studying a newspaper. He first made to look up and then return to his reading, but seeing six men crowding into the small space caused him to stand upright with surprise.

"We would speak to Mr. Borman," said Holmes with authority. The young man started to speak, then cleared his throat, said nothing, and rang a bell on the counter. In a moment, we heard the sound of approaching footsteps, and then the man whom we had met as Abraham Harden stepped in through a curtained doorway.

He had a false-looking smile on his face and was rubbing his hands, as if he were an actor stepping on stage to play the part of someone helpful. No doubt it was a role that served him well at the pawnshop, but it vanished abruptly when he recognized whom he was facing. Without a word, he turned and dashed back through the shop.

Thorndyke and I made as if to pursue, but Holmes threw out a hand. In a moment, we heard a scuffle, and then a slammed door and a call from a familiar voice. We passed the young man and through the curtained doorway into an open back room, filled with shelves containing a number of pawned items. In the center of it all was the nephew — identified by Holmes with his true name, Borman — in the grasp of Constable Mills, who had been sent around beforehand to watch the back door.

As he had when we confronted him at the Great New Street restaurant, he initially looked as if he were considering what possibilities he could manage before deciding to give up and discuss things in a friendly manner. With a smile that was just slightly more sincere than the one he'd presented when he'd entered the front of the shop, he asked, unable to keep the nervousness out of his voice, "What's up, gents?"

"Mr. Borman," Holmes began. "As you can see, we've had a chance to compare notes, and it seems as if you're attempts to both blackmail Mr. Harden about a non-existent event in his past, as well as get at his papers in Mr. Kirbishaw's office, had been kiboshed."

The man swallowed, and then said, obviously doubting it himself but willing to try and bluff it through, "I think you've got the wrong man."

Holmes smiled. "It won't do, Mr. Borman, it really won't. You've been under observation from the time we separated after our last meeting. In the days that followed, I've had a chance to do quite a bit of rooting around in your past. You aren't Abraham Harden, as you claimed, and as you were registered at the small hotel run by Mrs. Frobisher. You are Graham Borman, owner of this pawnshop, which was willed to you by the former proprietor, Walter Spaeth, following his death last year. You've lived in England for over a quarter-century, coming here from America in the late 1860's. You are still an American citizen, having been born in North Carolina. In spite of that state's association with the Confederacy, you had traveled north in 1861, along with two brothers, and joined the Union Army. My sources in the United States confirmed that you were in the same unit as the true Abraham Harden. In fact, it's been confirmed that you were friends, and so it was likely he who told you about his uncle, the tobacco millionaire, along with the true version of his father's death, and his subsequent move to Boston with his mother."

Holmes turned to John Vincent Harden. "I hope you understand, sir, that I took the trouble to verify your story."

The old man nodded. "Of course. I'm glad that you did."

Back to Borman, Holmes continued. "Young Abraham Harden was reported missing after The Battle of Gettysburg — where you served as well. His body was never found. I suspect that when he fell, you stole his identification, allowing him to be buried in an unmarked grave."

Borman laughed unconvincingly. I heard the front door open and shut — and then open and shut again. Then the second constable walked through the curtain with the young man in his grasp. "He was slipping out the front door."

"I don't think," said Holmes, "that he has anything to do with this. Could you keep him out front until we're done?"

The constable nodded and the two retreated. Then Holmes continued.

"You will deny that you took Abraham Harden's papers from his body, but I'm certain that you did. I found them upstairs when I searched this house last week."

At that, the man's rigid smile dropped. He snarled, "You have no right to do that!"

"He does," interrupted MacDonald. "We obtained a special warrant."

"What?" sputtered Borman. "Why — "

"Suspicion of murder."

Borman's face took on a wild look, and he jerked to one side, but Constable Mills' grip never eased.

"Seeing an opportunity," Holmes continued, "you took the papers from the dead Abraham Harden, perhaps believing that they might one day be useful in some as-yet unknown way. After all, you likely knew and understood that he hadn't seen his rich uncle in years. Possibly, if you waited long enough and the time was right, you might free up some of the man's wealth for yourself. But you didn't use them, and instead eventually drifted to England, where you became Mr. Spaeth's associate. Then, Mr. Harden came to London, and you devised your poor scheme to shake loose something from him, figuring that a rich man has secrets, and that even if the story you pitched wasn't true, he'd give you something to avoid any other scrutiny.

"By your own admission, you broke into his room at the Langham and read his papers, realizing that there were valuable bearer documents in Mr. Kirbishaw's office. In for a penny, you thought, and made a try for those as well. And here we are."

"You can't prove any of this," snarled the man, his long-ago American accent more obvious now.

"But I can. You see, after I became interested in you, every aspect of your life was suspect — including how you came to inherit this shop. We found arsenic stored here, and while that is a common-enough material, to be found in many places, it was enough to nudge me into examining the late Mr. Spaeth's medical records. He died from a wasting illness, it's true, something he'd had for a while, but it suddenly became worse at the end — with symptoms remarkably like arsenic poisoning. With this in mind, we obtained an exhumation order."

"Exhumation — ?" Borman growled.

"Indeed. Dr. Thorndyke?"

The young doctor cleared his throat. "I was present at the autopsy. Mr. Spaeth had clearly died of arsenic poisoning. In spite of the body's decomposition, the high levels of arsenic had remained. It was murder, without a doubt."

Holmes turned back to Borman. "I also cast my eye over Spaeth's will, such as it was. Knowing what to look for made spotting the signs of forgery quite obvious." He took a step closer to Borman. "It really was quite a seamy little crime, and you would have gotten away with it but for your greed for a piece of Mr. Harden's fortune, and the peculiar persecution that you carried out to get it." He shook his head. "The rest can wait. You'll hear it when Dr. Thorndyke and I testify at your trial."

"Take him away," added MacDonald. Borman began to curse and struggle, but he was no match for the burly constable, and in a moment, we heard the door to the alley close.

Over the next hour or so, further evidence was gathered. When his late nephew's papers were returned to Mr. Harden, with the Scotland Yard inspector's permission, the old man found himself unable to speak, except to thank Holmes for finally revealing the truth of his nephew's absence to him after to many years, even if the ending to the story was a sad one. Then he departed, having no further interest in the excavation of Borman's other secrets.

*****

Thorndyke, Holmes, and I gathered back at Kirbishaw's rooms, where he insisted on throwing an informal fete to celebrate the conclusion of the investigation that had wound through several weeks, from the time the old lawyer had first told his tale in our Baker Street lodgings. Then, the meal complete, Holmes explained in greater depth how he had traced Borman's past, by way of several associates that he had befriended through the years, and then made the connection to Abraham Harden. "It was fairly clear from the first that his shabby impersonation of the late Harden was ill-conceived. And knowing that he was willing to attempt that, I wondered what else he might have tried in order to improve his lot in life."

Kirbishaw gave a canny smile. "It didn't escape me that you let slip a little opening that any good attorney would be bound to pursue."

Holmes smiled. "The discovery of the arsenic?"

Kirbishaw nodded, and Thorndyke said, "I don't understand."

"Holmes indicated that arsenic was found *after* a warrant for a search was obtained," explained Kirbishaw, "but how did he convince anyone to obtain a warrant in the first place?"

I cleared my throat. "Borman's lock pick is not nearly as good as the set of them carried by Holmes." I looked his way. "You searched the house beforehand?"

"I did, and then when MacDonald obtained the warrant, on my advice, I was able to give him hints as to where to look without wasting any time. We had to get in and out, you see, on a Sunday morning when Borman had gone out to find some breakfast, and the shop was closed and his assistant absent from the premises."

Kirbishaw slapped his knee and laughed, but then said, "Still, arsenic is common enough. There's no reason that he shouldn't have had it there. How did you obtain the exhumation?"

"It was only after I examined the will that had been filed after Spaeth's death, leaving everything to Borman, and could confirm that it had been forged, that MacDonald was willing to go the next step. After that, everything fell into place, and Thorndyke was able to be present at the autopsy and testing of the remains as my representative."

"And fascinating it was, too." And he began to elaborate upon the procedure, seemingly unaware that Holmes and I knew it well, relating the story to Kirbishaw as if he were a boy who had caught a monster fish and wanted to share the details with his grandfather. And the old lawyer, in return, listened as if he'd never heard such a thing before, laughing and slapping his knee, or being shocked as fitting throughout the entire story.

It came as no surprise that Thorndyke soon after announced that he intended to add the title of lawyer to his medical credentials. Additionally, he began to haunt Barts, with a good word from both Holmes and me in the right ears, along with the chemical and physical laboratories and *post mortem* room at St. Margarets, in order to participate in those activities which would ground him well in the forensic arts. He became associated with Kirbishaw's practice, and his rise was meteoric. He was called to the bar the very next year, expressing to us in a conversation that he had hopes of getting a coronership. But soon after, one of the lecturers at St. Margaret's, old Stedman, retired unexpectedly, and he took that position instead.

He convinced Kirbishaw to straighten up the chambers, and to install a small laboratory, with an eye toward pursuing forensic cases. To run it, he hired a crinkly faced and incredibly capable fellow named Polton. Kirbishaw was more than happy to ease back on his own caseload, slowly turning more and more of the practice over to Thorndyke, who — in the meantime — was making a name for himself in the London medico-jurisprudence community. By the time he tried his first case for the defense, *Regina v. Gummer*, in 1897, his name was a byword for solid and workmanlike craftsmanship in his chosen field. And when old Kirbishaw passed in an omnibus accident later that year, the lease at 5A Kings Bench Walk transferred to Thorndyke, and there he remains to the present day.

The Curate's Curious Egg

by John Linwood Grant

I, Doctor John H Watson, must denounce myself. I must beg forgiveness for all that I have written in ire, frustration, or mere petty temper, on the habits of my old friend Sherlock Holmes. I have often mentioned his moods, his untidiness, his infuriating practice of withholding certain facts until he deemed it appropriate, and his many other small foibles — enough at times to drive a man to distraction. And yes, I have sniffed at his less than complimentary views on my own detecting and observational abilities, views which occasionally verged on the unkind, I felt at the time.

For the record, I will state that Holmes is the finest of men — polite, considerate, reasonable, and possessing every other social virtue to which one might aspire. And why must I do this, at such a late point in my association with the Great Detective? It is simple. It is because this autumn I encountered Professor Augustus S. F. X. Van Dusen, and learned my lesson.

I met The Thinking Machine.

*****

It was not common for a man of the cloth to be entertained in Holmes's rooms, and I was curious therefore when I received a scrawled invitation one morning, asking that I meet with my friend and the Reverend Edgerton Brice at Baker Street. I vaguely recalled Brice as an expert on church architecture, which was hardly Holmes's field; the clerical gentleman was the incumbent at St Melias's, not far from Blackfriars. What events must have prompted this summons, I could not imagine.

I hailed a cab, and when at last I saw myself up to Holmes's rooms, the two men were ensconced in comfortable chairs, clearly waiting. At the click of the door, Holmes leapt to his feet and strode over to pump my hand.

"Capital, Watson. Good to see you." And I believe he meant it, for it had been months since we had shared even the whiff of a case — though I expected that he would have been pursuing various investigations all the same.

"Holmes, I—"

"Take my seat, dear Watson. No, Reverend, pray do not rise — and let me say that I trust my friend here in all matters. He will wish to hear of your misfortune."

Edgerton Brice fiddled with his teaspoon, not quite looking at either of us. Wisps of white hair adorned a smooth pate, his eyes were pale, and only golden pince-nez gave him any real colour. I was reminded of the case of Yoxley Old Place and Professor Coram, and the startling Russian connections that emerged during our investigation. Was this to be another such convoluted business?

"Reverend Brice's curate is ill," said Holmes. "Very ill, in fact."

I blinked, and sat down.

"My, er, condolences." I refused a cup of tepid coffee. "There is some puzzle attached to his illness?"

Holmes laughed. "Indeed, indeed." The reverend gentleman looked a little put out, and Holmes amended his expression. "Forgive me, but this is all very interesting."

"My curate," said Reverend Brice, "Is in a grievous state in St Bartholomew's, though they have hopes that he will make a full recovery."

"Ah. A particularly virulent infection?"

"Strychnine, Watson," said Holmes more soberly.

"Good Heavens!"

The details which had brought Brice to Holmes's door came out in murmurs from the cleric and occasional lively interjections from Holmes. That Brice was here in particular was due to my friend having once done Brice's brother a kindness over a disputed legacy, and the reverend's inability to extract sense from Scotland Yard. For Scotland Yard were involved, and were being officious as usual.

That very morning, a Monday, the newly acquired curate of St Melias's, a young man called Bartholemew Grayne, came down to breakfast at his lodgings. He consumed (according to his landlady) a cup of tea, a bowl of porridge, and part of a soft-boiled egg. He was a slow eater, and halfway through the egg, he complained of a 'tightness' in his face, and a shortness of breath. Within moments, the landlady saw that the curate was jerking uncontrollably, enough to throw him off his chair. She immediately sent her maid to a doctor who practised only a street away, and that worthy, arriving with haste, pronounced that Grayne had been poisoned.

"The doctor," said Brice in his faint voice, "Administered an emetic and then bromide of potassium, I am told, and urged immediate hospitalisation."

"Very sound," I said, "Though I might have considered using tannic acid. I imagine Barts have taken all the necessary steps. But who on earth would wish to poison a curate?"

Holmes paced excitedly, enough that I wondered if he had been exploring his own medication once more. "More to the point, Watson, why does Inspector Yell of the Yard have his men outside the lodging house this very moment, eh? Why will they not tell the reverend of any apprehensions they may have?"

Reverend Brice shook his head feebly, his distress obvious. "It is all most vexing, gentlemen. I cannot understand a jot of it."

"Never fear, sir." I patted his knee as if he were a worried child. "Mr. Holmes and I shall shed light on the matter, you can be assured."

When Brice had gone, my friend rifled through his catalogue of cards and clippings, Debrett's open on the floor.

"Grayne — third son of a minor Kent family, of no importance whatsoever."

"Except to that minor family, perhaps?"

"Oh, probably, probably. But there is nothing obvious about the man that would interest Scotland Yard—"

Three sharp knocks upon the door to the street interrupted him.

"It might be Brice, having forgotten something," I suggested.

"Phh! A strong arm and a direct manner, hardly our clerical friend."

With Holmes's landlady away at her sisters, I went to see who was there —and when I drew the door open, I beheld one of the most peculiar sights of my life.

The man on the step appeared to be, in almost every way, the opposite of Mr Sherlock Holmes. Our visitor was perhaps only five foot two or three inches tall, with a great domed head fringed by lank yellow hair, a head which seemed as if it threatened to topple him. Beneath the dome, a small, narrow-eyed face tapered to a mouth which I might now describe as petulant. The eyes were sky-blue and watery, sheltering behind large spectacles.

"Montgomery Jones," he said in a sharp American accent.

"Oh." I opened the door wider. "Do come in, Mr. Jones."

"I am not Montgomery Jones," he snapped, entering. "Where is Holmes?"

Irritated already, I showed the American upstairs.

"There you are," said our visitor as he saw Holmes from the sitting room entrance. "Montgomery Jones is guilty. The limp is assumed — I made a thorough examination — and the Clyde Ruby will be in the built-up shoe that the police hold. The footwear is atypical, and was obviously manufactured for a purpose. The housekeeper was, of course, in love with him — he did not bother to inform her that the feeling was not reciprocated. Women like that open themselves up to mischief."

Holmes put down the manilla file he was holding.

"Professor Van Dusen. A pleasure to make your acquaintance."

"Professor Augustus S. F. X. Van Dusen, PhD, LLD, FRS, MD, MDS and—"

"Of course. From Boston, Massachusetts." Holmes gave a generous wave of his hand. "And you encountered Mr. Jones how, might I enquire?"

The American sat down on a straight chair by the breakfast table — without being asked — and fixed his watery eyes on Holmes, ignoring me completely.

"I have recently received a further honorary degree from the University of London; as I had a few days to spare, your Metropolitan Police Commissioner asked if I would be so generous as to speak to a number of his senior officers. My methods, and so forth."

"How interesting."

"Yes, yes. Anyway, it was mentioned that you were about to be approached concerning the Clyde case. I requested that I visit their suspect, Montgomery Jones, in his cell, to which they consented; once there, I merely utilised my medical knowledge, perused the file they held, and came to the logical conclusion."

"Logic is a powerful tool," said Holmes, half a smile at me.

"It is the only tool, sir." Van Dusen stood up. "The police may ask you for confirmation, being stupidly cautious of our modern American approaches, but you have your answer."

"I am sure that you are correct, Van Du... Professor. Will you take coffee before you leave?"

The American glanced around the cluttered room, noting the spirit burner, chemicals and stands of test-tubes by the window.

"You should invest in a proper laboratory, Holmes," he said. "Coffee? No thank you. British coffee is weak and unreliable. If you had a ham sandwich, however...."

"I am sure Watson can find ham in the pantry, for such an illustrious guest."

"Holmes, really, I must—"

"Whilst I tell the Professor about our earlier visitor, and see what he thinks of poisoned eggs."

The twinkle in my friend's eye was unmistakable this time, and although I grumbled, I adjourned to the pantry and made up a plate of sandwiches. My only pleasure was that I used the dry outer cuts of ham for those I would give to Van Dusen.

"...And I tell you, Holmes, that an emetic is of little real use in cases of strychnine. Furthermore..."

The American stopped at the sight of his sandwiches. "Good."

As if he were in a cheap Tottenham Road chop house, this extraordinary man began to wolf down what I had provided, without thanking me.

"Watson," said my friend, "We will have the pleasure of Professor Van Dusen's company today. He has graciously agreed to lend his expertise to the mystery of the poisoned curate, as an exercise."

Before I could comment, he continued.

"For the Professor is known in his home country for his scientific methods and his rigid application of logic to many a crime. Over there, I understand, they call him the Thinking Machine."

I already had a name for the man but chose not to share it.

*****

The lodging house where Bartholomew Grayne had been poisoned was a modest establishment on a respectable Farringdon street, less than a mile from St Melias's Church. The constable outside took one look at the three of us as we alighted from our hansom cab, and shot back through the open front door. I paid the cabbie and smiled to see the rotund figure of Inspector Harold Yell emerging from whence the constable had disappeared.

"Mr. Holmes. I don't believe we called you, sir."

"I am acting on behalf of my clients, the Reverend Brice and Mr. Grayne. The latter has, as you might imagine, Inspector, a keen interest in the case."

Though we had rarely crossed paths with Yell, he was said to have a tenacity and an honesty about him which raised him above some of his colleagues.

"And this," added Holmes, "Is the illustrious Professor Van Dusen, of Boston."

"Um… welcome to Farringdon, Professor."

Van Dusen, who was peering at the lodging house façade, ignored him.

"Um, yes. Gentlemen, you'd better come inside."

He ushered us into the house, quickly pointing out the basics — a breakfast parlour and a shared sitting room, with a kitchen and back parlour for the landlady.

Heavy furniture cluttered the otherwise airy breakfast parlour which looked onto the street. Near the open window stood a rectangular oak table with a place laid at either end. One was an untouched setting; the other a disturbed display – a side-plate with the top of an egg-shell and a half-eaten piece of brown toast, a teacup with the dregs of tea within, and an egg-cup holding a partially consumed egg. Next to these, a sugar bowl and an open salt cellar with a small silver spoon next to it.

"There is another lodger," said Holmes. "One who was called away before he could commence his breakfast. A bachelor, a man of at least moderate importance — a civil servant or advisor, probably to the Foreign Office. He likes simple privacy, and chose this street as it is unremarkable. There are now concerns that Bartholomew Grayne was poisoned, well, let us say not quite by accident, but as an acceptable casualty of war. The authorities believe the other man was the target, and that foreign agents are involved. Given the current political situation, a Balkan matter would be the obvious one — perhaps Serbia or Bulgaria."

Yell wet his lips. "I... that is, yes. You are, as I should have expected, entirely correct, sir. Astonishing."

"Hardly," muttered Van Dusen. "The hallway contains a newspaper in Cyrillic, and a hat of some quality, neither of which are likely to belong to a junior English clergyman. That the hat is still there suggests a hasty exit."

"Um... I see." Yell tried to recollect himself. "The landlady and the live-in maid occupy the top floor; Mr. Grayne and a man called Herrick the rooms on the floor in between. Mr. Herrick is, as you say, a civil servant. A major cog in the Foreign Office, but modest and quiet. I'm told he has been working on certain strategies, policies, what have you, which have some importance in the international arena."

"An obvious target," I said.

"Have you ascertained how the strychnine was introduced, inspector?"

"Not yet, Mr Holmes. The landlady, a Scottish woman named Mrs. Coombs, has been instructed to leave everything exactly as it was at breakfast time, in both kitchen and breakfast parlour.

"The garbage should be checked."

We turned to the American.

"The dustbins," Holmes explained. "The Professor refers to any hasty attempt to discard the origin of the poison, such as wraps, phials, or bottles. I dare say we should examine the eggs, as well."

A grey-haired sergeant entered, holding up a tray of eggs, from which one alone was missing. "The porridge bowl is in the kitchen, sir," he said, "But not washed. The landlady says she and the maid ate porridge from the same pan, in her own parlour, and has suffered no ill effects."

Holmes sniffed the eggs, and held one up to the light.

"No tampering. Irish eggs, by the smell of damp hay, not fresh but acceptable. Almost impossible to tamper with."

"Nothing is impossible, though I concur in this case." Van Dusen turned to me, his huge head quite intimidating. "Describe the common appearance of strychnine, Doctor."

I had no doubt he knew already, but I obliged. "Why, it's a white, crystalline substance, not unlike sugar at a glance. Nux vomica, we used to call it, in its original form"

The inspector nodded. "We are already examining the sugar from the larder and the sugar bowl, and will be sending samples for analysis. I do know my job, sirs."

"And how would a Scotswoman serve porridge, Watson?" Holmes was smiling, and I felt myself trapped between two inexorable intelligences.

"Plain. Or... wait, with salt. That's how I was brought up."

"Which is also the commonest condiment for a soft-boiled egg."

Holmes and Van Dusen looked at each other.

"The salt cellars," they said in unison.

Yell looked glum. "Then all the salt in the house must also be sampled."

Holmes disappeared into the kitchen to speak with the landlady and maid. He was there for some time, whilst I tried – and failed – to engage Van Dusen in polite conversation; Yell paced, occasionally receiving word from the sergeant, who tramped in and out with various items from kitchen and larder.

"Mrs. Coombs sits back there like an angry hen; the maid is subdued," said Holmes, returning. "Both have errands at various times of the day, and there is ample opportunity for a stranger to interfere. The kitchen door is wide open, and the trap to the coal-hole is loose, unsecured. There is a daily, and tradesmen call all the time apparently, as well as salesmen with their buttons and brooms. No one is watched; no one watches. Old Lestrade himself could blunder through the back gate or over the front wall, and be at the table and sideboard in here without anyone the wiser."

Van Dusen pulled a face. "The simplest knowledge of household routine would suffice. What of this 'daily' — some sort of cleaner, I imagine?"

"An elderly woman from the same street," said Yell. "In bed with rheumatism these last three days, sir."

"I see. And we must presume that the poisoner took aim at this Mr. Herrick, only missing due to unforeseen circumstances which drew the target away before breakfast. A poisoner who had no qualms about killing two men to get one. They will try again, of course, having gone to this effort."

"What were the circumstances?" Holmes rounded on the inspector.

"An urgent telegram, sir, about some unexpected Balkan matter that had arisen. I've been told no more."

"So, there was every reason to expect Herrick to be at breakfast." My friend's brows furrowed. "Why not poison Herrick's food alone? Because they had no way of doing so, when both lodgers shared their meals — Mrs. Coombs informs me that she provided the same fare for her 'gentlemen', and served it herself. Herrick had no interest in dining out; the curate's stipend rarely allowed for such extravagance. So, poison both, or none."

Holmes left once more to inspect the back and the front of the house in more detail, saying that as usual the hob-nail boots of the constabulary would likely have obscured anything of value. Unwilling to stay with Van Dusen, who was taking his own samples, I went to the kitchen where Mrs. Coombs, a plump and florid woman in her fifties, sat with a girl who was introduced as Sally Clarke the live-in maid, a plain young woman with clear blue eyes.

"I am Dr. Watson, an associate of Mr. Holmes. A tragic affair." I gave the two women what I hoped was a sympathetic look. "I expect that the police have been pressing all sorts of questions, which can be most distressing, but do not worry — we will find the scoundrel who did this."

"Sir," said the girl, "Will Mr. Grayne live?"

"I'm sure that the doctors have all under control. You will not do better than Barts — it is my alma mater, and Mr. Holmes himself studied in the laboratories there a while."

I would have said more, but the constable put his head in, and said that my colleagues were leaving.

Hurrying after, I found Holmes and Van Dusen on the pavement, arguing about tests for various African alkaloids, apparently nothing to do with our current case. As one point was conceded, another was raised, and I almost wished I was at my practice.

"Ah, Watson. I was about to suggest we adjourn to my rooms, whilst I make enquiries of young Inspector Dominick of Special Branch. He may be forthcoming as to details. And we should arrange to meet Mr. Herrick. If you agree, Professor?"

The American made a sound which might have been assent, and thus I found myself a gun dog trailing behind two masters….

*****

The St. Philip's Club, a common haunt for diplomatic staff, was awash with gossip from across the Empire, but none of it concerned Mr. Edgar Herrick, who sat primly in a leather armchair. He had the pale, worn look of a London civil servant, rather than the weathered look of those who serve from outpost to outpost across the globe. With his well-tailored, old-fashioned suit and his neatly cut grey hair, he resembled nothing so much as a rural bank manager who had attracted the unwanted attention of head office.

"I am shocked, gentlemen." Slim fingers interfered with each other nervously. "I am told… I understand, that I am to speak openly to you three, providing it goes no further."

"My services are entirely confidential," said Holmes.

"And it was strychnine, I understand? How was it—"

"The method is unimportant. Let us discuss your work, your routine and associates, Mr. Herrick."

I wondered at the rapidity of my friend's interruption. Van Dusen leaned forward to speak, and I cleared my throat, wondering if I should be more useful. "If you don't mind, Holmes, I saw Harry Bolsover coming out of the card room. I was at college with his brother, and you hardly need me here...."

"Of course, dear fellow. We shall not be long."

Relieved, I found Bolsover, brandy, and a comfortable seat in one of the other rooms, where we chatted of times gone, and anything which came into our heads. After a decent splash of soda in my second brandy, I smiled.

"Bit of a rumpus over the Balkans, eh?" I tried.

Bolsover raised his eyebrows. "Is there? I'm on Argentina and Brazil these days, old boy. The Turks, is it?"

"Did you hear about Herrick from the Foreign Office?"

"Edgar? Didn't even know he was here. He hardly ever visits. Quiet cove, keeps to himself."

I would learn nothing here, I realised, and sat back to enjoy my drink instead.

Holmes and Van Dusen emerged a half hour later, Holmes placid, the professor with an expression of ill-tempered boredom which seemed his natural state.

"Any luck?" I asked.

"Logic dictates the Serbians," said Van Dusen. "I have no interest in politics, but Herrick's role seems clear to me. This treaty may well benefit the Bulgarians, and they would hardly jeopardise a positive outcome."

Holmes nodded. "Inspector Dominick sent me a coded telegram just before we came here. He and I have an arrangement. He has heard of an agent in the country, Jovanović, who could be purposed with such interference by enemies of the Serbian Government."

"Is Herrick that important, then," I asked.

"Unfortunately, yes." Holmes led the way out of the St Philip's Club. "He speaks Russian, Serbian, Bulgarian and Greek – he is a brilliant if reclusive Oxford man – and may know more about the minutiae of the situation than any other man in England. An error on behalf of the Foreign Office, I believe, to have such a narrow approach."

"And his character?"

Holmes frowned.

"There you have me for the moment, Watson. On today's meeting, I would place him as an only child, raised in rural Oxfordshire, with likely no interest in the usual sporting or hunting activities. A copious writer, a scholar without social outlets. His fingers indicate he plays the violin; his demeanour suggests he plays it alone. He rarely visits his club, is a member only for form's sake, and I doubt he has ever deliberately sought preferment to any important position. Dominick will be able to add to this."

I pursed my lips. "So this was nothing more than a botched attempt to remove the fellow."

"Possibly," said Holmes. "Professor?"

"I still say that poison is a woman's weapon," said Van Dusen, who was observing the traffic along Pall Mall.

"Hmm? Oh, not always," said Holmes.

Eager to back up my friend, I grinned.

"There was our Cornish adventure, for example, where we—"

"Men rarely choose poison," the American insisted, interrupting me.

I could see that Holmes's earlier vitality was waning, and I knew that he would wish to sit and smoke, considering the problem with which we were faced.

"I must away to see to my own business and find some supper," I said, employing a brisk tone. "Professor, shall I summon you a hansom to your hotel?"

"Eh? I see. Yes, please do so." Van Dusen rose. "I shall see you tomorrow morning, Holmes."

The great detective said nothing, for his mind was already racing far from here.

*****

I cannot say that I slept well. I hardly needed an alienist or gypsy to tell me the meaning of my dreams, in which a wizened little man padded around me, shouting out chemical formulae – for this nightmare figure had a cracked egg for a head, an egg fringed with yellow hair, and spoke with an American accent.

In a poor temper because of my broken night, after breakfast I had a word with a medical friend who was used to acting in locum for me, and decided that I would go to the hospital and see how the unfortunate curate was progressing. Being back at Barts improved my mood, and I made for my target in a round about manner, chatting to various old colleagues.

I found Grayne in moderate health, and clearly on the mend. He was a lean, dark-haired young man — twenty-three years old, we had been told — clean-shaven and with muddy brown eyes.

"Reverend Brice was most concerned about you," I said, sitting next to Grayne's bed.

"So kind." The curate twitched, hopefully a last spasm of his recent misadventure. "I may never eat an egg again."

"The noxious substance was not in the egg, but in the salt cellar. I imagine that your first 'dose' was when you ate your morning porridge, and I assume you salted your egg, once opened?"

"I did. But... if you are Doctor John Watson, surely—"

"Yes. Mr Sherlock Holmes himself is on the trail of the culprit."

The poor fellow looked shocked.

"The others at my lodging – are they as I am?"

"Not at all – have no fear. They are all well."

I explained that his situation was most unfortunate, that the intended victim was his fellow lodger, Herrick. He moaned, and shook his head in disbelief.

"Herrick? He is a quiet soul. That it should come to this."

He sank back, his face as white as the pillow-case under his head.

"He needs to rest, doctor," said the attending nurse.

"Of course."

Grayne allowed the nurse to pull the sheet up on his chest.

"But she must not..."

He did not finish his sentence, drifting into sleep. As I rose, a young woman entered, fashionably dressed and quite pretty.

"You are a doctor?" she asked me directly.

"I am, Miss, but—"

"Will my poor Barty recover?"

Mindful of Holmes's admonition to observe and record everything to do with a case, I drew her aside, not disabusing her of the belief that the man was in my care.

"You are close to him?"

"I am Miss Enid Robinson, his fiancée."

"I see." I offered a reassuring smile. "Mr Grayne has, purely by accident, ingested a noxious chemical, but there is every reason to believe he will recover. He was attended to promptly, and is in the best possible hands."

"Thank God!"

Daring a little more, I took down her address in my pocket-book, asked a few general questions, and then took my leave quickly, before an actual hospital doctor arrived on the scene.

At Baker Street I found what I would call an uneasy accommodation. Van Dusen was at the table by the window, working with my friend's chemical apparatus and tutting; Holmes was withdrawn on an old divan on the far corner, his greasy black pipe building up a fug around him. He brightened when I entered.

"Watson. There is fresh tea in the pot."

I poured myself a cup.

"And what of our ailing curate?" asked Holmes.

"How did you—"

"Despite this unpleasant smoke, there is the faint tang of ether and carbolic upon you," said Van Dusen. "I am told you have arrangements to cover your practice at such times, and you are a man of apparent sentiment. It is logical that you visited the hospital."

"Oh. Well, I did. They believe he will make a reasonable recovery, due to a strong constitution and the prompt action of the local practitioner. Had he not received immediate attention, he would likely be dead."

Holmes drew on his pipe. "Did Mr. Grayne say anything of value?

I recounted the salient parts of our brief conversation and mentioned Miss Robinson, to which Holmes nodded and closed his eyes.

In an effort to be polite, I turned to the American.

"Doing your own analysis, Professor?"

"Obviously, though it was not needed. The salt from the larder is pure; that from the salt cellar has a considerable amount of crystalline strychnine in it, such might be found in domestic rat poison." He held up a broken eggshell. "Traces of strychnine in the half-consumed egg, of course. And nothing amiss with the remains of the porridge in the kitchen, or with the sugar. It is as I deduced — the salt in the breakfast parlour is to blame. Two and two always make four."

I pushed aside a wish to rap that swollen cranium with a teaspoon. Holmes had come to the same conclusion at much the same time, after all.

"Was any sign of rat poison found in the lodging house by the police?"

"None," said Holmes. "But it would not be, if some outside agent merely added strychnine to the salt cellar and then made off." He waved his pipe at a small heap of correspondence and telegrams. "But I have had word from various sources. My brother Mycroft says that the Bulgarian Treaty is delicate. Herrick has been whisked away, somewhat unwillingly, to a secure location; I have made enquiries of a 'friend' or two in the seamier parts of our city, and believe I can guide Dominick to where the Serbian has his lair."

"Then he will be taken forthwith?"

"He may be taken this very evening, if you care to join me."

"Of course. I have my service revolver with me – just in case."

Holmes turned to Van Dusen.

"Professor, Watson and I have work ahead of us, work which may present certain risks. Should I send word of any progress to your hotel tomorrow?"

The American drew his attention from a test tube of murky fluid, and sniffed.

"I shall accompany you. I can hardly assess your practice at second hand, can I?"

My audible groan I passed off, with apologies, as indigestion; my expression I left for Holmes alone to read.

*****

At seven that evening, as dusk fell, we set out for a particularly miserable part of Whitechapel, its name still shadowed by the terrible murders of a decade and a half before. One of Dominick's men had been posted to watch the house in question, where it was said we would find a certain Janko Jovanović.

"I have one or two contacts in the Greek and Italian criminal fraternities," said Holmes as our hansom clattered its way towards Christchurch. "It is their business to note visitors of Balkan origin, for more nefarious purposes than ours. A matter of territory, as they describe it. 'Laundry' Makarios, a dealer in stolen goods, was kind enough to give details of a Serbian who arrived in Whitechapel a few months ago. He matches what Dominick knows of Jovanović."

It might have been argued that this venture of ours should have been left to the authorities, but for my own part, I was strangely pleased to be in action again at Holmes's side, and the thought of moderate danger brought some relief from the presence of the querulous Van Dusen. Only moments before, I had mentioned a fascinating article in the papers, to be immediately rebuffed.

"I never read newspapers," the American said. "Gossip and nonsense. One must have facts to apply logic, not opinions."

"Dark times are coming in Serbia, I fear, and logic will play little part," said Holmes. "The papers may soon be full of dire news. Mycroft tells me that there may even be an uprising, led by various dissident Army officers. There is a group who some are beginning to call the Black Hand."

"Great Scott. Has it really gone so far?"

"It has not yet. This Bulgarian Treaty might alleviate some of their concerns, but I am no politician, Watson. I do not predict these things."

Our cab deposited us in shadow by Hanbury Street, and from there, dressed in overcoats of no distinction borrowed from Holmes's wardrobe, we made our way into the narrow world of taverns and tenements. Van Dusen cut an odd figure, his domed head bobbing above a worn tweed coat far too large for him – he looked like a child playing 'dress-up', not the supposed master logician and scientist he was.

We found Dominick's man, a swarthy Special Branch officer with a fresh cut over one eye, at the end of the lane in question.

"Many secrets come out during tavern brawls, doctor," the man said with a grin when I enquired if he needed medical attention. "Mr Holmes, sir – it is the third house down, a right stew of a boarding house. Jovanović is tall, with curly black hair – he has a room somewhere on the first floor, we think. Calls himself Ilić, for the moment at least."

"And he is in residence now?"

The officer assented, and we left him to watch our backs.

"This will not be a formal arrest, Professor," I said as we neared the house in question. "It is an enquiry, though from it warrants may issue. As a consulting detective of note, Holmes has a certain latitude allowed him."

"I had gathered that, thank you," sniffed the American.

At a gesture from Holmes, I knocked on the door of 26b. The toothless woman who opened the door must not have liked the look of me, for she let out a shriek in a language I did not know, and we heard a clatter of boots and slamming of other doors within.

I pushed my way past the woman, apologising as I did so, and Holmes was at my back as I ran up the stairs. I am not a young man, and was out of breath by the time a squat, thickset thug barrelled from one opening and tried to precipitate me back down to the hallway. Holmes thrust his cane forward, impacting directly on the fellow's kneecap. With a curse the thug staggered, and I was able to shove him from whence he had come.

"Not our quarry," said Holmes, pushing open the next door on the landing. I followed, and was in time to grab a pair of legs protruding from a window which gaped onto the cobbled yard at the back of the house.

"You'll injure yourself, man!" I pulled him back in, and we tumbled to the floor together. My back hurt, my old injury ached, and I felt a trifle dizzy.

"I think, Holmes," I gasped, "That we should have had… Dominick's man… do this part."

My discomfort was enhanced by the sight of Van Dusen standing unruffled in the doorway.

"Is this the Serbian?" asked the American.

Holmes nodded, helping me up. I took out my revolver, which I had forgotten during my charge upstairs, and the three of us regarded the panting agent sitting on the bare boards.

"Mr. Jovanović – or Ilić if you prefer. I am Mr. Sherlock Holmes., and I am here to ask you about a poisoning."

"*To nije moja krivica*!" said Jovanović. He was a handsome fellow, clearly as tall as Holmes and almost rakish, with a bronzed complexion.

"English, if you please."

"Is mistake."

Holmes paced around him. "It was a mistake, using poison in Farringdon, you mean? You intended for Edgar Herrick to die, but you failed.""

"*Ne*. No." His expression was not what I would have expected. Fear, yes, but also a peculiar openness. "Why would I try poison Edgar?"

We three glanced at each other. Holmes rapped his cane on the floor.

"Because with him out of the way, the Bulgarian Treaty might well fall through."

Jovanović's eyes widened. "That would be bad. I am not enemy of Serbia, I am not wicked people. Also, I cannot say it... Edgar is... *prijatelj*."

"What?" I asked.

"*Prijatelj*, special friend." The man seemed close to tears. "Very special friend. You know?"

I had the feeling something had gone rather wrong.

"See, I have picture." He reached slowly into his jacket, my revolver pointed at him, and drew out a simple brass cigarette case. Holmes took it from him, and opened it. Instead of cigarettes, the case held a photograph of Edgar Herrick, smiling, and a dried red rosebud.

"Ah." I reddened, catching the implication.

"Gentlemen," said Van Dusen, stepping forward. "The situation is quite clear. Your Mr. Jovanović is panicked because he too believes that an attempt had been made on Herrick's life, and fears for his own."

The Serb frowned, and his brow cleared as he caught the American's meaning. "*Da*! I think maybe someone at *ambasada*, embassy, is hearing..." He went momentarily shy. "That Edgar and I are... such friends. They do not like this. They hurt us, or make blackmail, da?"

Though I had caught my breath now, I was still confused. "The Serbian Embassy arranged to poison Herrick?"

"*Ne*," said Holmes with annoyance. "I mean, no. If Jovanović is telling the truth, we have this case completely wrong."

"Perhaps you are a competent medical man, Dr. Watson" said Van Dusen, in a tone so free of emotion that it was more annoying than a deliberate slur, "But you do not have a logical mind. Did I not say that poison was a woman's weapon?"

"Do either of these men have wives?"

Holmes put his hand on my shoulder. "Watson, dear fellow, I am afraid that the Professor has grasped the matter. Neither Herrick nor Jovanović are targets."

Replacing my weapon, I helped the Serb to his feet. He looked as puzzled as I was.

"Our fellow here is a Serbian agent, but has, as far as we know, done nothing untoward. Nor has Herrick — excepting that their... friendship would not be welcome in British or Serbian society"

I wanted to be censorious, and yet, had I not seen this sort of thing in my old regiment once or twice? Unwise at very best, rather tragic when genuine, and all to lose.

"But hang on, Holmes, if that's the case—"

"Watson, I grow old, and am too easily led by expectations of high intrigue. Without further information, we must conclude that the curate, Bartholomew Grayne, was the intended target all along."

"Pah! It is the perpetrator we seek, is it not? Method is established; identity can be obtained from reviewing the facts again."

"And motive?" I asked. "The emotional side of your equations?"

"Irrelevant, if method and identity are certain." Van Dusen pulled a face. "Logic cannot work without facts, without all the information."

"But what about this Serbian fellow?" I pointed to Jovanović, who had stood there through our discussion as if he were a lamb waiting to be led to slaughter.

"He will be watched by Dominick's people, or by others, but he is free to do what he must. I shall make no judgement, for I doubt that he and Herrick will ever associate – or be allowed to associate – again. Mr Jovanović, this is most important. Are you aware of any dissident groups – the Black Hand or others – who might be here to harm Mr Herrick?"

"*Ne.*" He spoke emphatically. "Black Hand, if exists, is not in England. Vienna, maybe Paris, not here. Yet."

"Thank you."

"If it was Grayne..." I had to intrude into the awkward silence that followed. "There was something else that he said, when I visited him."

"Out with it, Watson."

"I thought he was referring to the nurse as she attended to his bedsheets. He said 'But she must not...' That was all. He was too exhausted for more."

"A woman," said Van Dusen, eyes gleaming. "As I told you before. A secret wife or mistress. Women are vindictive enemies, not averse to poisoning two men if they also get the one they want."

"Could he have been referring to this Miss Robinson, the fiancée?"

"Possibly, though I cannot imagine her motive," said Holmes. "But I must consider a completely new line of enquiry. Let us return to Baker Street."

*****

Once more in his rooms, Holmes looked to Van Dusen.

"I believe that I know what must be done, but perhaps you wish to instruct us as to how you yourself would go about the next steps, Professor, if you were back in Boston?"

The small man gave my friend his usual irritated glance.

"I am not in the habit of chasing hither and thither after various unreliable strangers. My mind is my instrument. I require only pen and paper, and half a dozen addresses. With those alone, I can have your case solved within a few hours."

Holmes smiled. "Then let us each write what we must, and let Watson view the products of our ratiocination before they are consigned to their various destinations."

"If you wish," muttered Van Dusen, and cleared space on the laboratory bench in preparation for his task.

A half hour later, I stood — with some bemusement — holding several sheets of writing paper; one half of them were in Holmes's hand, the other half in the crabbed script I might have expected from Van Dusen.

"Er, Holmes, some of these appear to be virtual duplicates, requesting the same information."

"As I expected. Play the cavalier, Watson, and select which versions are despatched at random. I am sure that the Professor and I have both stressed the urgency of the situation."

I sighed, and did as he suggested.

He beamed at me when I was done. "The stamps are in the coal-scuttle; one of my young irregulars outside can deliver those letters with a local address."

"And in the meantime?"

"I shall amuse myself with an air on the Stradivarius."

Feeling that the two logicians deserved each other, I left to do their bidding, and considered that it might be best if I then spent a few hours at my practice. I was beginning to see the appeal of querulous old women with bunions, and children who had found where father hid the brandy....

*****

Returning to Baker Street at five in the afternoon, I was treated to the last notes of what must have been a long discussion on the nature of bullet wounds. After reference to a point Van Dusen said he had made twenty minutes ago, I interrupted with a 'Hulloo' cheerier than I felt.

"Holmes, Professor – have your communications borne fruit?"

"You must tell us, Watson," said my friend, gesturing to a tray on which sat a number of unopened envelopes and telegrams. "You are a vital part of this investigation."

"I am a postboy and unpaid letter opener," I said, but did as I was bid, reading out the gist of the replies as I went through the pile.

"Mr Herrick states that he prefers his food as plain as possible, and finds all commercial establishments too liberal with salt, pepper and other spices. Nor does he believe that salt is good for the circulation, so he uses it sparingly, and has often admonished his fellow lodger on the matter."

"Good, good," said the small man. "As I expected."

"Mr Coombs died in a railway accident whilst uncoupling a locomotive; his wife states that Sally Clarke offered herself with excellent references from the Bishop of Leatherhead, a week after Mr. Grayne took up residence at the lodging house. The Clarkes are a large family, Mrs. Coombs understands, respectable church-goers, and she does not think that Sally was meant to stay in service long."

I paused at the next one, a telegram, then read it out

"'Confirm B Grayne Esq previously secretary Guildford Diocese.' Holmes, Leatherhead is in that diocese, is it not?"

"Quite," said Holmes. "And the others?"

My mind raced, but I went through the rest quickly.

"The next is from Miss Enid Robinson. She considers the questions a little impertinent, but under the circumstances she vouches that she has been acquainted with Grayne for six months, and has only recently become affianced to him. His family is proper and respectable; her father was a clergyman, retired on grounds of ill-health, and she expects Grayne to have his own parish with a year."

"A woman with ambitions," said Holmes.

"This one's a scrawl, but it begs to say that yes, they had dreadful trouble with the rats, and that a portion of the chemist's preparation is indeed missing. Signed..." I held the letter closer, "Harold Clarke, Epsom."

"Near Leatherhead," my friend murmured to our guest.

"This note is from Inspector Yell. It says that he is on his way there immediately, but does not say where. And this last telegram is from Dominick. 'No other known connection. FO satisfied. Matter apparently closed.'"

Holmes forced a quantity of shag tobacco into his old pipe and hunted for the matches; Van Dusen's head nodded as if it might come loose.

I sat down. "Would one of you care to explain?"

"Not now, old fellow. We must away to Farringdon, though I suspect we will be too late."

The hansom driver, offered an extra shilling, did his best, but the traffic was at its height, the streets snarled with omnibuses conveying people from their places of work. We reached the lodging house, and hurried to the open front door.

Yell was already there, but he shook his head.

"Done a runner, I'm afraid, sir. I doubt we'll find her easily."

"Scotland or Wales, if she has sense. Ah well, we have our solution, at least. You will agree, Professor?"

"Mrs Coombs has fled?" I asked.

Holmes and Van Dusen looked at me.

"The maid," snapped the American. "Think of the communications you so recently read out, doctor. Sally Clarke is the culprit. Dear me, are you wilfully obtuse?"

Holmes stiffened. "Professor Van Dusen, without my Watson, I am without my good right hand. Please confine your observations to the case."

"Sentiment and logic do not mix," said Van Dusen. "Doctor, consider all the facts – and only the facts—"

"Might we at least sit down to do so?"

Yell agreed, and Mrs Coombs appeared, offering to serve us coffee in the breakfast parlour.

"I believe that Mr. Herrick will be returning to your care, Madam," said Holmes. "Though I cannot speak for Mr. Grayne."

"Aye," she said, glum-faced, "Weel, I'll have the better of the twa, then."

"You did not like Mr. Grayne?"

She set down the coffee-pot.

"I dinna say I disliked him, not enough to speak any ill when first you asked, Mr. Holmes. But he was ay a stuffed shirt with Sally, and o'er full of his prospects for my liking. Not modest, you understand, like Mr. Herrick."

"I do understand, Mrs. Coombs. I imagine he was more dismissive with Miss Clarke after his engagement was settled?"

"Aye, that's true."

When the four of us were alone in the parlour, Yell set down his cup of coffee.

"So, will one of you set out what exactly has happened, gentlemen? Can Scotland Yard get back to more urgent matters?"

Van Dusen's small blue eyes fixed the inspector in their glare.

"It is simple. Had I not been distracted by your politics and Balkan fantasies, I would have given you the answer far earlier. Sally Clarke, the maid, knew Grayne from service in Leatherhead, wherever that is. Intelligent and with her own ambitions, she no doubt made occasional comment as to Grayne's talents, spreading good word about him." He took off his glasses to polish them. "Whether his response came from carnal thoughts or genuine intent, I do not know, but I assume he offered her some sort of understanding."

I began to see a glimmer of light.

"But surely a cleric — and a young, rising one — would not marry a maid?"

"He would not," said Holmes. "I think we will find that Bartholomew Grayne is not a blameless victim, but a man of manipulative habit. When he was offered the curacy of St. Melias's, he gave her no thought, and yet she foolishly troubled to follow him taking up duties where he lodged."

Van Dusen put his glasses back on. "His engagement to this Miss Robinson is the key. Once announced, the maid had either to slink home, tail between her legs, or act. Any lingering thought that he might keep his word was banished. She chose to act as women do, and teach Grayne a serious lesson."

"But Herrick—"

"Avoided salt – remember his letter?" Holmes offered his cigarette case around. "Sally Clarke knew this well, as the live-in maid, and had no intention of causing Herrick harm. Nor did she let any portion of the 'borrowed' rat poison go in anything which might affect her or Mrs. Coombs. Her plan may have been to remove the poisoned salt entirely after the act, but she is no master criminal. Sent for the doctor, she found she had no time for further obfuscation. It must have been a relief when all immediately assumed Herrick, a far more important man, to be the intended victim."

I reached for the sugar, and then remembering the history of the parlour, decided not to bother.

"Unless she is more cunning than you credit, Holmes" I said. "Had the telegram not called Herrick away… well, he said he took little salt, not none. He would have undoubtedly felt unwell, had he sprinkled a grain or two on his porridge or in his egg."

"A pertinent observation, Watson. As for Herrick, Dominick confirmed in his telegram that there is no trace of international involvement. There is no reason why he may not know the full truth now – I withheld certain facts from him until I was sure that he was not involved in some complex situation. And I have chosen…" he glanced at Yell, "Not to mention anything of Herrick's private life. It has no bearing on this case."

"Woman trouble of his own, eh?" said the inspector.

I thought Van Dusen was going to speak up, but he pressed his thin lips together again.

I sat back. "Great Scott. We embark upon a search for Serbian or Bulgarian spies, and matters of national importance. And we end with a jilted girl's attempt at vengeance. What, then, of Bartholomew Grayne?"

"A victim of his own behaviour." Holmes drew on his slim cigarette. "I can hardly condone poisoning, but I have little sympathy. I shall tell the Reverend Brice that he should attend to his curate's moral development, and hope that Grayne has learned his lesson."

"I feel sorry for the girl," I said.

Yell had much the same scowl on his face as had Van Dusen.

"She was almost a murderer, doctor."

Holmes stood up. "We are all of us 'almost' a murderer, inspector, at one time or another in our lives. No doubt the regional constabularies will do their best, but whether or not she is taken eventually is not out concern. I do not expect any more attempts on either men's lives."

*****

The following day brought a promise of spring sunshine, and the greater promise of Professor Augustus S. F. X. Van Dusen sailing for Boston. The small man called on us at noon, when Holmes and I were sharing a brief, amicable moment before we once again parted ways for a while.

Subduing a weary sigh, I let Van Dusen in and asked if he would care for any refreshment.

"No," he said. "Holmes, I am leaving in an hour. It has been interesting meeting you."

"And my friend Watson."

"What. Oh, yes. The doctor. Anyway, One or two of your more scientific monographs are of interest. Please send copies of the following to my Boston office."

He passed Holmes a slip of paper.

"I would be delighted to do so. By the way, the Reverend Brice is not a poor man. He asks if you wish any sort of fee for your involvement. I have waived mine."

"Money does not hold any attraction for me," said Van Dusen. "When pressed, I pass any fees to charitable causes who may have some idea of what to do with it. Tell him to use it making more stringent enquiries about his curates in future."

Holmes rose from his chair and held out his hand. "We have been honoured to meet you."

Van Dusen brushed his pale, slender fingers against the tips of Holmes's fingers, and turned to leave.

"Indeed," he said. "For my own part, I admit you a most competent logician, Holmes, though I fear your medical colleague is beginning to infect you with a touch of typical human sentimentality."

Holmes smiled at me, a smile which I like to think came from years of acquaintance and common cause.

"I hope so, Professor Van Dusen," he said. "I do hope so."

With the American gone, I collapsed into an armchair and took a deep breath.

"That was kind of you, Holmes, what you said just now. And what did you really think of Van Dusen, eh?"

"What did I think of the 'Thinking Machine'?" He let loose a deep chuckle. "Watson, I found him like the curate's egg — good in parts."

The Case of William Wilson

by Richard Zwicker

I valued my friendship with Sherlock Holmes. It was impossible to imagine my life had our paths not crossed. The challenges presented by the medical field alone no longer satisfied me. Yet, there were times when his moods tested my patience. Mrs. Hudson had just set down a magnificent steak and kidney pie on the table, and after a long day, I planned to relish each savory bite. Holmes, on the other hand, stared at his plate. Even seated, he appeared tall. His deerstalker hat off, I could clearly see disturbed lines in his high forehead.

"Steak and kidney pie again?" he asked no one in particular.

"What do you mean, again? It's been weeks since we've had it," I said.

"That is true, but we've had it before, numerous times. We know what to expect when we eat it."

"Isn't expectation part of the joy of dining?" I asked, trying to be patient.

"Of course, but repetition deadens the senses. Eating becomes mechanical. Is it too much to ask that I be surprised by my food?"

"I suppose I could ask Mrs. Hudson to burn the dinner next time, but as she takes pride in her work, I doubt she would comply. Surely, you don't expect her to cook something different every day?"

"No," said Holmes, "but it would be gratifying if she mixed things up a bit. We have a limited amount of days on this mortal coil. Every time we repeat ourselves is time lost. Singularity is what I strive for, and singularity is what my life sadly lacks at the moment."

I nodded, knowing that further argument with him would be even more time lost. "Well, I intend to eat and enjoy my single serving of steak and kidney pie. If you don't want yours, I'll happily repeat myself by eating that as well."

Holmes cut into his pie. "A generous offer, Watson, but unnecessary. The body requires a certain amount of sustenance, which this pie will provide."

We ate in silence, Holmes finishing his portion well before me. He then proceeded to light his pipe. After inundating me with a couple of puffs, I asked him if he could delay his smoking until I finished my food.

"Oh, sorry, Watson. At least, at times, my insensitivity is singular." He extinguished the pipe, coughed, then gazed at me. "Have you plans for this evening?"

"I thought I might relax in my favorite chair and catch up with the news in the local papers."

"The problem with newspapers is they report what, when, and how, but rarely why."

"They need to leave something for you to do."

"Quite right."

Just as he rose, we heard raised voices from the foyer. The high-pitched feminine Cockney accent belonged to Mrs. Hudson, our landlady. The other voice was male, guttural, and slurred. After Mrs. Hudson said, "You shall wait here!" the male voice sputtered and then stopped. Our intrepid landlady then entered the room, looking harried.

The Case of William Wilson by Richard Zwicker

"There is a gentleman here to see you. I told him he had to wait until you finished your meal, but he insists."

"Don't tell me what he wants," said Holmes. "I'm keen to guess."

"He hasn't told me what he wants. He said it's for only you to hear. He is also intoxicated."

"Hmm. Whatever his problem, it embarrasses him. Well, Watson, though I have finished my meal, yours still demands your attention. Should we make him wait?"

"I am able to eat in conjunction with almost any other activity, and I'm curious to see if he deems my ears worthy of hearing his problem."

"Well said. Show the man in, Mrs. Hudson."

It wasn't necessary. At that moment the man in question forced himself through the doorway. He had a short beard and curly black hair in need of a comb. His clothes were fashionably cut but wrinkled. Though I guessed he was in his mid-30s, his face was lined and haggard. The quality that stood out to me was his eyes, which darted and pierced like a fencer's sword.

"Which one of you is Holmes?" he asked.

"I am Holmes," said my friend. "And this is my assistant, Dr. Watson. You are here today because someone is taking advantage of you, perhaps someone who has known you for a long time. The problem is more of an embarrassment than a financial worry. A difficult night has presented you with more worries than sleep."

Our potential client appeared baffled. It was a look I had seen many times. "You are not wrong, but how...?" he said.

"Your clothes tell me money is not a concern for you, but they were carelessly donned. Your blue socks don't quite match. The absence of a wedding ring suggests you are used to having your own way. Your liberal use of alcohol shows you have difficulty facing up to your problem."

"I don't like being read," he growled.

"Then you should make yourself less of an open book," said Holmes.

The man looked contemptuously at me. "Can he be trusted?"

"Implicitly, unless you continue to speak as if he weren't in the room," said Holmes.

The man hesitated, as if unsure he was being criticized.

"Very well. My name is William Wilson. If you can solve my problem, I'll pay whatever fee you require."

"In that case, pray tell us your story," said Holmes.

Wilson sat heavily in the third chair at the table. "I have been to the best schools and received an education that, had I needed money, would readily allow me to earn it. The truth is, I have an estate that provides a comfortable living."

"Yours sounds like a life many would envy," I said.

"Without doubt, but most would not act upon that envy. Unfortunately, there exists one person so consumed by that emotion that he won't leave me alone. His every action is a reaction to me. He attended the same upper school and university I attended. If I go for a walk, he finds me. If I have a party, he shows up at my door. I recently vacationed in Paris, and he found me there. He appears, he annoys me, and then, abruptly, he leaves."

"This is extreme behavior," said Holmes. "Clearly, he is also a man of means. How would you describe your direct interaction with him?"

"At first he was cordial enough. I think he wanted to be my friend, but I found him rather dull. He was the type of person who always followed the rules."

"And you weren't," said Holmes.

The Case of William Wilson by Richard Zwicker

Wilson shrugged. "I find them tiresome. When I questioned him about these unwanted encounters, he passed them off as coincidence. I'd have to be an idiot to believe that."

"Has he threatened you in any way?" I asked.

"Not overtly, but how would you feel if someone traced your life? I don't want to be the raison d'etre of someone else. When I rebuffed his advances, he took to criticizing me. For example, I've never had trouble attracting the opposite sex—I am a very handsome man—but I have to be careful as some women are only interested in my wealth. My nemesis has started to reach out to everyone I spend time with and denounce my behavior. The level of his interference has increased, and that's why I'm here."

"Have you tried hiring a guard to keep him from your home?" asked Holmes.

"For a time, but I gave up. He always got in because he looks just like me. He could be my twin."

"But he's not related to you?" asked Holmes.

"No."

"And his name?" I asked.

"William Wilson," said the man.

I thought he had misunderstood my question. "He has the same name as you?"

Wilson nodded.

Holmes scratched his chin. "This is extraordinary. I assume we are not the first people you have confessed this problem to."

"Certainly not! But for reasons that confound me, none of my acquaintances see this in the way I do."

"What do you mean?" Holmes asked.

"They admit it is odd that someone in my sphere looks like me and shares the same name, but they think I'm obsessed and should just ignore him. But he doesn't let me. At every turn he stands in my way."

"Have you reported your twin's actions to the police?" I asked.

Wilson shook his head. "In the past I've run afoul of them, so I'd prefer they not get involved."

"You've been convicted of crimes?" I asked.

"Minor disagreements, in the past."

"You say this man is very similar to you. Does he have any qualities that are different?" asked Holmes.

Wilson thought for a moment. "His voice. He never speaks above a whisper."

"And yet he insists on being heard by you. So, what would you like us to do?" asked Holmes.

"You are a famous detective. Meet this man and convince him to leave me alone. Use reason, threats—whatever works."

I watched Holmes's eyes darken as he pondered the case. It wasn't the type of thing we normally did. We wouldn't need to discover the identity of a criminal. Also, while Holmes could be most persuasive and was knowledgeable about certain human behaviors, his interaction with people was specialized. Did that specialty include convincing someone to mind his own affairs? I was unsure.

"You are dealing with a singular person," said Holmes. "To persuade him to stop oppressing you, we must learn his motivation. I will take the case."

"Thank you," Wilson said softly, using two words I guessed he rarely used in tandem. "I am giving a party at my house in three nights. I have no doubt my twin will be there at some point."

"I would prefer to move more quickly on this," said Holmes. "Can you tell me where your twin lives?"

"I cannot," said Wilson.

"You've never asked?" I said.

"No. I don't dare. If I knew where he lived, I might kill him. If you feel the need to follow him home from my party, that is your affair, but I beg you, do not reveal his address to me."

"Very well," said Holmes. "We will see you three nights hence." Wilson gave us his address, which was in Piccadilly, shook our hands, and left. After closing the door on our client, Holmes asked for my thoughts.

"Something is not right about it," I said. "If this fellow is identical to William Wilson and accosts him on a regular basis, why don't Wilson's friends recognize the problem?"

"Despite his parties, my guess is Wilson doesn't have many close friends," said Holmes. "Plus, his unwillingness to learn his nemesis's address sounds like denial. That said, the more pertinent mystery is the persistence of the twin. It is interesting that at first the twin downplayed the coincidence of their encounters but later became more critical. He hasn't tried to blackmail Wilson, so why does he persecute him? We will find out."

The next day we split up. Holmes went to city hall to see if he could locate an address for the second William Wilson while I talked to Lestrade at the police station to see if I could uncover anything about our client's past history. What I learned shocked me. He had been arrested three times in the past five years for assault, always while intoxicated. Two women reported that he'd made unwanted advances. Lestrade said, in his experience, that usually meant more went unreported. All in all, it was an unflattering portrait of our client, destructive of himself and others.

Holmes didn't return to Baker Street until early evening. There were five other William Wilsons in greater London. The two men that were home looked nothing like our William Wilson. Though Holmes didn't meet the other three, he was able to talk to neighbors. Two weren't remotely in right age range, but the third, in a rundown boarding house in Paddington, was.

"I talked to his landlady, a Mrs. Davies. She said he kept very odd hours and often didn't come home at all, but his appearance was similar to our client's, and she also described him as driven, quiet, and with a whispery voice. I slipped a message for the twin under his door. If he doesn't respond tomorrow, we will pay another visit."

We received no response, so we ventured to his address. The landlady, a squat, elderly woman, insisted he wasn't home. Holmes asked if we could inspect the rooms. At first Mrs. Davies refused, but Holmes made up a story that her lodger's whispery voice was possibly a result of consumption. Holmes insisted he must check that Wilson was taking proper precautions. Otherwise, the landlady might be at risk of the disease. She relented and unlocked the door. We discovered three rooms that appeared unlived in. The small bed in the bedroom was made up. A sitting room was spotless. We found no books or loose paper. It did not look like the living space of any bachelor I knew. The only evidence of the rooms being rented at all was a closet full of expensive eveningwear and a bureau of socks and underclothes.

After going through the drawers, Holmes turned to the landlady. "I think you are safe, Mrs. Davies. Apparently, Mr. Wilson is not suffering from consumption as he is using no medication."

As we left, I turned to Holmes and said, "I am not aware of any effective medication for consumption."

His eyes twinkled. "Neither am I. It appears the twin hasn't much of a life, at least in those rooms. He apparently spends more of his time at another address... or nowhere at all. We'll see if he is more of a presence at Wilson's soiree. At least he has an ample wardrobe to choose from."

The Case of William Wilson by Richard Zwicker

*****

When the butler admitted Holmes and me into Wilson's spacious home, I was immediately struck by its ostentation. Paintings adorned the walls. Ornate Indian rugs covered the floor. His furniture looked so expensive I thought twice about sitting on it. Though we arrived only fifteen minutes after the appointed time, the party was already well under way. Fifty people, most of them in their late twenties or early thirties, were scattered through the house, talking loudly, drinks in hand. This was the type of social gathering Holmes normally avoided. Too many people talking at once distressed him, and though he dabbled in cocaine, he felt disdain for those who overindulged in alcohol. I asked if we shouldn't seek out Wilson.

"In good time, Watson," he said. "Let's first get a sense of this party. It could tell us much about our client." We helped ourselves to drinks. He used his more as a prop than as an intoxicant, barely going through the motions of sipping. Our dress was formal yet unobtrusive. Holmes wore a black tailcoat, vest, and bow tie. I wore a dark brown coat with tan trousers. No one seemed to notice us as we drifted from one animated group to another. We found Wilson in the dining room, two pretty women tugging on his arms as if he were a chicken wishbone. Wilson was telling them about a heroic adventure he'd had in the Second Anglo-Afghan War. He held a half-empty wine glass in his hand, brandishing it like a torch. He was clearly drunk. Though we stood close enough to hear his narrative, his back was to us and we remained unnoticed. When he finished his tale, as if on cue, the women praised his bravery.

I nudged Holmes. "Wilson knows how to tell a war story."

"Indeed," said Holmes. "Yet I think he could have told one of Grimm's fairy tales to the same effect on these women. He wants to make an impression, and they want to be impressed: a fortuitous situation. But I think we've heard enough."

He reached over to Wilson and shook his hand. "William Wilson, thank you for inviting us to this stimulating soiree."

Wilson looked at us, trying to focus his eyes. "Oh, right." He turned to the women. "Could you will excuse me, ladies. I must speak to these gentlemen."

"But you promised to tell us how you singlehandedly annexed Burma," said one of them.

"And I shall, later. Don't go far."

Seeing that he was serious, the two women retreated, while Wilson gave us what was left of his wine-addled attention, putting his hand on Holmes's shoulder for balance. "I hope you enjoy parties. It may take some time for that fiend to appear."

"But you're confident he will," said Holmes.

Wilson's face grew dark. "Of that I have no doubt."

"We can entertain ourselves," said Holmes. "Is your twin much of a drinker?" asked Holmes.

"It's funny you should ask. I don't think that I've ever seen a drop of liquor pass his lips."

"Yet he regularly attends your parties where drinks are plentiful," I said. "This gin is quite good, by the way."

Wilson nodded, as if the high quality of his drinks was a given. "He doesn't come for the drinks or the people. He comes to criticize me. He doesn't drink because I do. He is alone because I enjoy the company of women. He lives in simple circumstances because I am wealthy."

"I thought you didn't know where he lived," said Holmes.

"I don't, but he has told me he lives in a simple one-bedroom flat. He says that's enough for anyone."

"It is important to act as you normally do at this party," said Holmes to Wilson. "Either I or Dr. Watson will have you in our sight at all times. Under no circumstances should you allow yourself to be alone with your nemesis. Someone who acts this oddly should not be trusted."

Time passed slowly, especially when I wasn't watching Wilson. I enjoy a good party, but this one became oppressively crowded. It would have been just the thing if I'd wanted to lose myself but, on the contrary, I was working. Wishing to fit in, I tried to find the two women Wilson had been talking to. They might have found details of my being wounded at the Battle of Maiwand interesting, but each time I spotted them, they'd latched onto another man. Holmes continued carrying his glass of sherry around, but its level never diminished. Eventually, an Irishman grabbed a guitar and started singing forlorn folk songs. These had an emotional effect on about fifteen people, who harmonized with him. I'm not a big supporter of Irish folk songs, but as they got increasingly grim, I found tears welling in my eyes. Though I had neither the voice nor a strong knowledge of lyrics, I found myself joining the melancholy group in song. I was belting out "Nay, no more will I play the wild rover," when Holmes tugged at my shoulder. William Wilson's twin had entered the house.

I followed Holmes into the dining room and saw Wilson in an agitated conversation with another man who not only looked like Wilson, but had chosen similar attire. Both wore a burgundy colored topcoat and pants and a flashy red tie. Both had brought black wolf-head canes. That couldn't have been a coincidence. But though both men were bearded with curly black hair, the twin had a younger face than Wilson. We edged closer to them.

The Case of William Wilson by Richard Zwicker

"This must end," said Wilson. "You have no right to trespass in my house and criticize my habits and lifestyle. Pattern yourself after someone else, someone you hate less!"

"Desist in your immoral ways and I will leave," whispered the twin. "Persist, and you will find me at every turn."

I looked at Holmes, but he raised his hand to hold me back.

"If you come into my house again, I will kill you," said Wilson, shaking with anger.

"Then you will truly be lost. I am the only thing that keeps you from the abyss," said the twin, who then turned and left the room.

Wilson turned and saw us. "You see?"

"Follow him at a discreet distance," said Holmes to me.

*****

Though we wanted to talk to the twin, Holmes deemed it more important to first learn if he returned to his boarding house rooms or some other place. We were led on a winding chase through some of the worst London neighborhoods. We passed prostitutes, beggars, and crumbling, abandoned buildings.

I turned to Holmes. "I'll say one thing for this man. He is brave to walk alone through these neighborhoods."

"Perhaps on other nights, but tonight I suspect he is aware that he has company."

"Why do you say that?" We had been careful to maintain a safe distance.

Holmes pointed to a boarded-up drug store.

"Have you seen this building before?"

"This is not an area of London I frequent," I said.

"This is the second time we've passed it. The man is leading us on a fool's chase. It's time for this charade to end."

But before we could shout out to the twin, he vanished inside another deserted building. A cracked sign said it had once been "The Tricolor Dog," but clearly no one had been served in this pub for many years. As we entered, the smell of mold and dust assaulted my nostrils. I nearly tripped over a broken floor tile.

"Why would someone of the twin's social status spend time in a rundown place like this?" I asked.

"He doesn't," said Holmes, scowling. "We haven't the means to search this building at night, but I think a return during the day would reveal that there is second exit onto another street. We've lost him."

As we stepped back outside, my heart nearly burst my chest as we smashed into two other men. Holmes stood dazed, staring at them in disbelief. I had enough of my senses left to demand that they watch their steps.

"A thousand pardons," said the taller of the two men, his words bearing a clear French accent. He had a clean-shaven, serious face and a full head of hair parted down the middle. He wore a black topcoat and a large red tie done in a bow. His voice was measured and authoritative. "We did not expect you to exit the building so quickly."

"What? Were you following us?" I asked.

"We were indeed," said the tall man.

"Why?" I demanded.

"The answer is obvious, Watson," said Holmes. "These two men could have only been hired by the twin. We are dealing with a savvy foe. Do you notice anything odd about these gentlemen?"

I looked closer. The taller, serious-eyed one was definitely the leader. The shorter, rounder man in a light overcoat stood behind him, somewhat bemused. Both were middle-aged.

"They look a little like us," I said. "But why follow us?"

Holmes shook his head. "To mock me. I was so focused on the twin that I didn't notice them."

"But who are you?" I asked.

"I am Marcel Berengar," said the tall man.

"You may call me Faucher," said his partner.

"I'm afraid those names mean nothing to me," I said.

"For years Marcel Berengar has been one of Paris's finest consulting detectives," said Holmes. "Some say his powers of deduction match mine. His work in the Pyrenees Strangler and Three-legged Poodle affairs was most impressive. I can add that he speaks excellent English. What brings you to London?"

"I find it necessary to change my setting and routine from time to time," said Berengar. "Shortly after we arrived, I got bored and advertised my services. Like you, happenstance brought us in contact with a man named William Wilson, though not the same person. He hired us because a detective named Sherlock Holmes had been harassing him."

"That's ironic, seeing as how your client is harassing ours," said Holmes. "Perhaps between the four of us we can solve this problem."

"That may be, but we are presently at cross-purposes," said Berengar. "You want William Wilson the younger to stop harassing William Wilson the older. We want the older to stop blackening the younger's name."

"But surely the older has a right to live as he sees fit," I said. "It is not his fault that someone else has the same name."

"You don't understand the relationship between these two," said Berengar. "Your client is on a dissolute path. Listening to the younger is his only chance of turning his life around. For that reason, you must leave my client alone."

"Why is your client obsessed with mine?" asked Holmes.

At that, William Wilson the younger stepped out from another boarded-up building and approached us. "I've known my namesake for many years, and once had high hopes for him and for myself," he whispered. "He has betrayed the name. When I tell people who I am, they back away in horror. 'Oh, that William Wilson.' And I say, 'No, not that William Wilson,' but it doesn't matter."

"Why don't you move to an area where the other Wilson isn't known?" I asked.

"But this is my area. I grew up here. I can't have this stigma attached to me. You two men want to change my behavior, but surely you can see it is the behavior of my namesake that must change."

Holmes frowned, as if he could see nothing of the sort. "I will think about what you've said." He faced Berengar. "At least tell me where you two gentlemen are staying so, if necessary, I can get in touch with you."

"You can reach us at the St. George's Hotel," said Berengar.

As we walked away, Berengar approached us. Wilson the younger had already vanished.

"Gentlemen, I could not speak freely before. You've no doubt noticed there is something strange about my client."

"I assume that is why you took the case," said Holmes.

"Indeed, and if we are to solve it, I believe the solution lies with Wilson the younger."

"Is the older in danger?" asked Holmes.

"Not yet. The younger's life revolves around your client. Though his desire to reform the older is genuine, I don't know how the younger would react if that actually happened. We must try to give him what he wants, but... tread with care. Do you think he is in danger from the older?"

"Like the younger, the older Wilson has limited his threats to words and is also making efforts to restrain himself, but he has a history of violence," said Holmes. "So it is a standoff. We must find a way to force a positive outcome."

As we left, Holmes kept muttering the word "extraordinary." I asked him if he was referring to Wilson the younger or the older.

"Actually, I am referring to Berengar. Do you see what the younger Wilson has done? In a way, he has put us in his situation. Berengar and Faucher are older versions of ourselves."

"But they don't cast aspersions on our names. They just happen to be in the same business," I said.

"No. From what I've heard, Berengar's methods are similar to mine. Or worse, mine are similar to his. I took this case looking for singularity. What I've found is evidence that I am not singular at all."

"Is that so important?"

"More than I wish to admit." He paused in thought. "Many a time our cases have brought us in contact with people who thought they were special, when they were merely arrogant. Berengar and I are on the same side, yet I feel compelled to somehow outdo him, to prove my worth."

"Your past history is such that you have nothing to prove," I said.

Holmes laughed. "We are not mathematical equations, Watson. We all require constant proof of our self-worth. But the best path to achieve that is to put the focus not on myself but the case."

Holmes said nothing about the affair for the next couple of days, and I thought it might become one of our rare open-ended adventures. As a result, I was surprised when, on the third day since we'd met Berengar and Faucher, Holmes

The Case of William Wilson by Richard Zwicker

informed me that we would be attending another of Wilson's parties.

"I don't see the point. We can't help Wilson until he wants to help himself."

"Quite right, Watson!" said Holmes. "Perhaps tonight we can be more persuasive." Certainly, I was proof of Holmes's power of influence.

When we arrived at the Wilson mansion, Holmes asked the coachman of our horse-drawn carriage to wait, implying that we weren't going to stay long. I didn't recognize any of the partygoers, though in truth they might have been the same guests in different attire as had attended the previous soiree. Whereas I'd felt a certain exhilaration at the first party, its repetition left me enervated. The point of a party is to deviate from routine. When it becomes routine, it turns pernicious.

We found Wilson holding court with three more young women. He was hanging onto one of them indecorously. This time Holmes immediately interrupted his host.

"William Wilson, I can see how your parties could become habit-forming."

Wilson's weathered face grew impatient. He released the woman. "Holmes, I wasn't expecting you tonight. Have you made progress?"

"Small and incremental, but the night is young. I'm afraid I must insist you leave your festivities and come with us."

"What? If I did that, my twin would show up and criticize me in front of all my guests."

"That is a chance we'll have to take." Holmes grabbed Wilson's arm. "Could you take the other arm, Watson?"

I was surprised but did as I was bid. Wilson wasn't a weak man, but in his befuddled state, he was no match for Holmes and myself. None of the revelers seemed to care or notice as we wrestled him into the waiting horse-carriage.

The Case of William Wilson by Richard Zwicker

Once we were all seated, the coachman urged the horse to proceed.

"Where are you taking me?" asked Wilson. I could have asked the same question.

"We are going to solve your problem," said Holmes.

Wilson rained epithets on us and threatened to call the police, despite his previously mentioned antipathy toward them. Holmes said he would be happy to put Wilson in contact with Inspector Lestrade if, after tonight, our client still wished it.

We pulled up to the rundown boarding house in Paddington, where we'd earlier tried to find the younger Wilson. Holmes's knock at the door was answered by none other than Marcel Berengar and Faucher.

"Bring him into the living room," said Berengar, and we followed the two detectives, ushering Wilson in front of us. On an old divan sat the younger Wilson. This time his choice of dress was modest and did not match his namesake's.

"Mr. Wilson," said Berengar to the elder. "My name is Marcel Berengar and this is my assistant, Faucher. Please have a seat. We need to talk, and it is my experience that discussion is more focused when all participants are anchored."

Wilson glared at his twin. "So now you're not content to go to my parties. You feel the need to bring me to you. This is an outrage!" He sat reluctantly on a high-backed chair. The rest of us sat on wooden chairs pulled out from a rectangular table.

"That was my idea," said Holmes to Wilson the older.

"You said if you knew where your twin lived, you would kill him. Now is your opportunity."

"You fool! I told you I didn't want to know where he lived!" said our client.

"So you did, but you and your twin are strong-willed men of similar polarity," said Holmes. "Like magnets, you repel—the opposite of what a magnet is meant to do. You asked me to change your twin's mind, but I believe neither of you will do that without a definitive face-to-face encounter."

A carving knife was set on the coffee table next to the younger Wilson. He picked it up, offered it to the older, and whispered, "Is this satisfactory?"

The older Wilson hesitated, reached for the knife, then dropped his hand. The younger placed the knife back on the table.

"The advantage of a knife is it's quiet. said Holmes. "The disadvantage is it requires some effort to accomplish the job. I am carrying a revolver, if you'd prefer that."

"This is absurd," said the older Wilson. "I go to you for help and instead you kidnap me and encourage me to kill? I am not a murderer."

"It is to find out what you are that we kidnapped you," said Berengar. "Holmes has a theory that it is not the younger Wilson that you despise. It is yourself. Hence, you regularly schedule Bacchanalias at your home."

"I thought it important to remove you to a setting where you are less comfortable, less shielded, and less important," said Holmes. "But I think it would be more instructive if your twin explained further."

The younger Wilson leaned forward and twisted his head like a raven. The fact that we had to strain to hear his whispered voice created an eerie aura.

"In the short run, there is an appeal to annihilation, and left to your own devices, you will eventually succeed," he said to the older. "But what happens after? You have abdicated responsibility. Your party continues without you. If you die, I can replace you as if you'd never existed. You could vanish without a trace in this boarding house."

The younger Wilson raised the knife and pointed it toward the older's belly.

"Do you think I wouldn't?" the younger hissed. "I would do a much better job of living your life than you. Everyone else would come out ahead, while you decomposed in an unmarked grave."

"You are insane!" He turned to Holmes. "Stop him!"

With a cry, the younger Wilson stuck the knife into the right arm of the chair the older was sitting in. The attacked man jumped away, falling onto the floor.

"Change your ways," whispered the younger.

"What's it going to be, Wilson?" Berengar said to the older. "Annihilation or redemption?"

His forehead lined with sweat, the older Wilson threw up his hands. "It is the constant criticism I can't tolerate. Were that to end, I might not need to seek escape through self-destructive acts."

"I am a doctor," I said. "I could help you overcome your addictions. It is not an easy road, but some have successfully navigated it."

"Annihilation or redemption," said the older Wilson. "When put that way, it doesn't seem like such a difficult choice. I can make no promises, but anything is better than this. I will try."

*****

I had mixed feelings about this affair. The older Wilson was self-destructive, yet so are many people. I also wondered if fear would be a lasting motive for reform. At any rate, if the older Wilson was to have any chance of success, he needed to avoid the sources of his temptation. I arranged for him to live in a boardinghouse within walking distance of Baker Street. Each day I checked on him. Since moving, he insisted he had drunk no alcohol. His shaking hands and irritable temper lent credence to his words. The younger Wilson was true to his promise. As long as the older avoided dissolution, the younger had not tormented him, at least not in person.

As for Berengar and Faucher, before they returned to Paris, we had a final meeting at the pub of the St. George's Hotel. Despite the fact that we were two pairs of similar looking detectives, no one did a double take as we sat in a booth. Each of us drank a cup of tea. Both Faucher and I found the young, attractive longhaired waitress enchanting, but only he flirted with her, asking her personal questions that she parried. I thought he looked a bit silly, then my face reddened.

"If William Wilson the older makes good on his attempt to reform, my colleague Dr. Watson will write up this case," said Holmes to Berengar. "One couldn't ask for a better publicist. We both came to the conclusion that William Wilson the younger was the key," said Holmes.

"I have Faucher to chronicle my cases but, in truth, I'm happy to give you the credit for this one," said Berengar. "The act of ratiocination is reward enough for me. If it ends up improving someone else's circumstances in real life, that's a bonus."

"You're a purist, Berengar," said Holmes. "I, too, enjoy mental puzzles, but as both William Wilsons proved, it is dangerous to live too much in thought without proper grounding in reality. Have you had subsequent contact with the younger?"

"I have not," said Berengar. "And I fear the final chapter of this tale has yet to be written. We all wrestle with our consciences. For the well-adjusted, the result is a draw. But it was as if Wilson the younger was the older's conscience, one that was out of the older's control. Faucher and I looked into the younger's past. We could find no trace of him prior to their university days."

"So his original name may not be William Wilson," said Holmes.

"And what will happen to the younger if the older no longer gives him any material to reprove? He may have to find a replacement. You, perhaps."

Holmes guffawed. "He'll find me a more difficult person to copy, but he is welcome to try."

After Berengar and Faucher left to pack, we lingered in the pub. Holmes sat lost in thought, and I asked Holmes if he shared Berengar's fear that the case was still open.

"Nothing in life is certain," said Holmes. "Wilson the older is taking definite steps toward reclaiming his life. The younger will have to figure out who he is. Somewhere along the way, both got lost. In part, I can appreciate the dilemma of Wilson the older. When we met first Berengar, I was unnerved. I felt I had lost my uniqueness. But even then, my brain told me that's not the way to look at it. Though our paths have intersected, I will continue along my road, taking all the cases that interest me. Berengar seems content to keep a lower profile. As such, there's little chance we'll end up in the same place. Are you bothered by the existence of Faucher?"

"Not in the least."

I saw some of my comical, less praiseworthy qualities in Faucher, but I've never felt the need to be unique. It is my job to point out extraordinary people like Holmes. Some call me an everyman, and I consider that to be the highest compliment.

The Case of the Spanish Bride

by Brenda Seabrooke

"*Cache-toi?*"

"Holmes, did you sneeze?"

The sound came from behind me but Holmes was slightly in front of me, and in the wan light leaking from the cloud-covered moon, I didn't see him move.

"Quiet, Watson."

Holmes had to be the sneezer because not another living soul knew where we were in the wood flanking the side lawn of Mauldin Hall.

"*Cache-toi, vite!*"

"Holmes, you sneezed again."

"Quiet, Watson. I didn't sneeze. Someone is coming. Quick, get behind that tree."

We crouched behind a bushy cone-shaped tree that seemed to tremble in a breeze though I could detect none.

How had we come to this, hiding ourselves behind a tree in the dark while danger lurked before us?

******

Mrs. Hudson had gone to her sister's, leaving us to fend for ourselves. On her second day away, all the dishes she had cooked for us were no more. We took ourselves out for midday nourishment and on our return, the temporary housemaid,

Bonnie Malone, informed us a strange man had called to see Mr. Holmes.

"Did he leave a note?" I asked her.

"Not that I noticed, sir."

"What was his name? Did he leave that?" Holmes asked.

Holmes was unfailingly polite to people in service but I could see he was annoyed.

"If he did, sir, I didn't get it. It sounded somptin' like 'dustpan', but I'm sure that couldn't be right."

"No, I'm sure it couldn't be either," he said.

She bobbed a curtsey though none were required in this house. We were not nobility but working men, a doctor and the world's best consulting detective.

Holmes had an appointment at two. He never liked to wait and took care to time our return within five minutes of the hour. He paced the room until the clock struck twice. "Watson, you know how I hate unpunctuality," he began when someone knocked at the downstairs door. Holmes glanced out the window and took his customary seat by the fire. I remained standing as a caller was sent up the stairs.

The man who entered was a commanding figure, tall and lean with a blade of a nose, dark hair and a dark moustache. An arrow of a beard accentuated the line of his thin, straight lips. He wore a long cape that found more popularity in other climes than in England where gentlemen tended to wear Mackintoshes in inclement weather or the Inverness capes favored by Holmes and myself. His compelling eyes were dark and hooded. On his right hand he wore a large ruby only somewhat smaller than the Black Prince's in the Queen's Coronation Crown.

"I am told you are the best detective in the world," he said in flawless English with only a hint of Spain.

"Good afternoon," Holmes said without rising. "Pray take a seat."

"I prefer to stand. I shall not be long."

"Suit yourself."

"Have you credentials that document your excellence in detecting?"

"No. Have you credentials that show you to be from the Spanish embassy?"

The man took a backward step, as if Holmes had pushed him. I smothered a laugh. One does not duel in matters of wit with Holmes.

The man bowed his head briefly, something he probably never did unless it was to a monarch or someone with a title greater than his. "I am Marques of Parandivar, Grandee of Espana."

"You are embarking on a journey and have stopped here at the last minute to discharge an obligation that you feel is beneath your importance. Nevertheless, you are a man of honor and are fulfilling your promise."

The Grandee stared at Holmes and sat in a chair he pulled up close to the fire. I gathered he was not accustomed to moving his own chair but he managed it without effort. "How can you possibly know all of that?"

Holmes waved a hand. "My credentials."

The man pushed the cape back to reveal its silky lining of a match to the ruby, perhaps chosen with that in mind. Men with the money to order every minute facet of their lives do so.

Holmes leaned back in his chair. He did not offer the man a smoke. "Now who is lost or missing that needs so urgently to be found?"

The missing person was a recent bride, her father a family connection. "The groom was Lord Mauldin of Mauldin Hall in Northumbria. I have made enquiries into this personage. There is such a man. I have sent messages which were ignored. Now I need someone whom I can trust to look into the matter. I've been called to Spain or I would go myself."

"What then is the problem?" Holmes asked before I could.

"The bride's family has not heard from her since she left for England."

"Nothing to say she'd arrived?" I asked.

"*Nada*. It is as if she sailed off the edge of the earth."

"What was her name before the marriage?" Holmes asked.

"Maria Isabella Constancia de Bracardez. A noble family without title. Her father owns vineyards. Perhaps you are familiar with de Bracardez wines?"

"I am," Holmes acknowledged. I didn't know if that meant the wine was cheap or dear.

"It is not well-known outside of Espana. The king prefers it when he is not drinking champagne from the Loire."

"That would explain the insularity of the wine," Holmes said. "Why doesn't her ladyship's father come to England for a visit?"

"His wife is seriously ill. That is another reason they do not understand the long silence from their daughter."

The clock on the chimneypiece chimed the half hour. The Grandee glanced at Holmes and rose. "I must not miss the boat."

"No, the tide waits for no man," Holmes said.

"Will you look into the matter for me?"

"Act as your factotum?"

"Yes."

"No. But I will look into the matter for you."

"I am most grateful."

He didn't look grateful but perhaps Grandees don't know how. He did look somewhat relieved. A worrisome chore could be crossed off his calendar. Now he could board his boat with a clear conscience.

"You must tell me how you did it," I said after the downstairs door had closed behind His Excellency the Grandee.

"Simple, Watson. I looked out the window and saw the crest on the carriage waiting at the kerb with fine trunks strapped on top. He wore no telltale pet hairs, no giveaway odours of oil or polish and that in itself was telling. He was perfectly barbered, immaculately groomed, and expensively dressed."

"Very expensively," I said. "His cape alone probably cost a year's rent for some."

"No doubt, but if one is a grandee one must dress the part." Holmes stood up and donned his Inverness. "I must go out. Make your arrangements if you plan to accompany me. We'll get the early train to York tomorrow."

I saw my patients and arranged to be away for a few days. I returned to Baker Street forgetting the situation there. Without Mrs. Hudson, we would have no tea and no dinner. Bonnie was incapable of cutting bread for sandwiches without needing my professional services to sew up whichever finger she had almost managed to sever.

I waited for Holmes, but when he didn't return at a late hour, I took a hansom to Simpson's where I encountered him entering that establishment.

"What ho, Watson, we are well-met."

"Indeed."

We didn't speak again until we were seated and had perused the Bill of Fare. We both ordered the roast beef which was soon brought to our table on a rolling cart and carved onto our respective plates where it was joined by a trove of complementary vegetables roasted to perfection.

"Have you made your arrangements for tomorrow?" Holmes asked when we were thoroughly sated.

"I have. And you? Did you do some preliminary sleuthing?"

"I did. I discovered Mauldin Hall was not in Northumberland but in the wilds of northern Yorkshire."

"Strange. Do you think he copied the address wrong?"

"We shall see."

After dessert of persimmon fool and as the evening was fine for September, we elected to walk back to Baker Street.

*****

"I was surprised you took this case," I said to Holmes the next morning after we were on the early train to York.

"Do you imply, Watson, I took it in deference to a Spanish grandee?"

"Not at all. You certainly put him in his proper place. No, I wouldn't have thought you'd find it interesting looking up a lost Spanish bride."

"Ordinarily, I wouldn't either, but something about this case is wrong."

"And you will set it right?"

"I may not be able to, but I'll certainly find out what is going on."

We reached York in time for a meal and bought sandwiches for a later one.

"We don't know what kind of accommodations we may find in this far corner of the county."

"Oh come, Watson, it is not the end of the world. I made reservations at the White Rose Inn. I'm sure we will be suited there but because we do not know the hour of our arrival, sandwiches are a good idea."

After two short train jogs we took a wagon to Wealdon and reached the inn at sundown. The White Rose was rustic but comfortable enough. We were shown to our rooms and I was ready to eat my sandwich and retire for the night but Holmes was not. "I want to take a look at the house before we besiege it."

He suggested we make use of the loaming light and take our sandwiches with us to eat while we walked. Not the most pleasant way to consume a brief meal but not the worst, and the roast beef and Colman's mustard washed down by tea we'd added a nip to did much to restore our energy for the task ahead.

Holmes had brought a lantern of his own invention, small with louvered shutters which allowed in air to keep a candle burning but not allow the light to show unless one were lying on the ground. The switch could close the louvers quickly if complete darkness were needed. It was smaller than the usual lantern and therefore lighter. It could be carried over the shoulder when not in use by a cord tied on the ring in the top or attached to a pole.

A pallid moon hung behind clouds giving enough light for us to make our way along the mile or so road to Mauldin Hall and that is how we came to be crouched behind this flimsy tree.

On the other side of the tree a light flitted on the ground. Something snuffled, breathing heavily. Was that the bearer of the light or a beast, those moor hounds of blood-curdling tales that nannies frighten children with in the nursery? For a blood-freezing moment I thought of slavering jaws and long-clawed paws. Then reason clamped down on my fears.

"Whassat? You find owt?"

The light searched the tree in front of us.

As the pair of hounds lunged closer, Holmes dug in his capacious pockets and tossed something in front of the tree. I caught a whiff. Pepper. I willed myself not to sneeze but it was difficult.

A sneeze erupted in front of us, but it was immediately joined by snuffling and human sneezing along with some from a canine or two. Those must be the guard dogs we'd been warned about. The human was the grounds keeper. What, then was the sneeze from the tree?

The keeper yelled something guttural to the dogs. They whined but backed away.

As the sounds of their movement receded, I stood up straight as did Holmes. Only the glimmer of the keeper's lantern was visible in the dark wooded night.

"A close call," I whispered.

"Indeed."

Holmes tracked the progress of the keeper as I did. "Do you have any more of that pepper?"

I felt him nod in the dark.

When the keeper's faint dot of light disappeared into the night, Holmes spoke in a guarded tone to the tree. "Chavalier Dupin, I presume."

Holmes was talking to a bushy tree? And calling it by name?

"*Oui*," the tree replied and raised two of its branches.

"Holmes! What the—"

"Surely, Watson, you recognize the Chevalier C. Auguste Dupin."

"I can't say as I do. He seems to have been turned into a bushy evergreen tree."

The tree's two branches analogous to arms busied themselves amongst the brush near the trunk and presently the Chevalier stepped out of his tree skin. Tall and aristocratic as he was when we worked on The Naval Man case with him. Maybe a little grayer, a little gaunter.

"Have you been eating properly?" I asked him with concern.

"Not so much these last few days, *parce que vous connaissez le cuisine.*"

"We regret we missed you in London. Remind me when this case is finished to tell you who the new maid thought you were."

"*D'accord. Je me souviendrai, mon ami.*" The former tree swayed but no wind was present.

"How did you arrive here?" I asked in hopes he had a cart and horse nearby.

"*En pied.*"

"I suggest we return to the inn to discuss our options," Holmes said, getting my drift. We needed to get the Chevalier back to the White Rose soon before we might have to carry him.

Our long day was beginning to take a toll on me. The bed at the inn was looking more and more comfortable by the minute as we returned to the road and followed it eastward to the village of Kelderton. We walked in silence to save the Chavalier's stamina. I did not know his age but he must be close to if not in his seventies.

We called for some libation on our return to the inn but were only able to procure ale at that hour. We were grateful for that and for the plate of scones with cherry jam as a restorative. Holmes and I each took one and pushed the plate toward the Chevalier. He took one, eyed it, and tried a bite.

"Ah *cerise!*"

Holmes explained why we were there.

"The Spanish bride! I am *ici* to find the French bride."

As we compared cases, we discovered they were the same with the only difference being one bride was from Spain and the other from France, each with a sizeable dowry due to be paid now.

Upon his arrival from Paris, the Chevalier had gone straight to Baker Street and finding us away had left a message which we explained Bonnie had construed to mean Mr. Dustpan had called instead of Auguste Dupin.

We had to laugh again at that. "I shall tell her to write down the names of future callers," Holmes said.

"I highly doubt she can write or read," I said. "We shall leave a pad by the door in the future for callers to write their own names and hope that Mrs. Hudson's sister recovers allowing her to return soon."

As to the two cases which were now one case, we heard what the Chevalier had done after his arrival the day before. He had tried to hire a conveyance to take him to Mauldin Hall but was told the only available horse in the village was lame. The villagers seemed not to know anything about Lord Mauldin or want to know anything. One old woman smoking a pipe in the sun had told him Lord Mauldin were 'nowt to do with this village' but at another one farther from Kilderton.

"Tweren't allus tha way," she said. When Lord Mauldin was a young man, he came to the village frequently, attended the harvest dance and opened Mauldin Hall at Christmas.

About four years ago, things changed. The Hall hired people from the far village. Kildertonians were hurt financially by this but they had learnt new ways of living, not as comfortable as before but they were getting by.

Holmes nodded as if he knew this already.

"I walked to the Hall and went to the door where I knocked and waited, knocked and waited. After some time, the door was opened by a rough sort of man who was not a butler and indeed did not work in the house. I told him I wished to see Lord or Lady Mauldin. He said the lord was not presently in. I asked about his lady. Yes, she was in.

"He led me to a lady's parlor where a finely-dressed woman sat reading a book of poetry.

"Tha's her.' he said. I introduced myself. My name meant nothing to her. I noticed the volume she held was in French, the poems of Rimbaud. I mentioned the poet who wrote of the Americas and she replied she liked travel poetry and hoped to see the places she was reading about."

"But Rimbaud didn't write poetry about the Americas," I said.

"Precisely, Watson. The lady doth pretend too much."

"Perhaps she is no lady," I said as realization hit me. "She is neither the Spanish bride we search for nor the French bride the Chevalier searches for. You knew this all along."

"I suspected, Watson. The question is what have they done with the two young ladies we seek and how can we rescue them if they are yet alive?"

I leaned back to contemplate the task. Never had I dreamed the Spanish bride might be dead.

The Chevalier nodded. "I have this conclusion *aussi*. I did not talk of the French bride but did inquire if the lady were from nearby. She said no she was from London where she met her husband a few years ago. I saw no sign of any other lady so I bade her *adieu* and left. I returned to the inn and availed myself of the costume I was wearing when you met me."

"That was a clever disguise," Holmes said.

"It is my own design."

"I must examine it later. I may need to be a tree myself sometime in the future," Holmes said.

We retired soon after discussing tomorrow's plan. Holmes and I would attempt to gain entry to the house. He didn't tell us how we would do that but seemed to have a plan in mind.

After a restorative night I could have spent on a hard floor for all I would have noticed, and a sumptuous breakfast, we went to talk to the owner of the lame horse. At Holmes's request I'd brought along my medical bag. The Chevalier spoke to the owner whose cart stood in the barn gathering cobwebs while the horse looked at us with morose eyes.

"*Mon ami*, I 'ave met *un medicin* — how do you say, 'doctor 'and bring him to look at your horse."

Instantly, suspicion overrode over the man's pleasant features.

The Chevalier introduced me, and I indicated my bag. "Shall I take a look?"

"How much do you be charging?"

"*Non, non, non, mon ami*, it is my *cadea*u to you. I have a great love of horses. I do not like to see *le cheval* in pain."

Holmes explained to the owner, a Mr. Dunton, what the Chevalier intended and why. "He is eccentric. You know, French."

Mr. Dunton nodded with understanding. Holmes nodded with him, and I got to work. We had procured some rags at the inn. The horse, a medium-sized gelded male was a dark red color with a lighter mane and tail, about four years old by the looks of his teeth. I had Mr. Dunstan lead him around in the yard. The horse favored his back left leg. I examined it and found no break. Indeed, the horse, responded to my ministrations with a whuff of pleasure, so I did the same to all of his legs. He closed his eyes and sighed.

"What is his name?"

"Willem."

"Well Willem, you don't seem to have any breaks or sprains, no swellings I can find. You do wipe him down after use?" I asked Dunton.

"Most of the time." He looked away.

"Got to take care of your horse," I said with a *tsk*. "Never put him up wet after a strenuous workout." I took some liniment out of my bag. I'd concocted it with some of the contents of my phials, and I applied it to the horse's legs with a rag. I wrapped that rag around his favored leg and applied it to his other legs, wrapping them as well. "Now he must be walked."

"Now?" Dunton was too busy earning a living to walk a horse, so I offered as part of the treatment to do it today.

"A nice leisurely long walk," I added.

He agreed to it and set off for his business which was fortunately in the opposite direction to Mauldin Hall.

"Quick, we need the saddle." Holmes lifted it off the sawhorse and onto Willem. He swiftly tightened the girth while the Chevalier bridled the horse, and we set off in the direction we'd taken last night.

Willem plodded along with us and soon began to walk the normal gait for a horse.

"Just as I thought," I said. "Willem was put up wet too often and when the lameness appeared, he was shut up in the barn. What he needed was to walk at a comfortable gait."

"The concoction you put on his legs may have helped," the Chevalier said.

"Thank you."

"Watson, we may make a veterinary out of you yet," Holmes said with a laugh.

About three quarters of the way to the Hall, Holmes halted our party. "You must remove the bandages now," he said to me.

"I don't understand."

"I plan to call at the Hall and say my horse has gone lame, I am out of liniment, do they have any to spare. Whatever they say or do, I will be able to assess the situation and formulate a plan."

"What should we do?" I asked. I didn't want to stand idly by but Holmes told us to do just that.

"Hide yourselves in the woods near the entrance and keep watch. Come along, Willem."

He led the horse through the unattended gatehouse arch and up the road to the hall. We found a good vantage point on the other side of the road where we could sit on some low boulders. I rubbed my hands with some aromatic oil from my bag to remove the strong smell of the liniment and hoped I was downwind from the hall.

The Chevalier lay on the ground and soon I could tell from his relaxed, even breathing he was asleep. I studied him. He seemed to be in good health, less gaunt than he appeared last night. Perhaps the scones and cerise had helped. I wished we had brought sandwiches with us. I resolved to feed the Chevalier every chance I found.

A nap would do for me now as well but one of us needed to be alert. I thought we were not in Mauldin's demesne, but I couldn't be sure. He might own this side of the road as well.

The day was fine for mid-September. I felt myself relax and jerked awake several times before a rider approached from the other direction. I crouched low though I doubted he could see me peering through leaves. He turned into the gateway.

About twenty minutes later, Holmes returned leading Willem.

The Chevalier woke up and wanted to know what happened. I told him Lord Mauldin had returned.

"Let's put some distance between us and the hall," Holmes said as we reapplied the rags to Willem's now-reeking legs.

Willem was stepping high after another application of liniment that smelled even stronger than mine. He looked like he wanted to pirouette from time to time but Holmes kept the reins short.

When we were about halfway back to town Holmes told us what had transpired. "I met Lady Mauldin. She was just as you described her, Chevalier, dressed in a green satin gown more suitable for a ball than a morning at home. Lord Mauldin is away, she said and sent me around to the stable where the man we encountered last night gave me a rag and liniment. He was not at all talkative but took himself off for some errand. With him out of the way, the stable boy talked a bit. He said the lord often goes away and brings people back with him. Sometimes they are couples but about every six months he brings a single woman with him and she is never seen again. He thinks they are mad and live in special buildings. He sees food taken out of the house but doesn't know where it goes. The most important piece of information from him is that they are taking food today. He saw it earlier."

"Excellent," the Chevalier said.

"Yes, one of the brides is still alive. Perhaps both. The Spanish bride's dowry is due to be paid now," Holmes said. "His reason for keeping them alive must be to have them sign papers which would eventually find their way back to the original bank from which they were drafted. He would have gone to different banks with each dowry so no bank knew about the other, then later move his funds into a central account."

"The French bride's also has been sent by now," the Chevalier said.

"Did you see Mauldin?"

"No, I was behind the barn. I heard him. He is an imperious lord of the manor. He belabored the stable boy for not being in front of the house to take his mount. The poor boy was afraid to tell him about me. I skirted the house and stayed in the cover of the park trees until I thought it was safe to return to the road. I was able to learn from the stable boy what buildings exist on the property."

No one said it, but we all knew we would be returning to Mauldin Hall tonight.

We took a happier Willem to his barn. He whuffed when we left him and seemed to want to continue with us.

"A most agreeable horse," I said as we walked back to the inn.

Holmes made arrangements to send telegrams to Scotland Yard and to the constabulary in York from the next town. We enjoyed a hearty English lunch though the Chevalier didn't look happy about it. "Simple country fare, *je sais, mais si anglais, si anglais. Je desire une clafoutis aux cerise, les madeleines.*"

"Later, when we are again in London, perhaps we can procure such for you," I said. "Meanwhile please avail yourself of healthy cuisine to keep your energy level high. We have much to do tonight."

"He is right," Holmes said. "And we'll need all our wits and energy about us. We don't know what we will find and must be prepared."

The afternoon was long and I spent a good part of it sleeping. I assume the Chevalier did the same. I don't know what Holmes did. He was often too anticipatory before the game was afoot to sleep but perhaps he snatched a few minutes as a restorative. We met for an early meal which passed without much conversation. Holmes bought a quantity of pepper from the innkeeper and parceled it out to us tied in a rag. "For the dogs."

He asked me to bring my bag and leave it by the gate in case it was needed and to keep my Webley with me.

"It has been with me every step of the way."

The Chevalier armed himself with a derringer. "It was sent to me by Henry Deringer himself for a case involving some of his friends."

On the quiet, Holmes told me not to get into a situation where I needed to depend upon that gun. "It has a short range."

The fine weather gave way to fog. As the sun set, wraiths of it hovered over the road, crouched in the hollows and clung to the woods. Holmes and I had donned our Inverness capes. The Chevalier carried a bag and wore a voluminous black cape with a black hood. "In case I need to disappear," he joked when we asked him about it.

We both laughed though I don't think he meant it as a joke. He didn't mention the contents of the bag.

At the gate, I rid myself of my medical bag, glad not to be encumbered with it for a while at least but comforted to know it was at the ready if we needed it.

Holmes had brought his lantern but kept it unlit as he led us up the road to a curve where I glimpsed Mauldin Hall for the first time. It was an imposing edifice built long ago of dark grey stone, added to from time to time, a tower here, a wing there. At some point, it had been crenellated, but later additions had left this behind as shooting arrows was no longer an adequate defense for a castle or fortress. No attempt had been made to soften the stern protective features of the house. The front door was massive enough to withstand a battering ram but probably not cannon of any size.

We leave the road here," Holmes whispered. "I wanted you to see the house, Watson."

"It's massive and formidable."

"This way." Holmes led us into the deep forested area and stopped to light his lantern with a Lucifer which he blew out and stuck into the ground. Nobody would follow Holmes's fire-starter.

"Keep the pepper handy, so you can get to it quickly if they loose the dogs," I said

"We are past the time I encountered the keeper last night," the Chevalier said.

"We are," Holmes replied. "Let's hope he has made his rounds and is drinking himself to sleep."

We followed Holmes's subdued lantern light through the trees, circling the stable where the dogs might be kept. On the far side of the Hall the land sloped gently downward to a lake. I heard a noise from the house behind us. I alerted the other two but they'd heard it as well. Holmes and I concealed ourselves behind trees but the Chevalier removed his cape and opened his bag. What was he doing? This was not the time for a picnic.

I looked at Holmes who shrugged in the dark. I need not have been concerned. The Chevalier removed his tree disguise from the bag. It was turned inside out to protect the needles. The inside of the tree was lined with sturdy green burlap. The Chevalier wound the costume around him and slid his hands into the armholes covered on the outside with realistic, needle-like material. I smelt the aroma and realized the needles were not just realistic but real from some evergreen tree. He buttoned the tree suit down the front with dark green buttons of a fairly large size which made it easy to don and remove. "I shall be invisible in this disguise. No one will suspect *l'arbre*. You follow behind me."

Holmes chuckled under his breath. "He is full of jokes. It must be the hearty English food."

As we watched, the tree took a few steps and stopped. The Chevalier made the tree sway while he looked around. He repeated the process.

We followed behind him. Ahead of us a man with a lantern walked beside another man. They were but black silhouettes in the darkness but I suspected they were his Lordship and the keeper without his dogs.

They rounded the lake to a ruin on the far side. We followed the moveable tree as it made a wide berth of the lake in order to remain in the concealing shadows. The two men unlocked a door and entered the ruin which seemed to have an actual room in it. Was this the place where the brides were kept?

We waited some distance from the ruin. The night was silent with tendrils of mist creeping across the woodland from the lake. I was glad of my Inverness.

The two men left the ruin. This time they prodded and pushed something between them. A figure of a woman in a dark dress. Was she one of the brides? I looked at Holmes. He must have the same thought. He nodded but didn't risk words. They would carry over the water and alert his lordship to our presence.

The three figures crossed in front of us and entered a copse of dark rustling trees. Beech perhaps. We followed our tree and hurried across an open area to enter the copse. We couldn't see our quarry but were able to follow a well-maintained path until the copse ended and in front of us stood an impressive mausoleum beside an ancient chapel. The men propelled their charge between them. Her hands appeared bound in front of her. She made sounds but they were inarticulate, designating a gag of some sort. One of them opened the door and shoved the young woman inside. They followed her, closing the door behind them.

"Shall I remove my disguise?" the Chevalier whispered.

"No," Holmes said. "It may be needed. Watson and I are going in. Watson, ready your weapon."

We both took our weapons out and ran across the open area in front of the mausoleum. The tree galloped alongside keeping pace with us. Perhaps the Chevalier was healthier than I thought. Fog swirled around our feet as if trying to impede us, but we made the door in time to hear his lordship order the keeper to remove the gag.

"Sor, tha mought screech."

"Let her. I enjoy hearing them scream," replied his lordship followed by a scream and a string of invectives in French, *les animeaux sauvages* being the milder of what she unleashed.

"Open it," Mauldin said and a long ominous scraping sound followed with more screams.

"Pleasant dreams," Mauldin said and laughed as the screams increased in intensity. Another scraping sound and the screams came to an abrupt stop.

I was horrified at what that meant. Holmes jerked open the door to a scene out of a lurid horror novel.

The lantern cast ghastly shadows amongst the tombs, some with knights and ladies carved on them, others of a plainer design. The two men were as we had thought, Lord Mauldin in a black cloak and the keeper in rustic woods attire. Both of their faces wore the slippery grins of amusement at another's misfortune. From the tomb beside them words and screams intermingled in a muffled version of the earlier eruptions.

Holmes stepped into view, his revolver pointed at Mauldin. I trained my Webley on the keeper who not being a thinking man, lunged at Holmes. I shot him, aiming at his heart, but he tripped and fell sideways, taking the bullet in his shoulder. That didn't stop him. He regained his balance and started for me. Again, a shot rang out, but it wasn't mine. The bullet hit him in the thigh.

I turned and saw the Chevalier in his tree costume holding his derringer in his right branch. Mauldin took advantage of this distraction and leaped for Holmes. The derringer spat a bullet into his arm. Mauldin gaped at the blood oozing onto his sleeve and the sharpshooter tree. The tree spoke in a deep voice. "Where are the brides?"

Mauldin possessed a brain intent on staying alive. Confronted by the three of us he slid down and lay against the side of the sarcophagus. His accustomed sneer turned into a grimace. The keeper lay beside him, one hand on each of his wounds.

Holmes gave his revolver to the Chevalier. "Hold this on Mauldin. If either of them moves, shoot them."

"*Avec plaisir.*"

Holmes and I tackled the lid of the sarcophagus where the French bride had not stopped screaming. He moved it a few inches letting light fall on the young woman. "Marguerite, le Chevalier Auguste Dupin has rescued you."

The screams subsided as we pushed the lid aside and the disheveled Marguerite sat up holding out her hands. Holmes removed the rope around her wrists. She climbed out of the tomb as Holmes pinned Mauldin's arms behind his back and secured them with the rope he had used on Marguerite. She stood over Mauldin and kicked him repeatedly until a word in French from the Chevalier stopped her but she continued to flash murderous looks at Mauldin.

At the sight of the walking talking tree, the keeper fainted but it could have been from blood loss. I would see to him but we had work to do. The Chevalier produced a length of rope and I used it on the keeper in the event he should wake up.

"Monsieur Holmes, she says Isabella, the Spanish bride was taken away earlier tonight and we should look for her."

Holmes and I opened another sarcophagus. It held many bones and rotted clothing but no recent interment. We opened two more and were lucky with the third one. A dazed young woman lay much like Marguerite, her hands bound, a gag slipped away from her mouth. I put a fingertip to her throat and detected a pulse. "She's alive."

As we freed her hands, she awoke and screamed.

"*Non, non*, Isabella. You are safe. *Segura. Segura.*"

Isabella appeared in shock as she took in Marguerite, the opened sarcophagi, Mauldin and the keeper both bleeding on the floor of the tomb and a tree holding a gun, but she broke out in laughter. I feared she was hysterical, but after a moment she said, "*Gracia*s, gentlemen. I never dreamed of being rescued by a tree."

"That is not a tree," Marguerite said with indignation. "May I present le Chevalier Auguste Dupin."

Isabella brushed her hair back and curtsied to the tree.

"Wot the –" A familiar voice spoke from the doorway. Inspector Lestrade in his trademark bowler entered the mausoleum

"Inspector. Delighted you could make it."

"It were close. Good you caught me in Leeds, but I see I've missed the excitement. Wot's going on here, Holmes? Why is this tree holding a gun?"

Behind him several uniformed policemen goggled at the sight in front of them, and I knew this story would be told for a long time amongst the constabulary of the land.

"May I present two missing brides?" Holmes began the long explanation while the policemen took custody of the two men. One of them left to bring transport for the prisoners. I told them where I'd left my bag. It would be needed for these two criminals.

"I am Lord Mauldin," his lordship said on gaining his feet.

"I doubt that," Holmes said. "I suspect we will find the bones of the real Lord Mauldin in one of the tombs along with those of several other young women who have been reported missing from other countries. This imposter killed the real

Lord Mauldin, grew a beard and stopped having anything to do with the village, preferring to go farther afield where the real lord wasn't well known. He and his partner, who may actually be his wife, have run this game for some years, four I believe. Every six months or so he took a trip and, posing as a lord, married a young woman who had a sizeable dowry. As soon as he got his hands on the money and she signed the papers, he interred the wife and went searching for a replacement. The French family was slow to turn over the funds to him. He was obliged to seek another bride to keep the lifestyle afloat while waiting. That is how two brides were kept prisoner.

"The funds for both brides arrived at the same time. He went to York to get his financial affairs in order and returned to remove the wives whose usefulness was over."

"That sounds as farfetched as a Chevalier in a tree suit," Lestrade said.

"And yet, there he is," Holmes said.

The constables drove up with my medical bag and prisoner transport. I examined each man and dressed their wounds. The bullets had gone through flesh without damage. The miscreants were stable enough to travel by wagon to York. The constables loaded them and the wagon left.

The Chevalier removed his tree suit as the constables persisted in calling his disguise. They brought his cape, too, but he insisted on wrapping it around Marguerite as she had nothing to protect her against the chill dampness of the fog. Isabella looked as if she thought she should get the cape but accepted my Inverness until we stopped at the house and both brides retrieved their clothing.

The constables searched but could find no sign of the woman who posed as Lady Mauldin. We surmised she'd heard the shots and seen the police vehicles and realized it was over. She slipped away while we were busy at the tomb.

Both brides, as I continued to think of them, insisted they never lived as man and wife. They'd been locked away on arrival. They saw the other woman once or twice but never close enough to speak to her. They never saw any maids or people on the estate. Their food was brought to them by the keeper. "We drove up in the coach and went straight to the prison in the ruin. I was first," Marguerite said, "A few weeks later Isabella came. If we'd not been together, we could not have survived this ordeal."

As it turned out, their dowries arrived on the same day, sealing their fates to die together.

"It was lucky for them you arrived when you did, Holmes," Lestrade said.

Holmes and I arranged to travel to London in a few days' time. We stayed a last night at the White Rose before moving on to York. The village was abuzz with the story of the murdered Lord Mauldin and the two brides. We learned from the innkeeper Mauldin Hall would go to a cousin.

Before we left the next morning, I took the recipe for liniment I had written down to Mr. Dunton. I told him how his horse aided in the rescue. He was proud of Willem's part and walked back with me to the inn where the coach waited. He headed for the bar with his part of the story which should be good for a few pints. Maybe Willem would get an extra bit of feed. He might even become famous as the horse what saved the brides after a few tellings of his story.

Six of us filled the coach, but it wasn't far to the next town with a train station. Holmes sent cables to the Grandee and the embassy. After we gave evidence in York, Isabella departed with an embassy escort from London. The Chevalier escorted Marguerite back to France leaving the port of Hull by steamer. Holmes and I took the train to London.

Examination of the sarcophagi revealed six brides and the real Lord Mauldin. They were identified by their clothing.

Mauldin had mercifully been shot, not left to suffocate in a tomb with his ancestors. I cannot dwell on the fate of those six brides. I think instead of the two we rescued.

"The Chevalier looked much better after we rescued the brides," Holmes remarked.

"Yes, he seemed frail when we first encountered him. It seems every time his partner has business outside of Paris, the Chevalier hares off to England on a case. Perhaps, he should take Dupin with him in the future."

"I should send him a telegram to that effect when we reach London. As a friend and a doctor but I think these cases seem to agree with the Chevalier. The tree disguise was masterful."

"It was."

"With real branches."

"Indeed."

"What, I wonder, will you call your account of this case? The Case of the Missing Brides?"

"Too simple."

"The Almost-Murdered Brides?"

"Gives too much away."

"How about The Murderous Bridegroom?"

"Same."

"The Entombed Brides? or The Moveable Tree?"

"Really, Holmes, leave the title to me."

He steepled his fingers and tapped two of them against each other while he raised his eyebrows as if he knew I hadn't a clue what to call this case. One thing I did know: I would be writing about it. After all, it was the most gothic case we had yet solved.

Special Thanks to Our Kickstarter Backers

A sincere thank you goes out to our Kickstarter backers who supported the campaign for Sherlock Holmes and the Great Detectives. Without their backing, the book you hold in your hands or read on your screen may not have come to fruition.

Thank you to:

Abi Hiscock
AKEE Krebs
Alan Hughes
Alessandro Caffari
Allyn Gibson
Anthony & Suford Lewis
Anthony R. Cardno
Anton Wijs
B+P-Snegg
Benjamin & Tiffany Moore
BKFortyTwo
Brett Timperman
Brian R. Boisvert
Carl W. Urmer, MHS
Céline Malgen
Cerise Cauthron
Chad Bowden
Charles C. Albritton III
Charles Warren
Chee Lup Wan
Chris Basler
Chris Chastain
Chris Patient
Christopher Davis
Conor H. Carton
Curtis B. Edmundson
David A Wade
David Darryl Bibb
David Galbis-Reig and Lisa DeFazio
David Lars Chamberlain
David Marcum
David Rains
David Tai
Dean S Arashiro
Deb Werth
Donna J. Hebb
Dr Douglas Vaughan
Dr. Noreen Pazderski
Dr. Wolfgang Ditz
DrLight
Edward Fitzpatrick
Edward Lee Love
Eldrich Nemo

Emily "Missy Boo" Adams
Eric Sands
Eron Wyngarde
Ewan Thomson
Fearlessleader
Frank M. Greco
Gary Phillips
Genevieve Cogman
Georgina Coates
Gilles Bourgeois
GMarkC
Greavr
Harry DeMaio
Harry Kay Lesser, Jr.
Howard J. Bampton
Ida Umphers
Jacinda Gift
Jack McGrail
Jaime Lawrence
Jamas Enright
James Bell
James Husum
James J. Marshall
Janice M. EIsen, NMSOBC
Jason Epstein
Jason Roberts
Jason VanNimwegen
Jay Shekelton
Jeff Lewis
Jeff Sigmund
Jeff Troutman
Jim Jorritsma
Jim Kosmicki
Joel Kovach
John Haines
John L. French
John N Wood

John Ver Linden
Josh King
JPD
Julia Morgan
K. Patrick Glover
Kaeleigh Post
Karen Lytle Sumpter
Keith Veitch
Kevin B. O'Brien
Kevin Schreur
Kim Watt
L.E. Vellene
Lark Cunningham
Laura Lea Davidson
Lauren Harrison Rossato
Lawrence J. Milo, Jr.
Lisa Black
Lowell Denning
Lucy Jefferies
Madison Lott
Mark Carter
Mark Robinson
Mark Rutjes
Mary Ann Raley
Mary Boelk
Matthew Kugler
Michael Barrett
Michael Howard
Michael Walker
Mike Brosco
Mike James
Niall Gordon
Oolie Smung
Patricia Miller
Paul Dent
Paul Leach
Paul Leone

Philip W Rogers Jr
PJK
Race Garber
Ray Riethmeier
Raymond Yamamoto
Richard Crowder
Richard L. Haas III
Rick Ohnemus
RIJU GANGULY
Robert Perret
Ron Bachman
Ronald H. Miller
Rusty Waldrup
Samee
Scarlett Letter
Scott J. Dahlgren
Scott Maynard
Scott Vander Molen
Shane "Asharon" Sylvia
Sharon Kouba
Simo Muinonen
Simon Mark de Wolfe
Stephen & Margaret Hiscock

Stephen Dye
Steve Smith
Stig Olsen
Tamara Michelle "Kat" Slaten
Tauriel Naismith Vorkosigan
Terry Cox
Thank Yoy
Thérèse Elaine
Thomas and Emily Hiscock
Thomas J. Shea
Thomas M. Colwell
Thomas Pheister
Tim King!
Tina M Noe Good
Tony Ciak
Trevor Prinn
Tyler R. Byers
Val Hiscock
Vivien Limon
Wanda Aasen
Yes
Zion Phan

For more adventures of Sherlock Holmes in the Great Detective Universe, join us in Volume One and Volume Two of 'Sherlock Holmes and the Occult Detectives', out now from Belanger Books.

Belanger Books

Printed in Great Britain
by Amazon